Y0-DBK-292

37814 00089 5889

VS Western
Blankenship, William D.
Yukon gold

NOV 0 6 1995

DISCARDED
BAKER CO. PUBLIC LIBRARY

Baker County Public Library
2400 Resort St.
Baker City, OR 97814

DEMCO

I've travelled the world twice over,
Met the famous: saints and sinners,
Poets and artists, kings and queens,
Old stars and hopeful beginners,
I've been where no-one's been before,
Learned secrets from writers and cooks
All with one library ticket
To the wonderful world of books.

© JANICE JAMES.

YUKON GOLD

Set in the Klondike during the gold rush of 1898, this is a rip-roaring story of Brian Bonner, a hard-drinking, unorthodox officer in the Royal Canadian Mounted Police, one of a handful of men dedicated to upholding the law in a time and place of near-total lawlessness. Gold is everywhere in Dawson: in huge seams called "cheese sandwiches", in the dust and nuggets men use to pay for drinks, in the gold fever that attracts thugs and inspires cheating, stealing, murder and riverboat hijacking.

WILLIAM D. BLANKENSHIP

Yukon Gold

Complete and Unabridged

Baker County Public Library
2400 Resort St.
Baker City, OR 97814

ULVERSCROFT
Leicester

First published in the U.S.A. by
E. P. Dutton, New York

First British Edition published 1978 by
Souvenir Press Ltd., London

First Large Print Edition
published October 1980
by arrangement with
Souvenir Press Ltd.
London
and
E. P. Dutton, a Division of
Elsevier-Dutton Publishing Co., Inc.
New York.

Copyright © 1977 by William D. Blankenship
All Rights Reserved.

British Library CIP Data

Blankenship, William Douglas
  Yukon gold.—Large print ed.
  (Ulverscroft large print series: western)
  I. Title
  823'.9'1F   PS3552.L366Y/

  ISBN 0-7089-0532-3

Published by
F. A. Thorpe (Publishing) Ltd.
Anstey, Leicestershire

Printed in Great Britain by T. J. Press (Padstow) Ltd.
Padstow, Cornwall

's
Western
Blankenship
(William)

The epigraph is a quotation from "The Law of the Yukon" from *The Collected Poems of Robert Service*. It is reprinted here with the permission of Dodd, Mead & Company and McGraw-Hill Ryerson Ltd.

All of the characters in this book are fictitious, and any resemblance to actual persons, living or dead, is purely coincidental.

This book is for my wife, Linda,
and for our children,
Lisa, Douglas, Kristen, Adam, and Beth.

This is the law of the Yukon,
and ever she makes it plain;
send not your foolish and feeble,
send me your strong and your sane.
ROBERT SERVICE

1

ON the evening of January 15, 1898, I witnessed the killing of Mike Lynch, a bartender at the Bank Saloon and Gambling House in Dawson, Yukon Territory. It was the first murder of the year in Dawson, and greeted as a welcome event.

There was nothing I could do to stop the crime. I could only arrest the killer, a handyman and occasional gold prospector named Rollo Moon. I was occupying my customary place at the Bank's bar when, out of the corner of my eye, I saw Rollo draw a knife. I managed to shout "Watch yourself, Mike!" but my warning came too late. Rollo reached across the bar and drove the knife deep into Mike's chest. Mike reeled backwards, toppling a pyramid of shot glasses, and fell to the floor. He was dead when I reached him.

Mike's parka was hanging on a peg behind the bar. I covered his body with it, then arrested Rollo. He put up no struggle and I marched him outside and down Front Street toward the police barracks without even drawing my revolver.

My name is Brian Bonner and in 1898, the year of the great Gold Rush, I was one of a handful of Northwest Mounted Police who kept the peace over two hundred thousand square miles of Canada's Yukon Territory. The town of Dawson was at the center of the rush, an isolated community located on the junction of the Yukon and Klondike Rivers six hundred miles from the nearest civilization and populated by gold prospectors, gamblers, traders, adventuring women, and assorted cut-throats.

In those days I was famous in the Yukon as The Man Who Killed Almighty Voice (having dispatched a notorious Cree renegade by that unlikely name) and many folks considered me the finest lawman in Canada. Like other men of large reputation, I also had my detractors. They whispered that I was a thief . . . drunkard . . . backshooter . . . and liar of grand scale. Unfortunately, that opinion of me has gained wide acceptance over the years.

At any rate, I locked Rollo Moon in Dawson's small jail and the following morning the place and date for his trial was set. It came as a surprise to the residents of Dawson when Inspector Constantine agreed to hold the trial in the Bank Saloon. True, the Bank qualified as *the scene of the crime*. But in the past Inspector Constantine had denied many other requests to add a flash of pageantry to his courtroom. Usually he convened his court in a tiny room at the police barracks that would hold no more than twenty people.

By contrast Silent Sam Bonnifield's Bank Saloon would hold up to three hundred people, tightly packed. Sam immediately began selling tickets to the trial at fifty dollars apiece. He raised the ticket price to one hundred dollars when it became known that Hannah Young had agreed to act as Rollo's defense counsel. The price was still a bargain. Everyone said so.

On the morning of the trial I arrived at the Bank half an hour early to find it swollen with ticket holders. I pushed my way through the crowd, reaching the bar with some difficulty, and waved for my glass and bottle. It was the management's policy to set a fresh bottle of Perry Davis Painkiller in front of me whenever I visited the Bank and to tear up my bartab when I left. In those days there wasn't a saloonkeeper in Canada who would take money from The Man Who Killed Almighty Voice. But for the first time in several years a bottle did not magically appear in front of me.

"Sorry," the bartender apologized. "No liquor for you 'till after the trial."

The man was new, Mike Lynch's replacement. I decided to show tolerance. "Look here, I'm Bonner. Constable Brian Bonner." Nice low voice, no fuss.

The bartender shifted uncomfortably. My temper is well known. On top of that I am a big handsome man who looks even bigger in a bulky elkskin parka with the brass buttons of the Northwest Mounted Police down the front. I was also wearing a pistol strapped to my waist over the parka and I suppose I was in one of my belligerent moods, which probably explains why the bartender hurried through his explanation. "Constantine passed the word about you, Bonner. Like I said, no liquor 'till after the trial."

"You mean he corked the bottle on me?"

Sam Bonnifield appeared at my side. "Come on, Brian. It's not our idea. Constantine says he'll shut down the Bank for three days if you aren't sober when you testify."

"By God, Sam, that's too much! They

4

can't treat me like a damned kid. I don't care whether I testify or not. I might not even be *called* to testify. To hell with Constantine! I'll do my drinking at the Aurora."

"The whole town is corked up. No one will pour you a drink against Constantine's orders."

People nearby were chuckling, but when I wheeled around they turned their heads or hid their grins behind glasses. "What are you *cheechakos* staring at!"

"Nothing, Brian," said Three-Inch White, who stood closest to me. "Not a thing." He moved down the bar.

"Relax," Sam coaxed in his warmest tones. "The trial starts in thirty minutes and it'll be over and done with in another quarter hour. Rollo is guilty as hell. We all saw him kill Mike Lynch. When the trial's over I'll break out my best stuff." he leaned forward, his mustache brushing my ear. "I've got a bottle of Napoleon brandy put away," he whispered. "I was saving it for spring, the day the damned ice cracks on the river. But you and me'll sample it this morning. What do you say?"

Only under very heavy pressure would Silent Sam make such a generous offer. I glanced around and began to feel that same pressure myself. The Bank was packed with Dawson's most important citizens. There was Thomas Fawcett, the Yukon gold commissioner, sharing a table with Swiftwater Bill Gates. Lord Avonmore, who had rafted downriver just before the ice jammed in September with a retinue of servants and chefs, a bulldog, a cargo of tinned hams, a lawn tennis set, and seventy cases of champagne that froze and went to vinegar, sat at the adjoining table in regal isolation. Antone Stander, one of the first Yukon prospectors to strike a million-dollar claim, shared his table with One-Eyed Riley, the Alaska Commercial Company's warehouse nightwatchman. And across the room sat Charles Berry, the six-foot eight-inch fruit grower from California who had pulled his bride over White Pass and down the Yukon valley by sled to stake his rich claim on Bonanza Creek. Dawson's most celebrated ladies were also present. Sitting together in their gaudiest silk dresses were Nellie the Pig, Gussie Lamore, Diamond Tooth Gertie, and half a dozen of their "sisters." William Ogilvie, the government surveyor who measured and certified the claims in the Klondike Gold District, was arguing about the depth of hardpan on Eldorado Creek with Deephole Johnson.

The loudness of my own voice made me suddenly self-conscious. They were all watching, anxious to see my full reaction to Constantine's order. If I tossed a chair through the mirror behind Sam's bar and stalked out of the Bank in a rage, that would be an added fillip to the morning's events.

So I swallowed hard and fought to bring my anger under control. "Okay, Sam. I'll have a shot of that brandy later." And I went to a chair that Swiftwater Bill had saved for me, aware of the mutterings of disappointment around me.

"Morning, Brian," Swiftwater Bill hailed. "Grab that chair before someone steals the damned thing."

Commissioner Fawcett nodded in his ponderous manner. "Hello there, Brian. You're the arresting officer, I understand. Tell me, is there any chance Rollo Moon will be acquitted?"

I shook my head. "I don't see how. Thirty people watched him kill Mike Lynch. Happened in two seconds, but we all saw it. It was a damned neat job of murder, speaking from a purely professional point of view."

"I shouldn't have done my gambling at the Aurora on Wednesday night," Bill groused. "Missed all the excitement." He winked at us. "They had a new gal at the Aurora, came upriver from Circle City by dogsled. I heard she was mighty fine-lookin' but it turned out she could've been one of the sled dogs herself." Bill's expression became more serious. "I hope Constantine hangs Rollo high. Mike Lynch was the best bartender in the Yukon."

Swiftwater Bill had become one of my closest friends among the Yukon prospectors. A little stringbean of a man, Bill had worked his way north two years before as a cook on a tramp steamer. After jumping ship in Nome, Bill found another cook's job on one of the stern-wheeled riverboats that plied the Yukon River between the Bering Sea and Dawson when the river was navigable. He had struck it rich on Bonanza Creek and now he wore a derby hat and Prince Albert coat at all times, even when working his claim. He gambled away as much as a thousand dollars a night in Dawson's saloons and frequently presented expensive gifts to the dancehall girls. The week before he had given Nellie the Pig a necklace of gold nuggets.

"Hey Brian," Axel Anderson called. "I hear Constantine's put you on the wagon."

Several people at nearby tables laughed.

"Just for the morning, Axel. I'll be at the bar two seconds after this trial ends, you can count on that."

"It might not end as soon as you think," Axel said. "Not with Hannah Young talking for Rollo."

The conversation trailed off as each of us indulged in his own thoughts about Hannah Young.

Moments later the doors of the Bank opened to admit Captain Scarth, Inspector Constantine, and the prisoner, Rollo Moon. Another storm had begun outside and the three men's clothes were covered with a fine layer of snow. The Yukon snow is peculiar. It seldom falls wet or mushy. Instead it comes sweeping through the Yukon with a hissing sound, scarring trees and cutting men's faces. The temperature outside had fallen to thirty degrees below zero.

"We'll set up court over there," Constantine told Silent Sam, indicating the far wall across from the bar.

"Right away, sir." Sam grabbed his new bartender and together they quickly dispossesed a half-dozen people from their tables and rearranged a small area so that two tables facing the room served as a magistrate's bench with a witness stand to one side. Usually a slow-moving, taciturn man, Sam was quick as a cat for Constantine.

A place was made for Rollo Moon near the magistrate's bench and the prisoner was given a shot of hooch and a tin plate heaped with pemmican. He drank the hooch straight down and began picking at the dried meat with his fingers. In place of drinking I studied Rollo. I was surprised that little Rollo had found the nerve to murder anyone. The man had previously struck me as completely harmless. He was a tenderfoot, a *cheechako* in Yukon slang, who had come up to Canada from Seattle when the first rumors of the great Yukon gold strike reached the outside world. A man of slight build, receding sandy hair, and unshapen nose, Rollo's only prominent feature was a large Adam's apple. He had been a streetcar conductor in Seattle, hardly the kind of man to commit murder. But then gold had turned many supposedly timid and God-fearing men into killers.

A stirring among the crowd caused me to turn in my chair in time to see Hannah

Young sweep through the doors of the Bank. *Sweep* was just the word for it, too. The damned woman never walked anywhere. She moved through the frozen streets of Dawson like royalty. Even on snowshoes she seemed to glide where others were forced to stamp holes in the snow.

"Hello, boys!" she sang out. "Good morning, Sam. . . . And a good day to you, Inspector Constantine. . . . Captain Scarth, you look very distinguished today."

Scarth and Constantine rose. Constantine even bowed slightly. Hannah flashed them a brilliant smile and sat down next to Rollo, putting her arm around the little man and giving him a hug of support.

At that moment I would have gladly traded places with Rollo even though it meant going into the dock for murder. "That redhead could have any man in this territory," I said.

"You're telling me?" Swiftwater Bill drained off the last of his hooch. "I offered Hannah a trip to Europe and a whatdayacallit—villa— for one night with her. She turned me down flat and that's a fact."

"She's been offered more than that," Commissioner Fawcett confided. "Antone Stander asked her to marry him. She turned him down, too. The woman's too independent by half."

Captain Scarth began hammering on the table with the butt of his Enfield pistol. "Quiet, everyone! Quiet! This is a court of law now, so shut your mouths. That goes for you, too, Deephole Johnson. And Sam, the bar is temporarily closed."

The crowd settled in and fastened its attention on Scarth and Constantine. Constantine cleared his throat. Like myself, he and Captain Scarth were dressed in elkskin parkas with pistols strapped to their waists. Constantine was tall and arrow straight, Scarth shorter and wide as a door. Both men exuded the stuff of stern authority. It's a manner both natural and cultivated by the Northwest Mounted Police. With fewer than thirty mounties to keep the peace over the thousands of square miles of the Yukon Territory, our reputation was our most powerful weapon.

"This court is convened to ascertain the facts regarding the death of Michael Lynch," Constantine began. "Most of you know the special ruling by which the Mounted Police are allowed to operate in this Territory. For those who may not understand, let me just say that the government in Ottawa has decreed that two officers of the R.C.M.P. have the power of a magistrate in these remote outposts."

Constantine glared around as if daring any man to speak out against his authority. No one did. "Now you may also be wondering why Captain Scarth and myself have allowed the court to be convened in these . . . uh . . . unconventional surroundings. There are several factors. First, this crime is more serious than most we have tried here at Dawson. Our usual punishment is a term of hard labor on the government woodpile or a blue ticket out of the territory. The punishment for murder is death. Second, Miss Hannah Young, who is acting as counsel to Rollo Moon, has insisted that the facts can be brought out only by holding this hearing at the scene of the crime. I yielded to her argument in this instance."

That admission by Constantine launched a ripple of whispers and chuckles. So even the Inspector could be moved by Hannah's charm. I should have realized she was the only person who could have talked Constantine into transferring his court from the police barracks to a saloon.

The reaction to this statement caused Constantine's face to redden. "Let's get on with it," he said sharply. "Mr. Moon, step to the chair."

Rollo put aside the plate of pemmican and slouched forward to the witness chair. His doleful expression and the slump of his shoulders advertised his slim hopes for acquittal.

Captain Scarth went right to the question. "Rollo, did you stab Mike Lynch to death Wednesday night here at the Bank Saloon?"

The little man looked at his boot tops as he replied in a low voice, "Yes, I did."

"Did you have any provocation?"

"Any what?"

"Did Mike Lynch threaten you? Did you stab him in self-defense?"

Rollo hesitated. "No, he didn't threaten me."

"Is this the weapon you used?"

Rollo glanced at a knife Scarth put on the table in front of him. It was a crude tool, rusted and pitted along the shaft and bearing a large nick in the hand grip. "Yes, that's my knife."

"Did you bring this knife into the Bank for the purpose of killing Mike?"

"No, sir," Rollo said slowly. "I carry that knife for chopping ice and cutting bacon. I didn't come in here to kill Mike, if that's what you mean. All I wanted was a drink and some company."

"Why did you kill Mike?" Constantine asked.

"He cheated me." For the first time Rollo showed some spunk, lifting his head and looking directly at Constantine as he answered the question.

"Cheated you?" Constantine frowned. "How did he cheat you?"

"I don't know exactly." Rollo squirmed as he attempted to answer the question. "I gave him my poke. He poured some dust on his blower, weighed out the price of the drink, then poured the leftover dust back into my poke and handed it to me."

"I don't understand," Constantine said. "I've seen bartenders do that a thousand times, Mike Lynch included. How did he cheat you? Did he weigh out too much dust?"

"No," Rollo admitted.

"Did he spill some of your dust on the bar? Did you think his scales were rigged?"

Silent Sam Bonnifield stood up abruptly. "Now just a damned minute! Everyone knows my scales are honest. No one's ever questioned the Bank on that."

"Sit down," Constantine commanded.

Rollo was shaking his head. "No, none of them things. I can't tell you how, but I'm sure Mike Lynch cheated me. I've been swindled . . . hustled . . . outsmarted . . . ever since I came to this territory. And this was one time too many. I couldn't take it. Mike cheated me and I saw red. The next thing I knew my knife was in my hand and I shoved it into Mike's chest." Rollo put his hands over his face. "God! I don't know how he did it, but he took too much of my dust. I didn't have that much to begin with, so I could tell. But Jesus, I shouldn't have killed a man over the price of a drink. I'm sorry . . . dear God, I'm sorry. . . ." And Rollo began sobbing quietly into his hands.

Hannah Young stood and the crowd drew in its collective breath. This was the scene they had come for, the moment for which many of the spectators had struggled thirty miles through snow and ice to watch.

"Inspector, now that Rollo has admitted killing Mike and given you his reason, I'd like to ask him a few questions myself."

Constantine and Scarth exchanged a quick

glance. They were touchy about the influence Hannah had already exerted on them, but her request couldn't be seen as unreasonable. Constantine said, "Go ahead, Hannah."

"Thank you." Hannah took off her marten fur cap and heavy mackinaw jacket. As she stepped forward she tossed her hair to straighten out the tangles and three hundred men ached for her, including me.

I had spent a good many long winter nights analyzing the way Hannah affected men. She was pretty, yes, and young, tall, firmly built with a longish face framed by tangles of red hair. But her eyes were her most stunning feature. Green and probing, they could strip away a man's surface toughness and leave him stuttering like a tongue-tied kid. Her eyes challenged you to live up to old expectations of yourself. And she had that bold way of moving, as if expecting seas to part in front of her. Hannah was ambitious, too. She bought, sold, and traded gold claims as if they were trinkets. No one knew whether she would come out of the winter a millionaire or a bankrupt, her business affairs were so complicated. Hannah drove tough bargains, tougher than any man in Dawson. But just when you started to forget she was a woman,

Hannah would do something softly feminine, like giving Rollo a hug to buck up his spirits or calling on a sick miner with a fruit jar of hot soup or showing up at the Aurora in a green dress instead of her usual pants and mackinaw and dancing with every man in the house.

She was a tigress and a kitten and I loved her. From the first moment I set eyes on her, I knew she was trouble. Vast, magnificent trouble, like the Yukon itself. And I have always been drawn to trouble. She had turned me inside out the way no other woman had ever done, but loving her would never do me any good. Hannah had made it clear a dozen times that she considered me a loafer and drunkard who would never amount to anything.

Now she stood waiting for Rollo to get hold of himself. She showed no sign of impatience or disgust at Rollo's breakdown, only an attitude of calm concern. When Rollo finally did raise his head and straighten his back, Hannah put her hand on his shoulder and squeezed it gently. "It's all right, Rollo. Of course you're sorry for what you did. But you were right about Mike Lynch. He did cheat you."

"No speeches, Hannah." Inspector Constantine's rebuke was sharp. "Just ask your questions."

"All right." She fixed her green eyes on Rollo's face. "How much gold did you have when you came into the Bank?"

The little man shrugged. "Maybe an ounce."

"And how much did you have after Mike took out the price of your drink?"

"Hardly anything at all. Less than half an ounce, I'd guess."

"What grade of dust do you carry?"

"Commercial dust, like most everyone else."

Commercial dust was a coarse grade of gold liberally laced with sand. It brought only eleven dollars an ounce compared to clean dust, which was worth sixteen dollars an ounce. Most of the miners in the Klondike District used commercial dust to pay their bills. Some even salted their pokes with brass filings to make their money go farther.

Hannah did a little quick calculating for the benefit of the gallery and Rollo's judges. "So you gave Mike Lynch eleven dollars worth of gold dust. From that amount he was supposed to take the price of a shot of hooch, one dollar. That would be about one-tenth of an ounce. And instead he took almost your entire poke, am I right?"

"Yes, that's what happened. But I still don't know how he did it. I was watching him every minute."

"One more question, Rollo. How have you been earning a living since you came north?"

"Well, I staked a claim on Henderson Creek as soon as I got here, but it was a skunk. Wasn't worth the filing fee. Then I worked for Joe Ladue snagging stray logs off the river for his lumber mill. Now I'm doing handywork mostly. I made a few dollars last week salvaging nails from the old burnt-out Opera House. Axel Anderson bought them at thirty dollars a pound for building sluice boxes."

"Thanks, Rollo. You can go back to your seat now."

Rollo left the witness chair with everyone wondering exactly what Hannah was up to. So far she hadn't put forward much of a defense for Rollo. All she'd done was bring out some cockeyed story about Mike Lynch taking too much gold for Rollo's drink.

"Can I call a witness?" Hannah asked.

"Of course," Constantine replied. "There

20

were about thirty people present at the time of the killing. You know who they were. Take your pick."

"I call Constable Brian Bonner."

I went to the witness chair with a heavy stride to prove my sobriety to Constantine. When I sat down Constantine said, "I'd like to ask a few questions before you start on him, Hannah. Constable Bonner, did you see Rollo Moon stab Mike Lynch to death last Wednesday night?"

I nodded forcefully. "I did, sir. And I arrested him immediately afterwards."

"Did Rollo say anything to Mike before he killed him? Was there an argument of any kind?"

"No sir. Poor Mike had just poured a drink and the next thing I knew Rollo drew his knife and did for him in the chest. I saw the whole thing from over there." I motioned to a spot at the end of Sam Bonnifield's bar. "I was too far away to help poor Mike, but I saw everything that happened."

"Did you see Mike Lynch do anything suspicious?" Scarth asked. "I'm referring, of course, to Rollo's accusation that Mike stole some of his poke."

"I saw nothing like that," I answered firmly.

21

I am a damned convincing witness when I put my mind to it.

"Thank you, constable. Go ahead, Hannah."

Hannah smiled at me and came forward with her hands in her pockets and her shoulders thrown back. It took all my self-control to keep my eyes from wandering to her breasts. They were dancing around like two cats in a bag.

"Constable Bonner, I'd appreciate it if you didn't refer to the late Mr. Lynch as 'Poor Mike'. It sounds as if you've already dismissed Rollo's story as untrue."

I grinned back at her. "Okay, Hannah. And I'll be glad to call your client 'Poor Rollo' a few times to even up the score."

The gallery burst out laughing and I winked broadly at them from the side of my face that was hidden from Scarth and Constantine.

Hannah continued to smile. If anything her grin was even wider and more friendly. "Tell me, what were you doing here at the Bank on Wednesday night?"

I had come prepared for that one. "I was inspecting the premises for fire hazards."

"Very commendable. Do you inspect the Bank for fire hazards every night?"

"Of course not."

Hannah put her hands behind her back. "That's right. I'm told that other evenings you inspect the Aurora or the M and M Saloon. And still other nights you can be seen sniffing out potential flames at the Blue Ox or Diamond Tooth Gertie's. I've heard it said that if the old Opera House had a bar, Constable Bonner would never have let it burn down."

The gallery roared again. This time I didn't join in. My face had gone hot with embarrassment and I knew without looking that Constantine and Scarth were glaring at me. Neither officer would have much sympathy for a mountie who laid himself open to ridicule.

"I do my duty," I said seriously, and was dismayed when my reply drew still louder laughter.

"That's enough!" Constantine drummed for order again with the butt of his pistol. "I've told you not to make speeches, Hannah, unless you want this court moved back to the barracks."

"I'm sorry, Inspector. I didn't mean to make sport of Constable Bonner. I was only trying to point out that he's familiar with the Bank and its employees."

I watched in amazement as Hannah worked her charms on the two officers, wringing a grudging smile out of Scarth in reply to what I could see was a totally insincere apology.

Hannah continued with her questions. "Tell me Constable Bonner . . . Brian . . . did you notice Mike Lynch do this . . . ," and she pushed back her hair from her forehead, "While he was measuring out Rollo's poke in the blower?"

"I didn't see poor . . . I didn't notice Mike do anything like that."

"Forget Wednesday night. Haven't you often seen Mike Lynch at other times brush his hair back like this . . ." and she repeated the action.

Gradually I recalled that I had seen Mike push the hair out of his eyes, many times. "Yes, I guess I have. I suppose his hair got mussed up when there was a crowd at the bar and he was working hard. So what?"

"I'm asking the questions. I have one more. Did you ever notice the length of Mike Lynch's hair and fingernails?"

I couldn't resist the opening. "I haven't been in the Yukon *that* long, Hannah."

The answer drew another long laugh. This time even Scarth and Constantine chuckled.

"I'm glad to hear it," Hannah continued. "For the record, Mike had very long fingernails and hair. Those are all the questions I have for you."

I left the witness chair and returned to my seat at Swiftwater Bill's table more confused than ever. I could see no connection between the length of Mike's hair and fingernails and Rollo's reasons for killing him.

"I have one exhibit for the court," Hannah was saying. "Can I have it brought in?"

"Brought in?" Constantine was as confused as everyone else. "I don't see why you didn't bring your evidence to court to begin with."

"That might have been difficult," Hannah replied. "My evidence won't last long indoors." She turned and waved at two men standing just inside the front doors of the bank. "Carry him in, boys."

Phillips and Crowley were two miners who sometimes worked Hannah's claims for wages when they weren't trying to coax the yellow metal out of their own claims. When Hannah waved they giggled like kids and went outside with their collars turned up against the wind and snow. They were back in less time than it takes me to polish off a shot of Perry Davis Painkiller, Phillips at the front and Crowley at the foot of a six-foot wood plank. A body lay on the plank covered with a canvas tarpaulin. The corpse could only be Mike Lynch, who had been laid out in the open behind the N.A.T. & T. warehouse with only the tarp to cover him, preserved by the sub-zero temperatures.

Constantine exploded. "Hannah, I won't have you turning my courtroom into a three-ring circus!"

"I'm not doing any such thing!" Hannah fired back. "Mike Lynch's body is evidence and I demand the right to examine that evidence in open court."

"Examine it? Examine it for what?"

"I'll show you." Phillips and Crowley had laid the plank bearing Mike's body across the roulette table. Hannah went over to it and turned back the tarpaulin, revealing Mike's head and shoulders. Mike was a fine figure of a man in death, as he had been in life. Though with the face muscles contracted around his mouth, his teeth looked yellower than I had recalled. "I had Mike's body moved inside the warehouse this morning so he'd thaw out in time for the trial," Hannah explained.

"This is disgusting," Captain Scarth objected.

"What I have to do won't take long. Did you bring the pan and soap?" she asked Crowley.

"Right here." Crowley handed her one of the shallow twelve-inch pans that miners use to wash gold and a bar of Orange Flower Skin Food, a toilet soap popular with Dawson's whores.

"What the hell is that woman up to?" Swiftwater Bill whispered.

"I don't know," I whispered back. "But she sure as hell is giving these sourdoughs full value for their hundred-dollar tickets."

That was true enough. The Bank had become so quiet that even at the rear of the saloon the spectators could hear the faint sound Hannah's hands made as she lathered them with soap and water. When she nodded to Crowley he lifted a large pitcher and began pouring water slowly over Mike Lynch's head. As Crowley did so, Hannah began washing the corpse's hair with the soap. She had positioned the pan on the floor directly under Mike's head so that the soapy water flowed into the pan.

Hannah spent a good five minutes washing Mike Lynch's hair, shampooing it slowly, rinsing it, shampooing again, rerinsing. Not a word was said during the strange scene, not even by Constantine or Scarth. Everyone understood that Hannah would make whatever point she was after in her own way and in her own sweet time. Besides, the sight of Hannah Young washing a dead man's hair was an event to be savored in later conversations.

At last Hannah finished washing Mike Lynch's hair. But those who hoped she would now make her point were disappointed. Next she drew out Mike's hands and began cleaning the dirt from under his fingernails with a pocketknife. Once again the pan was positioned so that the dirt from under Mike's fingernails fell into it. She cleaned each of Mike's fingernails slowly and thoroughly. I knew Hannah understood the powerful impact her strange acts were having on the crowd in the Bank.

"Are you finished?" Constantine asked.

"Yes," Hannah answered.

The inspector sighed in relief. "Thank

God. Perhaps now you'll tell us what that was all about."

"I'll do better than tell you. I'll show you. Give me a little room, boys."

Hannah held the pan out at arm's length and began rotating it gently. Gradually the pan dipped lower and the water began sloshing out. In two minutes Hannah washed all the water and dirt from the pan. Then she tilted the pan so that everyone could see what was in the bottom.

"Gold!" The word came from several throats at once.

"That's right," Hannah confirmed. "Gold. Mike Lynch covered his hands with grease so that gold would stick to them when he was making change from your pokes. Some of it would get under his fingernails. The gold that stuck to his hands would be transferred to his hair, which was also heavily greased. That's why you'd often see Mike running his hands through his hair."

"The slick bastard," Swiftwater Bill muttered.

"Give me your blower," Hannah said to Sam Bonnifield.

Sam passed it to her nervously. "I didn't

know Mike was cheating people," he wailed. "I swear I didn't."

"We all know that," Hannah said. "Mike Lynch was a small-time chiseler. No one who's seen you drop twenty thousand in a game of cards without batting an eye would ever say that about Sam Bonnifield."

Hannah poured the gold from the pan into the scales. She adjusted the counterweight and announced, "Seven ounces. Mike would go home after work every night and clean close to a hundred dollars out of his hair and fingernails. Rollo didn't know that when he killed Mike, but he did know Mike had somehow cheated him. Mike probably cheated all of you at one time or other. I often saw Mike pass his hands through his hair. When Rollo explained what happened to him, the reason behind Mike's habit clicked into place for me."

The sentiment in the Bank had shifted violently away from "poor old Mike Lynch" in favor of Rollo. At my table Commissioner Fawcett was saying, "Mike Lynch never was any good. He deserted a wife and two children in Denver, you know. And there was talk about the way he left Denver; someone told me very confidentially that Mike skipped town with the insurance money from a widow lady he'd been seeing."

"Mike was a rat," Swiftwater Bill agreed. "There wasn't an honest bone in the man's body. I've said so many a time."

"I want quiet and I want it right now!" Constantine barked. He and Scarth had been whispering together while everyone else in the Bank had been discussing Mike Lynch's newly discovered faults. "Captain Scarth and I have reached a decision in this case. Rollo, you are hereby acquitted of the charge of murder. However, you did kill a man without very much *direct* provocation. You should have brought your suspicions to the police barracks. Therefore we're issuing a blue ticket out of the territory. You're banned from the Klondike Gold District for a period of six months. We have a mountie going to Circle City by dogsled tomorrow with some mail; you'll go with him."

"That's better than hanging," Rollo grinned.

Constantine and Scarth stood together. "This court is adjourned. God save the Queen!"

"God save the Queen!" the Canadians in the crowd echoed.

31

"And the drinks are on the Bank," added Sam Bonnifield, anxious to obscure the fact that his bartender had stolen thousands of dollars from his customers. A shout of appreciation and a mass exodus in the direction of the bar greeted Sam's offer. The trial was over.

I watched Hannah hug Rollo and offer her hand to Constantine and Scarth. They accepted it warmly. That didn't surprise me. What did surprise me was that Hannah next came up to me.

"Brian, I'm sorry if I embarrassed you in the witness chair. You made me sore, though. I knew Rollo had cause for what he did and I wasn't about to let him hang. You understand, don't you?"

"Yeah . . . sure . . . I suppose so." I cursed myself for stumbling over my words. But with those green eyes turned on me I found it difficult to talk straight. "No hard feelings," I said in a steadier voice.

"Good. And listen, I want to talk to you about something. Can you stop at my cabin tonight when you're off duty? Any time will be fine. If I'm not in the cabin I'll be down in the shaft. Just give a yell."

"I guess I can make it."

I had no idea why she wanted to see me, and at that moment I didn't care. It was enough that every man in the Bank was watching us and that several people standing nearby had heard the invitation.

"Here's a better idea," Hannah said. "Have dinner with me. I bought some fresh venison from a Chilkoot hunter yesterday. You must be tired of the bacon and beans they serve at the barracks. I don't have any vegetables to go with the meat, but I do have an apple left from a bag of fruit I bought off the *Mary Dwyer* last fall. Can you make it for dinner?"

Dinner with Hannah! I could hardly believe my ears. "I'd like that, Hannah. And I'll supply the refreshments, a bottle of Napoleon Brandy."

That drew a gasp of surprise from her. "Napoleon Brandy! I thought Perry Davis Painkiller was your drink."

"Oh, I like a taste of good brandy now and then." I tried to keep the swagger out of my voice. Hannah didn't go for men who swaggered, I knew that about her.

"Then bring it along, Brian." She smiled and moved toward the door, stopping to accept congratulations and turn down offers for drinks.

When she was gone I grabbed Silent Sam from behind the bar and pulled him into a corner. "I'll have that brandy you promised me, Sam. And I'm afraid I'll need the whole bottle."

"The whole bottle?" Sam looked stricken. "Not a chance." He shot a glance at his customers, who were doing their best to clean out his stock while the drinks were free. "Look at those thirsty bastards. Today will cost me a fortune as it is. I'm not passing over a full bottle of Napoleon brandy, too."

"Look, Sam. Hannah Young invited me to dinner and I promised her a bottle of Napoleon brandy. If you don't hand it over I'll find myself a nice piece of cordwood and just about bust this place down to the ground. The only thing I'll leave in one piece will be that moldy old moosehead over the bar."

Sam studied my expression and knew that I wasn't bluffing. The fact that I'd once actually destroyed a saloon in Circle City helped convince him. And then, none of Sam's customers would be inclined to stop me after the tricks Mike Lynch had pulled behind Sam's

34

bar. He sighed. "I'll get your brandy. Just let me have one drink before you take the bottle. Christ, I need it."

2

I WAS ordered to report to Inspector Constantine immediately after the trial. When I arrived at his office in the barracks Constantine was going over some documents with a pained look. I should have known they concerned me.

"Brian, I've just had some disturbing news about you." he brandished a paper in my face. "I have here a letter from a Mr. Andrew Rose, managing director of the Bank of Montreal. He's lodged an official complaint against you at headquarters in Ottawa."

"Why, this is outrageous. I don't even know this man Rose."

"He obviously knows you. His description is accurate right down to the stubble of beard on your jaw. I see you didn't stand close enough to your razor this morning, as usual. And your uniform is none too clean, either."

I rubbed my jaw and found that he was correct. I hadn't shaved very close. Actually, I hadn't shaved at all that morning. It's not safe to draw a razor across your throat with a hangover. I almost did for myself that way once. "I'm sorry, sir. I'll buy myself a new razor, my old one doesn't seem to hold an edge anymore."

"Never mind that right now. The fact remains that Mr. Rose does seem to know you. Apparently he shared a Canadian Pacific coach with you and the prisoner Jack Dunnock when you took Dunnock to Edmonton last fall."

"I still don't remember him."

"Do you recall a man from whom you confiscated three quarts of whiskey on the train trip to Edmonton?"

"Yes, I do. But his name slipped my mind. Andrew Rose? Yes, that could have been his name. And I did confiscate three bottles. Very fine whiskey, too. But my actions were completely legal and in accordance with the Act for the Preservation of Peace in the Vicinity of Public Works, which I'm sure you know prohibits gambling and drinking for an area of ten miles on either side of a railroad line."

"I know the law," Constantine snapped. "And I'm aware that you've used that particular law many times to your own advantage."

NOV 0 6 1995

Baker County Public Library
2400 Resort St.
Baker City, OR 97814

37

"My own advantage? I don't know what you mean, sir."

"I mean that you took the whiskey for yourself. Mr. Rose states in his complaint that he was not drinking on the train, that he merely opened his valise to show another passenger some extremely expensive whiskey he had purchased in Vancouver. He says you were sitting near him with your prisoner, saw the whiskey, and confiscated it illegally. He further charges that you used highly abusive language and that he later saw both you and the prisoner drinking from one of his own bottles in an Edmonton restaurant."

"That can't be true, sir. I deposited those bottles with the mountie post at Edmonton."

"You did?" Constantine looked unsure of himself for the first time. "Then you must have a receipt. Give it to me and I'll forward it to Ottawa, along with your explanation."

"I'm not sure they gave me a receipt for those bottles."

"They must have."

"They don't run the Edmonton post with an eye on the regulations, I'm afraid. Not like you do, sir. I was distressed, in fact, to see the sloppy condition of the post. I don't believe I'd care to serve at Edmonton, sir."

Constantine made a humming sound which I had come to identify over the months as a signal of frustration. The sound bucked up my spirits considerably, as it meant he was about to abandon his complaints of my conduct on the Edmonton train. It happens that I did remember Andrew Rose. Who could forget the loudmouthed dude. And yes, I drank his liquor. It was too good for him anyway, him and his scented handkerchiefs, putting them to his nose every time I passed his seat. If he'd just chased a bank robber to ground, sleeping in his clothes for a week, he'd have had a ripe old aroma himself.

"Brian, you've given me more disciplinary problems than any mountie I've ever commanded. If it weren't for your heroism at Duck Lake you'd have been discharged from the force long ago. I mean that. You're a good constable when you put your mind to it, but the drinking, the brawling, the other infractions have *got* to stop. Do you understand?"

"Yes, sir."

Of course I had no intention of abandoning a set of habits that had served me well for all of my thirty-two years. We both knew that the Northwest Mounted Police wasn't going to cashier its most renowned hero, The Man

Who Killed Almighty Voice. A year before I had tracked down Almighty Voice, a Cree Indian who had murdered several people. I cornered him and three of his men at Duck Lake. They shot me up pretty good, but I finished the four of them and that fight made me famous. Now my post was safe unless I hacked up a clergyman with an axe or exposed myself on the Parliament floor. I was more popular with the public than with the mountie command, however. The High Commissioner himself had shipped me off to the Yukon because it was the most isolated and desolate territory in Canada.

Imagine the High Commissioner's annoyance when the Yukon produced the biggest gold strike since the California bonanza of '49. There were already more than five thousand people in the Klondike Gold District, with another twenty or thirty thousand stampeders waiting for the spring thaw in order to get into the territory. Not a very good spot to hide the black sheep of the Northwest Mounted Police. I say kick me to hell out or let me do the job my way. It takes more than a close shave, a clean uniform, and a sober breath to stay alive and get the job done in a wild country like the Yukon.

"We'll let headquarters sort this one out." Constantine put aside Mr. Rose's complaint. "I have more urgent matters at the moment. In fact Captain Scarth and Constable Van Ness are supposed to join us. Ah, here they are. . . ."

We could hear the snow being stamped off four big feet outside the door and presently Captain Scarth and Constable Evan Van Ness came into Constantine's office, ducking their heads to avoid the low-hanging door beam.

"Sorry we're late," Scarth apologized. "The snow is coming down hard. Looks like she might be a bad one tonight."

Constable Van Ness was exercising his face muscles to work off the effects of the stiffening cold. He was fairly new to the R.C.M.P., less than a year's service, but Constantine thought well of him. Van Ness always had a nice clean shave and he made a practice of volunteering for nasty pieces of business. You rarely saw him in a saloon, but he was often at Father William Judge's makeshift infirmary helping tend the victims of scurvy and meningitis, the two most serious health problems in Dawson. He enforced rigidly the law against gambling and drinking in Dawson on Sunday. Anyone he caught breaking that law invariably spent a four-day term on the government woodpile.

I didn't much care for Van Ness.

"Hello, Brian. I hear Hannah Young chewed you up good at the trial this morning."

He didn't care much for me, either.

Constantine cleared his throat and shuffled some papers. "Do you think the patrols will be able to get out of Dawson tomorrow?" he asked Scarth.

The captain nodded. "I think so."

"What patrols?" I asked.

"We're sending out two patrols in the morning," Constantine explained. "There are several prospectors who haven't been seen for three weeks or more. Some of them might be too starved to make it into Dawson. You know what the food situation is. We'll be lucky to avoid a famine." The inspector took out his pipe and began packing it carefully with a small amount of tobacco. Even tobacco came dear in the Yukon in the winter of '98. "I want this kept strictly between us; the A.C.C. and N.A.T. & T. warehouses have barely enough food on hand to last until the first week in May. If the ice breaks late on the river this year . . ." His face darkened. "Well, gold won't mean much then."

"How's the whiskey holding out?"

I didn't plan to ask the question. It just popped out. In fact it gave me quite a start to hear my own voice.

Scarth had the decency to laugh, but Constantine just sucked in his cheeks and looked grim. "I think you'll survive, Brian."

Scarth changed the subject to take me off the hook. The captain liked a drink himself, you see. "Evan has volunteered to go downriver with Father Judge. We want you to go upriver Brian."

"That's fine, but who'll go with me? Father Judge is a medical missionary. About all I know of medicine is how to stuff a rag in a bullet hole."

"Hannah Young has agreed to go with you."

Good God! Was it my birthday? I had never been presented with so many fine gifts on one day. First Hannah Young invites me for dinner, then she volunteers to go upriver with me.

"How far am I to go?" Van Ness inquired.

"From Forty-Mile to the Alaska border," Scarth said. "You'll be carrying two hundred pounds of dried fish and fruit. That's the best we can do. Brian, you and Hannah will go upriver as far as the Stewart. You'll carry the same amount of supplies. Be frugal with them, help those who are in the worst shape."

I wasn't surprised that they had asked Hannah to make the swing upriver, just that they were letting her go with me. Hannah and Father Judge were the closest we had to doctors in Dawson. The Father knew some medicine but Hannah simply liked to take care of people, or to boss them around when they were too weak to talk back. Whatever her motives, Hannah was always prepared to do some quick doctoring. She kept a medical kit in her cabin that included such items as compound catharitic pills for moving the bowels; carbolic anica salve for cuts, running ulcers, and fever sores; Boll's Remedy for freeing the system of boils; Bromo Vichy, a popular nerve steadier and morning bracer; pure Norwegian cod liver oil that would stop the advance of scurvy in the most emaciated person; effervescent lithia tablets, known to work wonders in cases of subacute and chronic rheumatism, gout, and irritable bladder; plus a dozen other remedies the names of which escape my memory.

"Is your dog team in good condition, Evan?"

"Yes, they're all right, sir."

Constantine didn't even bother to ask me that question. When it came to my gun and dogs I was always prepared.

"We have one other problem to discuss today. In the long run this one may be as bad as the food situation." Constantine puffed at his pipe. "Captain Moore came in from Skagway this morning with the mail." The inspector's face glowed with admiration. "I don't see how the old seadog does it, running a dogteam five hundred miles downriver with a load of mail at his age. He must be over seventy."

The old sea captain also carried a few bottles of liquor in his mail sacks. And he didn't shave or bathe more than was necessary to keep the fleas from multiplying too fast, but Constantine didn't want to hear that.

"He brought me a report from Colonel Steele," Constantine said, referring to Col. Samuel Enfield Steele, commander of all mountie forces in the Yukon Territory. "Steele says the number of people coming over White Pass is increasing every day. By May he expects twenty thousand to be camped on Lake Bennett waiting for the ice

45

to break on the Yukon. On the Alaska side of the line Soapy Smith and his gang are growing powerful and dangerous. There's a murder almost every day in Skagway. Hundreds have landed at the Skagway docks only to be robbed of their stakes before they could reach the Canadian border. The colonel suspects that Smith has a plan for moving his operations into Canada this spring. Smith may already have sent some of his men in here to sniff out the possibilities, so keep your eyes open."

Colonel Steel's information didn't surprise me. I knew Soapy Smith from the old days, when I made a living smuggling whiskey across the border from the U.S. into Canada. Soapy had a lively sense of villainy. When I first met him in Colorado he was selling ten-cent cakes of soap at five dollars apiece, somehow convincing suckers that each cake of soap contained a twenty dollar gold piece. That's where he earned the nickname Soapy. His given name was Jefferson Randolph Smith and he was rumored to be a Southern Baptist minister gone bad. When the gold rush began Soapy moved up to Skagway, a small port on the Alaska panhandle only thirty miles from the Canadian border. Now he ruled the town like one of those tinpot South American dictators, with his own private army to put down any challenges to his authority and a gang of confidence men and killers who fleeced the *cheechakos* coming off ships at Skagway.

Constantine dismissed us after issuing some further instructions about the patrols Evan and I were taking out in the morning. I hardly listened to him. My thoughts were about dinner with Hannah Young. If I could jolly her into a good mood tonight, anything might happen on the trail.

That evening found me tramping down Front Street through ankle-deep snow toward Hannah's cabin in the gold fields.

The gold fields around Dawson were a fabulous place in those days. Dawson itself is in the middle of nowhere on a river that starts near Alaska, goes like hell for five hundred miles through Canada, then flows back into Alaska some fifty miles downriver of Dawson and on toward the Bering Sea. Every river in northwest Canada and southern Alaska feeds into the Yukon.

Dawson was built on a one-hundred-and-seventy-acre town site owned by just two men, Joe Ladue and Art Harper, who bought the parcel of swampland from the Crown. Bill Ogilvie, the government surveyor, laid out the town so that every street is exactly sixty-six feet wide. Front Street, the main avenue, faces on the Yukon river.

As you walked down Front Street you passed most of the town's landmarks: the M & M Saloon, the Pioneer Saloon, Diamond Tooth Gertie's Saloon, the Aurora, the Bank Saloon and Gambling House, the Blue Ox Saloon, and others of lesser reputation. The two big trading companies that operated on the Yukon River also had their stores and warehouses on Front Street. They were the North American Trading and Transportation Company and the Alaska Commercial Company. The A.C.C. was so well established on the river that it was often referred to simply as the Company. I was an N.A.T. & T. man myself. Give me the upstart every time, he'll do you a better deal than the big fellow.

The recording office, run by Commissioner Fawcett, was also located on Front Street. You could usually find a line of prospectors there waiting to file claims. The line wasn't long in the winter of '98 because everyone had already filed and no one could stake more than one claim in the Klondike Gold District. You could trade and buy claims to your heart's content, of course. That was Hannah Young's favorite game.

In between the buildings on Front Street were smaller businesses, many of them housed in tents, lawyers, barbers, tinkers, and the like. You might think barbers would starve in the Yukon but they did a brisk business. Most sourdoughs shave regularly because in sub-zero weather the moisture from your breath will collect in a beard and freeze. Only *cheechakos* grow beards in the Yukon.

Inspector Constantine mentioned the food problem and he didn't exaggerate. A dinner of boiled potatoes and an apple went for five dollars. Eggs were fifty dollars a dozen and salt cost its weight in gold. Most people made do with hardtack, bacon, and a little dried fruit and fish. Real coffee brought forty dollars a pound and I have seen a handful of old coffee grounds go for ten dollars.

Most of the folks in Dawson lived in shacks built from green spruce. I knew millionaires who felt lucky to have a twelve-by-twelve-foot cabin with a reliable stove and flue. The whores had the best places in town on a back street known as Paradise Alley. They didn't have red lights, though. Coal oil was too expensive. Instead they advertised with red curtains.

I lived in the police barracks at the foot of Front Street and got by as well as any man. The pay was only two dollars a day, but bed and board went with it and most of my liquor was free because I'm The Man Who Killed Almighty Voice.

The whiskey situation was both good and bad in the winter of '98. By that I mean the supply was holding out, but the quality was terrible. There were no decent brands available. No real whiskey at all. Just hooch. Hooch is sometimes called "fifty-foot whiskey" because its aroma has been said to kill small animals at that distance. Personally, hooch agrees with me. They sold four different brands in the Dawson saloons: Red Tiger, Juice of the Snake, Chilkoot Dynamite and Perry Davis Painkiller. I'm partial to Perry Davis Painkiller. My affection for it goes back to the days when whiskey was outlawed on the Canadian frontier except in medicinal compounds. In those days I seemed to have a chronic sore throat that required liberal daily doses of Perry Davis Painkiller. My sore throat didn't clear up until that damnable whiskey law was struck from the books.

I crossed the footbridge spanning the Klondike a few hundred yards upriver of the Yukon and started towards Hunker Creek. Hannah's newest claim was Hunker Thirty-Nine Above. Each claim in the Klondike Gold District measured five hundred feet along the creekbed, and from one rim of the creek to the other. Claims were numbered beginning at the first claim filed on the creek, which was known as the Discovery Claim. So Hannah's claim was the thirty-ninth above the Discovery Claim on Hunker Creek.

Up and down the creek prospectors had driven shafts down to bedrock, creating a valley of craters. Most of the timber on the slopes had been cut to build cabins and shore up the shafts. The floor of the Yukon valley is frozen in winter, which forced the prospectors to devise a unique method for making their shaft holes. They simply set fire to large logs and burned holes in the ground, shoveling out the muck of melted earth after a day's burning. A permanent haze hung over the Klondike from the hundreds of shaft fires in the valley.

I always made a point of passing Charles Berry's cabin when I went up the Klondike.

Berry was a gentleman of rare quality. A weary traveler would always find a bottle of whiskey and a tobacco can full of gold nuggets sitting on a tree stump in front of his cabin. Over the stump, nailed to his cabin wall, was a sign that read *Help Yerself*.

After refreshing myself at Berry's hospitality, I continued up the creek to Hannah's cabin. It was your standard twelve-by-twelve-foot shack, but nicely fixed up. Hannah had installed windows of genuine glass, using the bottoms of vinegar bottles set into the frame and chinked together with clay. The roof, which was covered with sod, served a double purpose. Hannah would plant radishes and lettuce up there in the spring and have her own vegetable garden.

I knocked on her door but received no answer. I went on in. The cabin was snugly fitted out inside with a small sheet-iron stove used for both cooking and heating, a shelf for her groceries and personal things, and a mattress stuffed with spruce twigs. There was also a water trough in one corner, used for everything from cleaning and cooking to washing small amounts of dirt to provide gold dust and nuggets for buying groceries and other necessities.

I put the brandy on the shelf and went out looking for Hannah. She had started a new shaft since the last time I had come past her cabin. I found her down in the shaft excavating the dirt that had been thawed in the day's burning.

"Hey down there! It's dinner time."

"Brian? Do me a favor and lift this one last bucketful."

"Sure." There was a windlass positioned above the five-foot-square shaft. I grabbed the handle and began turning. When the bucket rose aboveground I swung it out and kicked it over on a conical-shaped mound of dirt next to the shaft. That was Hannah's "dump". There wasn't enough unfrozen water to wash large amounts of dirt in the winter, so every miner concentrated on building his dumps until the spring thaw. Then the dumps would be washed in sluice boxes and the prospectors would learn for sure just how rich . . . or how poor . . . they were.

"Hannah?" I peered into the hole but couldn't see her. The heavy log from the afternoon's burning still smoldered, sending a thin mist of smoke up the shaft.

I hoisted my leg over the side and scrambled down the ladder to the bottom. The mining shafts in the Yukon go down eighteen to twenty feet before hitting hardpan. At the bottom I found myself standing in a cavern. Hannah had been "drifting" her claim for about two weeks, enlarging the bottom of the shaft by digging out the walls on all sides.

She emerged suddenly from the gloom of the cavern dressed in pants and shirtsleeves and carrying a pick. Her long face bore lines of disappointment.

"I was right," she announced.

"That's good. What were you right about?"

"This claim is a skunk."

"A skunk? It can't be. You paid seventy thousand dollars for this claim, or so I heard in the Aurora."

She nodded. "From Axel Anderson no doubt, gloating over the deal he made. Well, I asked for it. I thought this claim would pay a thousand dollars a foot and I'm getting tests that show more like sixty dollars a foot. Axel took me to the cleaners all right."

I was dismayed for her. I knew Hannah had put every cent she could scrape together into this claim, selling off three other promising properties to buy it. She had gone through her booms and busts before, but this one might just finish her off.

To my surprise Hannah smiled and said, "Let's eat. I'm starved." Then she scampered up the ladder like a kid.

I followed. By the time I reached the cabin she was already plunging her face and arms into the water trough. "Oww! This water is colder than the ice on the river. Throw another log in the stove."

A few minutes later we were sitting knee to knee across a packing crate near the stove. The crate served Hannah as a desk, dinner table, butcher's block, and breakfront. I watched as long as I could stand it while she rolled a large piece of venison around in a pile of flour she had sprinkled on top of the crate. Finally I snatched the meat away from her. "That's no way to handle good venison. Give me your kettle and let me do the cooking."

"You're the guest," Hannah said. "So I suppose I'll have to do what you say. But I'm going to be mad if you turn out to be a worse cook than I am."

"I don't know if I could fix a fancy dish like those crepe suzettes I once had in New Orleans, but when it comes to a game dish I know my business."

She watched closely while I cubed the venison and re-rolled it in the flour. From inside the pocket of my parka I took a jar of clean fat and some vegetables swiped from the barracks kitchen. I poured about three tablespoons of fat into the kettle, melted it over the fire, and added the meat. I let the meat brown a while, then produced a bottle of red wine from another inside pocket and poured about ten ounces into the kettle. When the whole thing was simmering nicely I sliced an onion into it along with a couple of potatoes and carrots and a sprig of parsley. Each item I produced made Hannah's smile grow wider.

"You win," Hannah said. "You're a better cook than I am. What do you call that?"

"Hunter's stew."

The cabin was beginning to fill with the aroma of the stew. Hannah closed her eyes and inhaled deeply. "Lord! If I weren't half frozen I'd swear I was sitting at the best table at Grissom's Steak House in San Francisco."

"San Francisco?" I uncorked the bottle of brandy. "Is that your home town?"

Her eyes opened and narrowed at the same time. "I don't have a home town," she said coolly.

I shrugged and took two tin cups from the shelf. One thing about a twelve by twelve cabin, you can reach most everything without standing up.

"Sorry," Hannah said. "I didn't mean to snap at you. I was raised first in an orphanage and then in foster homes, *lots* of foster homes. I didn't finish school so I couldn't find the kind of work I wanted. It was either marriage or the Yukon, so I struck out north."

"What's so bad about marriage?"

"Nothing." Hannah sipped the brandy I had poured for her. "Mmm, that's good. I'm not even going to ask where it came from. You probably did something horrible to get it." She returned to the subject of marriage. "No, there's nothing wrong with marriage. It's just not for me, that's all. Have you ever been to San Francisco?"

"A couple of times. Nice town."

"It's a beautiful city, the greatest in the country. I intend to make it mine." Her face was even more striking than usual against the pale glow from the single candle on the make-shift table.

"You could make it yours without working up to your ass in mud, Hannah. Just find the richest man in San Francisco and snap your fingers."

"No. I want San Francisco on *my* terms."

"Nobody can corral a town that size anyway. You can live high, meet a lot of people and such, but you can't own it."

Hannah disagreed. "I've seen the men who own San Francisco. They're railroad barons... publishers... meat packers... shipping line owners. You know the type. When they pull out a cigar twenty people jump to light it. They have the best box at the opera. The biggest house on Nob Hill. The best table at Grissom's. Fresh roses the year round. And when they buy something they don't ask the price. Universities and museums are named after them and when they take a mistress or stagger under drink everyone looks the other way." Her face was shining with determination. "That's what I want, San Francisco on a platter. And I'll have it."

"You got my vote, Hannah. But when you pull out that cigar, don't expect me to jump to light it." And I laughed so hard at my joke that an ounce of precious brandy splashed out of my cup.

"You never take anything seriously, Brian."

"I don't take civilization seriously, that's a fact."

She picked up a wooden spoon and began

stirring my hunter's stew, which was smelling sweeter and juicier every moment. "You don't even know what civilization is."

"Sure I do."

"You think civilization is a big city. I'm talking about a certain way of life. I'm talking about . . . style . . . class . . . quality. Do you know what those things are?"

"Hell, yes. I've got class I haven't even used yet."

She snickered at my style of speech and that made me mad. "I'll tell you something else, lady. I've seen your civilization up close and I don't give a damn for it. I remember coming into Chicago on a train one day. A windy fall day it was, just after dawn. I stepped down from the coach and looked across the railyard. Over by the freight cars they were stacking buffalo bones. The bones made a pile seven feet high that stretched for half a mile down one track. They had been shipped back to Chicago from the west to be ground up for fertilizer. I went behind a tool shed and puked my guts out. That's civilization, Hannah. Slaughtering the most beautiful animal the world ever saw and grinding his bones for fertilizer."

My own eloquence surprised me until I

noticed how much of the brandy I had put away. Half a bottle of good stuff nudges me into loud conversation and a full bottle drives me to singing lewd ballads. "Let's eat."

Hannah began ladeling out the stew into deep tin plates. Steam rose in gray curls and the meat rolled invitingly in the sauce. I cleaned my hands on my shirtfront like a gentleman and we plunged in with spoon and fork.

"You're a genius!" Hannah declared between bites.

I suppose we looked pretty crude wolfing down that meal. Hannah would have been asked to leave her favorite San Francisco restaurant if she bolted her food the way she was doing just then. But you have to remember how scarce good food was in the Yukon that winter. The closest I'd come to venison since December was an occasional slab of stringy moose, unsalted.

We ate for probably half an hour without talking. When the meat was gone we finished the vegetables. When the vegetables had been eaten we sopped up the juice in pieces of sourdough bread. Then . . . and I'm not ashamed to tell it . . . we took turns licking the kettle.

Hannah was the first to sit back and stretch. "God," she moaned. "I feel like going to bed for a week."

"Suits me."

Her chuckle was low and friendly, a soft rejection. "Tell me something, Brian. Don't you have any ambition at all? Isn't there anything you really want out of life?"

"I've got my dream. It may not be on your scale, but it suits me."

"What is it?"

Before answering I burped behind my hand in the polite fashion. "The Crown grants one hundred and sixty acres of prime farmland to any man who serves out a five-year enlistment. That's what I want, Hannah. I've got my parcel picked out. It's over near Wilcox in Saskatchewan, close enough to the rail line to ship my products. The earth there is good, Hannah. Real good."

"Somehow I didn't picture you as a farmer."

"Farmer? Hell, no! I plan to open a distillery. I can grow enough barley, rye, and corn on a hundred and sixty acres to make all the whiskey I can sell without working too hard. I've got the license and I've already picked out my brand name: *Brian Bonner's*

Old Dependable Canadian Whiskey. How do you like it?"

"You'll be your own best customer."

"My name alone will sell a thousand barrels a year."

Hannah's lazy mood disappeared. "How'd you like a thousand acres and a distillery that could turn out ten thousand barrels a year?" The steel was back in her voice. I'd forgotten that Hannah wanted to talk to me about something. Dinner was over and it was time for me to pay my bill. Hannah always collected one way or another.

"What's this all about, Hannah?"

"Business," she said briskly. "I've told you this claim turned out a skunk. I have to get rid of it and go to work on something else fast. There are just five months left before the ice breaks on the river and thousands of stampeders hit this territory. The price of claims will triple overnight. We have to be well on the way to our first million before that happens."

"We?"

"That's right, we. I've decided to make you my partner."

"Partner?" I found it hard to get a grip on the direction of our conversation. Hannah never went into deals with partners, everyone knew that. She bought and sold and sometimes leased. But take a partner? Never.

"I'm in trouble, Brian. I don't have any choice. You still own that claim on Pure Gold Creek don't you?"

"Yeah, but it's a skunk, too. I don't see how my claim is going to do either of us any good."

"Don't be too quick about that. Look, I'll show you my plan." And Hannah began clearing the crate so she could stretch out a map of the Klondike Gold District.

I did have a claim, Fourteen Above on Pure Gold Creek. But the claim was a skunk, as I said. The whole creek was a skunk, in fact. The prospector who staked the Discovery Claim and gave the creek its fancy name should have called it Disappointment Creek. You could find more gold in a Canadian maple leaf than in that sorry stretch of water.

"Here we are." She smoothed out the map. "Let me show you something. This is the Klondike River." She put her finger on the spot where the Klondike met the Yukon river. "Now the richest diggings seem to be right here, Bonanza Creek. That's our target."

Bonanza was the next major creek downriver from Hunker. It emptied into the Klondike just across the river from the town of Dawson itself. There were plenty of other good claims on an upper section of the same water called Eldorado Creek. Pouring into both creeks were at least twenty "pups", very small creeks that were little more than rivulets. Despite their small size most of the pups had been staked, too.

"Come on, Hannah. How are you going to buy a claim on Bonanza? Even unproven ground there'll cost you a hundred thousand dollars."

"I didn't say we'd be able to afford Bonanza Creek right off. We'll have to wheel and deal some first."

"Wheeling and dealing is how Axel Anderson stuck you with this skunk," I reminded her.

"I haven't forgotten that."

"Well, what's our first move?"

She grinned and gave me her hand. "Thanks, Brian. You won't regret it. From now on you and I are partners. I'll run your old skunk on Pure Gold into a fortune for both of us. You'll be taking baths in *Brian Bonner's Old Dependable Canadian Whiskey*."

"That would be a sad waste of good liquor."

Now you might be wondering why I jumped into a partnership with Hannah so fast. The truth is, and I won't mealy-mouth about it, I figured going partners with Hannah in a business deal put me first at the foot of her bed. Besides, I didn't have anything to lose. My claim on Pure Gold Creek was worth less than the brass buttons on my coat. It was just something Hannah needed to make a trade with.

What happened next put my teeth on edge, though. Joe Rudolph showed up out of the night carrying a battered old leather satchel filled with his papers. Rudolph was one of Dawson's two lawyers at the time. The other was Pete James. They did a fine business, too. With so many prospectors buying and selling claims, Joe often drew up ten or twelve deeds of conveyance every day at fifty dollars a deed. That's where the real gold is, in thick sheafs of paper that no one can make sense out of except another lawyer. That's why one lawyer in a town starves to death, but two get rich together.

"Hello, Hannah. Bitter night." He flopped his old briefcase on the packing crate and began unfastening the straps. "Congratulations, Brian. I think you're making a smart move going partners with Hannah. She'll make her mark in the Yukon if anyone does."

You can see why my back was up. Hannah had told Joe Rudolph we were going partners before she even talked to *me* about it! I knew she was a twister but that was too much. I was on the verge of walking out on her when Hannah rationed me one of her warm smiles.

"I hope you're right, Joe. If I must take a partner, I'd rather have Brian than any man in the territory."

That stopped me, of course. The chances are she saw my temper rising and threw out the compliment to quiet me down. The tactic worked, damn her eyes. I didn't even put up an argument when Joe slipped a paper in front of me, a partnership agreement. He had brought along one of those new stylographic fountain pens that carries ink right inside the pen; leave it to a lawyer to own the latest thing for signing papers. I put my name to the document with a flourish and passed the pen to Hannah. She signed in her own quick, no-nonsense way and we were partners.

"Good." Joe whipped the agreement off the crate and put another in front of me. This was a deed of conveyance giving Hannah half the rights to my claim on Pure Gold Creek. We both signed that one, too.

Then he put still another document in front of me, a second deed of conveyance. "What's this?" I asked.

"It's simple," Joe began. "You and Hannah are now partners in the Young and Bonner Mining Company. The company has two assets. One is this claim, Hunker Thirty-Nine Above. The other is your claim, Pure Gold Fourteen Above. You're going to sign both those properties over to Axel Anderson in exchange for Five A Below on Little Skookum Creek."

"What? Five A Below on Little Skookum! Hannah, that's not even a full claim. It's just a damned fraction."

"I know that." She spoke with a quiet reasonableness that maddened me all the more. "But Little Skookum runs into Bonanza Creek. I've got a hunch about that piece of dirt, Brian. I think there's a rich streak down there. The claim's hardly been worked at all. Axel Anderson picked it up from old Drew Adams, who fell sick in December. He sold it to Axel for only five thousand dollars. Axel has several claims on Little Skookum but he's been too busy elsewhere to develop them."

"It's a skunk, Hannah. Everyone knows that. Even if there were gold on it, the claim's not big enough to give us a good-sized dump. Exactly how big is Five A anyhow?"

Even Hannah had to look embarrassed about the size of that claim. After some throat-clearing and lip-licking she gave me the hard facts. "It's ninety-six feet."

"Ninety-six feet? Hannah, you're crazy."

But the damned woman wouldn't take no for an answer. She just kept on repeating that she had a hunch there was a streak under that fraction on Little Skookum. The papers were right there. Axel Anderson had already made his mark, and she wanted me to stop arguing and start writing.

In case you're wondering, a fraction is a claim that's less than the standard five hundred feet in length. When the word got out about rich diggings around the Klondike, the first thousand or so prospectors staked their claims by pacing off five hundred feet along the creek. Now some of the prospectors don't count as well as others, and here and there a man might have stepped off a six-hundred-foot claim when he thought he could get away with it. The whole mess wasn't straightened out until Bill Ogilvie, the government surveyor, arrived on the scene. He remeasured all the claims and found those that ran longer than the law allowed. Those fractions of claims were put back in the Crown's domain and other prospectors were allowed to file on them. And that's what Hannah wanted, a ninety-six foot fraction on Little Skookum Creek.

"All right!" Her badgering made my ears ring. "I'll sign the damned thing just to watch Axel have a second laugh on you. What the hell, my claim isn't worth beans anyway."

"That's my point, Brian. Neither is this one. But together our claims are worth something as trading material. And I just know there's rich dirt on Little Skookum."

"I know . . . I know . . . you've told me a dozen times." I signed the paper and pushed it across to Hannah, who snatched it up before I could change my mind.

"There goes your fortune," I warned her.

"We'll see." She passed all the documents to Joe.

"I'll register these at the recorder's office in the morning." Joe dropped the papers into his briefcase. "You'll be there, Hannah?"

"No, I'm going upriver with Brian tomorrow. Inspector Constantine is sending out patrols to call on some of the boys who haven't been seen for a while."

"Oh? Who's going downriver?"

"Van Ness and Father Judge."

"A couple of my clients haven't been in town lately. One is Red Lewiston, he's got a cabin on one of the pups down there. The other is an old fart . . . excuse me, Hannah . . . an old and valued friend named Herman Ganz."

"I know Ganz," I told Joe. "He wears red suspenders over his coat and smokes a briar pipe."

"That's Herman," Joe confirmed. "He was supposed to see me last week about a licence to sell liquor. Ganz did pretty well off his claim and wants to open a saloon right on the river at Forty-Mile."

"I'll tell Van Ness to look for him," I offered. "Where's his cabin?"

"He's using an old Hudson Bay Company shack on Forty-Mile."

"We'll see to him," I promised.

By the time Joe left I was feeling up to the mark again. What the hell, I hadn't actually lost anything of value and I'd gained Hannah as a partner.

Those thoughts went through my mind as Hannah was washing her kettle in the water trough. When she rose to put the kettle on the shelf I slipped my hands around her waist. It was so narrow my fingers completely encircled her. "It'll be nice having you for a partner, Hannah, I guess you know I've always . . ."

But before I could get all my words out she whirled like a wolverine and fetched the kettle up against my skull with a short chopping blow. It *thwanged* off my head and filled the cabin with yellow and pink butterflies. I staggered back, my senses so clouded that it took several moments for me to realize I had backed into the red-hot stove. The message was delivered to my brain by my ass, which was hollering for relief in its own language. I screamed and bolted forward, putting my foot in the icy water trough. As I tried to decode the conflicting messages from my ass and foot, my feet tangled up and I pitched to the floor at the foot of Hannah's shelving.

The damned woman burst out laughing!

"Hannah . . ."

"Oh, shut up, Brian," she said between gulps of laughter. "And get up, too."

I struggled to my feet, trying to bring off my recovery with some dignity. "What the hell did you do that for?"

"To make a point. You and I are partners in the Young and Bonner Mining Company *only*. Our partnership doesn't give you the right to run your big greasy hands all over me."

"I wasn't running my hands *all* over you. They aren't greasy, either."

"Just remember that you don't have any claim on my body."

"That never occurred to me," I protested. But I sounded like a preacher caught in a whorehouse. To cover my embarrassment I asked Hannah if she was still willing to go upriver with me in the morning.

"Certainly," she answered promptly. "I told Constantine I'd go, and I will."

"You can go with Van Ness if you'd rather."

"I know that. But we understand each other now, right?"

"Absolutely." I picked up my cap and jammed it down over my ears. "See you in the morning, then. And thanks for the venison."

"You turned it into a meal. I'll never forget your hunter's stew."

I was sliding out the door, already gauging how much Perry Davis Painkiller it would take to drown my humiliation, when the damned woman grabbed my arm, pulled my face down, and planted a big kiss on my cheek just under the left eye. Can you understand that? Two seconds after knocking me flat with a kettle for a harmless little squeeze she grabs me and kisses me like a Paradise Alley harlot.

I didn't even stop to think about it. I mumbled my farewell and cut for the Aurora before she decided I'd enjoyed the kiss too much and did for me again with her kettle.

3

VAN NESS and I rose at an early hour the next morning. Constantine joined us for breakfast, which consisted of thick pieces of bacon washed down with hot tea. He had prepared hand-drawn maps indicating the prospectors he knew of and the locations of their cabins or diggings in the area. Hannah and I would be covering the stretch of territory between the Indian River and the Stewart. Constantine's thinking was that anyone between Dawson and the Indian would be able to reach the town. It was the people farther upriver who might have a tough time getting in.

Van Ness and Father Judge would cover the river between Forty-Mile and the Alaska border, where our authority ended.

"Remember that the food you're carrying is as valuable as gold itself," Constantine warned us once more. "Use your best judgment in the way you distribute it."

The first order of business after breakfast was to ready our dog teams. The dogs slept in kennels behind the barracks. There were four teams, twenty-seven dogs in all including three pups being groomed to take the place of some of the older animals. You might think you have the power to imagine how noisy twenty-seven dogs can be, but whatever is in your mind is wrong. Multiply it by sixty and you might have some idea what the Queen's Dogs sounded like on a cold winter morning.

Malamutes are more wolf than dog, you see. They don't bark much. When they want to communicate they sit back on their haunches and howl. Sometimes they howl for hours. They were kept chained in three rows in the kennels, well away from their food supply. It was the food dump that Van Ness and I went to first. This consisted of a pile of frozen moose carcasses covered with snow. We brushed off some of the snow and separated one carcass from the rest of the pile. I used a hand axe to chop it into hunks. It wasn't easy work. Moose is stringy to begin with. After sitting out in the cold for a few months it becomes damn near as tough as a banker's soul. "That should do it." I gathered up an armful of meat and went off to feed my dogs.

They greeted me in their usual frisky way,

several of them snapping at my legs by way of fetching up a morning appetizer. But as I tossed the meat they forgot my legs and went into a frenzied fight over the pieces of moose. Asleep or sitting quietly a malamute can almost be mistaken for an ordinary dog, but when he goes after a piece of meat he shows his true colors as a savage beast.

I watched the leader, a thick-chested brown brute called Kamu, leap on one of the team and sink his fangs into the hunk of meat the other dog had picked up, and retreat to the end of his chain snarling. The unlucky dog, a bitch named Daisy, wasted no time in wheeling to fight her neighbor for one of the other hunks. Anyone watching my dogs rip and tear at each other for their breakfast would soon drop any illusions that they would make good pets.

"Good morning, Brian."

And there was Hannah, sassy as ever with her medical kit slung over her shoulder by a rope, dressed in her plaid mackinaw and trousers with marten fur cap and high boots, looking spectacular.

" 'Lo, Hannah. Ready to move out?"

"Sure." She sniffed the air and made a face. "Phew! Don't you ever clean these animals?"

"They don't take kindly to Saturday night baths. They're healthy enough, though."

Hannah had never paid much attention to my team, but now that her own survival depended on the dogs she was giving them a close examination. She had the ability to study a thing so closely that nothing about it escaped her notice. "I used to think all those dogs were alike. I see now they aren't."

"That's right."

"He's the leader." She pointed at Kamu.

"Right on the money, Hannah." The woman had judgment, no doubt about that.

"What are their names?"

"You've met the leader, Kamu. He's got a nasty disposition, so stay out of his way."

"What kind of dog is he?"

"Malamute. They're all malamutes. That's an Eskimo breed. You can tell a malamute by the white face and the dark markings on the head. They're part Siberian husky and part wolf."

"They look like wolves. Are you sure they're tame?"

I laughed at that. "I'm sure they're *not* tame. But they'll work, so long as they have a good leader. Kamu here was born to be a leader. Now that one with the gray and white patches along his back is Chuka. Daisy there is my only bitch. I won't have two in a team. When bitches fight you can't break them apart without losing a couple of fingers. That big black fella over there is Sitka. He and Kamu hate each other's guts, that's why Sitka works in the middle of the team even though he's nearly as strong as Kamu. The one that looks to be part Labrador is Duke, and the brown dog making a pig of himself is called Hungry, I'm sure you can see why. He'd kill his own pup to steal his food. You won't find a more vicious pack of animals this side of the hounds of hell, but *I* like them."

While I was making my introductions a fight broke out between Hungry and Sitka, who were chained next to each other. In thirty seconds they both drew blood, but after a few more snarls and lunges they separated and went back to their breakfasts.

The combat had excited the other dogs and two more fights broke out. Chuka and Duke were mauling each other and making fierce sounds without hurting each other at all. The two dogs were great friends and fought only because it was expected of them. They often made a noisy show of jumping each other and rolling around in the snow locked in angry combat. They never bloodied one another, though.

Kamu was a different type, mean as original sin and a bully in the bargain. He went for Daisy, swiping at her private parts with his fangs. He knew all the best places to hurt an enemy. One time he sank his teeth into Duke's upper lip and hung on for five minutes. Old Duke almost lost the entire lip in that fight.

Hannah watched Kamu's cruel antics with disgust. "Why don't you stop him? He's hurting Daisy."

"Kamu is the leader. The way he treats the other dogs is his business."

She shuddered and looked away.

"Just pretend Kamu is a San Francisco millionaire," I chided. "Then whatever he does will be all right."

Her eyes drilled into me but she didn't say anything.

I hauled out the dogsled and anchored it to one of the kennel posts with a length of chain so the dogs couldn't run away with the sled while I was harnessing them. Then I grabbed Kamu and put him in the lead traces. The lead dog is always harnessed first. It's his right and he expects it. I harnessed Daisy . . .

Sitka . . . Duke . . . Chuka and Hungry in that order. By the time Hungry was in harness the other dogs had wandered around tangling their traces. Getting them back in position was Kamu's job.

Over on the side of the kennels Van Ness had real problems. A tremendous roar of yelps and howls had started.

"What's wrong with Evan's dogs?" Hannah asked, stamping her feet against the cold.

"Van Ness has two bitches in his team. Remember what I told you? He'll be half an hour quieting them down. Evan isn't very good with dogs."

"Your dogs fight."

"Sure. They rip off pieces of each other's ears and slash their partner's flanks. They cut each other to the bone sometimes. But that's just clean, healthy fun for my dogs, a way to liven up the day and start the blood circulating in the morning. Fighting is their idea of harmless amusement, like me taking a shot of Perry Davis. But when females fight, stand back! Don't pet them and for God's sake don't try to feed them. Leave the handling of the dogs to me."

The food we were to distribute was brought from the A.C.C. warehouse by three clerks and loaded on the sled. While that was being done I returned to the food dump and wrapped half of one carcass in a tarpaulin. With the dogs' food added to our supplies, I helped Hannah settle herself in to a narrow groove reserved for her at the rear of the sled.

"Where will you sit, Brian?"

"Nowhere. I'll stand on the back runners when the trail is smooth. Otherwise I'll be running alongside."

It afforded me some satisfaction to see her impressed by that.

Van Ness was still wrestling to bring his team under control as we moved out. Father Judge stood nearby hugging himself under the arms while Van Ness punished his dogs with a whip. I don't use a whip myself and I don't much care for people who are too handy with one.

"Aren't you going to help Evan?" Hannah called from under the big buffalo robe I had put over her.

"I never interfere with the way another mountie handles his dogs or his women. You can get your head blown off that way. Several have."

On a smooth trail my team could haul a five-hundred-pound load sixty miles in a single day. We cut straight up the middle of the Yukon River, making good time. There was a covering of about four inches of snow on the river. The only sound in the air was the hissing of the runners and the pounding of dogs' feet.

The dogs were working well. They loved it, of course, needing a good ten hours of work a day plus three or four nasty fights just to maintain their health.

We reached Indian River in three hours, which must have been a record, and began looking for the first prospector on Constantine's list. I expected most of the miners to be easy to find. Their claims and cabins were strung along the rivers and creeks, and while the Indian wasn't thick with prospectors they would still be no more than a mile or two apart.

First on our list was Coatless Curly Munro. Curly had staked a claim on the Indian near its junction with the Yukon. Early in the rush he had convinced himself the real strike would be made on Indian River, that Joe Ladue had suckered everyone into staking claims on the Klondike in order to populate the town of Dawson. Nothing could convince

Curly otherwise, not even when the claim holders on Bonanza Creek began washing twelve hundred dollars a foot.

A plume of smoke rose from one of the shafts on Curly's claim. We ran the sled as close to the cabin as possible so that I could chain it to Curly's doorpost. The dogs flopped down with their backs to the wind and began eating snow.

"Curly! Where the hell are you?"

His voice boomed up from the shaft. "Is that a real human being up there? Or is it only Brian Bonner?"

"Two humans," Hannah yelled back.

"And one a woman? Goddam, I'll be right up."

A minute later Curly's soot-streaked face appeared as he hauled himself hand-over-hand up the windlass rope.

"Hannah Young! What the hell are you doing here?" Coatless Curly Munro was in his shirtsleeves, as usual. He never wore a coat, not even in the coldest weather, though he often bundled up in six or seven shirts of gradually escalating sizes. He claimed to have more hair on his body than a full-grown husky and certainly his head was covered with shaggy gray bristles closely resembling the pelt of a timber wolf.

"We're checking the upper river," I explained. "Constantine thinks some of you elderly citizens up here might be perishing from shingles and scurvy."

"Not me. I'm fine. But come in for a drink anyway."

"We have a lot of territory to cover," Hannah said.

Curly wouldn't take Hannah's refusal. "I don't see a woman but once every six or eight weeks. You gotta come in for a drink, Hannah. And tell me all about the trial. Did they hang Rollo yet?"

"No, and they're not going to. We won. Rollo was acquitted."

"Acquitted! I want to hear all about that." And he ushered her inside his cabin.

I sighed and saw to the dogs. This wasn't going to be a fast swing. The people this far upriver didn't get into town very often. To them a visitor was better than a Christmas turkey. Curly was good for an hour of conversation before taking his second breath.

When I went in for my drink Hannah was just telling Curly about the gold in Mike Lynch's hair.

"That dirty bastard!" Curly exploded. "And to think of all the drinks he poured for me. Why, I'll bet he cheated me out of two hundred dollars over the past year."

"We have to push off," I insisted. "You're all right but others might not be." I downed the drink he handed me in one draught.

"Sure, I understand. It's just . . . well, it's so damned lonely out here."

"I know," Hannah said. "Come to Dawson when you can. We'll go dancing at the Aurora. And by the way, I've got a new claim on Little Skookum. Brian and I are partners on it now. The cabin's not as good, but I'm betting the dirt is richer than my last claim."

"Little Skookum?" Curly shook his head. "You're making a mistake." He jabbed his finger downward. "This is where the real dirt is, Indian river."

"Have you hit a streak?"

"Not yet," Curly admitted. "But any day now, Hannah."

Curly came outside to bid us goodbye, still in his shirtsleeves. "Ha! It's warming up again. Can't be more than twenty below zero. Worse than the tropics. I may have to move farther north if this hot spell don't let up."

As we pulled away, the dogs scrambling for

purchase on the snow, Curly called out: "Next time bring me some of them Chinese fans from Paradise Alley! I need somethin' to fight the damned heat!"

The story was about the same at the next five places we stopped. People were holding out despite the cold, eating carefully to stretch their food supply and getting plenty of exercise hauling up paydirt from shafts and building their dumps. There was gold on Indian River, Curly had been right about that. One prospector showed us a large flat nugget that weighed three pounds. Prospectors call a big nugget flattened between layers of rock a "cheese sandwich." And everyone wanted to talk with Hannah, especially about Rollo Moon's murder trial. Very few Indian River people had been able to make it downriver for the trial. Our "mission of mercy" was rapidly turning into a Chautauqua lecture tour.

But the seventh stop paid off.

We found Shep Naylor's cabin about mid-afternoon. It was set farther back from the river than most. His cabin had been built originally by the Hudson Bay Company in the days when they were heavily into the Yukon fur trade. You could always tell a

Hudson Bay Company cabin by the initials H.B.C. burned into the front door. That outfit was so arrogant that many people claimed H.B.C. stood for "Here Before Christ."

Anyway, the cabin was set about a quarter mile back from the river. There were two shafts near the river, neither giving evidence of having been worked in several days. The charred logs in the bottoms of both shafts were cold and covered with drifting snow.

"Maybe he went into Dawson," Hannah suggested.

"I doubt it. Shep is kind of old for long winter hikes. Most likely he's visiting another prospector somewhere on the Indian."

Hannah looked in the cabin. She came out to report that the stove hadn't been fired up for at least one full day. We were discussing whether to look around the claim site or push on to the next stop when Hannah shushed me. "I heard something."

Sitka's ears perked up and a low growl rumbled from his throat. "Sitka heard it, too. Look, he's staring in that direction."

We climbed a steep slope behind the cabin. The footing was treacherous in the snow. We reached the top to find ourselves looking down through the arctic darkness on a gully of scrub timber. Something moved down there, a red ghost in the trees, and we heard a feeble call of "Help . . . please . . . help."

"There he is." Hannah charged down the hill, slipping halfway down and sliding the rest of the way like a schoolgirl. At the foot of the hill she bounded to her feet and ran to Shep. I followed, taking somewhat more care to keep my neck in one piece.

Shep had dragged himself into the shelter of the trees and covered himself with spruce branches against the cold and wind. "I thought I was done for," Shep rasped.

"What happened?"

"Came down here for firewood . . . twisted my ankle . . . tried to climb back up the hill . . . no strength."

"Lie still while I look at your leg." Hannah peeled back Shep's trouser to take a better look at the injury. Shep's ankle was somewhat swollen, but that wasn't his main problem. It took only a glance to see that the old man was racked with scurvy. His face was puffy and gray, his skin dry. Shep's customarily bright brown eyes had sunk into his head. His breath smelled as foul as rotten fish and when he opened his mouth he revealed swollen and bleeding gums.

"How do your joints feel?" Hannah asked. "Can you bend your arms and legs?"

"Not too good, Hannah, They ache like hell when I move. If I try to stand my heart jumps around in my chest like a damned squirrel."

"You've got scurvy," Hannah told him. "A bad case. What have you been eating?"

"A few potatoes is all I have left."

"You're in luck, Shep. Constantine sent us out looking for broken-down cases like you." I grabbed hold and eased his body up on my back. " 'Watch out for old Shep Naylor, he'll probably need a transfusion of Juice of the Snake,' Constantine said to me."

Shep tried to laugh but it came out a wheezy cough. "Constantine offering whiskey? That don't sound like the inspector."

"You go ahead." Hannah was busy stripping bark off one of the spruce trees. "Get Shep into his cabin and start a fire. I'll be along soon."

By the time I had climbed the hill, picking my way carefully down the other side to avoid taking a fall with old Shep on my back, Hannah had caught up with us.

She helped me put Shep into his bunk and shooed me outside again to find firewood. When I returned she was working at pouring a big spoonful of Norwegian cod liver oil down Shep's throat. The old prospector did his best to fight her off, but he lacked the strength to defend himself. Especially when Hannah put her knee on his chest to hold him down.

"Brian, don't let her feed me that stuff!"

"It's cod liver oil, Shep. Best thing in the world for scurvy."

"But she already gave me a shot while you were outside! This stuff smells like a dead seal! For God's sake . . ."

"Be quiet, Shep." Hannah seized his nose with her free hand. "There, now you won't be able to smell it. That's it, swallow it down."

Shep turned green when the oil slid into his gullet. As soon as Hannah let loose of his nose he started coughing and gagging. His head lolled to one side and for a moment I feared Hannah had done for him with her doctoring. But presently the old-timer's eyes opened and he drew a few long breaths.

"I'll start the fire." Hannah bustled around in her bossiest manner. "You go out and bring in some of that fish and fruit. Then you can help me break up this bark. I'm making a big pot of spruce bark tea."

Give a woman a little authority and it turns her into a dictator; I've seen that happen many times. But I did as she said and in the next hour Hannah poured about a gallon of tea into Shep and sat him up to feed him some of the fish and fruit. She fed him very slowly, making him chew each morsel thoroughly before he swallowed it. You'd be surprised how much better Shep looked after just a little of Hannah's doctoring. To be honest, I believe it was Hannah's attention as much as the nourishment that improved Shep's appearance. A man just naturally responds to having a beautiful woman look after him.

Shep improved so much, in fact, that he was able to rise by himself and wave goodbye from the cabin door when we left.

"What's the next stop?" Hannah inquired.

"About two miles downriver there's a pup off to the south with a dozen claims on it. Good dirt I've heard. That's our last call on the Indian. We'll double back and head up to the Stewart after that."

We left Shep with ten pounds of food,

enough to put him back on his feet so that he could do some ice fishing or trade for food with other prospectors in the area. In the next five hours we found two more miners with cases of scurvy, but neither was as bad off as Shep. They were in a more populated area where others were willing to share some of their meager supplies. We passed out another thirty pounds of food on that pup and, after Hannah told the story of how she had saved Rollo Moon several more times, we pushed back to the Yukon.

By evening we were exhausted. We stopped for the night at a cluster of claims on a very small stream that ran directly into the Yukon. Five men shared one cabin but that didn't stop them from inviting us to spend the night. The fact that they hadn't seen a woman in two months might have had something to do with their hospitality.

Hannah told her tale about Rollo Moon again (she had boiled it down to a standard act complete with dramatic gestures) and we slept side by side with the miners on the dirt floor of the cabin with only some boughs for a mattress. Hannah never complained about the accommodations. I couldn't figure her out. Why would a woman who yearned to become the toast of San Francisco be willing to risk her time and health searching the Yukon for scurvy cases? It didn't make sense.

The next morning Kamu and Sitka were in a fighting mood.

Sitka had been working himself up all winter to challenge Kamu's leadership and he saw this trip as an opportunity to make his bid. While I was feeding the dogs Kamu tried some of his bullying tactics to steal a bit of meat from Daisy. I had been forced to chain the dogs closer together than usual and Sitka was able to leap to Daisy's defence and retrieve the meat for her.

No dog had ever interfered between Kamu and another member of the team. Kamu went mad with anger at the insult. He leaped for Sitka but I managed to jerk the chain taught before they could get into a tangle. Sitka was just as ready to fight. Both dogs bared their fangs and strained to reach each other. I slapped them both across the face with my gloved hand and backed them down, but I knew that was only the beginning.

Sure enough, the next five miles were torture. Kamu was determined to work the other dogs as they'd never been worked before to pay back the insult. He strained in his harness, leading the team up steep grades along the riverbanks instead of looking for flat stretches that made easy running.

"Kamu!" I yelled. "Heely! Heely!"

Hannah twisted in her narrow seat to talk to me. "What are you telling him?"

"I'm trying to get him to veer back onto the riverbed. He'll kill the other dogs if he tries to pull grades all day."

"He's not doing me any good, either," Hannah complained.

The sled bounced like a cork in a rough sea. I had to hold on tight myself to stay on the runners.

Sitka bore as much blame for the rough going as Kamu. He was pulling with twice his ordinary speed, and with purpose. He had come up with a simple tactic for making Kamu's life miserable. He was forcing Daisy, who ran in harness between himself and Kamu, to increase her own speed just to stay ahead of Sitka. As a result Daisy was running almost on Kamu's heels, sometimes butting his rear legs and causing him to falter in his pace.

Poor Daisy was caught in a war between the two with no place to hide. I could have stopped and hitched a different dog between Kamu and Sitka, but that wouldn't have stopped their feud. And putting Sitka at the rear would only ruin the pace of the team.

I had only one choice, to occasionally drag my foot in the snow to slow the team and give Kamu a chance to catch his breath and increase the distance between himself and Daisy.

Despite the problem with the dogs, we made decent time and found eight more prospectors before noon, one a former professor from Seattle who had come north after being caught tutoring a young lady in his underclothes. He fell in love with Hannah on sight. Not even his scurvy could keep him from wooing her with poetry while she forced cod liver oil down his throat.

By the time we reached the Stewart River that afternoon the dogs had declared a temporary truce, more from fatigue than improved humor. The first cabin on the Stewart was another old Hudson Bay Company shack. A French Canadian named Pierre Lavelle reportedly lived there, but the door stood wide open to the elements. Even more puzzling was the appearance of the interior. Someone had ripped up an old mattress and emptied flour and coffee cans littered the floor. The floor-boards were also torn up, exposing the frozen earth underneath.

"What happened here?" Hannah wondered. "Brian, look at this." She knelt just inside the cabin door to point out a pattern of stains on the floor that might have been blood.

"That could be anything." But I slipped my revolver out from under my parka and held it behind me so as not to frighten Hannah. "I'll look around. Why don't you straighten up this place. See if there's food. That'll tell us whether anyone's here."

"All right. I suppose Lavelle might have gotten fed up with his claim and smashed up the cabin before he left. I've seen others do that."

"So have I. That's probably how it went."

But I didn't really think so. There were too many other signs pointing in another direction. For one, Hannah hadn't noticed the way my dogs were acting. She wasn't accustomed to their different moods. I could tell they were upset. They stood in their traces with heads down, sniffing the ground and whining.

Then there was the lack of firewood. Whoever had been the last to leave the cabin had taken all the firewood with him. No one but a thief or murderer would do that. It was an iron-clad law of the territory that a man replenished any firewood he used before leaving a cabin. Anyone caught breaking that law would be given a blue ticket out of the territory, or worse.

I walked slowly around the cabin, testing the air in much the same way my dogs had done. I couldn't tell you what I was sniffing for. When I could find nothing I walked down to the river.

Hannah came out of the cabin. "There's no food! Nothing!"

That convinced me Lavelle had been murdered. The stains were blood and the cabin had been looted of everything, even firewood. And suddenly I knew where to find him.

I hastened back and went to the shaft Lavelle had been burning out.

"Where is he?" Hannah said.

"Down there, in the shaft."

"How do you know?"

I gestured in the direction of the river. "I just saw a place where someone started to chop a hole in the ice. They were going to throw his body in the river but the ice was too thick or they were too lazy. The shaft is just the place a lazy killer would choose to dump a body. Here, you let the bucket down while I hang on."

Hannah turned the handle on the windlass, lowering me into the shaft as I held tight to the rope with my feet in the ore bucket. The bottom of the shaft had drifted over with snow. I located Lavelle a moment later. The killer had pushed him into a corner and collapsed a portion of the shaft wall onto him in a careless effort to hide his body.

"Did you find him?" Hannah called.

"I found him."

"Do you need any help? Are you going to bring him up?"

"No. Might as well leave him here, it's the next best thing to a grave." I turned him over and brushed the snow off his face. Lavelle had been a swarthy man with a bristling black mustache. I had seen his face in Dawson once or twice. The back of his head was missing, blown off, and there were two bullet holes in his back.

"What are you doing?"

"Looking him over. You keep a sharp eye up there. The men who did this seem to be

98

long gone, but you can never tell." I pulled out my old Montana Stockman's jacknife and opened the long blade. It was nasty work digging the two bullets out of Lavelle's back, but I knew Constantine would want them. The man was a stickler for evidence. Fortunately Lavelle had frozen solid so there was no blood to deal with. I had both bullets in my hand after five minutes work.

I also went through Lavelle's pockets but did not find any papers or other valuables. Before going back to the surface I had Hannah toss down a blanket to cover the body.

When I scrambled out of the shaft Hannah was waiting with the big Ithaca shotgun from my sled. "Did you bury him?"

"He's as buried as he needs to be for now."

"Why did they do that?"

"Put him in the shaft? I don't know, can't figure it. They'd have been better off to leave him in the shack and set fire to it. They might have passed it off as an accident."

"I meant why was he killed."

"For his poke, of course. There's supposed to be some rich dirt here on the Stewart."

"You seem pretty sure there were more than one."

"Had to be. Lavelle was shot twice with a

pistol and his head was shotgunned. That means two killers for sure, maybe three. I don't understand why they didn't take more care in getting rid of his body. They could have dropped him in a gully where no one would ever find him. Sloppy work."

Hannah looked around uneasily. "What do we do now?"

"I want to find out whether anyone else on the Stewart is missing."

"You think someone else has been killed?"

I took the shotgun out of her hands. "That could be the reason their housekeeping was so casual. You might cover up the murder of one man, but two or three missing Stewart prospectors would be tough to hide."

Hannah saw what I was driving at. "You think we might find several bodies around here!"

"That's right. Look, you can stay here while I go along the Stewart. I'll set you up in that stand of trees. You'll have food and firewood. The men who killed Lavelle won't be back. Even if they did pass by you'd be under cover."

Hannah's mouth tightened in anger. "Someone up there may be hurt instead of dead. Did you ever think of that? Let's get on the trail." She stalked back to the sled, climbed into the nest I had fixed for her, and pulled up the buffalo robe around her shoulders.

Hannah always had to be right. I didn't mind that so much, but she always had to be right in such a loud voice. I followed her to the sled and put the shotgun in its scabbard. When I climbed on the rear runners the dogs were happy to get moving. They dug in their feet and we headed up the Stewart at a fast clip.

My guess turned out accurate. We found another dead prospector at the next cabin, an old sourdough named Rufus Polk. He, too, had died from a combination of shotgun and pistol wounds. Once again the cabin had been stripped of food and presumably Rufus Polk's gold dust. They had been even more careless with Polk's body, leaving it in plain view in front of the cabin. Polk had probably come out of his cabin to greet his visitors and they gunned him down on the spot. I hauled the body into the cabin and dug out three bullets before wrapping him in a handy tarpaulin.

The story was roughly the same at the third cabin we visited, except that some wolves had found the body and carried it several hundred yards as they ripped it apart and devoured some choice pieces. The man was named Ted McCone. I knew him. He had taken ten dollars off me in a game of Acey Deucey one time in Whitehorse. His sister was a Baptist missionary who traveled in China carrying the Good News to the heathens. She would have many a prayer to say for her brother.

McCone was the last man killed on the Stewart. About two miles up that river the claims were closer than fleas on an Irishman and the murderers had evidently shied from going in among too many people. We reported to them what had happened to their neighbors on the Stewart, and you can guess the commotion it caused. But no one had seen any strangers and I doubted that the killings had been done by anyone on the river. For one thing, the people there were too under-nourished to do much mischief. We distributed the balance of the food and told the miners to pass the word and keep a weapon handy if they had one. Most had traded their guns for food long ago. But I thought their numbers lent them safety if they took precautions. The Stewart River Miners' Association pledged to recover and bury the bodies of their neighbors, and with everything under control I didn't feel derelict in my duty leaving those people to return to Dawson.

Constantine had to have this news as soon as possible. The murderers wouldn't stop at three killings.

4

WE encountered one more siege of trouble before reaching Dawson. I blame myself for what happened.

That night we found ourselves on the Yukon twenty miles upriver from Dawson when a snowstorm with winds up to fifty miles an hour came blasting down the valley. I pitched a fly in a grove of trees and bedded down the dogs in the snow.

Pitching a fly is an old northwoods way of sleeping warm in the open. You tie a blanket between two trees at an angle, anchor the bottom of the blanket to the ground, and start a fire a few feet out from the blanket. Starting the fire with wet wood is the toughest part of the exercise. But once the fire is going the wind throws heat into the shelter of the blanket, if you have positioned everything correctly. Add some spruce branches as a mattress and you'll keep your body off the snow.

It worked well enough. Hannah and I snuggled together in the shelter, each under a different buffalo robe but sharing the warmth of the fire.

"This is marvelous," Hannah murmured from deep in the folds of her robe. "I can't get this warm in my cabin. But what about the dogs? They're already covered with snow. Won't they freeze during the night?"

"Not those dogs. They curl up with their backs to the wind and their tails over their noses and go to sleep. Cold doesn't bother them at all. They love it."

"So do you. I used to think you were just too big and dumb to let the weather bother you. I'd see you stomp into Diamond Tooth Gertie's covered with snow, laughing, calling for your bottle, and I'd think. 'There goes one of God's great idiots.' Now I realize you're one of those men who thrives on a rough life. Freezing weather . . . rotten food . . . murder . . . bad whiskey . . . none of it slows you down. I remember when Tom Deacon's shaft caved in on him last fall during that big rain. You shoveled for five straight hours even though everyone knew Tom was dead. Twenty or thirty other men took turns digging next to you down there, one at a time, but you worked straight through until Tom's body was found."

"I had to do my best for old Tom. He owed me thirty dollars."

Usually the sharp angles of Hannah's face made her look serious and determined. But the fire was throwing shadows over us, giving the long lines of her features a softer appearance, and her small smile conveyed a feeling of admiration for me. That's right, *admiration*. Hannah had never looked at me with such high regard. It was one of the best moments of my life, ranking right up there with the time I confiscated forty cases of genuine Scotch whiskey off a border smuggler who was willing to trade the entire shipment for his freedom.

"You joke about everything," Hannah scolded.

"Not everything."

"No, not about whiskey. Why are you so devoted to the stuff? A lot of men need whiskey to keep going. You don't strike me as one of those."

"I don't need it," I told her. "I just like it. Look, here we are in the middle of nowhere. How many things are there to do around here? You can't go to the opera. I haven't seen a newspaper since November. There are only two books that I know of in the whole territory, the two volumes of *The Decline and Fall of the Roman Empire* that Old Man Hunker owns. The only sporting event that's taken place in Dawson all winter was Rollo Moon's trial. That leaves gambling, drinking, and whoring as the principal recreations. Of the three, drinking is the cheapest and its pleasurable effects last the longest. Not that I totally ignore the other two."

"Someone told me you were once a whiskey smuggler."

"That's right. I worked out of Fort Whoop-Up. That was the center of the illegal whiskey trade up here. When Ottawa finally legalized whiskey on the frontier I joined the mounties. You know why. I want that free land and my own distillery."

"Don't people still smuggle whiskey?"

"Sure. But these days it's done to avoid the tax. That's no fun. I started running whiskey because the blue laws made me mad. I figured folks had the right to drink if they felt like it and I did my best to see they could. It was a civic duty, sort of."

"I'm surprised the Northwest Mounted Police took you with that kind of background."

"They didn't exactly know what they were

getting. I passed myself off as a wheat farmer from Manitoba when I joined up. By the time they found out different I had become The Man Who Killed Almighty Voice and they couldn't afford to kick me out. They posted me to the Yukon instead. I was supposed to turn blue from the cold and disappear. Things didn't work out that way."

Hannah snuggled around until she lay on her side looking directly at me. Our faces were no more than a foot apart. They might as well have been on different continents. As friendly as she had become, I didn't detect any carnal desire in her attitude.

"Now I've got a question for you, Hannah. How did you come to start doctoring people?"

My question caused Hannah's eyes to go cold again, as they had when I raised the subject of her home town during dinner in her cabin. "I told you I was raised in foster homes and in an orphanage. It was an orphanage for girls in Sacramento. Terrible place. One of the problems was medical care. There wasn't any. When a kid took sick she'd just lie in bed until she got well . . . or died. I was about five when I began going around with my doctor's bag. I handed out colored water and baking soda and pretended to take temperatures. Sometimes I'd put a cold rag on a girl's head or just sit and hold someone's hand. And you know what? Fewer kids died. Years later it hit me that loneliness and lack of attention were the worst diseases in that place. When I finally got out of the orphanage I began reading books on medicine. Before coming up here I worked in a medical clinic for a couple of years. I wasn't a nurse, just a clerk. But I kept my eyes open. So you see, I'm pretty much a fake as a doctor."

"No, you aren't. Ask old Shep Naylor."

"Even so, no one will ever call me 'Doctor Young'. Which reminds me, I've always meant to ask why people call you The Man Who Killed Almighty Voice. That's a strange nickname."

Her comment left me thunderstruck. "You mean you don't know who Almighty Voice was?"

"I didn't even know it was a person."

"Didn't know! My God, woman, where the hell have you been? *Everybody* knows who Almighty Voice was and how I came to kill him."

"I don't." She erupted in mischievous laughter. "Really, I thought it was a reference to *your* voice, which can be rather loud when you're angry—like you are now."

"You're damned right I'm angry! A man risks his life to bring the most dangerous renegade in Canada to justice and you . . . *my own partner* . . . know nothing of it. It's humiliating."

"Almighty Voice was a renegade?"

"Hannah, he was the all-time renegade, a Cree brave with more murders to his name than you could count, including three mounties and a highly respected postmaster. When I finally cornered him and three of his men at Duck Lake they pumped three bullets into me. But I did for them just the same. That fight made me famous all over Canada and a good part of the United States, and *you* never heard about it."

"You know, Brian, some people have more pressing business to occupy their attention than your exploits."

What she said was true, of course. I was so wrapped up in my fame that I had come to believe it was everybody's duty to know about me. It's a common failing among certain types of people, politicians in particular. The possibility that I had taken on the coloring of a politician brought me up short. Had I really fallen that low?

"Okay," I grumbled. "I suppose there are some isolated communities that haven't heard about me."

"San Francisco . . . Chicago . . . New York . . ."

"Shut up and go to sleep, Hannah."

And sleep we did, with the wind howling above our heads and sheets of snow clawing the air.

Our trouble came the next morning.

I awoke first and set about making the coffee. The storm had blown itself out overnight and the morning was calm and dark. The coffee was ready and a breakfast of dried meat and fruit fixed by the time Hannah crawled out from under her buffalo robes. By then, too, an ominous howling had begun in the hills to the west of our campsite. Wolves. From the sound there were a dozen or more and all hungry. The storm had driven most game into hiding and probably drifted over whatever kill the wolves may have left on the ground the previous day. They were out for fresh game and we were handy.

"How close are they?" Hannah asked, sipping her coffee.

"Mile or so."

"Will they attack us?"

"They'd like to. I don't think we'll give them the chance." I pulled my Ithaca shotgun from its scabbard on the sled and cocked one hammer. "Easy, Kamu." The report of the shotgun made an enormous sound in the still winter landscape, echoing off the surrounding hills three or four times before silence returned.

The wolves stopped howling and Kamu kept the other dogs from bolting at the shot by issuing a low warning growl.

"That shut 'em up. By the time they get up the nerve to take another look at us, we'll be gone. Eat your breakfast while I harness the dogs."

And that's where I made my mistake. I had already fed the dogs and I thought they were calm enough to be harnessed quickly. I also believed they were as anxious as myself to put distance between us and that wolf pack. And so instead of handling one dog at a time, I quickly unchained the first three dogs in the team and began harnessing them together. Kamu was in the lead position, of course, with Daisy and Sitka behind him.

But Kamu hadn't forgotten Sitka's insult

on the previous day. Without even a warning growl Kamu tore from my grip and launched himself at Sitka. He landed on Sitka with his forelegs, knocking the surprised dog on his back in the snow. While he had him in that exposed position Kamu leaped in and tried to slash Sitka's throat with a lightning sweep of his fangs. Sitka recovered quickly though, and Kamu's bared teeth missed the younger dog's throat by several inches. Sitka regained his footing immediately and charged into Kamu's flanks, drawing blood with a diving attack that sent Kamu reeling backwards.

Daisy growled and tried to leap into the fight on Sitka's side, but I held fast and dragged her back to the tree where she had been chained during the night. My first thought was to settle Daisy and then break up the fight. But in the precious seconds I lost rechaining Daisy, Kamu and Sitka locked themselves in a fierce battle that no man could have stopped without shooting one dog or the other.

"Brian, stop them!" Hannah was watching the fight with a horrified fascination.

"It's too late." My voice was hoarse from the cold and the exertion of my struggle with Daisy. "They've been building to this all winter." I turned my attention to the other dogs, who were howling excitedly and straining at their chains. "Shut up! Hungry, get down. Ho!"

When I looked back to the fight Kamu was still on the attack, driving into Sitka's chest and going for a killing throat hold.

I picked Kamu to win. He was heavier, at least eighty-five pounds to Sitka's seventy-five, and he had spent all his life as a leader. Kamu was totally without fear and he had fought a hundred battles with dogs seeking to take his place. He knew every killing hold and his stamina was unmatched. I hated to lose Sitka, but the younger dog had brought it on himself. There could be only one leader and Sitka would no longer be satisfied with less. So be it.

"Brian, look at that!"

Hannah's words come in reaction to Sitka's surprising counterattack. The younger dog suddenly twisted out of Kamu's grip and danced around him in the snow, dealing out a half dozen slashing bites to Kamu's right shoulder. The leader's brown coat oozed blood from the wounds.

Kamu roared and sprang high in the air, coming down squarely on Sitka's back. Sitka yelped as Kamu's teeth sank into the nape of his neck. But he rose on his hind legs, carrying Kamu with him, and whipped his head forward. Kamu flew forward, landing on his back at Sitka's feet. The young black dog ripped at Kamu's genitals, then leaped to one side as Kamu jumped up and charged.

Once more Sitka managed to avoid Kamu's teeth. Instead Kamu found himself in danger as his opponent punished his wounded right shoulder and side with a second series of bites. The snow around both dogs had gone bright red with their blood.

Hannah stepped farther back from the fight. "You've got to stop this, Brian. They're tearing each other to pieces."

"It's almost over. Sitka's winning."

I suppose I shouldn't have been surprised. Kamu's superior age and experience had become a liability instead of a strength. He was seven years old and some of his teeth had been worn down to stumps from years of chewing on rock-hard frozen moose meat. Perhaps his large bulk was no longer all muscle. And certainly his arrogance had made him over-confident.

The fight ended abruptly when Sitka clamped his massive jaws over Kamu's right foreleg. He ground his teeth into the flesh and shook his head violently. Kamu tried to fight loose, but Sitka's strength was greater. Suddenly we heard a crunching sound as a bone in Kamu's leg crushed in Sitka's grip. Kamu wailed, a sound I had never heard from him, and rolled over on his side.

Sitka released Kamu's leg and separated from him, standing to one side with his furred chest heaving. His head dipped and he gulped up several mouthfuls of snow to refresh himself, then turned and trotted slowly away from Kamu to the harness traces I had laid out on the ground. He stepped into the leader's spot and turned his eyes on me.

I had a new lead dog.

Meanwhile Kamu had regained his feet. Shakily, but with much of his old arrogance, he stood there on three legs studying the other dogs. Then he began limping up the hill to the west.

"That was awful," Hannah said in a rush.

"I know. But it was bound to happen."

"Where's Kamu going?"

"To meet the wolves." I went to Sitka and began strapping the harness over his shoulders. Snow and ice had packed into his fur during the fight. I brushed off his coat and checked his wounds. He was in good shape considering the ordeal he had just been through. I rubbed some of the snow into his cuts to clean them out. The frigid temperature had already stopped the bleeding.

Hannah was staring at me in disbelief. "You aren't going to let Kamu do that."

"He wants it that way."

"The wolves will devour him."

"He understands. But he wants to go out his own way . . . fighting."

"That's horrible." Hannah watched Kamu struggle up the hill. "Don't let him suffer any more. Shoot him."

"That's not what he wants." I tried to explain it to her. "You seem to think he's suddenly become a frightened, pitiful thing. That's not the way it is. Kamu isn't scared, he's mad. Mad clean through. He wants to kill something, to taste blood once more. I'm not going to take that away from him."

Hannah ran to the sled and pulled out the shotgun. She probably couldn't hit Kamu at thirty yards on a dark winter morning, but I didn't intend to let her try. So I yanked the shotgun out of her hands before she could use it. "I told you when we started this trip . . . leave the handling of the dogs to me."

Her eyes punched at me like fists. The admiration had disappeared from her eyes. Disgust had taken its place. "Nothing you've said makes sense, Brian. Letting Kamu go to those wolves is just plain cruelty." And without another word she gathered up the buffalo robe and went to her place in the sled.

We were on the trail a few minutes later. As we picked up speed the wolves could be heard making their attack on Kamu on the far side of the hill. Not that they howled; wolves are quiet when they go in for a kill. What we heard was wolves shrieking in pain as Kamu fought back. It lasted several minutes. From the sound of it Kamu put up one hell of a fight.

Hannah didn't speak to me during the rest of the trip back to Dawson.

Inspector Constantine held the bullets I had taken out of the dead men on the Stewart. He rolled them around in his palm. "Twenty-two caliber, I'd say."

"Twenty-five," I suggested. "Probably from a Derringer or a Stevens pocket pistol, the one with the tip-up barrel."

"Could be from a small Harrington and Richardson," Van Ness said. He wasn't one to be left out of an important conversation, and this was the biggest meeting Constantine had called since the snow began. There were twenty-five mounties in the barracks room. They had been called in from Fort Cudahy, Fort Reliance, and Fort Selkirk.

It seems the three dead prospectors I found weren't the only murder victims on the Yukon. Van Ness had discovered Joe Rudolph's missing client, Herman Ganz, dead in his cabin. Ganz, too, had been killed by a combination of shotgun and pistol fire. Jim Carney from Fort Selkirk had stumbled across the bodies of two other miners as far upriver as the Pelly, a tributary running into the Yukon near Fort Selkirk. Still another murder victim had been found at the bottom of his shaft not five miles from Fort Cudahy below Forty-Mile.

"Seven murders in the course of a week," Captain Scarth said. "Are we all agreed that the killings were done by the same person or persons?"

General agreement on that point was voiced. Sgt. Mark Mahafey from Fort Reliance added, "I'd say there were two killers, one armed with a shotgun and the other with a pistol."

"Correct," Constantine said crisply. "The

point is, who and where are they? Anyone have an idea?"

"I say they came into the territory from Alaska," Van Ness said, standing to make his point. "I'd guess they decided to make a quick strike across the border. They came in by dogsled, searching the rivers along the Yukon for miners working isolated claims. You'll notice they never strayed farther off the Yukon than five miles. Naturally they gave Dawson a wide berth, and when they reached the Pelly they turned back. I'd hazard a guess on two other points. One: there are probably other dead miners we haven't found. Two: the killers are already back on the Alaska side of the border where we can't touch them."

Having said his piece Van Ness sat down well satisfied with himself. Several of the mounties in the room nodded agreement with him. Jim Carney said, "They'd certainly be fools to stay in the territory. They must know that every mountie on the Yukon will be after them."

"Crossing the border into Alaska would be the wise move," Constantine agreed. "But I wonder . . . Captain Scarth, what do you think?"

Scarth had warmed to Van Ness's theory. "The fact that they stuck close to the Yukon could indicate they don't know the territory well enough to wander very far from the main waterway. Yes, I'd say Van Ness could be right."

"Any other ideas?" Constantine's eyes swept the room. "What do you think, Brian?"

I weighed my reply. "Well, I'd say those men came from somewhere right around Dawson and that they're still here."

Van Ness greeted my statement with a scoffing laugh.

"Continue," Constantine said, in a way that cut off Van Ness's derision before it could spread.

"First of all, the killers knew exactly who they were after. Every victim owned a successful claim. Anyone making a random raid from across the Alaska border could hardly be lucky enough to hit seven jackpots. No, the killers had information. The best place to pick up information like that is right here in Dawson. Each of the dead men had been in Dawson sometime in the last month. Each was known to live alone. And the reason the killers hugged the Yukon is simple. It's the only fast route through the territory and the killers wanted to do their business in a hurry. They could move forty miles south of Dawson, kill the victims they had picked out, and still strike forty miles north of Dawson within a couple of days, traveling by dogsled. That's the way I see it."

Sergeant Mahafey chimed in after I finished. "Brian makes sense to me, Inspector. I've got only one quarrel with him. I doubt our murderers are still around. Brian, wouldn't you run like hell for the nearest border after killing seven men?"

"I would, unless I'd been ordered to stay in Dawson."

Constantine tugged at his chin. "Ordered? I don't understand."

"I think we've had our first run-in with Soapy Smith's gang," I said.

The room came alive with excited comment, some supporting my remarks and others openly doubtful. Van Ness led the skeptics. "There isn't one bit of proof that Soapy Smith had anything to do with these killings, Brian. Frankly, I think you're just edgy. You know that Colonel Steele is worried about Smith and that's made you jumpy about him yourself. Soapy Smith is five hundred miles away in Skagway."

Constantine took the pipe out of his mouth and rapped it on the table for quiet. "Let's hear Brian's thinking on this."

The fact is, I wasn't certain about Soapy Smith's role in the killings. But I was stuck with my theory. There was little else to do but flesh out the idea. "I've known Soapy off and on for some years, starting back in Colorado. Soapy isn't a killer himself. He doesn't even carry a gun. He began as a confidence man working simple schemes and branched out into bigger operations. Now he has teams of men working for him: other confidence men, sneak thieves, gunmen, all brands of crooks. But wherever he operates, Soapy has followed one simple rule: leave the locals alone. That's how he's built his power in Skagway. He's never stolen a cent from the people who live there. His victims are all people passing through Skagway on their way to the gold fields.

"Now my idea is this. Soapy is too big a crook to be satisfied with bilking the prospectors heading into the Yukon. He'll want to rob the successful ones when they come out, too. I think he sent a couple of men into

Dawson last fall to keep their eyes open and gather information. They probably staked claims and are pretending to work them. Maybe they've even found a little gold. They hang around the saloons listening to the talk. They're finding out who's making the big strikes, where they keep their gold, how they plan to take their gold out of the Yukon this summer. When the territory opens in the spring Soapy's gang will know just where to find the fattest pigeons and how to take them."

Constantine was listening carefully, but I couldn't tell from his expression whether he thought my theory was any good.

I continued. "But there's a fly in the buttermilk. The men Soapy planted here are thieves. They see lots of heavy pokes around and it makes them greedy. So they decide to knock off a few easy targets, prospectors they know hold good pokes and live alone in the wilderness. They also take care to follow Soapy's principle of Let the Locals Alone by hitting targets to the north and south of Dawson. Soapy won't give a damn as long as they're here in May and they have the information he wants. And that's where they are right now, living somewhere around Dawson, rubbing shoulders at the saloons, still watching and listening. I'd bet on it."

I had convinced myself as I went along. By the time I finished I was certain that Soapy Smith's gang really had done the killings and that the killers were still in Dawson. Knowing Soapy, it just made sense.

My story had gradually registered an impression on Inspector Constantine. He seemed genuinely shaken when I finished. He sat behind the broad barracks room table with his hands clasped together and his pipe clamped between his teeth in an unnaturally tight manner. "If you're correct, we're in for more trouble this spring than we may be able to handle."

After a few moments of silence Sergeant Duryea from Fort Reliance said, "Aren't we getting additional forces this spring, inspector?"

Constantine removed the pipe from his mouth. "Ottawa, in its infinite wisdom, is sending us an additional ten men to keep the peace in the Yukon Territory."

"Ten men!" Duryea threw his fur cap on the floor. "Don't those lunatics know what's happening out here?"

"I'm afraid they can't grasp the size of our

job," Constantine replied. "The only man genuinely in touch with our problem is the Minister of the Interior, Clifford Sifton. Unfortunately he hasn't the influence to get us the men we need."

"Tight bastards," someone groused, refering to the members of Parliament.

"We'll just have to do our best until Ottawa comes to understand our situation," Constantine said. "That's the only positive aspect to these killings. They may arouse Ottawa to what's happening out here." The inspector turned to me. "Brian, I think your observations are sound. I'm sending Constable Reynolds to White Pass tomorrow to inform Colonel Steele about the murders. I'll pass on your suspicions to him, with my opinion that you may very well be correct. Gentlemen, we're looking for two men who have access to a dogteam. Stay on that. They may be living or working separately, so study individuals rather than pairs. Keep a special eye on the saloons and gambling houses. That's where blood money usually turns up."

I cleared my throat. "You've raised a good point, inspector, if I may say so. With your permission I intend to put a very close watch on Dawson's saloons."

Evidently my theories had raised my stock with Constantine, for he allowed himself a wintry smile. "I couldn't think of a better man for the assignment, Brian."

5

ON our return to Dawson Hannah plunged into the task of making something out of our new claim.

The other prospectors in Dawson gave Axel Anderson high marks for unloading another skunk on Hannah and I feared they were right. A ninety-six foot claim off the main streak of placer deposits was hardly the chance of a lifetime Hannah considered it. But if gold did exist on Little Skookum, Hannah would find it.

She began by hiring three miners at one hundred dollars a day per man. That was about a hundred times higher than the wage scale in the rest of Canada or the United States and twenty percent above Dawson's prevailing rate. Hannah was forced to pay the bonus because most men considered it degrading to work for a woman, even Hannah Young. The bonus became a way of overcoming their masculine pride. Hannah had three thousand in cash left in her kitty, enough to keep the men at work for ten days.

The three hands were Roy Teal, who sometimes worked as a bartender; an out-of-work riverboat engineer named Howard Jasper; and Three-Inch White.

Three-Inch White was Dawson's standing authority on fractional claims. When Bill Ogilvie began remeasuring the claims in the Klondike Gold District and declaring some fractions available for filing, Jim White wanted one. He bided his time, hoping to find a really rich fraction. According to his own measurements there was a fifty-foot fraction directly in the middle of the richest section of Eldorado Creek. He filed on that fraction at the recorder's office even before Bill Ogilvie declared its existence. Questions arose about the legality of his claim, but Commissioner Fawcett decided in White's favor. Jim White waited anxiously for several days before Ogilvie got around to remeasuring Eldorado Thirty-Six and Thirty-Seven. Sure enough, a fraction did exist between those claims. But instead of measuring fifty feet wide, as Jim White had estimated, it was exactly three inches wide. Jim White tried to have his claim declared invalid so he could refile elsewhere, but Commissioner Fawcett ruled that White was stuck with his three-inch claim. From that day Jim White was known as Three-Inch White.

Late one Tuesday night Three-Inch came looking for me in Dawson. I had taken seriously my promise to watch the saloons for murder suspects and was examining the patrons at Tom Chisolm's Aurora Saloon and Dancehall from a vantage point at the bar when Three-Inch approached me. "Come on," he said, tugging my arm. "Hannah wants you out at the claim right now."

"What's the hurry?" I waved to Tom Chisolm for another glass. "Have yourself a drink, Three-Inch. It's too damned cold to rush right back out into the night. Warm your insides first."

"But *Hannah* wants you *right now*."

"Right now is it? Let me tell you something, Mr. White. Brian Bonner doesn't come running at the beck and call of *any* woman. Now relax and enjoy your drink."

I managed to keep a smile on my face even though my insides were churning. Since our return to Dawson Hannah had frequently sent for me at odd hours to consult with her on matters related to the Young and Bonner Mining Company. While I wanted to be informed on progress at the claim, I did not enjoy being summoned like a toady. Her bossiness had begun to attract attention around Dawson. Only the night before Antone Stander had made a joking remark in my presence about Hannah's habit of ordering me about, forcing me to reward his impudence by laying my pistol barrel across his skull. Antone's wealth hadn't completely ruined his manners. After he had been revived with a sip of Chilkoot Dynamite, Antone apologized for the remark and we shook hands in a gentlemanly fashion. But it just wasn't practical to lay open the head of every man who whispered about the "arrangement" between myself and Hannah.

When I had resisted Hannah's summons long enough to demonstrate my independence, I said in an offhand way, "We might as well go on up to the claim now, Three-Inch. Looks like a quiet night here." And I strolled out of the Aurora whistling a little tune.

But as soon as we reached Front Street I grabbed Three-Inch by the arm and hustled him along at a fast clip. Because she still held a grudge against me for letting Kamu go out to face the wolves, my other meetings with Hannah since returning to Dawson had been cool and businesslike. I hoped that this urgent request for my company signaled a softening of her attitude.

Hannah had started two new shafts on the Little Skookum claim in addition to the one that had previously been sunk on the site. Three-Inch led me to the newest shaft and hollered, "We're here, Hannah!"

"Come on down," she called back.

I followed Three-Inch down a ladder, blinking back tears as smoke from the log at the bottom stung my eyes. The air became clearer down below and I found myself standing in the middle of a huge cavern. "Hannah? You've really been busy. I didn't know you'd begun drifting already."

"Come over here, Brian." A candle fixed to the cavern wall threw just enough light to reveal Hannah kneeling in muck about fifteen feet away. "Hurry!" she added.

I waded through mud to the narrow section of the drift where Hannah was chipping at the wall with a pick. "Look at this," she said.

I bent over her shoulder and quickly understood her excitement. Along the face of the wall between two horizontal layers of rock ran a streak of gold four inches thick, a cheese sandwich that extended at least three feet in length and God only knew how far in depth. "My God, you've hit a streak!"

"Better than a streak," Hannah said. "There are placer deposits all over this section. Look, while Three-Inch went to find you I washed some of this dirt in the cabin trough." She handed me a pan covered all over with gold at the bottom.

"How much dirt did you have to wash for all that dust?"

"Only one bucketful."

"She'll pay two thousand dollars a foot," Three-Inch announced from behind me.

Mathematics has never been my best subject, but it didn't take me long to figure out that our fractional claim could wash out as high as two hundred thousand dollars. "We're rich," I croaked.

"It's a start," Hannah agreed. "Let's see how far this streak runs. Three-Inch, go to work with Roy and Howard in the other shaft. Tell them to expand the west wall of the drift. That's the direction the deposits are running."

Three-Inch scrambled back up the ladder and I took the pick out of Hannah's hands. "Give me that thing and stand back." I swung the pick and watched splinters of frozen muck fly past my face. "I told you to stand back!" My feet were planted ankle deep in freezing mud, but I didn't care. I've known men with gold fever, seen them go crazy at the sight of the stuff. I thought it could never happen to me. It could and did. That night I went gold crazy. The demon didn't own me for long, but while he did I was a man possessed. For three solid hours I punished that cavern wall, spurred on by the riches I found. Every tenth or twelfth bite of the pick uncovered a new deposit. The cheese sandwich soon ran out, replaced by hunks of frozen muck bearing good-sized nuggets, some as large as walnuts.

Hannah brought a bucket down into the shaft and began filling it with nuggets. "Brian, this is the richest strike they've seen around here yet."

I didn't bother to reply. At that moment nothing could have kept me from my work, not even a full bottle of Perry Davis Painkiller . . . which shows what terrible changes gold can make in your personality. In the end I gave up the pick not because I had returned to my senses, but in answer to the promise of still greater riches. Three-Inch White suddenly appeared halfway down the ladder and said, "Hannah, we've hit the same streak in the other shaft."

The pick fell from my hands like a hot poker and I raced Hannah to the ladder. She won. I followed her out of one hole and dived down the other right behind Hannah without once feeling my usual desire for her extraordinary bum, another illustration of the horrible effects of gold.

"There it is." Three-Inch pointed at the streak with the air of a father showing off his newborn babe.

"We hit it five minutes ago," said Roy Teal. "Right where you guessed it would be."

Hannah went to the wall and ran her hands over the frozen dirt. "This shaft is sixty feet from the other one. That means the rich digging runs at least that far."

Howard Jasper, Hannah's other hired hand, spoke up out of the darkness. "We figure you owe us a big bonus."

"Watch yourself, Jasper," I warned. "Your pockets are probably full of our nuggets already."

Jasper stepped forward. He was a beefy gent with the ruddy complexion common to steamboat engineers and his manner threatened.

"I don't take that kind of talk, Bonner. Not even from one of the Queen's yellowlegs. It don't matter how many sick Cree Indians you shot from ambush, you don't scare me one damned bit. The three of us have a bonus coming for hitting paydirt."

"Shot from ambush!" I started for the windy bastard's throat but Hannah stepped between us.

"Stop it, Brian. Howard's right. They do deserve a bonus. And you'll get one, provided you don't open your mouths about this strike until noon tomorrow."

The three men exchanged glances. "How big a bonus?" Teal asked.

"One thousand dollars apiece."

"Two thousand," Three-Inch countered.

Hannah thought about that. "Five hundred apiece in U.S. dollars and all the nuggets you can stuff in your pockets."

"We'll take a flat fifteen hundred apiece," Jasper said.

Hannah stuck out her hand. "Done! But only if you stay in my cabin until noon."

After some discussion the three agreed to the last part of the deal. I added nothing more to the negotiations, satisfied that I had been right about the three of them stealing some of our gold. They could have only one reason for turning down Hannah's offer to fill their pockets with nuggets—they had already done so. Hannah knew how to drive a bargain.

What she wanted, of course, was to buy the adjoining claims before anyone else heard of this big strike. The claims on either side were both owned by Axel Anderson, another reason for trying to get them on the cheap. I didn't blame Hannah for wanting to give Axel some of his own. He had built his business by tricky dealing and couldn't squawk if Hannah paid him back in kind.

We climbed up to the surface and installed our three hired hands in the cabin. They grumbled about it but Hannah stood firm. "You'll stay here until noon tomorrow, unless we let you go sooner, or lose your bonuses." She looked boldly into Jasper's eyes. "And I'll have Brian turn each of you upside down and give you a good shaking besides."

When they were safely put away Hannah said. "You'll have to keep watch on them. There's no lock on the door. Even if there was, I wouldn't trust them not to break it open. Do you know where I can find Axel?"

"He was in the Bank earlier. By now he's

probably worked himself over to the Aurora. He likes to gamble there on Tuesday nights, that's when Tom Chisolm deals poker himself. Axel says Tom is the easiest dealer to beat in Dawson, though he hasn't had much luck at it so far."

"Axel thinks too much of himself. Maybe we can teach him a lesson."

"I know you want the two claims on either side of us. But where will you get the money?"

"I'll try to talk Axel into taking a thirty-day note for the other two claims. He's been trying to sell them off anyway. He might consider this a good opportunity to put me out of business once and for all. Axel hates to have a woman as a competitor. Then we'll use the nuggets to pay the bonus to those three and the cheese sandwiches to hire more help."

Her soaring ambition made me nervous. "I don't know. We're standing on a fortune. Why risk losing it? The other two claims might not be as rich as this fraction."

"They are, Brian. *They are.* This is just the beginning, can't you feel it?" Hannah gripped my shoulder. It was almost a religious gesture, a laying on of hands. And somehow it worked. My doubts vanished. I found myself saying, "All right, you go sweet-talk Axel while I watch these three."

And off she went down the creek, brushing the hardened mud from her pants, fingers probing under her cap to straighten her hair. From a distance no one would ever imagine that a beautiful woman inhabited those dirty work clothes. I had no doubt that Hannah would strike a deal with Axel. This was just the beginning, as she had said. But the beginning of what?

I pushed open the door to Hannah's cabin and joined our three workmen. "Gentlemen, we are all about to come into a sizable sum of money. So let's relax and play a little Acey Deucey."

Hannah made the deal. She gave Axel a note for one hundred thousand dollars payable in full in thirty-five days. If we failed to pay on time Axel would repossess all three claims, including whatever dumps had been built on them. Hannah roused Joe Rudolph from bed and brought him down to the Aurora in his nightshirt and greatcoat to draw up the papers. When Axel and Hannah had signed, she rushed back to the claim for my signature.

Although I had no sleep that night I was on time and closely shaved for once when I reported to Inspector Constantine at eight A.M. Van Ness was already there, looking pious.

"What's the trouble?" I could see they were both upset.

"Your friend Bill Gates is about to plunge this territory into a civil war," Van Ness said grimly.

"Swiftwater Bill? He's too busy with women and gold to start a civil war. What the hell are you talking about, Evan?"

Constantine confirmed Van Ness's fears. "Swiftwater Bill has started hoarding food. Last night he bought up every egg in Dawson, fifty of them, for five thousand dollars. One hundred dollars an egg!"

"I didn't know there were any eggs left in Dawson."

"A few here and there," Constantine said. "Last night Gates went into the Bank for dinner. He ordered a plate of potatoes and apples. Halfway through the meal he told Sam Bonnifield he wanted to buy every egg in the kitchen. Sam had seven eggs in the food vault under the floor of his back room. They were frozen, of course, part of the last food shipment from Skagway in October. Gates bought them all, then went around town buying up every other egg he could find. Five thousand dollars' worth.''

Van Ness and Constantine watched me as if I might have a clue to my friend's strange behavior. All I could say was, "That doesn't sound like Bill. Hell, he throws away gold about as fast as he finds it.''

"That's only gold,'' Van Ness snapped. "We're talking about food.''

"Has the word gotten around?''

Constantine claimed that it had. "At first everyone took it as one of Swiftwater Bill's pranks. Then they started talking among themselves. What if every millionaire in Dawson started buying up food? The rest of the territory wouldn't be able to survive. The only people who could afford to eat would be the Swiftwater Bill's . . . the Charles Berrys . . . the Antone Standers.''

"You'd have to be a millionaire to buy a plate of beans!'' Van Ness burst out. "There's only one way to discourage hoarding. Throw Swiftwater Bill in jail.'' Van Ness pounded his fist on Constantine's desk. "Put him to work on the government woodpile until spring. Show what will happen to anyone who tries to corner part of the food supply."

"Wait . . . wait just one minute." No matter how hard I worked at it, I couldn't picture Swiftwater Bill Gates hoarding anything. Several days earlier I had run across him leading a bunch of Paradise Alley whores to his claim. Each of the girls carried a lard bucket. It seems Bill had drifted across a new streak and his first thought was to invite some of his favorite girls to a party in the shaft. As party favors the girls were invited to fill lard buckets with nuggets. "There's something wrong here. Before you drag Bill off to the woodpile let me talk to him. Maybe I can straighten this out."

Constantine nodded. "All right. I don't know what good it will do, but go talk to him."

"He's at Diamond Tooth Gertie's right now having breakfast," Van Ness said. "Eggs, of course."

"I'll join him."

As I left Constantine said, "We have to settle the problem this morning. If one more of our millionaires goes on a food-buying spree we'll have a full-scale panic on our hands."

"I'll be back inside an hour."

On my way up Front Street I saw that Constantine hadn't exaggerated the problem. Knots of people were gathered in front of the N.A.T. & T. and A.C.C. warehouses. The topic of conversation undoubtedly centred on the amount of food left. If the crowd became a little bigger and uglier they might decide to break into the warehouses and find out for themselves just how much food Dawson had to live on until spring. Then the panic surely would be on. Many of the crates in the warehouses were empty. Constantine had conspired with the warehouse managers to make the food supply look more plentiful than it was.

I found Swiftwater Bill breakfasting contentedly on a plate of scrambled eggs at Gertie's place.

"Hey there, Brian. Sit down. Gert, how many of those eggs did you thaw out for me?"

"Six, Bill. You got three left."

"Put em on the skillet. How do you like your eggs, Brian?"

Bill was placing me in a tricky ethical position. On the one hand I had come into Gertie's to stop him from hoarding food. On the other hand the aroma of Bill's eggs made my knees weak. "Sunny side up." If Constantine asked I would say I had examined the evidence. Maybe all Bill's eggs had gone rotten. Then he couldn't be accused of hoarding.

Bill mopped up the yolk with a piece of bread and popped it into his mouth. "What's this I hear about you and Hannah making a big strike. Is it true? I ran into Axel this morning. He was cussing you and Hannah at the top of his voice."

"We hit some good dirt last night. Hannah mortgaged the claim to Axel in order to get her hands on two other Little Skookum titles."

Swiftwater Bill threw back his head and laughed. "That Hannah! She'll own us all one day."

"Unless our new claims turn out skunks. Then we'll be broke thirty-five days from now."

Bill shrugged his narrow shoulders. "That's the game, Brian. That's the game."

"Anyhow, I didn't come over this morning to talk about gold. I was wondering, Constantine wants to know too, why you bought up all the eggs in Dawson."

"Oh you *do*!" Bill threw his knife and fork

on the table. "Well, I'll tell you. I did it because of that bitch."

"What bitch?"

"Gussie Lamore!" Swiftwater Bill rolled his eyes. "I'm in love with that woman, Brian. And she's driving me crazy."

"Some woman is always driving you crazy. What does Gussie Lamore have to do with your eggs?"

The little prospector hunched forward and lowered his voice. "Last night I asked Gussie to have dinner with me after she finished her shift dancing at Tom Chisolm's place. She told me no, she didn't feel like dinner. Claimed her feet hurt. I said, okay, get some rest, I'll see you tomorrow." Swiftwater Bill's ears began to turn red. "So about ten o'clock last night I'm sittin' in the Bank by myself over a plate of potatoes. In comes Antone Stander and who's on his arm? You guessed it . . . Gussie! The two-timing baggage didn't even have the decency to look embarrassed at finding me there. She smiled over at me sweet as you please. And cool? Butter wouldn't melt in her mouth."

Sometimes Bill could talk for an hour without unloading an answer to a straight question. "Eggs, Bill. I want to know about the eggs."

He pushed his plate away. "I'm gettin' to the eggs, dammit! Gimme some talkin' room."

I waited while Bill pulled out a pouch of tobacco and papers and began rolling a smoke.

"Eggs . . ." He struck a match and lit up. The extra paper at the tip of his handmade cigarette flared. "Eggs, you want to know about. I'll tell you about eggs. That . . . that . . ." Bill waved angrily at the cloud of smoke between us. "That damned woman loves eggs. Gussie, I mean. Last night she says to Antone, 'Oh, Antone dear, I'd like a plate of scrambled eggs for dinner.' I could hear her all the way over at my table, as could half of Dawson. So Antone orders eggs for both of 'em."

A slow smile spread over Bill's face. "But they didn't get 'em. I nipped out to the kitchen and bought up every egg in the place. Then I went all over town buyin' up eggs, fifty of 'em. Gussie won't be able to eat another egg until the stern-wheelers start bringin' in supplies next spring."

"You spent five thousand dollars just to

keep Gussie from having eggs with Antone Stander?"

"That's right." Swiftwater Bill chuckled behind his smoke and pushed his makings across the table to me. "You should'a seen the look on Gussie's face when Sam told her I'd bought up her eggs. Off they go in a huff to the Blue Ox, where they discover I've also got my hands on Paddy Malone's three eggs." Tears rolled down the little man's cheeks as his laughter built. "I never had so much fun, Brian."

I waited until his jubilation eased. "This is serious, Bill. You don't understand what's happening. People think you're hoarding food. There's a mob down by the warehouses already. People are worried that Dawson's high rollers are out to corner the food supply. Unless we straighten this out fast we'll have a full-scale food panic in Dawson."

The cigarette fell onto the table as Bill's mouth dropped open. "Hoarding! Me? Why, Brian that just ain't possible. You know me better. I'll take my chances with everyone else."

"Hell, I know that. It's the rest of Dawson you have to convince."

My news scared Swiftwater Bill. He had

been around long enough to have seen other food panics. He stubbed out the cigarette on his plate and sneaked a furtive glance around. "I get it now. When I came along Front Street this morning hardly anybody gave me the nod. Now I know why." He rubbed his palms together. "What can I do?"

"I don't know, Bill. You could sell back the eggs, but folks would think you did it because you were caught out. I'm afraid everyone would still worry that you or another of Dawson's millionaires might start buying up all the food."

"Jesus." Bill straightened his French cuffs and brushed a piece of lint from the sleeve of his Prince Albert coat. "I really started somethin'."

"Yeah, you did."

The waiter appeared and put a plate of eggs in front of me. They smelled so inviting that the fork sort of drifted into my hand. Before I could argue out the rights and wrongs with myself, the plate was half empty. "Hey . . . these are yours, Bill. I shouldn't be eating them anyway."

"I don't want 'em. I feel sick."

And that's what gave me the answer to Bill's problem. "You feel sick?"

"I surely do."

"That's it! There's your answer. How many eggs are left?"

"Forty-four of the damned things."

"Great! I'll tell you what you're going to do. You're going to donate those eggs to Father Judge's infirmary."

Swiftwater Bill scratched his nose. "The infirmary?"

"Sure. That's why you bought the eggs, as a donation to the patients at Father Judge's infirmary."

"I did?" A shadow of comprehension crossed Bill's face. "That's right, I did!"

"You're a goddam humanitarian."

Bill threw his arm around my shoulder. "By God, that'll fix it, Brian. I can get myself off the hook and look a hero from it. You saved my bacon."

"Not to mention your eggs."

That's how a Yukon food panic was avoided in '98. People settled down and trusted Constantine to see that the food supply would last the winter, which it did.

There were other problems not so easily settled.

About a week after the incident of Swiftwater Bill's eggs one of the dancehall girls from the Aurora, a chunky little blonde named Dolly Morgan, dumped a different kind of problem in my lap. She approached me in the Aurora as I was about to pour myself a well-earned six ounces of Perry Davis Painkiller. Constantine had dispatched me on patrol seven days in a row looking for signs of the murderers of those seven prospectors. All I wanted was to be left alone with my friend Perry Davis for a few hours, but Dolly wouldn't hear of it. "I need your help, Brian."

"All right, let's go sit down." I carried my bottle and glass to a table where Three-Inch White and Howard Jasper were sitting and evicted them with the toe of my boot. I offered Dolly a chair. "Now what the hell's so important that you can't let me poison myself in peace?"

Dolly had placed both her hands in front of her on the table. A crumpled white handkerchief lay in them. The chubby hands worked endlessly on the handkerchief, twisting and pulling at it. "I can't take this life anymore." The first taste of Perry Davis brought a glow to my cheeks and tears to my eyes. "All right, quit. Get yourself a job as a waitress.

Sam Bonnifield's short of help, he told me so himself."

She shook her head, tossing blonde curls. "That's not good enough. I came up here to make some real money. Tom Chisolm keeps seventy percent of the dollar a minute we get for dancing with the customers, and with the cost of goods so high I'm not saving much more than I did at home in Portland."

"There's plenty of cribs on Paradise Alley."

"I'm not a whore, either," she flared.

"All right. Okay. I apologize. Have a drink."

Dolly accepted a glass. As we were drinking Deephole Johnson came stamping into the Aurora full of laughter and covered in mud. He announced to one and all that the Yukon had made another millionaire . . . himself . . . and proceeded to prove it by dumping the contents of a salt box on the bar. Nuggets spilled across the mahogany and a cheer went up. Johnson bought drinks for everyone. He was pounded on the back and his hand pumped by every loafer in the place. As Johnson recounted in detail how he discovered a rich vein of placer gold, people began slipping out of the saloon in ones and twos. I had seen it happen many times.

Johnson's claim was located up on Last Chance Creek. The men slipping away would drift into the wilderness carrying light stampede packs, hoping to piggyback on Johnson's luck. Most would return from Last Chance Creek in a few days, the pain of one more false promise written on their faces.

"What do you want from me, Dolly?"

She stopped twisting the handkerchief. "I had an idea this morning. Larry Bartleman decided to quit trying to get rich and go home, so he auctioned off his tools. He got five hundred dollars for his pick, shovel, and sluice box. That gave me the idea of auctioning myself."

"Auctioning yourself? Why that's foolish, Dolly. There's twenty women over on Paradise Alley auctioning themselves every night. Besides, you said you didn't want to go into whoring."

"That's right. I want to auction myself off as a wife. Not a real wife. I figure someone will pay a pretty good price to have a woman live with him the rest of the winter. I'll cook, mend clothes, do everything else a wife would do."

"But only for the winter?"

"Yes, until the first stern-wheeler arrives

from the outside. I want you to run the auction, Brian. People trust the mounties. Whatever money I bring can be kept in the safe at your barracks until spring. That'll be a guarantee for both me and the man who buys me. He'll pay in advance so there's no chance of his welshing, and you don't give me the money in the spring unless he agrees I was a good wife to him."

Dolly had everything planned down to the last detail. She had even painted posters in bright colors announcing the auction in three days' time. The conditions were spelled out just as she had explained them to me. Dolly advertised herself as twenty-three years of age, in good health and free of social disease, adept as a seamstress and cook, amorous in nature, and willing to learn new skills.

"*Willing to learn new skills*? You know what people will make of that, Dolly."

She smiled brazenly. "Let them think what they want. That's salesmanship. Will you do it, Brian? Will you run the auction?"

"Let me talk to Constantine first to see if he'll hold the money in our safe until June. He might kibosh the whole idea."

"Fair enough. You talk to him and let me know."

I did talk to Constantine and you can guess his reaction. But despite his feelings he didn't intend to stop the auction. You can't police people by trying to fit them out with your own moral code and Constantine was smart enough to understand that. He even agreed to let me run the auction and to keep the proceeds safe in the barracks until summer.

With Constantine's approval I began nailing up Dolly's posters around Dawson. They created such a sensation that I soon came to appreciate the shrewdness of Dolly's thinking. Having no use for a wife myself, I had not realized how deprived many of the men felt, especially those who did have wives back home. They were the ones who quickly announced their intentions to bid for Dolly. It seemed that the men who bragged the loudest about their happy marriages were the most eager for the auction to begin.

Only a few people voiced doubts about the auction. One was Evan Van Ness, who couldn't believe Constantine would approve such an event. Another was Father Judge, whose apprehensions had a religious basis. Old man Hunker took his nose out of *The Decline and Fall* long enough to make comparisons between Rome and Dawson. But the most vocal opposition came from Hannah Young.

Her opinion was made known to me on the afternoon before the auction. I hadn't paid a visit to our three claims on Little Skookum for almost two weeks, owing to the heavy schedule of patrols assigned to me. When at last I did get out to Little Skookum the activity amazed me. Hannah had hired six additional men and sunk three more shafts on the claims. The dumps next to the shafts were each more than twenty feet high and all the timber along the ridges had been cut to brace the walls of the shafts.

I found Three-Inch White and asked him where Hannah might be.

"Up there." He waved at the rimrock above the creek.

And in the arctic darkness I saw Hannah working in the snow just below the top of the ridge. She had a pick in both hands, chipping with it at the rock face of the ridge. "What the hell's she doing?"

"Damned if I know what gets into her mind," Three-Inch said. "We've been hitting good dirt down here but that don't satisfy her. She seems to think there's gold up on the ridge, too."

"That's a crazy idea."

"I know," Three-Inch agreed. "But you can't tell Hannah anything. She'd give Moses an argument about the Ten Commandments. She'd want twelve."

I climbed the steep slope to the top of the hill. "Hey there, Hannah. Haven't you got the world turned upside down? The gold's in the creek bed, not up here on the ridge."

She laid the pick against her leg and studied me at her leisure. "I'm surprised to see you out here."

"Constantine's had me on patrols sixteen hours a day. I would have been out otherwise, you know that."

"Would you? I understand you're keeping yourself quite busy these days peddling flesh."

"Peddling flesh? Oh, you mean the auction. Look, Dolly came to me and asked . . ."

"Pimp!"

"Don't you call me a pimp, you little . . ."

Hannah turned her back on me and continued chipping away at the crevice between two heavy layers of rock.

"Turn around and talk to me. You can't call me a name like that and then just turn your back."

"I don't have anything to say to you, Brian. As far as I'm concerned you're pimping, whether Dolly suggested it or not."

"Listen, she's going to do it anyway. All I care about is that she gets a decent price for herself."

"I've never heard a more clear-cut definition of a pimp."

"Stop using that word!"

"I won't," Hannah countered, concentrating on her work.

At times the best way to deal with Hannah was to change the subject. I asked what she was doing up on the ridge.

"Crevicing," she answered shortly.

"For gold?"

"No, for sunflower seeds."

I ignored her sarcasm and pointed out that the gold was to be found down on the creekbed.

"Let me ask you a question, Brian. How do you think the gold got down to the creekbed?"

"The water carried it there over a period of thousands of years, I suppose. Being heavier than the water and dirt, the gold collected between and around the rocks under pressure of the water."

"Look at these ridges. They were cut away by water. A million years ago all these streams and creeks were huge rushing rivers. Why couldn't the river have deposited gold in the crevices up here as well as on the creekbed?"

"Because it didn't. Gold is where you find it. That's the only rule in this business."

"It's a good rule." Hannah picked up a bucket at her feet. "But before you can find gold you have to look for it. I looked up here and this is what I've found." The bucket was half filled with chunks of gold. "I came up here yesterday, following a hunch. After two minutes of crevicing I found my first nugget. I filled a whole bucket yesterday afternoon. The only reason I don't put the men to work on the ridges is that this kind of gold is too easy to steal. We have only fifteen days left to come up with Axel's hundred thousand dollars."

For the first time I really believed we might become millionaires. "How much do we have so far?"

"About thirty thousand in nuggets and cheese sandwiches. The real money is in those dumps, but I can't think of a way to wash enough dirt in this weather to come up with the money to pay Axel. All we can do is hope to hit enough deposits of pure gold to make a hundred thousand dollars before the note comes due."

I discovered that I wanted very badly to keep the three claims. "If we can come within a few thousand, Swiftwater Bill will loan us enough to make up the balance."

"I know. So you'd better go back to your work and let me get back to mine." She swiveled around on her rocky perch to continue chipping at the face of the hill.

"Hannah, I don't think you're being fair about Dolly Morgan. Even Constantine is going along with the auction."

She wanted to withdraw the crude name she'd called me, that was clear from her discomfort. But there was a principle at work that would not allow her to apologize. "I'm sorry, Brian. I can't 'go along'. I'm sick of the way you men use women. That's why I'm out to get rich. No man is ever going to buy me for a few dollars."

That's how we left it.

6

THE auction took place as scheduled on Front Street on the steps of the A.C.C. general store. One-Eyed Riley had built a platform onto the front steps and promptly at ten A.M. I mounted the platform in my cleanest uniform and with my boots polished to a high gloss. I had never looked better even on parade.

More than a thousand people crowded Front Street, some on hand for the bidding but most simply to enjoy the festivities. Extra coal oil lanterns had been hung on the storefronts to illuminate the street. The twenty-four-hour-a-day darkness of the Yukon winter creates a gloom that is hard to dispel, but on this occasion everyone seemed happy and excited.

You could tell who the bidders would be. They carried heavy moosehide pokes the size of soccer balls. Amateur oddsmakers favored Antone Stander or Lord Avonmore to top the bidding. Axel Anderson had announced he would not bid at all unless Dolly stripped naked during the auction so that he could examine the merchandise. Several friends of Axel got up a petition supporting his position, but sentiment in that direction withered under the strong argument that a naked Dolly would freeze to death before the auction could be completed.

I raised both my hands to signal for quiet and the crowd hushed obediently. Everyone was anxious for the bidding to begin. "Good morning. You all know what we're here for. Dolly Morgan has decided to put herself out at auction as a temporary wife. She will perform all the services of a wife beginning today and continuing until the day the first sternwheeler reaches Dawson from the Bering Sea. The bid money will be held in the Mounted Police barracks until that day as a guarantee that Dolly will faithfully perform the duties to which she has subscribed. Are there any questions?"

"Get on with the bidding!" someone shouted.

"Where's Dolly?"

"Dolly is waiting inside the A.C.C. store. There is one more announcement before the bidding begins. Commercial dust will not be accepted in payment for Dolly. Only nuggets and clean dust will be recognized as legal tender. Let me also add that gold submitted for payment will be examined for brass filings and other evidence of salted pokes."

Cries of "Outrage!" and "Bad faith!" rose from the crowd. Several prospective bridegrooms quit the field in disgust, taking their salted pokes with them.

As I opened my mouth to introduce Dolly, a wind came driving down Front Street with the power of a locomotive. My breath was temporarily taken away. The temperature registered twenty-five degrees below zero on the A.C.C. thermometer. There had been no snow for three days but plenty of wind, the kind that strips bark from trees. I held my breath until the wind abated, then went on quickly, "And here she is . . . Dolly Morgan!"

The doors to the A.C.C. store opened and Dolly Morgan stepped out. Cheers went up, followed by whistles and lewd catcalls. Dolly wore a handsome fur cape borrowed from Gussie Lamore for the occasion. She had wisely wiped all makeup from her face to accommodate her appearance to the wifely virtues advertised on her posters. "Hello boys!" Dolly smiled demurely and waved to the crowd. Out of the corner of her mouth she whispered, "Let's get this damned thing going. My knockers'll freeze off before you can sell 'em."

I cleared my throat and yelled into the wind, "The bidding will now commence!"

"Thirty dollars," Three-Inch White yelled. The crowd roared its disapproval at such an uncomplimentary bid. Several hands snatched at Three-Inch. In a split second he was hoisted off the ground, passed along overhead by dozens of willing hands, and pitched headfirst into a snowbank between the barber shop and the M & M Saloon to a round of laughter and applause.

"Thank you one and all," I said. "You're quite right. The bidding should open at one thousand dollars. Do I hear a thousand?"

Antone Stander raised his hand. "You've got it."

"A thousand. Do I hear two thousand?"

Deephole Johnson bid two thousand.

"Dawson's newest millionaire bids two thousand dollars for the hand of Dolly Morgan."

"I bump that another thousand," said Thomas Lippy. Lippy was a former YMCA instructor from Seattle whose claim on

Eldorado Creek could have bought a hundred Dolly Morgans. There were a few chuckles at Lippy's bid. He had given several lectures at the old Opera House on the subject of "How to Live Happily in Sexual Abstinence." Apparently he now felt the need for a live-in audience for his lecture.

Frank Conrad followed up with a four-thousand-dollar bid and Antone Stander raised that another thousand. Then the small-timers jumped into the bidding, bumping each other a hundred dollars a crack. Most had no intention of sticking in the auction to the end. They would settle for the thrill of taking part. It took only ten minutes to work the bid up to ten thousand dollars, which seemed to be the level separating the serious bidders from the thrill seekers. Suddenly only two men remained in the bidding, Antone Stander and Deephole Johnson.

"Twelve Thousand," Antone said.

People stepped aside to let the two competing bidders advance to the foot of the platform.

"We have a bid of twelve thousand dollars from Antone Stander," I reported with suitable eloquence. "Before continuing the auction I will place on exhibit two articles that should be of interest to the bidders."

I signaled to One-Eyed Riley, who was waiting just inside the A.C.C. door. He came out bearing two items wrapped in brown butcher paper. I took one and unwrapped it, holding it high above my head. "This is a man's shirt, medium size. Yesterday at four P.M. when I handed this shirt to Dolly it was in terrible condition. There were holes in both elbows. The seam under one arm had come loose. It was covered with mud and caked with grime. The shirt belongs to Three-Inch White. If he were still present at this auction I know he'd testify that this shirt has not been in such good condition since the day he was overcharged for it by the A.C.C."

To demonstrate Dolly's skill as a seamstress I pulled on both arms of the shirt and prayed it wouldn't come apart. It held together, prompting numerous compliments to Dolly.

"And now I take pleasure in unveiling an example of Dolly's cooking." One-Eyed Riley handed me the second article, which I uncovered with a flourish.

Gasps could be heard over the sound of the wind.

"An apple pie!"

"That's correct. The first apple pie ever baked in Dawson. And it will be consumed this very evening by the man who wins Dolly's hand at this auction."

"Fifteen thousand!" Deephole Johnson cried.

"Sixteen," Antone Stander countered.

"Sixteen-five . . ."

"Seventeen . . ."

"Seventeen-two-fifty . . ."

The bidding seesawed back and forth until the grand figure of twenty thousand dollars was reached, put forward by Deephole Johnson. For the first time during the auction Antone failed to follow right up with a higher bid. He simply stood with his back hunched against the wind and his eyes fastened on Dolly, clearly making up his mind whether she was worth a higher bid. After several tense seconds he made his decision and spoke out in a loud and challenging voice, "Twenty-two thousand!"

It was a bid designed to break Johnson's spirit by indicating Antone's willingness to push forward. Privately I believed Antone was about ready to quit and that this newest bid of his was a bluff. I felt certain he would abandon his bidding if Johnson topped him again.

"Twenty-three thousand," Johnson countered.

And I was right. Antone kicked the snow and gave Johnson a contemptuous glare. "She's yours."

"Three cheers for Deephole Johnson!" Frank Conrad shouted.

The crowd cheered lustily while Johnson blushed under the layer of grime he had carried to the auction from his diggings. The twenty-three-thousand-dollar bride stepped down from the platform and went to Johnson's side, slipping her arm through his. Johnson escorted Dolly through the crowd with the dignity of a king bringing his new queen to the coronation. More huzzahs went up and the happy couple was hustled off to the Aurora Saloon where Dolly turned in her resignation as a dancehall girl. Tom Chisolm, always a gentleman, not only accepted her resignation with grace but laid on a wedding breakfast of beans and bacon for the couple.

During the festivities someone stole Dolly's apple pie. I was called on to find the culprit and retrieve the pie. Although my investigation was thorough, I was not able to locate the thief or the apple pie. The bride and groom were angered by the loss, but determined not to let it mar the occasion. I told them they would be wise to put the incident out of their minds and promised to continue my investigations throughout the winter, if necessary.

The apple pie was delicious.

Constantine's observation that blood money usually finds its way into saloons and gambling houses proved accurate two nights later.

Lord Avonmore had persuaded me to join him in tasting something called a rum melt at the Bank, where Sam Bonnifield kept His Lordship's private store of liquor under lock and key. Always interested in extending my knowledge, I agreed to the experiment and met Lord Avonmore at the Bank at the appointed hour of nine P.M. I was on time as all considerate guests should be. Lord Avonmore had arrived early to instruct Sam on the complicated business of concocting the rum melt, a drink of his own invention.

"You must . . . ahem . . . heat this iron until it is sufficiently hot. Not . . . ahem . . . red hot. *White* hot. Can that be . . . ahem . . . accomplished in your sheet iron stove, Mr. Bonnifield?"

Lord Avonmore came from somewhere in

the south of England. He had a peculiar little catch in his throat, but his account at the Bank of British North America in Edmonton was so large that he seldom had trouble making himself understood. Along with a host of servants, the bulldog, lawn tennis set, and the seventy cases of champagne that quickly spoiled in sub-zero temperatures, he had also brought several cases of rum that survived. Lord Avonmore had never staked a claim. He appeared to be a traveler by profession, one of those nomads who follows every new road in search of fresh experience. Everyone liked him. He was quick to buy drinks and always interested in listening to the complaints of his fellow man, a rare gift indeed. Liquor and conversation were the two mainstays of his life. He often spent twelve hours at a stretch standing drinks and swapping stories in the Bank. Many people called him "Lord Have-One-More," Tall, spare and in his early fifties, he wore a mustache that stood to attention.

"That's it," he was telling Sam. "Now I will plunge the . . . ahem . . . poker into the drink for exactly seven seconds."

Lord Avonmore slipped the white-hot poker into an iron mug. The liquid quickly boiled, causing some of the rum-based drink to overflow. His lordship removed the poker after exactly seven seconds and plunged it into the second mug.

"I will leave the poker in the . . . ahem . . . second mug for nine seconds. One must offset any cooling effect caused by . . . ahem . . . the heating of the first drink."

We each took a mug and Lord Avonmore urged me to drink as quickly as possible while the mixture was at the height of its powers. I followed his advice. By the time the last drop found its way to my stomach I was a new man . . . a warmer man . . . a quieter man. "You may have stumbled on something very important here," I said, my voice coming in a rasp.

I was about to ask his opinion on the possibilities of a Perry Davis Painkiller melt when Sam Bonnifield signaled for my attention. He had turned over the mixing of Lord Avonmore's drinks to one of his bartenders and stood aloof from the flow of business with a worried expression.

"What's the trouble, Sam?"

He opened his fist to show me a sizable gold nugget. "Does that look to you like a shamrock, Brian?"

On close inspection the nugget did resemble a shamrock. There were three distinct lumps of gold connected like three pods on a shamrock. "Yes, I can see it."

"So could Herman Ganz. This was his goodluck piece. He showed it to me several times. That was the first nugget he found up on Forty-Mile and it brought him luck, he said. Herman always carried it in his pocket."

"Where did you get it?"

"From Jules Pelletier and his partner. Jules paid for their dinner with it.

"Where's Pelletier now?"

"Right over there at the roulette wheel."

Without making a sideshow of it, I turned toward the roulette wheel and examined Jules Pelletier and his partner, Ira Wade. I knew them both slightly. They were partners on a claim on Too Much Gold Creek. I watched Pelletier place a large bet on double zero and snarl at the croupier when number thirty-two came up instead. Pelletier had a temper that flared when he gambled. I recalled once breaking up a fight over cards between him and Tom Chisolm at the Aurora.

Pelletier and Ira Wade had come down together from Skagway last November by dogsled. That was another reason to hold them suspect in the seven killings; they owned a dogteam of malamutes with a Siberian husky for a leader. A pretty good team. Pelletier was the taller of the two, topping six feet by a couple of inches and with shoulders like an ox. His skin and hair were dark, advertising his *métis* blood. He dressed expensively in a wool Norfolk jacket with cavalry riding pants and fleece-lined boots and he often smelled of hair oil. I'd heard rumors that Pelletier had taken part in the Saskatchewan Rebellion. He wore a short black beard, which he kept trimmed and combed, and when he laughed he barely moved his lips.

Ira Wade had less to brag about in the way of looks. He stood six or eight inches shorter than his partner and ran to fat. A long scar that could have been made by a knife ran across his right cheek. It was the only interesting feature to his face, which otherwise resembled a lumpy potato.

"Thanks, Sam. I'll have to take that nugget for evidence."

In approaching Pelletier and Wade I unsnapped my holster flap. There was not much danger involved, neither man appeared armed. They could be carrying concealed weapons, however, and if they were responsible for the seven killings they wouldn't come quietly. I relished the idea of a lively brawl. Except for patrols and Dolly's auction, things had been awfully quiet.

Pelletier was involved in one of his running arguments with the croupier when I came up behind him. He claimed that he had put his chip on number six, which came up a winner, instead of the number five square next to it.

"You put your chip on five," the croupier argued stubbornly.

"I put it on six," Pelletier insisted. "You knocked it off with that damned stick, which I'm about to break over your head."

"What's the trouble here?" The argument offered me an excuse to slide in between Pelletier and Wade at the table. I always like to separate a pair of rattlesnakes when I can.

"Hello, Bonner." Pelletier tapped his finger on the chip on square number five. "About time I had some help from you yellowlegs. This place is cheating me blind."

"That's right," Wade chimed in. "Jules put his chip on six. I saw him and so did half a dozen others, but they're all Bonnifield's friends."

I took the shamrock-shaped nugget from my pocket and showed it to Pelletier. "Have you ever seen this?"

Pelletier squinted at it impatiently. "I don't know. It's just a gold nugget, isn't it?"

"This particular nugget belonged to Herman Ganz, sort of a goodluck piece. He always carried it."

"So what?"

"You paid for your dinner with it." I dropped the nugget back in my pocket.

Wade began to ease cautiously away from the table. "Stay where you are, Ira. How about it, Jules? Can you explain how you put your hands on a murder victim's goodluck piece?"

The *métis* laughed. "I didn't give that nugget to Sam. He's lying. Sam's had it in for me ever since I started complaining about how he runs his tables."

"Has he? Then you won't mind if I look around your cabin. Just to make sure Sam didn't slip any of Herman Ganz's other goods onto your property to make you look bad."

Pelletier and Wade exchanged glances.

"What kind of deal are we getting here?" Pelletier demanded. "I make a little fuss about Sam's roulette wheel and all of a sudden you're accusing me of . . . well . . . I'm not sure what."

"Murder," I supplied.

Our exchange of words did not pass un-noticed by the other patrons of the Bank. Everyone's first instinct was to jam in close in order to hear every word. But at the accu-sation of murder people moved back as if fearing contamination. Ira Wade went pale at the charge but Pelletier's only reaction was a faint frown. "You'll play hell proving that," he said in a voice just above a whisper.

"Let's talk to Constantine about it." I stepped away from the table. "Walk outside and down Front Street to the barracks. Stay at least three feet apart and don't make any sud-den moves."

Pelletier stared at me. "Are we under arrest?"

"Not yet. Just do as I say, Jules."

The *métis* shrugged. "You'll owe us an apology, Bonner."

"Jules?" Ira Wade was a born follower. He needed some signal from Pelletier before he could move.

"Let's try the street, Ira."

I didn't like Pelletier's remark. Its meaning was unclear to me. But his words did start Wade moving toward the door. A wide path opened in front of us. The situation stayed under control until they reached the heavy oak doors of the saloon. Pelletier then reached out to open the door and Wade shoved his hands into his pockets as a man might do before going out in the cold.

But half a second later a muffled *click* reached my ears. At the instant of the sound I drew my Enfield pistol and fired at Wade. My bullet pierced his back just below the collar, jack-knifing him forward into the wall.

I fired a second time as Pelletier bolted through the door, but someone jostled my arm and the shot went wide. People began milling and shouting as I tried to reach the door. By the time I shoved my way through and gained exit to the street, Pelletier had vanished into the darkness.

I cursed my vanity at trying to take them alone and returned to the Bank.

"You shot him in the back," someone said. "Coward!"

"Get out of my way." I was in no mood for criticism. When Antone Stander stepped in front of me I yanked him aside by the neck. Ira Wade's body lay in a growing pool of blood. My bullet had evidently cut an artery, for the blood kept erupting from him in spurts. That at least indicated he was still alive. But as quickly as I noticed the rhythmic flow of blood, it stopped. I turned Wade over and felt under his coat for a heartbeat. There was none. His life had slipped away under my eyes.

I became aware of the voices around me. The words ran together in a jumble but their meaning came through clearly: *backshooter.*

I couldn't have made myself heard if I had cared to, which I did not. Words don't mean much when people grow hysterical. Some of the more ugly comments did filter through. Axel Anderson could be heard saying, "Bonner has been spoiling to kill Ira Wade for weeks. Someone told Brian that Ira Wade was sparking up to Hannah Young. I've never seen a more cold-blooded murder."

And Antone Stander's high-pitched voice came through with the most vicious lie of all: "That's how Brian got Almighty Voice. In the back."

When you wear a uniform you make enemies, that's taken for granted. To your face people say, "Good morning, Constable Bonner." But out of sight you're just another yellowleg. So I did not respond. Instead I bent over Wade's body and slipped my hand into his jacket pocket. When I straightened up I was holding a palm-sized .25 caliber

Derringer with two barrels, one mounted over the other. The sound that had caused me to fire was the click made by the pistol being cocked. I've heard that sound too many times to mistake it. Wade had palmed the gun as he put his hands in his pockets. When Pelletier told Wade "Let's try the street," he was signaling him to wait until they were outside, then use his Derringer on me. Wade had made a fatal error by cocking his piece before drawing it.

I held the Derringer above my head for all to see. A number of people looked embarrassed about the slander they had been talking. When I had made my point I lowered the hammer on the Derringer and put it away in my own pocket.

"Good show," Lord Avonmore piped up, raising his mug of rum melt in salute. "You gave the . . . ahem . . . sly little brute exactly what he . . . ahem . . . so richly deserved. Come have another melt to settle . . . ahem . . . your nerves."

"Maybe later," I answered, grateful for his support. "Pelletier is still out there somewhere."

"Quite so," Lord Avonmore said with a serious nod.

I found Constantine in his office fidgeting over paperwork and gave him a one-minute report on what had happened. As usual his questions were quick and to the point: "Where's Pelletier?"

"I don't know, sir. He escaped into the dark."

"Is he armed?"

"Probably. I'd guess they both carried pocket pistols."

"What do you think Pelletier will do now?"

"Bolt for the downriver border. It's only fifty miles away and once he's in Alaska we can't touch him."

Constantine jumped to his feet and threw on his parka. "We'll send a patrol to Fort Cudahy. Perhaps they can catch him crossing the border."

As we left the barracks Evan Van Ness came racing from the direction of Front Street. He almost crashed headlong into us. Constantine had to step aside and catch him by the arm.

"Inspector, Jules Pelletier just broke into the A.C.C. warehouse. He was stealing food. One-Eyed Riley caught him at it and Pelletier shot Riley. Riley's dead!"

"Where did Pelletier go?"

"I don't know." Van Ness looked astonished at the question.

Constantine swore and let go of Van Ness's arm. "Pelletier is one of the killers we've been after. His partner, Ira Wade, was another. Brian just killed Wade in the Bank. Pelletier is probably making for Alaska."

"And he has one of the better dogteams on the Yukon," I reminded them.

Constantine immediately split us up to look for Pelletier. Van Ness went out to Pelletier's cabin with a shotgun. I was ordered to continue scouting the town while the inspector organized the other four mounties on duty in Dawson into patrols. One patrol would head upriver to Fort Selkirk in hopes of catching Pelletier if he decided to head in that direction. The other patrol would rouse Fort Cudahy to close the downriver border with Alaska.

By that time everyone in Dawson had come into the streets. The news of Wade's death in the Bank and the murder of One-Eyed Riley had spread through town in a hundred versions. Any hope of catching Pelletier in the streets was destroyed by the presence of so many people wandering in the dark and in the half-light from the windows. The best I could do was enlist their help.

"We're looking for Jules Pelletier!" I shouted. "Has anyone seen Jules Pelletier?"

"I did." One of the miners from Carmack's Fork stepped forward.

"Where'd the bastard go?"

"Downriver. I was comin' back from gettin' my wick lit in Paradise Alley when Pelletier's dogs comes whooshin' out of the dark. Damned near run me down, he did."

"You're sure it was Pelletier?"

"Course it was. Didn't he yell that I cheated him at cards one night in Gertie's? And didn't I lay a fist up t'side of his head? Yer damned right I did. Saw his ugly face clear as sin. Came six inches from knockin' me off my feet. He was headed down-river sure enough. Skidded on the ice when he hit the river, but the dogs dug in and his sledge straightened out."

"Thanks." I ran to the barracks to warn Constantine but arrived too late. He had already sent patrols in both directions. I harnessed my own team as quickly as possible. We were on the river within ten minutes.

During the night I passed the mountie

patrol that had started downriver ahead of me. That gave me hope of overtaking Pelletier before he reached the border.

I didn't, though. Morning found me at the gates of Fort Cudahy, the last Mounted Police post before the Alaska border. The duty constable reported that a dogteam and driver had passed beneath the gates of the fort an hour ahead of me, moving fast. The constable had hailed the driver, who continued without replying.

Pelletier was safely across the border.

Constantine seemed to be the only person in Dawson who didn't blame me for something. There were those who thought I had shot Ira Wade without due cause. Others said I should have sent for Constantine and the other mounties on duty instead of trying to bring in Pelletier and Wade myself. A few of One-Eyed Riley's friends blamed me for his death because I had let Pelletier escape.

Even Hannah found cause to criticize. "You shouldn't have taken a chance with them," she said. "Suppose they'd killed you. Your estate would be tied up in legal knots for months. How could I operate if that happened?"

"Thanks a hell of a lot! Never mind that I'd be dead. That doesn't matter so long as the damned Young and Bonner Mining Company isn't hurt."

"Oh, Brian." Hannah patted my cheek. "You don't have any sense of humor at all. I'm teasing you."

"The claims are all you think about anymore," I grumbled.

"I said I was teasing. Now be quiet and sign these papers." We were sitting in Hannah's new cabin on Little Skookum. It was bigger and had a stouter stove than the one on Hunker Creek, but I liked it less. The meal of Hunter's stew in her old cabin had brought me closer to Hannah than I'd dared hope.

"What are these?" In the past month I had signed more papers than in all my previous years. It was tiring work. Aggravating, too. The elaborate loops of Rudolph's handwriting taxed my eyes.

"The first is a deed of conveyance," Hannah explained. "We have sixty-five thousand dollars in gold. We're selling the dump of ore on Five Above for sixty thousand to Thomas Lippy. That gives us enough to pay off Axel plus twenty-five thousand to spare."

"You mean we'd be out of debt? Then I'm

for it." I signed the paper right under Hannah's name.

I should have known that wasn't the end of it. Before I could suggest that we adjourn to the Bank to celebrate our solvency, Hannah whipped out another paper. "Now this is a letter of agreement between the Young and Bonner Mining Company and the Klondike Investment Bureau, Ltd."

"The Klondike Investment Bureau? What the hell is that?"

"It's a development company owned by Alex McDonald and Pat Galvin. We're borrowing three hundred thousand dollars from them to buy five claims on Bonanza, putting up the Little Skookum properties as collateral."

"What! Borrow three hundred thousand dollars? Why, you're mad, woman! Stark raving mad! We just climbed out of debt and now you want to bury us even deeper under notes. I won't have any part of it."

Hannah had an irritating way of smiling calmly whenever I tried to talk sense to her, as if I were the crazy one. "Brian, look at the five claims we're buying. They're on the best stretch of Bonanza." And she produced five more deeds of conveyance for the properties on Bonanza.

"I don't care how good the claims are. Three hundred thousand is too much money. And why would Galvin and McDonald lend us so much money anyway?"

"I imagine they want the interest. We're paying ten percent a month for three months."

"Ten percent! That's not a loan, that's a holdup."

"We'll own eight claims, Brian. Even if two of them turn out skunks we'll have plenty of gold to pay off Galvin and McDonald. There must be a million dollars in the dumps already built on those claims."

My head was swimming with so many figures that I didn't know what to say. "Let me get this straight. We pay off Axel with sixty-five thousand in Little Skookum gold and sixty thousand from Thomas Lippy for one of the dumps on Little Skookum . . . then we borrow three hundred thousand and buy five more claims . . . and then what?"

Hannah went coy. "I don't understand what you mean."

"That's not the end of it. I know you too well by now. You're holding back something.

What else are we buying or selling or leasing?" When she hesitated in answering I knew my instinct was right. "Come on, Hannah. Give it to me in one lump. I can't take two shocks like this one."

"All right." Hannah smiled with the relief of someone released from a great burden. "I do have another deal worked out. It's kind of tricky and calls for some cooperation on your part. That's why I've hesitated talking to you about it."

"What kind of 'cooperation' am I supposed to give?" I inquired, not liking the sound of this new deal at all.

Hannah wasn't about to tell me straight out. She had to work around to it in her own way. "Do you remember the night we had to bed down in the open during the storm? You were telling me your theories about liquor. One point you made stuck in my mind: people drink so heavily here because there's no other entertainment. That's why Sam Bonnifield was able to sell tickets at a hundred dollars a seat to Rollo Moon's trial. The idea hit me later that if we had genuine entertainment to offer we could make some really big money. Do you agree?"

I did. Most of the miners around Dawson

would pay a hundred dollars to see a lantern slide show about the pyramids of Egypt or the mating habits of eels. A real piece of entertainment would be worth a fortune. "Yes, but you'd have to find a good draw to make the kind of money that interests you."

When Hannah became excited her eyes glittered like a cat's. "I've found a big draw. There's a miner working up on Henderson Creek who hasn't had much luck. He's hard up for cash. His name is Frank Slavin. Have you heard of him?"

The name seemed familiar. I couldn't place him, though.

"He's a prizefighter. Four years ago he was the light heavyweight champion of the British Isles. Slavin is an Australian and I'm told he has a large following outside Canada."

I snapped my fingers. "That's right. Now I know him. Frank Slavin, the Sydney Slasher. He's a damned good fighter. Hannah, you've latched onto a great idea this time. I'd pay a hundred dollars myself to watch Slavin fight. The man's a killer. Who are you going to match him against?"

Her silence puzzled me until I realized who she had selected as Slavin's opponent. "Oh,

187

no. Listen, Hannah, I'm no boxer. I can handle myself in a saloon brawl, but a professional boxer like Slavin would take me apart."

"Brian, a fight between the two of you would be a natural. *The Sydney Slasher Versus The Man Who Killed Almighty Voice.* I've already talked to Slavin and he's agreed to take forty percent of the receipts. You and I will stage the fight and take the other sixty percent. We'll make a fast and easy twenty thousand dollars."

The woman's brass astounded me. "Haven't you wondered why Slavin is called the Sydney Slasher? Because he cuts his opponent's face to pieces with his bare knuckles, that's why. Fighters have come out of the ring with him looking like strips of raw steak."

"There are three more claims up on Quartz Creek that we can have for a song," Hannah continued. "All we need is a twenty-thousand-dollar binder against a purchase price of seventy thousand. By summer we'll have the other fifty thousand. You can't let those claims slip through our fingers just to avoid a few cuts and bruises."

"The hell I can't! If you want those Quartz

Creek claims so much, you can use the twenty-five thousand that'll be left over after paying off Axel."

"We can't do that," Hannah explained patiently. "That money is needed to pay hired help to work the claims."

"Then let's pass up Quartz Creek. For God's sake, Hannah, we're sitting on a mountain of gold as it is. I'll sign the note to the damned Klondike Investment Bureau if you'll just forget about matching me with Frank Slavin." And to get her off my back I snatched up the pen and hastily signed my name to the three-hundred-thousand-dollar note and the deeds to five new properties on Bonanza. She let me sign, then calmly gathered up the documents and put them into a manila folder.

"Thank you, Brian. But I still want you to fight Frank Slavin."

"No! And that doesn't mean maybe."

She rubbed her hands together crossly. "Your reputation could stand some polishing after that business with Ira Wade. A fight with Slavin would show people you aren't . . ."

She broke off the conversation and reached for the coffee pot on the stove.

"That I'm not a coward?"

"I wasn't going to say that."

But the meekness of her reply confirmed that she had started to say something close to it. "Hannah, I don't have to prove I'm not a coward. I shot Ira Wade because he was about to draw a cocked pistol on me. Some people may not believe that. If so, a fight between me and Frank Slavin isn't going to change their minds. Don't try to shame me into fighting him."

She poured coffee for both of us. The grounds had been reused many times, giving the brew a slightly rancid odor. I drank mine anyway wishing all the while that I had not come out to the claim. I thought Hannah would understand my actions. It was a kick in the teeth to find she didn't.

"Phew!" Hannah smacked her lips. "This coffee is worse than yesterday's. Guess I'll have to throw away the grounds. They're only a month old, too." She put down the cup and toyed with it. "I didn't mean that, Brian. I was trying to make you sore enough to fight Frank Slavin. I got carried away. Apology accepted?"

"Apology accepted, so long as you stop trying to match me with Slavin."

"Fair enough." Hannah added with a

wistful sigh, "But we could have made a potful of money."

Hannah was right, as usual. Later that year a down-and-out gambler named Tex Rickard picked up Slavin and matched him against someone else, making the potful of money that Hannah had wanted. Rickard found such easy pickings in fight promoting that he later made a career out of it. Just about every one of Hannah's hunches that winter paid off. Crevicing is one example. When Hannah began chopping away at the hillside everyone thought she'd lost her mind. But when she found nuggets all the other prospectors on the Klondike hiked up in the hills behind their claims. Damned if a lot of them didn't hit rich dirt up there, too. In just a couple of weeks crevicing had become big business, thanks to Hannah.

Suddenly, without warning, a thunderous pounding shook the entire cabin.

"What the hell?"

"Someone's trying to knock down the door!" Hannah screamed.

I jumped for the door with my gun drawn and pulled it open. Sheets of snow swirled in the night. Directly in front of the door stood a slightly larger than life snowman. The snowman shook its head, sending white flakes flying in the wind and uncovered the large shaggy head of Coatless Curly Munro.

"How do, Brian. Is Hannah t'home?"

"Jesus, I thought you were Father Christmas. Sure, she's here. Come on in, Curly. Brush off some of that snow first."

Curly shook himself like a bear, revealing a heavy wool shirt but no coat or hat, as usual. He stepped inside and his eyes glowed as they located Hannah. "I'm here for that dance you promised me. Remember? You said to come on down to Dawson and we'd go dancing at the Aurora. Here I am, Hannah. How about it?"

Hannah slapped her hand on the packing-crate table. "Curly, your timing is perfect. Brian is brooding over something and I've been making things worse. A night out at the Aurora is what we all need. You two step outside and try to keep warm while I change into my green dress. You'll have to carry me to the Aurora to keep my dress and dancing shoes dry."

And that's just what we did. Curly and I carried Hannah three miles into Dawson and deposited her on the dance floor of the Aurora. I ordered the piano player to strike up "The Denver Trot" and claimed the first dance for myself. Twenty other men who wanted to dance with Hannah quickly formed a line at the side of the floor, much to the displeasure of Curly. He managed to hold onto Hannah for three dances, letting go of her only when he heard someone at the bar make a slighting remark about the dirt on Indian River.

One dance was plenty for me. I took my pleasure in standing at the bar watching Hannah. It wasn't often that anyone saw Hannah in anything except her wool shirt and work pants. Even in those clothes she managed to look beautiful. In a green dress cut to show off her arms and a neckline plunging down between her breasts, she became spectacular. And could she dance? I never saw a woman move around the floor the way she did. It didn't matter whether her partner had two left feet, Hannah would waltz him around in circles until she had him prancing like a Vaudeville headliner. She annoyed the other dancehall girls, of course. No one would pay a dollar a minute to dance with Nellie the Pig when he could have a five-minute spin with Hannah for nothing.

Swiftwater Bill came into the Aurora with

Gussie Lamore, who had quit her job as a dancehall girl some days before. They had recently become engaged to be married. Bill had won Gussie's hand by offering to pay her a dowry of her weight in gold on their wedding day. They planned to be married in June in San Francisco. As soon as they came in, Gussie sat down at a table and ordered a big bowl of boiled potatoes for dinner. She had been eating steadily since her engagement and had already gained ten pounds.

I stuck out my hand to Bill as he joined me at the bar. "Congratulations, Bill. You finally got Gussie, I hear. But did you have to offer Gussie her weight in gold? That'll cost you a fortune."

"I know it will." Bill shrugged. "What the hell, when summer comes and I can wash my dumps I'll have more gold than I can spend. But there's only one Gussie Lamore."

"Doesn't it make you sore to watch her gulping down potatoes to gain weight, just so she can gouge you for more gold? At the rate she's eating, she'll double herself by June."

"No, that don't bother me. I think it's kinda cute."

There was no way to convince Swiftwater Bill that Gussie didn't give a snap for him, that she was the greediest female north of Sixty. Bill might even agree, but he'd still shrug and smile fondly at her. Of all the millionaires on the Yukon, only Swiftwater Bill Gates seemed completely free of greed.

Hannah danced with upwards of two hundred men that evening. She danced all through the night, in fact, and went back to working the claims at six in the morning. Curly and I shared a bottle of Perry Davis Painkiller for breakfast. With patrol duty facing me in an hour, I climbed into the kennels with my dogs for a few minutes of badly needed sleep before beginning the new day.

7

TWO weeks later Constantine received a message from Colonel Steele ordering me and one other mountie of Constantine's choice to report to him at White Pass on the Alaska border. He wanted us to go into Skagway for information about Soapy Smith's gang. Constantine's report on my encounter with Jules Pelletier and Ira Wade had convinced Steele that Soapy Smith was behind the seven murders along the Yukon. It seemed that Pelletier was well known in Skagway and had been seen often in Soapy's company. Pelletier had killed two men in Skagway the previous summer, both *cheechakos* passing through the town on their way to the gold fields. Steele needed to identify the other members of Soapy's gang in order to stop them from coming over Chilkoot Pass and White Pass in the spring.

When Hannah learned that I was headed all the way upriver she demanded to go along. She wanted to take five thousand dollars to Skagway to buy dredging equipment. Purchasing equipment in Skagway and shipping it downriver would be much cheaper than trying to buy it in Dawson in the summer. She ragged me about it and I finally agreed to approach Constantine on the subject.

The inspector rejected the idea until I pointed out that I would be less suspicious as a mine operator going into Skagway with my partner to buy equipment than as a mountie on the snoop. He thought that over and agreed that Hannah should go with me.

The second mountie assigned to the patrol was Evan Van Ness. I'm sure that Constantine matched me with Van Ness to prevent Hannah and me from bundling on the trail. His concern was flattering, though unnecessary.

The three of us left Dawson by dogsled on the morning of March twenty-first in the middle of a snowstorm. Despite the bad weather we moved rapidly, arriving at Lake Bennett five hundred miles upriver of Dawson exactly eight days later.

I'll always remember my first view of Lake Bennett on that cold morning in late March. We came across the lake with Hannah riding in my sled under buffalo robes and blankets and Van Ness using his whip to keep his animals moving as fast as mine. At first I thought the slopes around the lake had already begun to thaw. The snow over large areas seemed to have melted away to reveal expanses of dark earth. But as we approached the far shore the dark masses could be seen moving like bees on a hive.

Hannah was the first to recognise what lay ahead of us. She dragged one arm out from under the buffalo robes to gesture grandly around the lake. "People, Brian! Thousands of them!"

There were perhaps seven or eight thousand people at Lake Bennett, with additional thousands on the other side of the mountains struggling to bring their supplies across White Pass and the Chilkoot. Whichever pass they took from the Alaska panhandle, their destination was Lake Bennett, the jumping-off place for the Yukon.

At first I wondered why they were all standing around freezing when they could be hiking or sledding downriver. As we drew closer the reason became obvious. Tons of supplies littered the lake shore, stacked everywhere in untidy mounds. Ordinarily a gold hunter is the least provident of God's creatures. He'll run off into the wilderness with nothing but the clothes on his back, certain he'll find a pot of gold and a side of lean beef at the end of the trail. Instead he starves to death or turns criminal and kills his fellow prospectors for their food. Colonel Steele had acted to save the gold hunters from themselves and each other. Every person crossing into Canada was required to bring enough supplies to last six months, which came to about one ton of goods per person. The mounties posted at the top of each pass enforced that law. So the gold hunters were stuck on Lake Bennett until the ice broke on the Yukon.

In the meantime they packed their supplies over the pass and began building the boats and rafts that would take them and their goods downriver. Hundreds of men worked on the slopes trying to fell the frozen trees with whipsaws. Some rafts and boats had already been built. They sat on wood blocks along the bank of the lake while their owners caulked them with oakum.

We reached the bank and mushed the dogs up from the ice onto the snow. Our arrival caused a great commotion. Hundreds of curious onlookers pressed around the sleds, completely halting our progress while they pelted us with questions from all sides.

"Where's the richest diggings?"

"Are there any claims left on Bonanza?"

"Do you have to dig for the gold or is it lying around on the ground?"

"How long does it take to make a million dollars?"

"Should I stop at Dawson or go on to Forty-Mile?"

"Are there any women down there?"

"How many claims can I file?"

"What's gold look like?"

"Will the Indians let us go downriver or will they try to kill us?"

"Is there enough gold for everyone?"

The questions came so fast and from so many directions that we didn't even attempt to answer them. They also showed a sorry lack of knowledge among the gold hunters. I didn't expect the *cheechakos* to know much, but I thought they'd know *something* about what they were getting into.

"Mush! Pull, you damned mongrels!" The team dug in and rushed at the wall of people. Sitka slashed someone with his fangs, which helped to drive back the crowd. He used the opening to jam himself and the other dogs through the mob. Suddenly we were moving at top speed again past stacks of supplies and boats under construction and stiff canvas tents packed with people. Pack animals skittered out of our way as we began the long haul up to the top of White Pass.

The trail to the top of the pass was crowded with men coming down, some dragging handmade sleds loaded with supplies and others leading pack animals. A few women worked in among the men. The animals were the oldest, weakest collection of bones I had ever seen in one place.

One mule, overloaded with such heavy equipment as picks, shovels, and sledge hammers, stumbled and fell onto his front knees, blocking the trail. The mule stayed in that position for several minutes while he tried to muster the strength to rise. The owner, a *cheechako* in fresh store-bought clothes, began flailing the mule with a whip by way of encouragement.

"Heely!" I called to Sitka, who veered right and led the team off the trail. "Ho!" The team came to a halt.

"Why are we stopping?" Van Ness yelled from his position behind us.

Hannah answered for me. "I think Brian

wants a talk with the owner of that mule."

She was getting to know me real well, or else she had mind-reading ability. I walked over and tapped the *cheechako* on the shoulder as he was drawing back to lay the whip across his animal's back for the twentieth time.

"What the hell . . . Who are you, mister?"

I peeled back the front of my parka enough for him to see the red coat. "Constable Brian Bonner, Royal Canadian Mounted Police. What's your name?"

"Anson Black."

"Where are you from, Anson?"

"Omaha, Nebraska."

"Did they teach you how to use a whip in Omaha, Anson?"

The prospector puffed himself up. "Look here, constable. How I treat this mule is my business. You mounties don't own this territory, however much you act it. I just gave that old geezer at the top of the pass a good tongue-lashing about the damned fool mountie law that says everyone has to have a ton of supplies to get into this territory. It's criminal!"

"Well, I sympathize with you, Anson. But we do have a good many regulations up here in Canada, as you've noticed, and one regulation concerns the manner in which mules may be whipped."

Anson Black looked puzzled. "Regulations for whipping mules? I never heard of such a thing."

"I'm afraid we have them. Look, I'll show you what I mean." And before he could say yea or nay I took the whip out of his hand.

"Say, give that back."

"I will, in just a minute. Now watch carefully." I flicked the whip to draw it out full length on the ground. "This is how you have to start. It's against the law to bring the whip down overhand. In Canada you're supposed to make sidehand strokes, like this." My arm jerked and the whip flew out and lashed itself around Anson Black's legs.

Black howled "Oh, you damned yellow-leg!" and fell to the ground.

"Now, you don't have to give up overhand strokes altogether. Every third day one lash can be delivered overhand if you've gone to church the previous Sunday, as I'm sure a Christian soul from Omaha would do. But the overhand stroke should be short and businesslike. The law doesn't allow a stroke that causes the whip to wrap itself around the mule in this manner." And I pulled down a hard overhand chop that laid the whip over Anson Black's shoulder . . . across his back . . . and down around his chest.

"*Eeeeee!*" Black screamed and rolled on the ground at his mule's feet. It's a funny thing about mules. You can yell and coax and tug at their harness and they'll just sit there. But sometimes a high-pitched sound will cause them to stand up and move away. And that's exactly what Anson Black's mule did.

"There. Do you see what I mean, Anson? A mule just naturally reacts to a whip when it's applied in a lawful method."

Van Ness stamped up. "Are you through? We've wasted enough time here."

"I'm done." I dropped the whip. "You remember the law now, Anson."

But to show how ungrateful a man can be, that Anson Black never even thanked me for showing him the proper way to whip his mule. He just sat huddled on the ground whimpering and spitting out curses at me while his mule clomped on alone down the trail.

An hour later Hannah was the first to spot the Union Jack flying at the top of White Pass. Soon after that we reached the summit and Colonel Steele's headquarters, which were not much. A log cabin served as the headquarters and a place for Colonel Steele to sleep. Two other cabins had been dug out of the mountainside to house the other mounties on duty at the summit. A maxim gun stood above Steele's headquarters on a rock ledge that afforded a clear field of fire along the trail. I recognized the mountie manning that position as Freddy Loomis, an old comrade and drinking partner from warmer climates.

"Halloo, Brian!" Freddy hailed.

"Freddy! Anything to drink up here?"

"Not a damned drop."

"I've brought my own. See you later."

"You bastard! I knew you'd have something for old Freddy. Don't make it too much later."

The other mounties broke off their activities to welcome us. Their main job appeared to be collecting duties and verifying the amount of supplies each stampeder brought over the mountains.

Colonel Steele heard our arrival and came out to greet us with the others. He shook hands with Van Ness and myself, gallantly helped Hannah out of the sled, and escorted her into his cabin. We followed them. Steele made us comfortable with hot mugs of tea laced with honey. "I only expected two mounties," he said when we were settled. "What are you doing here, Hannah?"

"I'm here to buy dredging equipment in Skagway. It seemed a good idea for Brian and me to go into town together. Brian could say he's quit the mounties, which wouldn't surprise Soapy since he's bound to have heard that we're partners. Constantine agreed and he thought you would, too."

Steele produced a sparkling white handkerchief and began polishing his spectacles. "Smith certainly expects us to make a move against him. You might be able to catch him off guard posing as a mine owner. Brian, do you think you can get close to him?"

"I do, sir."

"Will he swallow a story that you've given up the mounties in favor of full-time gold prospecting?"

"Yes, I'm sure he will. Quite a few mounties have done that already, and Soapy knows me from days when I was a whiskey trader with plenty of money jingling in my pockets. He wouldn't see anything strange about a man giving up the mounties. Just the opposite, Soapy would consider anyone a fool who'd take our low pay, dangerous work, and bad food over a chance for gold."

As usual, I spoke without thinking. Steele reddened from his neck to his hairline at my remark about the mounties who had quit the force to look for greater rewards elsewhere. To Steele, one of the most dedicated men in the service, they were little more than traitors. He had been fighting for his country all his life, going back to the days when the Fenians were raiding into Canada from the United States. Steele helped organize and shape the Northwest Mounted Police. A dozen times in Canada's history Col. Samuel Enfield Steele had been the one man with the courage and bold common sense to bring a dangerous situation under control. After Sitting Bull massacred Custer, the Indian chief brought his warriors up to Canada. He had the men and the will to start a frontier war that might have gone on for ten years. But Colonel Steele rode into Sitting Bull's camp alone and negotiated a peace pact between the Indian leader and the government. Steele made the agreement stick, too, and won Sitting Bull's respect in the bargain.

Steele also commanded the force that put down the Saskatchewan Rebellion started by

Jacob Riel and his *métis* followers. So Colonel Steele was not a man who appreciated a slur against the Northwest Mounted Police.

"I understand what you're saying, Brian." Steele spoke in his blunt voice. "But don't ever put that idea to me in the same rude terms or I'll back you up against a whipsaw and cut about three feet off your hide. Understood?"

"Understood," I echoed meekly. There is no way I would ever disagree with Steele. I would fight the Sydney Slasher with both hands tied behind my back before taking up an argument with the colonel. Although in his fifties, Steele still possessed the muscled reflexes of a mountain cougar and the temper of a nest of hornets. I had once traveled with Steele all the way from Edmonton to Whitehorse. The only stops we made on the trip were for the purpose of resting the animals. Steele never considered the possibility that either of us might need more than an occasional catnap alongside the trail. Yes, he was a ferocious old buck and looked the part with his stiff white mustache and closely cropped gray hair.

And if you think he scared me you should have seen Evan Van Ness. From the moment we entered the cabin he kept his mouth closed tight, quite a feat for the fat-lipped toady. Van Ness sat with his teacup balanced on his knee, his eyes bugged out and fastened on the colonel. He managed to paste a smile on his face but it hung there like a crooked picture.

When Steele fixed his eyes on Van Ness, my fellow constable trembled so violently that the teacup on his knee rattled. "Van Ness, I've had good reports about you from Inspector Constantine. I asked the inspector for a fresh young face, someone Soapy Smith and his gang wouldn't know. You fit that bill pretty well. With Brian out in the open and you undercover, we have a good chance to discover what Smith is up to. Did you meet Pelletier when he was in Dawson?"

It took several seconds for Van Ness to answer. First he cleared his throat and screwed up his face like a member of Parliament with a bowel problem. "Ummm . . . I never met Pelletier face to face and . . . ummm . . . to my knowledge we were never in Dawson at the same time."

"How long since you shaved, constable?"

"Not since we left Dawson, sir. It seemed too much trouble on the trail. but I'll get rid of these whiskers immediately, sir, I promise you."

"The hell you will! Keep 'em on in case Pelletier did catch a glimpse of you." Steele reached over and whacked Van Ness on the shoulder. He may have been aware of Van Ness's discomfort and meant the punch as a comradely gesture. However, Van Ness didn't take it that way. His eyeballs rolled and he seemed about to faint.

Steele gave up chumming with Van Ness and turned his attention to Hannah. "By God you're as beautiful as ever, Hannah. I doubt if anyone will give these two rascals a second look when you arrive in Skagway."

"You haven't changed either, Colonel. If anything you're looking even more distinguished."

Steele's mustache damned near curled at the compliment. "Ha! Well. Thank you, Hannah, but I know better. Getting up in years is no fun, believe me."

"Up in years?" Hannah laughed as if Steele's remark was the funniest joke she had ever heard. "Why, Colonel, a man doesn't become interesting until he reaches your age."

You would have thought Steele had been

presented with a jug of water from the fountain of youth. His ramrod back became even stiffer and his face glowed with health and happiness. "My dear, what nonsense," he clucked, but he did not push his denial too vigorously.

The conversation then turned to the more serious matter of Soapy Smith and his gang. "You'll have your hands full finding out exactly who his people are," Steele said. "The gang seems to consist of a shadowy network of supposedly legitimate citizens plus a hard core of outright cut-throats like Jules Pelletier. Smith has built his power through secrecy and intimidation. On the surface he's a legitimate businessman. I don't know how you'll be able to identify his men, I'll leave that to your imagination."

Steele pointed a long finger at Hannah, "And you, young lady, will stay out of this. Avoid Smith. Buy your equipment. Make your arrangements for shipping it to Dawson. Then clear out of town."

"We'll see to her safety," Van Ness promised.

His air of authority over Hannah brought out my worst instincts. I moved my leg casually, letting it brush against the saucer holding Van Ness's teacup. The cup and saucer tipped and fell into Van Ness's lap, drenching the poor fellow in hot tea. He jumped to his feet dancing a jig of pain.

"Careful there, Evan," I chided.

Hannah had observed my little ploy and glared at me in disgust. I ignored her while offering Van Ness my sympathy and some good advice on the care of minor burns. Fortunately Steele hadn't noticed the disservice I did Van Ness, which was just as well. He never would have understood how a mountie could do such a thing to a fellow officer.

Our meeting ended with Steele producing a jar of ointment and urging Van Ness to salve his burns while the three of us left him alone in the cabin. He also cautioned Van Ness to take more care with hot tea in future. In the confusion Hannah kicked me in the shin.

Outside Steele said, "Van Ness seems an alert young man. I just hope he's mature enough for this assignment. Keep an eye on him Brian."

"I'll do that, sir."

Steele left us to supervise the inspection of a string of mules carrying a mixed load of food and tinware.

As soon as he was out of earshot, Hannah

said, "That was a rotten thing to do to Evan. He could be badly burned."

"Oh, Christ. A little tea."

"A little *hot* tea. What on earth got into you?"

"I didn't like the way he acted with you. 'We'll see to her safety,' he says. Since when has Evan Van Ness been extending his personal protection to you?"

Hannah sputtered like a volcano about to blow its top. "Since . . . since *what?* Listen, Constable Bonner. Never mind Evan. Who gave you the right to declare yourself my personal protector?"

"I never . . ."

"You act like no one but you has the right to say hello to me."

"That's not . . ."

"I saw you frown when Colonel Steele passed me a compliment."

"Passed a compliment? The old lech did everything but look down your shirt."

"So what? If a man wants to look down my shirt that's his business, and mine."

"I'm your partner," I reminded her.

"You're my *business* partner. That doesn't give you license to scald Evan's leg because you didn't like something he said about me."

"Well . . ."

"You make me furious sometimes." Hannah turned on her heel and stalked away.

Colonel Steele called me over to the checkpoint where every stampeder had to show his goods for inspection. "Brian, we're not collecting all the duties for the Crown that we should. Whiskey is one of the prime trading goods up here, yet only ten or twelve barrels a day seem to be coming over White Pass, and about the same over the Chilkoot."

"That doesn't sound right."

"Of course not. Obviously the smugglers have found some clever wrinkles. An old whiskey runner like you should be able to sniff out the goods, show us why we're missing so much liquor."

"Sir. I don't know what you've heard about me. I did trade for whiskey at one time, but as for smuggling I resent . . ."

"Oh, shut up and take a look at these shipments. My men can't open every crate. There's too much coming over the pass for that."

"I don't know how much help I can be, but I'll be happy to take a look at the problem. A fresh approach might make a difference."

"Yes," Steele said with a wry smile. "A

fresh approach. That's just what I was thinking of."

I joined the other mounties at the checkpoint and began eyeballing the stream of people and goods.

The people coming over the pass could be broken into three groups. The first and biggest group were the prospectors. Their goods consisted of the thousands of pounds of supplies required by Colonel Steele. Most pulled small sleds piled high with supplies. They couldn't haul more than two hundred pounds on one of those sleds, so each man was forced to make ten or more trips over the pass. Each time they crossed, the mounties would check off the amount of supplies the prospector had brought over so far. If a man tried to beat the one-ton rule by losing himself among the mass of people on Lake Bennett, he would be stopped at one of the checkpoints Steele planned to set up downriver when the ice broke. It was a good system, though rough on those who did not have sufficient funds. No doubt many people would die trying to find some other route to Dawson through the frozen wastes. But anyone going down the Yukon via the White or Chilkoot would do it Colonel Steele's way or not at all.

The second group coming over the pass were the professional mule packers and backpackers. They both charged a dollar a pound to bring goods from the town of Dyea over Chilkoot or from Skagway over White Pass. The backpackers were mostly Chilkoot Indians. These mountains were their home and they knew every foot. The Chilkoot packers stood out from the others along the trail by the huge loads they carried on their backs.

The third group consisted mainly of traders. They had no intention of digging for gold on the Yukon. Instead they were bringing in things to sell the miners: coats, boots, pots and pans, pick handles, coal oil, candles, soap, machine parts, washboards, socks, shirts, heavy underwear, cheap jewelry, tooth powder, shaving brushes, and the like.

Other traders had given a good deal of thought to specialized goods that might sell well in the Yukon. One trader was bringing thirty crates of kittens to Dawson. He was convinced that miners living alone in the wilderness would want the companionship of a pet. Another merchandiser carried five thousand jars of mosquito repellent. I expected him to make more money than

Hannah and Antone Stander combined. The mosquitoes in the Yukon Territory are so big in the summer that I've seen people break off their stingers, tie them to a pick handle, and use the stingers to dig for gold.

Another trader carried fifty gross of perfumed garters, which he expected to sell to prospectors as something they could fondle during the long winters to remind them of their women back home; he also carried a stock of lewd photographs and postcards showing naked women doing unspeakable things to men. I confiscated one of each view and sent the wretched little snake down the pass with the toe of my boot.

Others planned to sell their services in Dawson and along the river. A tinker with a grinding stone on his back came over the pass while I was there, as well as an assortment of barbers, lawyers, gamblers, a doctor who would be a welcome addition to Dawson even though he smelled of strong drink, a bootmaker, several restauranteurs, a dozen or more bartenders, a mortician with a greedy smile, and a fellow who called himself a "practicing philocubist." I looked that up later and discovered the word means "lover of dice games." And there were a number of whores heading for the gold fields. A strawberry blonde caught my eye and winked at me. If Hannah hadn't been around I might have sampled her wares in one of the mountie barracks.

Many of these people were probably thieves. Gold fields attract the dregs of the earth. Our few mounties couldn't possibly keep the situation under control once all the stampeders scattered down the Yukon River. Unless the politicians in Ottawa took their thumbs out of their mouths long enough to send us more mounties, we'd be in deep trouble by summer.

I put those thoughts aside and concentrated on finding whiskey smugglers for the colonel. The assignment was not one I would have volunteered for. To my mind whiskey should be allowed to circulate freely like the geese and caribou and other forces of nature. Sniffing out illegal whiskey seemed almost a sacrilege.

It didn't take me long to find my first runner. I began by explaining the basics of the business to Colonel Steele. "Never mind the prospectors. They might have a few spare bottles tucked among their goods, they'll need them to ward off the cold. Study the traders with big shipments."

"But that's just what we've done," Steele insisted.

"You're not looking at them closely enough."

Just then a packer leading three mules approached the checkpoint and I knew the man was running whiskey. Don't ask me how I knew. Maybe there was a tenseness in the way he moved, or maybe I've run enough whiskey across borders myself to develop a sixth sense. "You! Bring those mules over here." I waved the packer out of line.

"What's the trouble, mountie?" The packer spat on the ground at my feet. "I've got two loads to haul over this pass today. I can't waste time jawing with you yellow-legs."

"What are you packing, mister?"

"Coal oil."

"How many gallons?"

"Two hundred."

"Let's take a look."

The packer didn't like it, but he pulled the covering off one of his coal oil tins and unscrewed the cap on the top of the drum. I put in my finger as far as it would go. It came out smelling of coal oil.

"You see," the packer growled. "Coal oil. Do you want to inspect the other tins?"

"No, that won't be necessary."

The packer was smiling. "Go ahead. Stick your nose in them if you want to."

I pulled out my pistol and the packer stepped back. "Hey now, mountie. I was only passing a joke."

"Don't worry, mister. Just stand back and hold your mules." I cocked the weapon and aimed at the centre of one of the drums. When I fired the mules kicked their hind legs and shied back, then stood firm.

"What the hell are you up to?" the packer roared. "That's personal property. You can't go blowin' holes in my goods."

Coal oil spurted out the hole I had drilled in the drum. Then the flow of black oil gave way to an amber fluid. "I'd stick my nose in that for you." I bent over and let the stream of liquid flow into my mouth. It was whiskey. Pretty good whiskey, too. I didn't straighten up until I had consumed a pint or so, gathering evidence in case Steele wanted to charge the packer with smuggling.

Steele joined me and took a smaller taste for

himself. "That's whiskey all right." He glowered at the packer, who swore at his bad luck and glared in my direction.

"Yes, sir. This packer's gone to a lot of trouble to avoid his duties. He built hidden compartments inside these coal oil drums."

The colonel collected a hundred and fifty dollars in duty from the packer on a hundred gallons of liquor, plus a five-hundred-dollar fine for trying to smuggle the goods across the border without paying duty.

During the balance of the day I gave Steele and his men a few more lessons on techniques of running liquor. We caught three other smugglers, though none was carrying as much whiskey as the packer. By the end of the day the man Steele had sent into Dyea for civilian clothes arrived with outfits for Van Ness and myself. Steele congratulated me on my day's work and suggested Van Ness and I get a good night's sleep. He gallantly offered Hannah his cabin and bunked in with us.

8

THE following morning Hannah and I started down White Pass toward Skagway on horseback, leaving my dogteam in Colonel Steele's care. Van Ness would follow an hour later so that no one on the trail or in Skagway would see us together. The civilian clothes felt uncomfortably tight, particularly across the chest, and Hannah still was not talking much.

"I can't understand why you're sore," I complained. "Van Ness was hardly burned at all. He told me so himself."

"You're a bully," she retorted. "From now on stop being so possessive or I'll have Joe Rudolph dissolve our partnership. No man owns me, Brian Bonner. Especially not you." She spurred her horse ahead of me.

Shortly after dropping below the summit we began meeting the first travelers coming up the pass. Many had stopped along the trail to adjust the blankets on their animals' backs, hoping to cover running sores and other signs of abuse. Colonel Steele had given an order to shoot any crippled or badly mistreated animals found among the pack trains.

We soon learned why the three-mile stretch leading to the summit had been given the nickname Dead Horse Canyon. I've never seen men treat animals as brutally as those gold hunters did in their frenzy to pack their goods over the mountains and down into the Yukon valley.

"What's that stench?" Hannah pulled out a bandana and covered her mouth and nose.

"Dead mules and horses," I informed her. There were hundreds of animals lying in the ravine alongside the trail. They had not been able to climb the steep thousand-foot hill that made up the last part of the journey to the summit. They lay on their backs, most of them, with their legs sticking out at all angles like broken tree limbs. Thousands of crows worked noisily at the bodies, pecking out the animals' eyes and digging deep into their bowels.

When the line of horses and mules came to a halt, as it often did, no one bothered unloading their animals to give them a bit of rest. Mules stood all day with hundreds of pounds on their backs. I had never let a man torture any animal within my sight, but the cruelty in White Pass was on such a large scale that nothing I could do would stop it. Some of the animals weren't even horses or mules. I saw a number of reindeer with amputated horns pressed into service as pack animals. I later learned that Soapy Smith had hit upon that idea, selling the reindeer to *cheechakos* who couldn't tell the difference between mules and wild reindeer, or who didn't care. There's no one quite as low as a gold hunter after the yellow stuff, except perhaps a politician after votes.

A couple of hours later we had to dismount to lead our horses down Devil's Hill, a particularly dangerous section of the trail. The path measured less than five feet wide at that point, with a solid wall of slate on one side and a drop of three hundred feet or more on the other. We hugged the wall, letting the ascending line of men leading mules and dragging sleds take the outside. They were all too willing to give us the inside of the trail; sharp rocks jutting from the walls cut at our arms and legs and the flanks of our mounts. Even so, the protection of the wall was worth the discomfort.

Halfway down Devil's Hill we saw one of the mules slip on an icy patch of slate and slide down towards the edge of the trail. "My goods!" yelled the mule's owner, not giving a hang for his animal. He grabbed his mule's harness to halt its slide. Unfortunately his hand jammed between the harness and the mule's head. The mule went over the side with its owner helplessly attached and screaming in fear. The terrified howl lasted several seconds while man and animal plunged to their deaths below. No one took particular notice of the incident, except to watch their own footing more closely.

We witnessed death once more before reaching the foot of White Pass. The trail had widened into meadowland dotted with frozen marshes when we came on a man seated on a tree stump.

"How far to Skagway?" Hannah called to him.

The stranger didn't answer.

"Is the trail good the rest of the way to town?"

Still the man didn't respond to Hannah's questions.

"Oh my God, Brian!"

I had been aware of the stranger's condition for a few minutes, but didn't know how to tell Hannah.

"He's dead!" She said. "How can everyone just leave him here to . . . to . . ."

I dismounted and walked up to the corpse. He was a man of about forty with bright blue eyes still open and staring in the direction of White Pass. "There's not much to be done for him, Hannah. He's frozen solid. Must have been here for weeks. Maybe all winter. Look, his pockets are turned out. Someone's already robbed the corpse so there's not even any way of telling who he was."

"There must be a marshal or sheriff in Skagway."

"We're in Alaska now, Hannah. There is no law in Skagway except for Soapy Smith." I closed the dead man's eyes and we continued into Skagway.

It was a bigger town than I'd expected. There were three or four hundred tacky wooden buildings arranged around the main street, which was called Broadway. Four saloons dominated Broadway: the Pack Train, the Bonanzan, the Grotto, and the Nugget. Soapy Smith owned pieces of all of them. There was a photographer's studio, a barber shop, a laundry, a hotel, and at the end of the street a restaurant advertised by an old pair of trousers flying from a flagpole with the word "Meals" painted on the seat. A number of packing companies had their offices along Broadway, along with the steamship lines and other enterprises organized to profit from the gold rush.

The Skagway docks had been built out into the mudflats only a few months before. Until then ships had been forced to unload cargo onto smaller boats capable of being poled far enough up onto the mudflats to be unloaded. The docks were one of Soapy Smith's "civic improvements" and he was said to be enormously proud of the accomplishment.

Huge piles of cargo from the boats littered the waterfront. Most stampeders had hooked up with a partner so that one could guard their belongings while the other made arrangements for shipping them over the pass.

A dozen ships were tied up at the docks, each a relic of the past. Only one looked less than fifty years old and none looked seaworthy. The biggest, a cargo ship with two smokestacks, listed dangerously into the dock. They were all coated with four or five inches of ice from bow to stern, making them look like giant icicles. Workmen were busy on one craft carrying lumber out and stacking it on the docks. The owner of that craft, not content with making a fortune packing the boat to overload capacity with passengers, was now ripping out the bunks and other wood parts from the guts of the ship to sell as lumber.

We edged our horses up the crowded center of Broadway until Hannah halted her animal in front of a building bearing the sign "Reliable Packers and Equipment Brokers." "I'll try this place. They might know where I can find dredging equipment."

"Okay. But don't flash any gold around."

She gave me a withering look. "I didn't just get off the boat, Brian. Leave the business deals to me."

"Whatever you say, boss lady."

Hannah dismounted and went into the building without acknowledging my sarcasm. I tied my horse next to hers and sauntered on down Broadway. My last bottle of Perry Davis Painkiller had been consumed the previous night on White Pass with my old friend Freddy Loomis, so I naturally drifted toward the saloons to replenish my stock.

The Pack Train looked as good as any other saloon for that purpose. I went in and studied the prices written in green chalk on a blackboard over the bar. Prices weren't as bad as

Dawson, but they were high just the same. A full bottle of any brand of hooch cost twenty-five dollars. As I was deciding between the various brands, a hand clamped on my shoulder and turned me around.

"Brian Bonner! I'll be damned, son, if it ain't just grand to see your homely old puss again."

I found myself facing my old friend Soapy Smith. "Soapy!" I grasped his outstretched hand and pumped it enthusiastically. "By God you're looking great for an old man."

He laughed in his silky Southern voice and continued wringing my hand. "We're growing old together, partner."

In truth Soapy did look healthy and prosperous. In the old days in Colorado his best clothes were often in hock. The suit he wore when I met him in Skagway was of the finest dark wool and pressed to perfection. The old twinkle leaped from Soapy's eyes. He always seemed to be holding back a good joke until you were in just the right mood for it. He wore a wide-brimmed white hat tilted down over his long face, which was covered in part by a short and neatly-trimmed beard, another difference from the old days.

"You look good with that brush on your kisser."

"Well thank you, Brian. I needed something to make me look more distinguished. A beard seemed to do the trick." He kept hold of my hand and drew me away from the bar. "Sit down and let's have a drink together, unless you've gotten religion and given up the stuff."

"Not likely!"

The two people at the table Soapy led us to jumped up and evaporated into the crowd.

"That's it." Soapy nodded in the direction of the bar. "Henry, bring a couple of bottles of my private stock over here."

"Right away, Mr. Smith," the bartender barked.

We sat back and examined each other as old friends do when they haven't met for some time.

"I've heard your name over the years," Soapy said. "The Man Who Killed Almighty Voice. Isn't that what they call you?"

"That's right."

"Sounds impressive."

"It's worth a free drink anywhere in Canada."

Soapy laughed. "You haven't changed. Still got that stuff in your blood."

"Keeps me warm."

"But where's your uniform?"

"Uniform? Oh, the mountie uniform. I quit the mounties a few weeks ago. Threw in on a mining deal with a gal named Hannah Young, damndest woman I ever met. She's making us both so rich that I don't need the mounties anymore. I told Inspector Constantine where he could put his two dollars a day."

"Ahh. That's it, then. I heard you were tied up with that woman. I'd like to meet her myself. Sounds like she knows how to get what she wants."

"Well, sure, Hannah's in town right now. We came into Skagway together to buy equipment before prices go through the roof."

"Staying long?"

The question came too quickly to be idle conversation. "A few days."

The bartender arrived with the bottles and glasses. Soapy uncorked one and poured generous drinks for both of us. The second bottle he pushed across the table to me. "Keep this one, if you like the brand."

I did like the brand. The whiskey was old

and mellow, the best stuff I had tasted since the Napoleon brandy I shared with Hannah. "Damn, Soapy! You don't know what it means to me to drink something smooth for a change."

"I'm glad it meets your expert approval." He began to say something else but a cloud passed over his eyes. The customary twinkle died and a flat stare of exasperation took its place. "Brian, we're about to have a little problem here. I want you to sit still and let me handle it."

"What kind of problem?" I worked my hand around under the table so that I could reach my revolver fast.

"I'll take care of it," Soapy promised, rising from his seat.

He was looking past me at someone else. I moved my chair around to see who it was. Pushing through the crowd came my old friend from Dawson, Jules Pelletier. I didn't recognize Pelletier at first. If I had recognized him, I'd have pulled my pistol and finished the job I started in Dawson. But Pelletier's appearance had changed so drastically that I scarcely noticed his face. My attention was drawn to his left ear. The damned thing had grown almost as large as his head! I've never seen anything so grotesque. Pelletier's ear, which had previously looked pretty much like any other ear, was now the size and shape of a large head of lettuce. The swollen thing had become wrinkled and blue-red in color in the bargain. By the time I realized Pelletier was attached to the great puff of flesh, Soapy had stepped in front of him and halted his progress.

"Settle down, Jules."

"I'm going to kill him, Soapy!"

My revolver crept into my hand.

"No, you're not. Sit down and have a drink if you want, but cool off."

The words had no effect. Pelletier poised to draw his weapon. In turn I looked forward to blasting his *métis* body to pieces. But before Pelletier could make his move, two huge brutes appeared at his sides and clamped hold of his arms.

"Let go of me!" Pelletier struggled in vain.

Soapy stepped forward and struck Pelletier across the face with his open hand. "I won't have any trouble with you, Jules. Brian says he's quit the mounties and that's good enough for me. Even if he hadn't, I wouldn't especially want a mountie killed in Skagway. The mounties are clannish; they might come down to Skagway in numbers and do us some damage. So get hold of yourself."

Hatred oozed out of Pelletier. The man was literally sweating hate. You could smell it in the air, his feelings against me were that strong.

"Take him out of here and make sure he understands me," Soapy told the two human apes holding Pelletier.

They dragged Pelletier away as if he were a side of beef.

"Who the hell are those walking gorillas?"

Soapy chuckled and returned to the table. "My bodyguards. I've got a few enemies, you know."

"One of them looked Chinese, except he's too big."

"That's Yea Mow Hopkins, he's half Chinese. I met him in San Francisco when he was working as a bodyguard to a rich Chinese family. His name means 'wildcat' in Chinese. All those wealthy Chinese are afraid of being killed or kidnapped by rival tongs, you know. Hopkins killed twenty or more tong hatchetmen, but when he killed a white man he had to leave town."

"What about the other one? He looked familiar."

"You remember Big Ed Burns. He worked for me in Colorado."

"Yeah, I remember him now. Isn't he the one who used to eat cigars?"

"He still does. Big Ed eats more cigars than food. Costs him a fortune."

"You should feel safe enough with those two around."

"Oh, I do. Don't get the wrong idea." Soapy tapped the table with his finger. "This is my town. Nobody makes trouble for me in Skagway."

"So I've heard. But what the hell happened to Pelletier's ear? It's as big as a coconut!"

"Jules holds you responsible for the accident to his ear."

"Me?"

Soapy nodded. "He told me how you chased him out of Dawson. I'm not saying he didn't deserve what happened, but when Jules cut for the border he didn't have much time to pick up supplies."

"He had time to burglarize the A.C.C. warehouse and kill the nightwatchman."

Soapy sat back in his chair. "You're talking like a yellowleg. I thought you quit the mounties."

"I'm talking as a friend of One-Eyed

Riley, the nightwatchman Pelletier killed."

"I see. Well, that's between you and Jules. It's got nothing to do with me. I'm just trying to explain that Jules had to cut for the border fast. He got caught in a snowstorm while he was doubling back to Skagway and his left ear froze. When it thawed out it began to swell." Soapy laughed. "It just kept on swelling. He went to a doctor who told him the swelling may never go down. The doc wants to amputate the ear but Jules won't have that. He thinks the swelling might go down sometime."

I couldn't help smiling. "Ruins his good looks, doesn't it."

"You don't know the half. Jules used to be a big man with the ladies. Now he can't get one to bed down with him for money."

"You're making me cry."

Soapy put his hands up in a protesting manner. "Brian, I told you the trouble between you and Jules has nothing to do with me. That's why I kept him from jumping you. I don't want to see anybody killed."

"Don't worry about me, Soapy. I can take care of myself where Jules Pelletier is concerned."

"Sure you can. But you'll pardon an

old friend for trying to do you a favour.''

I wanted to tell Soapy to give Pelletier free rein so I could finish the job on him. I didn't though. That might have spoiled my pose as a miner. So instead I thanked Soapy and let him pour me another drink.

We began chatting about the old days, recalling people and places and trading bits of information about what had happened to those people. Many of them had died off, most by violent means. The afternoon slipped by and I admit to enjoying myself. Soapy was good company. That was one of the reasons for his success. You've heard about the man who could charm birds down from the trees; Soapy could talk them into marching into a bird pie.

Presently he looked at a gold watch that dangled from his vest by a gold chain and said he had business to attend to. "Why don't you bring Hannah Young to dinner at my place. I own the best oyster house in Alaska. Ask anyone where it is, they'll direct you.''

I agreed to that and we parted company.

Later I bumped into Hannah on the boardwalk in front of the general store. Hannah carried several packages wrapped in brown paper and tied with bows. "Brian, wait till you see the dress I just bought! It's red . . . redder than Gussie Lamore's Saturday night dress. She'll *die* when she sees it."

"Good, you'll save Swiftwater Bill the price of a bad marriage. I'm glad you've bought some new clothes for another reason. Soapy Smith just invited us to dinner at his oyster house."

"You've seen him then."

"Yep. He greeted me like a long lost brother. You'd have thought we went to Bible school together, he treated me so fine. Look what he gave me."

"I don't have to look. I can smell what he gave you. You'd do well to hold down your drinking if you expect to outfox Smith."

It had taken some time, but I had finally learned how to deal with Hannah. When her tongue got sharp I simply changed the subject. "Did you have any luck finding dredging equipment?"

"Yes, we're in luck. Reliable Packers recently took in a dredge in part payment of a bad debt. I went over and looked at it and it's just what we need. It's a dragline dredge, solid wood, with ten buckets that can each scoop up as much as three cubic feet. Reliable is willing to let it go for twenty-five hundred dollars if they get the contract to haul it over the mountains and down to Dawson; That'll bring the price to a total of four thousand dollars."

"That's a good price," I admitted. "Are you sure the dredge is in good condition?"

"It's used. But a new dredge would be out of our price range anyhow."

"You didn't give them any money, did you?"

Hannah became vexed at my suspicious nature. "For heaven's sake, of course I did. He took a twenty-five hundred dollar deposit, which was reasonable. We'll pay the balance on delivery in Dawson."

"Did you get a receipt?"

"Certainly I got a receipt." She dug into her coat pocket and showed me a receipt made out to the Young and Bonner Mining Company and signed by a Mr. Raymond Ross, President, Reliable Packers.

"This receipt is on plain paper. Don't they have any letterhead?"

Hannah's exasperation became complete. "Brian, I've had to drag you kicking and screaming into wealth. The least you can do is credit me with some business sense. No, Mr. Ross did not have any stationery with

Reliable Packers on it, and for a very good reason. Do you see any printers in this hellbox of a town? Plain pieces of paper are scarce enough in Alaska. A printed letterhead would be a miracle."

I couldn't deny that. Every saloon, restaurant, and store employed blackboards and chalk for price lists because of the shortage of paper. It was reasonable for Reliable Packers to give a receipt on plain paper. Even so, I had my doubts about the bargain Hannah had struck.

As usual Hannah felt no such doubts. If anything the successful deal for the dredging equipment fed her ambitions. "I'll tell you what we'll do," she went on, excitement in her eyes. I had come to both fear and admire that sense of excitement. It always meant new speculations, economic dangers, tipping over one apple cart to lunge at another. "Since we don't need the full five thousand in gold I brought along, we'll invest what's left in mercury."

"Mercury? What the hell for?"

"We'll have tons of ore to wash this spring, especially with the new dredge. Separating gold from the dirt is going to be a big job. Mercury forms an amalgam with gold. You just wash the dirt over copper plates coated with mercury and the gold sticks to the plates. For a thousand dollars we can buy the copper plates and enough mercury to last through the summer and part of next fall."

"Hannah, you're making me dizzy with your ideas. Can't you ever leave well enough alone?"

She threw up her hands almost sending the packages in her arms flying. "Maybe we are biting off more than we can chew! Maybe the Young and Bonner Mining Company will go bust! But I won't be satisfied until we've tried everything we can think of to get that gold out of our claims."

You can't imagine the energy that woman could generate. People all over the street turned to look at her. And it wasn't because she was spilling out her ideas to me in a loud voice. On the contrary, she spoke in low husky tones. But when Hannah became excited the air around her crackled with electricity. You could almost see sparks flying from her red hair.

I gave in to her, as usual. "All right, Hannah. You go shopping for mercury tomorrow while I nose around Skagway. Meanwhile let's invest some of our capital in a few more bottles of whiskey and some oysters at Soapy's restaurant. I'm starved to a shadow."

She slipped her arm through mine and we began walking up Broadway. "First I'll need a place to clean up and change. I saw a hotel at the other end of town. We'll see about lodgings for both of us."

As we headed for the hotel I told her about my meeting with Jules Pelletier, giving special care to my description of his left ear. To my surprise Hannah found no humor in the story. She became very serious. "That settles it. You won't have another drop of liquor while we're in Skagway. If you let down your guard for a minute Pelletier will kill you and worry about Soapy Smith's orders later. Soapy will be watching you closely, too. Why else has he invited us to dinner?"

"Hannah, I'm not giving up my reasonable refreshments just because a yellow dog like Jules . . ."

"You *will* stay away from liquor while we're in Skagway." She stopped on the boardwalk with people jostling us and cupped my chin in her hand, pulling my head around so that I was looking directly into her eyes.

"If you don't let the whiskey alone, our partnership is finished. Do you understand? I'm serious, Brian."

Hannah didn't make idle threats. She meant every word, forcing me to choose between the two things I valued most: Hannah and whiskey. Choices like that give me a headache. The only sensible course was to lie. "All right, Hannah, I'll give it up, but only until we leave Skagway."

Her features softened and she slid her arm back inside mine. "Thank you, Brian."

I left for Soapy's oyster house before Hannah. Sure enough, the first person I stopped on the street was able to direct me to his place, as Soapy had predicted.

The restaurant was first class. It featured a long bar of polished mahogany, large tables covered with genuine linen, potted palms in the corners, and heavy drapes covering the windows. The bartender wore garters over his arms to keep his shirtsleeves out of the drinks and a diamond stickpin in his tie. Nothing but the best in Soapy's place.

The proprietor wasn't in view, but Jules Pelletier came striding out of a back room toward the front door just as I entered the place. My first thought was that I'd been lured into a trap by Soapy. I put my back against the nearest wall and prepared myself for a fight.

"Relax," Pelletier sneered. "I'm not looking for trouble with you tonight."

He was obviously telling the truth. His posture was too relaxed for a man about to go into a fight. "What changed your mind about calling me out?"

Pelletier ran a finger over a long red streak along his jaw. "Yea Mow Hopkins and Big Ed Burns changed my mind. Temporarily, at least. Soapy doesn't want trouble with you so that's the way it'll be . . . for now. We'll tangle some other day." Pelletier nodded to emphasize the point. As he did so his enormous left ear jiggled like a circus balloon. I couldn't take my eyes off it. Pelletier stiffened and drew himself up. "Take a good look at it, you bastard! You gave it to me and you're going to die for it."

"Just so long as I don't have to eat it."

Pelletier might have forgotten his promise to Soapy for that remark. But his boss came out of the back room just then and said one word: "Jules!" Pelletier clenched his fists and shouldered past me.

Soapy came up and apologized. "Sorry,

Brian. I didn't expect you so early. Jules and I just talked again about the problem between you two. I had him cooled down, I thought. What did you say to get him riled again?"

"Nothing much. Does Pelletier hang around here a lot?"

"Sometimes," Soapy answered cautiously. "Jules used to work for me as a bartender. I can't use him for that now, of course. My customers couldn't stand to look at that ear over their oysters. But I give the poor fella a few dollars now and then to tide him over."

I didn't doubt that Soapy was keeping Pelletier in funds. Not as a bartender or out of the goodness of his heart, however. Throat cutting was Pelletier's profession and that's what Soapy paid him for.

We sat down at the best table in the place. I took the chair that would put my back to the wall, not trusting Pelletier to keep his promise to Soapy. For that matter I didn't know for sure that Soapy was really keeping Pelletier away from me. The clash between them could have been a piece of playacting designed to throw me off guard.

"Where's Hannah Young?" Soapy asked. "She isn't going to stand me up, I hope. I've been waiting a long time to meet that gal."

"She'll be here. Hannah bought a new dress today. I expect she's fussing with it right now. You know women."

We drifted into a conversation about women, a subject Soapy could talk about for hours. He had known the best and worst of them, to hear him tell it. As he approached the middle of a story about a banker's wife who had run off to New Orleans with him when he was a sixteen-year-old seminary student, our conversation was interrupted by the sound of pistol shots. The shots came from just outside in the street and were accompanied by cries of warning, the clatter of feet as people tried to get out of the line of fire, and finally a deathly moan as some unfortunate caught a fatal dose of bullets.

Soapy frowned at the interruption, waited patiently until the fireworks and shouting had quieted down, then eagerly proceeded with his story as if nothing out of the ordinary had occurred. "This banker's wife . . . her name was Esther and she could have stepped right out of the scriptures . . . had the most beautiful gold hair I ever did see. It fell down her back almost to the ground. Well, she kept me in high style in New Orleans for three months. Then her money started to run out. I had tired of her by that time anyhow, so while she slept one night I cut off all her hair, packed my things, took the last dollars out of her purse, and tiptoed down the stairs. I sold her hair to a wigmaker near Jackson Square in the French quarter and never saw the woman again." Soapy smiled over the memory. "Her hair brought thirty dollars, would you believe it? That's when I realized that a smart man can sell anything . . . anything at all. There's a buyer somewhere for every damned thing you can think of."

"What happened to the banker's wife? Did you ever hear?"

"Oh, sure," Soapy said. "She killed herself."

The door to Soapy's restaurant opened and three men came slamming in. It was plain they were looking for Soapy, their eyes settled on him right away. They stamped toward us, bumping into the other tables and upsetting one customer who was just digging into his oysters. I noticed Soapy's bartender duck behind his bar and come up with a shotgun, which he concealed behind the glasses and bottles in front of him.

"Smith, we're looking for you," one of the three men declared.

"You've done a right smart job of finding me, too," Soapy replied without turning a hair. He stood up. "Let me introduce you to an old friend of mine. He . . ."

"I don't care to meet any friend of yours, Smith," the same man anounced. He was obviously the spokesman for the other two, who did little but stand in the background and watch Soapy with sour expressions.

"But this is one of the greatest lawmen in the northwest," Soapy said. "You've been crying for law and order, Frank. Here it is in the flesh. Brian Bonner, The Man Who Killed Almighty Voice."

The three men reluctantly took their eyes off Soapy and studied me.

"Brian, this is Frank Reid, the civil engineer who laid out the town plan for Skagway, and Bob Clampett and John Regan, two of Skagway's leading citizens."

Frank Reid grunted a greeting. "I've heard about you, Constable Bonner. But I never expected to see a man of your reputation in a friendly conversation with Soapy Smith."

"I'm no longer with the mounties, Mr. Reid. My business these days is mining for gold."

"Sorry to hear it." Reid turned his attention back to Soapy. "Your other good friend Jules Pelletier just killed a man named Rawlings outside on the street. I understand Rawlings refused to sell you a string of mules he brought up here from Seattle. Rawlings had an idea he wanted to go into the packing business. You didn't want him to. I strongly suspect that Pelletier murdered him at your order."

I expected Soapy to throw a fit over the accusation, but he just shook his head as if unable to believe anyone would utter such slander. "That's just not true, Frank. I haven't even talked to Jules Pelletier in several days. Certainly not since Rawlings arrived in Skagway. Yes, I offered to buy Rawlings's mules. He turned me down and that was the end of it. I didn't bear him any grudge. I'm sorry to hear he's met a bad end."

"Pelletier is one of your hired killers," Reid insisted. "Everyone knows that."

Still Soapy did not flare up. "If that's what you really believe, Frank, you should take your suspicions to the law. You know very well there's a deputy U.S. marshal head-quartered right here in Skagway. Marshal Ben Taylor. I'm surprised you didn't go to him in the first place. If Pelletier killed Rawlings without due cause Marshal Taylor will arrest him on the spot, I'm sure of it."

The man Soapy had introduced as Bob Clampett spoke up for the first time. "Taylor won't blow his nose without your permission. You own the marshal body and soul and everyone knows that, too."

"Don't credit me with too much influence," Soapy smiled. "I'm just another citizen, like yourself."

Frank Reid shook his fist in Soapy's face. "We will talk to the marshal. And if he won't do anything about Pelletier I'll write the attorney general in Washington about finding a new deputy U.S. marshal for Alaska." And with that warning the three men heeled around and stalked out.

When Soapy sat back down he was shaking with laughter. "The damned fools. They'll never get anywhere that way."

"How much opposition do you have, Soapy?"

"Oh, a few soreheads like Reid and Captain Moore, that's all. Hell, I'm on the town council myself, along with half a dozen close friends. I've got friends all over town. Next Sunday I'm delivering the guest sermon at the Church of the Good Shepherd and the week after that the town is putting up a plaque on the dock recognizing my civic contributions. Now I ask you, how are Reid and his friends going to stop me with all that support?"

"Sounds like you're still following your own Golden Rule: Leave the locals alone."

"You're damned right." Soapy bit off the tip of his cigar and spat it into a cuspidor. "So long as I don't steal from the people who live here, I'll be all right. Nobody cares what happens to the gold hunters passing through town. They're fair game."

"You must have quite a payroll."

For once Soapy looked mildly unhappy. "I'll say. Half the palms in town are out to me. Why, just this morning I shelled out two hundred dollars for a new church bell. There's always something like that. I'm aiming for one big killing to set me up for life, then I can sit back and let my organization protect me." Soapy glanced at me out of the corner of his eye and launched into a story about another of his women, a fake Russian countess he had met in St. Louis. I guessed he regretted letting his desire for "one big killing" be known to me.

I had two quick drinks while talking to Soapy and covered my tracks with Hannah by slipping Sen-Sen into my mouth. About that time a number of Soapy's friends began showing up for dinner. He jumped up and greeted each in his courtly manner, introducing me all around. If Soapy had a blind spot it was his almost childish desire to be an intimate of well-known people. I remember from the old days in Colorado his great pleasure at sharing a box at the Denver Opera House with the popular writer Mark Twain.

One of the people he introduced me to happened to be the deputy U.S. marshal for Alaska, Ben Taylor.

From across the room Taylor had appeared to be a menacing character. He wore a pair of guns in a holster belt outside his coat and stood well over six feet in his boots. His face was rough-cut with deep-set eyes and a broken nose. But seeing him up close when we were introduced told me why Taylor would bend to Soapy's will. Taylor's eyes darted all over as he talked to me, everywhere except into my own eyes. The man was a coward, pure and simple. That made him a perfect tool for Soapy. Soapy introduced me as The Man Who Killed Almighty Voice just as Taylor began shaking my hand. His flabby grip dissolved altogether and he drew his hand back as quickly as manners would allow.

"I take it you aren't visiting Skagway on a law enforcement matter," he said with a nervous smile.

"No, I'm here with my partner on mining business. I've resigned the mounties."

"Fine . . . fine. Make yourself at home. And let me know if I can do anything for you. Always glad to help a friend of Soapy's."

"Thanks, marshal. I may call on you."

"Yes . . . er . . . do that."

Soapy was watching Marshal Taylor's discomfort with amusement. He would use Taylor, but he could never like him. Say what you want about Soapy, he had nerve. At last he decided to enter the conversation and put Taylor back at ease. "Frank Reid came in here a while ago with Clampett and Regan. They tell me Jules Pelletier killed that fellow Rawlings tonight. What's the story on that, marshal? Did Jules start the trouble?"

"Jules! No, of course not." The question surprised Taylor, but he composed himself when he realized Soapy had asked it for my benefit. "Rawlings started an argument with

Jules and ended it by drawing a pistol. Jules fired in self-defense." He paused. "There are witnesses to that," he said directly to me.

"I'm sure there are," I commented.

"Damned shame," Soapy murmured, finally getting around to lighting his cigar. "Say, didn't Rawlings own a string of mules?"

"Yes," Taylor said. "I've impounded them since Rawlings didn't appear to have any business partners or relatives in the territory."

"What do you intend doing with those mules?"

"Well . . ." Taylor chose his answer to Soapy's question carefully in my presence. "I thought I might auction them off next week. The marshal's office can't afford to feed those mules for very long. We don't have the budget for it."

"I just might put in a bid myself," Soapy said casually.

I had no doubt Soapy's bid would be accepted, no matter how low it was. Soapy suggested we return to our own table. I was happy to escape Marshal Taylor's company. Worms like Taylor and Pelletier disgust me. I know Soapy was just as bad, or worse, but at least there was nothing petty about him. He went at life on a grand scale. From his point of view life was just a rigged game of cards that someone had to control, and it might as well be him.

The next customer to enter Soapy's oyster house carried a large metal box and a camera tripod. "Soapy! Here I am!" He bustled over to our table, plump and sweating, and deposited his equipment on the floor.

"Thanks for coming, Billie." Soapy pulled out a chair for him. "Brian, this is one of my very special friends in Skagway, Billie Saportas, editor of the *Skagway Alaskan*. I asked Billie to bring his camera and notebook and do a story about you."

"Me? What for?"

Saportas chuckled and brushed aside any objections. "Mr. Bonner, you're a famous man in the Northwest. Perhaps *the* most famous." Saportas paled and added quickly, "Next to Soapy Smith, of course. Why even in the East they know your name."

"You're from the East?"

"Billie used to work for the *New York World*," Soapy supplied. "He was one of their most famous correspondents."

A bartender had put a very large glass of whiskey in front of Saportas. Saportas hadn't ordered the drink. It appeared the way drinks appear in front of me. However, I pride myself that my hand doesn't shake the way Billie Saportas's hand did as he coaxed the drink to his lips.

"Ahh!" When he put down the glass it was empty. "First the picture."

He set up his equipment, which was quite a job in itself. First he ran out the telescoped legs of the tripod. Then he took a huge Conley View Camera from his equipment box, pawed through the box until he found a portrait lens, attached the lens and loaded the back of the camera with a plate holder of film, and finally ducked his head under a focus cloth. "There." He pronounced himself ready and asked Soapy and me to step in front of a blank white wall.

"We'll need a smile from both of you."

Soapy put his arm around my shoulder and we both grinned self-consciously into the camera. A flash went off with a puff of noxious smoke.

"One more."

We repeated the process and returned to our table. Saportas packed up his equipment and began to interview me while Soapy took care of some business in the parlor at the rear of his restaurant. The bartender kept Saportas supplied with liquor during the interview. I probably learned more about him from the interview than he learned about me. I found that Saportas had come out to Alaska to cover the gold rush for the *World*. He lost all the *World*'s expense money at one of Soapy's roulette wheels, and on top of that gave Soapy a note for two thousand dollars he didn't have and couldn't raise. To repay the debt Soapy had forced him to quit his job with the *World* for the *Alaskan*. Soapy had an interest in the paper, and with Billie Saportas's help, it served as his personal publicity sheet. Saportas didn't seem troubled by his misfortune. He was the amiable sort who drifts whichever way the wind blows.

"You'll be seeing yourself on the front page of the *Alaskan* tomorrow morning," Saportas promised. "Provided I was sober enough to get the focus right on the camera, which is doubtful." He lurched to his feet, stuffed his notebook into a pocket, and took his equipment away.

I had another drink and ate more Sen-Sen. Soapy rejoined me and asked again what had become of Hannah.

Before I could think up another excuse,

Hannah made her entrance. All conversation in the oyster house stopped as she took off her coat. Under the coat she wore her new red dress, silk stockings, and red shoes. The dress fit so tightly that her breasts seemed in danger of escaping their skimpy lace bodice. She had never looked so beautiful. *No one* had ever looked so beautiful. Even her mass of red hair was under control. It had been washed and combed out until it shined with golden highlights. "That's Hannah Young."

"Yes, indeed." Soapy went to the foyer, where Hannah waited like a queen for her consort. She took his arm and let herself be escorted to the table.

"Hello, Brian. I'm sorry to be late. It took me forever to get into this new dress."

"Even then you didn't quite make it."

She set her teeth and smiled politely. "Dear Brian, always joking."

"I'm sure he meant that you couldn't possibly find a single dress to contain your full loveliness," Soapy said smoothly.

Hannah put her hand on Soapy's arm and squeezed it gently. "What a beautiful compliment. You must be from the South, Mr. Smith."

"I am, and proud to admit it." He motioned

for the waiter. "I've taken the liberty of putting champagne on ice. I'll have it brought over now. I'm only sorry it isn't the very best vintage, your beauty calls for the best. But any kind of champagne is difficult to acquire up here."

"Champagne!" Hannah clapped her hands together. "I haven't had champagne since I left San Francisco."

"San Francisco? Is that where you're from?"

"Yes."

"Marvelous city. Have you ever been to Grissom's?"

"That's my favorite restaurant!"

"I wish I could offer a comparable bill of fare. This is a simple oyster house, but I think you'll find we do some interesting things with our speciality."

"I'm sure the cuisine will be superb. You have a reputation for demanding the best, Mr. Smith."

"Please call me Jeff. Some folks call me Soapy, but Jefferson is my Christian name and I don't hear it nearly enough."

"Of course."

The waiter put the champagne glasses in front of us. I was reaching for one when Hannah said, "You can take Mr. Bonner's glass, waiter. He isn't drinking tonight."

Soapy's eyebrows rose. "Brian not drinking? That's hard to believe."

"He's been having stomach trouble and I've had to insist that he give up drinking during this trip. Partners have to look out for each other."

"You're a lucky man to have a partner like Hannah," Soapy said to me.

His admiration was genuine, which made things all the worse. I was fuming and having a difficult time not showing it. Hannah had set out to get even with me for my jealousy on White Pass by sparking up to Soapy. She knew I couldn't afford to treat Soapy as I had Van Ness.

They continued fawning over each other all through the champagne, while I sat sipping at a glass of apple juice Hannah had impudently ordered for me. *Apple juice.* They talked about "cuisine" and "the symphony" and "*haute* fashion" and other such rubbish. I might as well have been back in Dawson for all the notice anyone took of me. It didn't do my humor any good to see all the other men in the place ogling Hannah. But what really drove me around the bend was Hannah's

260

laughter. She usually laughed with the zest of a stevedore, but to Soapy's stale jokes she gave off tinkling laughs that sounded like little bells ringing.

They kept it up all through dinner. Now and then Soapy did try to bring me into the conversation, but Hannah would charge off in some direction she knew I couldn't follow, like a discussion of the new European ascots that "society gentlemen" were beginning to wear. I've never heard so much tripe in my life. When I tried to steer the talk back to a sensible subject like the subtle differences between Kentucky and Canadian whiskey, she would give me a half-polite smile and return to her own topics.

It was a terrible evening. I thought it would never end. But after lingering over dinner for two hours, Hannah evidently tired of torturing me and told Soapy she felt like "retiring," another word I'd never heard her use. Many times at our claims I'd heard her say, "I'm caved in, boys. I'll have to pile into my bunk for awhile." *That* was Hannah.

Soapy kissed her hand and detailed Yea Mow Hopkins to see Hannah safely back to her hotel. Hannah smiled wickedly as she said good night, knowing she had tied me in knots. "Now Jeff, don't give Brian any whiskey when I'm gone. I don't want to listen to him belching all the way back to Dawson."

The comment brought a burst of laughter from Soapy. He never knew how close he came to losing most of his front teeth.

"By God, that's a woman," Soapy declared when she had left. He looked me over with new interest. "No offense Brian but you and Hannah are like sandpaper and velvet. How did you ever talk her into a partnership? You must have powers of persuasion that I've missed."

"She needed my claim." That was a tough fact to admit to Soapy, but I had to face the truth of it. "Bring me some whiskey," I told the waiter.

"Hannah said . . ."

"She's my partner, not my keeper. Have your man find me a bottle of that fine stuff we had this afternoon." Soapy shrugged and ordered the waiter to bring me a bottle. Apple juice is a foul drink. I washed away the taste with whiskey and returned to the chore of cultivating Soapy. He suggested we adjourn to his parlor at the rear of the oyster house where there were some things he wanted to show me.

The parlor was comfortably furnished with overstuffed chairs, settees, and a big rolltop desk which Soapy unlocked and opened. "I don't know whether you realize it, Brian, but I've become quite a well-known man myself. Take a look at this."

There were letters and documents crammed into every one of the rolltop's numerous pigeonholes. He picked one at random and flourished it in my face. "You see, here's a letter from William Jennings Bryan. I sent him some of my ideas for improving the postal system and he replied within a month. You can see what he says: 'I have often heard your name in connection with the opening of Alaska. You have my congratulations on your achievements.' That's from *William Jennings Bryan.*" He snatched up another letter. "And look at the signature on this one."

I saw that it was signed by James Corbett.

"That's right. Gentleman Jim Corbett, the best prizefighter in the United States for my money. I was at the ringside last year on St. Patrick's Day when that chicken thief Bob Fitzsimmons was given the decision over him. It was an unfair decision and I wrote Corbett to tell him so. He's a gentleman, just like they say. Answered me by return mail. I told Corbett he can have a fight in Skagway any time he wants one. I'll promote the fight and guarantee him a purse of twenty-five thousand dollars. He has other offers to consider, as he says here in this letter, but he appreciates my support. And look at this . . ."

Soapy went on for another half hour showing me his correspondence with the great and near-great. Apparently he spent a good part of each day writing to famous people and every reply he received boosted his ego that much more. There were letters from people like Mrs. Theodore W. Birney, thanking Soapy for a ten-dollar founding contribution to the National Congress of Mothers; a note from the actor Richard Mansfield acknowledging Soapy's letter of congratulations on his successful opening night at the Garden Theater in New York playing *Cyrano de Bergerac;* a terse reply in answer to Soapy's complimentary letter to songwriter Paul Dresser about his new tune "On the Banks of the Wabash"; and a long letter from William Allen White, editor of the Emporia, Kansas *Gazette* thanking Soapy for his favorable comments about White's editorial "What's the Matter with Kansas?" which had been picked up and reprinted in newspapers all over the world.

There were more, I can't remember all the famous signatures Soapy showed me. The most unusual piece of correspondence was a copy of a letter Soapy had sent to President William McKinley. It was dated March 1, two weeks after the American battleship Maine was blown up in Havana harbor with two hundred and sixty U.S. seamen lost. In this letter Soapy announced to President McKinley that he was throwing his full support to the president in the coming war against Spain. Soapy told President McKinley that he was organizing a military unit in Skagway and had commissioned himself a captain in the U.S. Army. He asked McKinley to confirm the commission in writing at the earliest opportunity so that he could proceed with his recruiting plan.

"Soapy, you can't issue yourself a commission in the U.S. Army!"

The bearded con man waved aside my objections. "It's just a formality. The commission will come from Washington any day. I've got friends there; you've seen that. Meanwhile I've already started to organize my militia. We hold drills and parade reviews every Wednesday morning on Holly Street."

Soapy showed me the badge each member of his unit was required to wear on parade. It said: *Freedom for Cuba . . . Remember the Maine! . . . Compliments of the Skagway Military Company . . . Jeff R. Smith, Capt.* "We'll show the Spanish they can't blow up our battleships!" he said with feeling.

Soapy was explaining the strategy he had recommended to President McKinley for driving the Spanish from Cuba when a lean man in a black suit rapped on the wall outside the parlor, then stuck his head through the curtains. "Am I interrupting, Mr. Smith?"

"Why no. Come on in, Reverend Bowers."

The clergyman entered the parlor in the company of another man, a *cheechako* judging from the smoothness of his skin. Anyone living in the Yukon for more than a month develops a rough windburned look which this stranger didn't have. The *cheechako* wore a hangdog expression that begged sympathy.

"Mr. Smith," Reverend Bowers began, "this is Ernest Lane from Philadelphia. He came into Skagway yesterday on the *Mary Lou* and it seems that someone has swindled him out of most of his funds."

"What?" Soapy looked outraged. "How did this happen, Mr. Lane?"

The poor mark gnashed his teeth and went into a long story about cashing a nine-hundred-dollar bank check made out on the Mellon Bank of Philadelphia at a place called the Merchant's Exchange on Broadway. Later, when he tried to purchase equipment, he was told his money was counterfeit. Lane returned to the Merchant's Exchange, but the manager swore he'd given Lane legitimate U.S. currency. "I went to the marshal," Lane complained, "but he says Merchant's Exchange enjoys a good reputation in Skagway. I don't know what to do! That nine hundred dollars was the biggest part of my stake."

"Let me see one of the bills," Soapy said.

Lane handed him a twenty dollar note. Soapy held it to the light and examined the bill carefully. "Yep, it's counterfeit. Very good workmanship." He handed the twenty back to Lane. "Tell me, is there any chance a pickpocket could have stolen your money and switched this counterfeit in its place?"

"No, sir," Lane assured him. "I keep all my funds right here in this moneybelt." And the fool showed Soapy exactly where the rest of his poke was located.

Soapy smiled slightly. "Well, I don't know how I can help you, Mr Lane."

"But Reverend Bowers said you're the most influential man in town."

"I said he *might* be able to help you," Bowers corrected. "There doesn't seem to be much anyone can do. This is a very puzzling case."

"Puzzling! There's nothing puzzling about it," Lane insisted. "The Merchant's Exchange swindled me, that's all."

"Now, now," Soapy cautioned. "I know the manager at the Merchant's Exchange and he's an honest man, a church deacon in fact."

"That's true," Reverend Bowers agreed.

Just then a door leading from the back yard of Soapy's oyster house opened and two men with drawn pistols rushed in. "Get your hands up!" one of them barked. "Don't try anything."

"Oh my God!" Lane moaned.

"You dirty . . ." Soapy began.

"Shut up!" One of the gunmen struck Soapy across the face with his pistol barrel. Soapy staggered against the wall but stayed on his feet. Miraculously, the blow didn't leave a mark on Soapy's face.

"I'll take that gold timepiece," the thief

said, and snatched Soapy's watch and chain off his vest.

"My mother gave me that watch. You'll both pay for this," Soapy promised.

"Never mind the preacher," the second gunman said. "He don't have nothing. Clean out the fat one."

The first gunman went straight to Lane's belt and ripped it off the *cheechako*'s ample waist. Lane's pants fell and his knees could be seen trembling.

"Forget the big dude, too," the number one man said, meaning me. "We've got what we want."

I hadn't put my hands in the air because I didn't intend to be robbed. But the two gunmen carefully kept the clergyman and Lane between us, giving me no opportunity to draw my own weapon and fire without endangering them.

The two men backed out the door and slammed it shut behind them. My gun was in my hand as I raced for the door. "Stay back!" I warned Bowers, but in his confusion he stepped into my path and jostled me. When I finally reached the door I threw it open and hurled myself through the opening as low and as fast as I knew how. I landed on my stomach in the back yard of Soapy's establishment, my pistol in front of me.

To my amazement no target presented itself for my weapon. Although the yard was enclosed by a solid fence at least ten feet high on all sides, there was no one in sight. It seemed impossible. The two thieves had beat me out the door by no more than a dozen seconds, not enough time for both of them to scale that fence.

I got to my feet slowly. By that time the others had pushed through the door behind me.

"Where did they go?" Reverend Bowers wondered.

"I don't know." I was stumped. "They just disappeared."

"My money!" Lane was holding his pants up with one hand and massaging his head with the other. "That was every cent I had in this world."

Soapy examined his back yard carefully. "I don't understand. This fence is ten feet high. How did they get in here, and then how the hell did they get out so fast?"

"It's cold out here." I shoved my pistol back in its holster. "Let's go inside."

Reluctantly the four of us filed back into Soapy's parlor.

"I'm very sorry about this," Soapy told Lane. "Look here, there's a boat leaving tomorrow for Portland. Since you were robbed in my restaurant I feel obliged to stake you to a ticket home." Soapy rummaged in his pocket and came up with two fifty dollar bills. "Here." He tucked them into the pocket of Lane's coat. "That'll buy you a ticket to Portland and enough food for the voyage."

"That's extremely generous of you, Mr. Smith," Reverend Bowers said.

"It's nothing," Soapy said.

Lane didn't seem as impressed with Soapy's generosity as the good reverend, but there was not much else he could do but take the money and return home. "I don't understand what's happened here," Lane whined. "All I know is I've been robbed by your friend at the Merchant's Exchange and now I've been robbed in your restaurant. I guess I'll have to thank you for the hundred dollars to get home, Mr. Smith. But I'll always wonder how I ended up in your parlor." He looked at each of us suspiciously, then left through the curtains with his hand still clutching his pants.

Soapy and Reverend Bowers grinned at each other. "Make sure he leaves," Soapy said.

Reverend Bowers took up a station by the curtains while Soapy went to his back door and stuck his head out. "All clear, boys!"

When Soapy turned back to me his eyes were twinkling above the soft beard. "Did you see that chump's knees shake?"

Two men followed Soapy in from the back yard. Even with the masks off their faces, I could tell they were the two who had robbed Lane.

"I was afraid he might have a stroke before I could get his belt off," the taller of the two said. "Here's your watch, Soapy."

Soapy took his watch and fastened it on his vest. "How much did he have?"

"Another five hundred," said the second gunman, a young kid not more than eighteen. He watched me while Soapy counted Lane's money. "Is this big dude all right, Soapy?"

"Sure, he's an old friend. You've probably heard of him. Brian Bonner, meet Slim Jim Foster and Blue Jay. Blue Jay's the one who isn't old enough to shave. He's a prime gunhand, though. And of course you've met Reverend Bowers."

The preacher bowed. "God bless you, sir. And now, if you'll excuse me, there are other poor souls out there in the night who need the word of the Lord." Reverend Bowers slid through the curtains.

"Brian Bonner!" Blue Jay dropped his suspicious manner. "They say Almighty Voice plugged you three times before you killed him and his braves. Is that right?"

"That's what happened."

"Can I see the scars?"

"Hell, no! I'm not your private circus freak."

Slim Jim Foster still had suspicions about me. "Brian Bonner is a mountie."

"Brian's all through with that," Soapy assured Slim Jim.

"He wasn't last month when he ran Jules out of Dawson. Does Jules know he's in town?"

"Yes. Don't worry about it. Brian traded his red coat for a gold mine and a woman. And what a woman! You boys get yourselves lost now. Don't show yourselves around town until Lane catches the boat tomorrow. He didn't see your faces but he might recognize your clothes." Soapy frowned at Blue Jay. "Especially that red jacket of yours, Blue Jay. Get rid of it. Find something that blends in."

"I paid fifty bucks for this coat," Blue Jay objected.

"Get rid of it," Soapy repeated.

Blue Jay and Slim Jim left by the rear door. I followed them and looked into the back yard. Once again they had disappeared. "Okay, Soapy. How do you do it?"

"I'll show you." Soapy led me outside and went to a section of fence near the doorway. He reached under one of the cross-rails and pushed a hidden catch. A three-foot section of fencing swung out on concealed hinges. Soapy winked and closed the hidden exit. We went back into the parlor.

"Now I know how you did it," I said. "But why? Your goons could have relieved Lane of his moneybelt in any dark alley."

Soapy poured us both drinks. "Why do I do it? For fun! I'm like any old con man. Watching the sucker take the bait is the biggest enjoyment I get in life. So once or twice a week the boys steer a mark into my parlor so I can have the pleasure of setting him up myself. Did you see how fast I got Lane to show me where he kept the rest of his poke? Blue Jay and Slim Jim were outside with their ears to the door just waiting to hear that."

"It was a nice touch having Blue Jay snatch your watch."

"It makes the mark feel better when he thinks you've lost something, too. And I always give the sucker the price of a ticket out of Alaska, unless he tries to stick around and make trouble."

"What then?"

Soapy pointed in the direction of White Pass. "That mountain is the biggest natural graveyard on the continent."

Soon after that I left the oyster house and returned to my hotel, satisfied that I'd put in a profitable day. I had identified several of Soapy's key people and learned something about his operations. I wondered, though, whether Soapy genuinely believed I had quit the mounties. I couldn't ignore the possibility he was playing on my gullibility just as he had the luckless Mr. Lane.

9

THE following morning Soapy and I stared out from the front page of the *Alaskan* looking foolish and friendly. The picture didn't do me justice. I was also annoyed at being advertised as such a good friend of Soapy Smith's. But the picture and the story did help me in my immediate mission. Dozens of people looked me up after reading the paper to shake my hand and offer me a drink. During the conversations that followed I learned a great deal more about Soapy and his people.

But earlier in the morning, before the paper was distributed, I met Hannah for breakfast. I found her in the hotel dining room going at a plate of bacon and biscuits with both hands. She had the appetite of a mule driver.

"Good morning, Miss Young," I said stiffly.

She looked at me with some amusement. "Good morning, Mr. Bonner. Sit down."

"Thank you." I sat but declined to place an order with the waiter. "I'm not hungry this morning. I only came in here to tell you that you performed like a damned whore at Soapy's place. Gussie Lamore never laughed more falsely or batted her eyes more brazenly than you did last night. And all that talk about 'society' and 'fashion'. Neither you nor Soapy ever got within spitting distance of real society in your whole lives."

Hannah choked on her biscuit when I used the word "whore." She threw down her fork and leaned over her plate. "Don't you ever use that word with me!"

"You once called me a pimp," I reminded her.

"Because the word fit the occasion."

"Well the word 'whore' fits last night's occasion, if I'm any judge."

"You're not a judge. When I have dinner with Jeff tonight I'll do . . ."

"Dinner with who?" It dawned on me who she meant by "Jeff." "Dinner with Soapy? We aren't having dinner with him again."

She smiled sweetly. "I didn't say *we* were having dinner with him. *I'm* dining with Jeff."

"No you aren't. And stop calling him Jeff. He's Soapy Smith and he's just about the most dangerous man you'll ever meet, except for me when I'm sober."

"Which is a rare sight," Hannah threw in.

"I'm not fooling about this. You can't take on a man like Soapy. He'll eat you alive."

Hannah scoffed and went back to her bacon. "He's just a man. I had him twisted around my finger last night and I'll do the same tonight. Don't worry about me, Brian."

I couldn't make her listen. "Colonel Steele told you to stay out of this business. You've got your dredging equipment. Look for the mercury you want, buy it, then go back to White Pass and wait for me."

"I'll do no such thing. Skagway isn't much, but it's the biggest town I've seen in two years. I intend to do as much shopping as I can. When you're ready to go, I'll be ready. Meanwhile I can help you by keeping Soapy Smith occupied. I'll see that he doesn't begin to wonder whether you really resigned from the mounties."

"I don't need your help and I don't want it." I explained it as simply as I could. "At best you're a nuisance. At worst you might get yourself into real trouble."

Hannah stared at me. For just a second I thought she might cry. I must have been mistaken. Hannah never cried. Presently she shook her head. "You are the dumbest man who ever lived. Go away! Leave me alone!"

She spoke with such emotion that I didn't know quite how to react. Even though nothing had been settled I couldn't bring myself to give her the full tongue-lashing she deserved. "All right, I'll go. But remember what I said. Stop interfering in the business of the R.C.M.P."

It was a weak warning, the best I could master in the face of Hannah's hostility.

I spent the balance of the day in the saloons drinking with Skagway's loafers and listening to talk of Soapy Smith. For the record, I considered my promise to stay away from liquor null and void. Hannah's rudeness at breakfast was one reason. For another, how could I stand around saloons all day without taking a drink? It would draw suspicion to me and wreck my mission. That would be my excuse to Hannah, anyway.

What I learned about Soapy and his methods convinced me I was wise in telling Hannah to avoid Soapy. By conservative estimates Soapy was behind more than a hundred killings that had occurred in the Skagway area in the past year.

In whispered asides the more knowledgeable drinkers in the Pack Train also pointed out the other members of Soapy's gang. Many were confidence men posing as legitimate businessmen, like the managers of the Merchant's Exchange and the Cut-Rate Ticket Bureau.

Soapy also operated a telegraph office in Skagway. For only five dollars he would telegraph a message anywhere in the world. Upwards of eighty *cheechakos* stopped by the telegraph office each day to send their loved ones a last message before heading into the wilderness of the Yukon. There was one catch: Skagway wasn't connected to the outside world by any telegraph lines. The manager of Soapy's telegraph office would simply tap out a message on a dead key while the sucker watched, happy for the chance to contact his wife or family. Soapy didn't miss a trick. I made a mental note of the "telegraph operator's" name and description for Colonel Steele.

But it was the hardcase types like Jules Pelletier, Slim Jim Foster, Blue Jay, Yea Mow Hopkins, and Big Ed Burns who could cause the worst trouble if they got over the passes and down into the Yukon. So I concentrated on learning what other gunmen Soapy employed.

One of the first I spotted looked hardly strong enough to lift his feet, much less a gun. Old Man Tripp they called him. Real name, Van Triplett. Old Man Tripp sported a flowing white beard and spoke in a soft voice. He also faked a hacking cough. His story was simple. He was a poor old man who had lost his health in the Yukon. But he did know a shorter and easier trail to Lake Bennett than over White Pass, a route that avoided the mountie checkpoints. He only confided his information to well-heeled gold hunters who had somehow slipped through Soapy's other traps in Skagway. When the gold hunters were far enough along Old Man Tripp's "secret" trail they would be met by Jules Pelletier, Slim Jim Foster, and a few other of Soapy's friends. The victims would never be seen again.

Another of Soapy's men called himself Yank Fewclothes. His speciality involved begging along the trail in a tattered coat and pants. He didn't expect anyone to give him a handout, but often a mark would put his hand over his purse to make sure the panhandler didn't try to relieve him of it. Yank Fewclothes would note where the mark kept his poke and the other gang members would take it from him farther up the trail.

Doctor Malone wasn't a doctor, though he advertised himself as such with a sign above a storefront on Holly street. When a mark came to the doctor with a medical complaint he would be given a spoonful of "elixir" that consisted of cherry-flavored knockout drops. The good doctor would have ample time while the patient lay unconscious to relieve him of his valuables.

Kid Jimmy Fresh looked even younger than Blue Jay. He worked along the waterfront offering to help people carry their goods into town for a dime. He was an engaging freckle-faced kid with a helpful manner, and when he recommended to people that they cash their bank checks at the Merchant's Exchange, they usually took his advice. About Blue Jay, I heard rumors in the Pack Train that he was wanted in Missouri for killing his father and mother while they slept and robbing their house of fifty dollars and a pair of silver candlesticks. The story was apparently true; Blue Jay had bragged about the deed.

But the worst of Soapy's crew was Fatty Green. Fatty was wanted in California for murder, arson, burglary, assault with a deadly weapon, and having sexual relations with animals on government property. No one would say exactly what duties Fatty Green carried out for Soapy. Fatty lived alone in the worst-smelling cabin in Skagway, a town boasting any number of vermin-infested dwellings. People said he had not changed his clothes once since coming to Skagway six months earlier. He weighed more than four hundred pounds and licked his fingers whenever a pretty girl passed by. Rape was his favorite sport.

There were others in Soapy's gang, but that should give you an idea of the obstacles the stampeders faced. The majority of Skagway's residents turned their eyes the other way, even if they didn't openly support Soapy. Everyone profited from the stampede and Soapy was generous with "his people." Most important, the residents knew Soapy would leave them alone.

One piece of information I acquired positively tickled me. It seemed that the outfit with the worst reputation in Skagway was Reliable Packers and Equipment Brokers. Soapy owned that, too. They specialized in bidding low on packing jobs, taking a deposit, and then never following through on the job.

A client who left goods in their care might never see the stuff again. Scores of stampeders on the other side of White Pass were building boats to go downriver and expecting the balance of their goods to follow by pack train. The manager of Reliable Packers, a crook named Bascomb, would sell the goods to someone else at a cheap price. Anyone who complained was out of luck. Bascomb signed all receipts with the name Raymond Ross, then denied that the signature was his. Marshal Taylor backed him up, of course, and with all receipts issued on plain white paper and no letterhead at the top, no one could prove Reliable Packers guilty of anything. I could hardly wait to tell Hannah. For once her business sense had failed her. Reliable Packers had no intention of shipping that dredge to Dawson for her. Hell, they'd probably stolen it from someone else to begin with!

I was entertaining myself by considering different ways of breaking the bad news to Hannah when Evan Van Ness came sliding up to me. I had seen him around town making conversation with a few people. He didn't have the gift for small talk, though. I doubted he'd picked up any information as solid as mine and it annoyed me to be approached after we'd agreed to avoid each other in public.

"So you're The Man Who Killed Almighty Voice," Van Ness said loudly, doing a terrible job of pretending we'd never met. "I saw your picture in the paper this morning, Mr. Bonner. Just thought I'd like to shake your hand."

"Why, thank you." And I took Van Ness's hand.

Under his breath he said, "Meet me at midnight just south of town on the mud flats." And louder, "Sure a pleasure to meet you, Mr. Bonner."

Van Ness drifted away into the crowd. The man was a damned fool but Steele had stuck me with him. I didn't care to meet him at midnight or any other time. I needed a good night's sleep after a day of heavy drinking and spy work. But I supposed I'd have to meet Van Ness. Otherwise he might step in a bog hole and get sucked up.

"Brian?"

"Quiet down!"

I walked through the slush of mud and snow toward the sound of Van Ness's voice.

My hands were thrust into the pockets of my coat and my collar was turned up against the cold. Midnight on a mud flat!

"Is that you, Brian?"

"No, it's Father Judge with a new hymn book. Who the hell did you think it would be at this hour?"

We came face to face and Evan sighed with relief. "Thanks for coming. This is important or I wouldn't have approached you at the Pack Train."

"What's so important?" I shivered, crinkling up my toes to keep them from freezing in my boots.

"I've found someone who can tell us all we need to know about Soapy Smith and his gang."

I wondered why I had ever cared if Van Ness got sucked up. "So that's it. You've got an informer with a few scraps of information and you had to trot him out for me. I wish you'd set up a meeting someplace warmer."

"My contact is afraid to be seen talking with strangers. He promised to meet me here and to bring someone who can tell us the name and background of every important member of Soapy's gang."

"You didn't give him my name, I hope."

Van Ness took offense at the question. "Certainly not. What kind of fool do you take me for? Steele said to work alone and that's just what I've done. But I knew you'd want to talk to my informant, since you've already worked your way in with Soapy." A tinge of jealousy showed through in his words. "How did you manage that, by the way?"

"Luck and pluck." The night was too cold for wordy replies. "Where are your informants anyway?"

"They'll be along."

"And who are they?"

"I don't know the name of the man my contact is bringing, but the contact himself is a pastor in one of the churches here."

"Are you by any chance talking about the Rev. Charles Bowers?"

"That's right. How did you know?"

I cursed Van Ness and scanned the darkness. "He's one of Soapy's gang, you great blundering lunatic."

"He can't be. Reverend Bowers is pastor of the Church of the Good Shepherd."

"Are you certain you didn't drop my name to him? Think about it!"

"I told you I didn't. He thinks I'll be here

alone. What makes you say he's a member of Smith's gang?"

"I met him last night in Soapy's parlor. He was helping Soapy fleece a dumb *cheechako* out of his life savings."

"Reverend Bowers? I can't believe it." Van Ness sounded unconvinced. "When he gets here I want you to face him with that accusation."

The man's stupidity knew no limits. "He's not coming alone, or with one other man. If you've told them you're a mountie sent in here by Colonel Steele to snoop around, they'll send three or four men to kill you. Unless I save them the trouble."

"Kill me?" Van Ness repeated stupidly.

"Why do you think they set up a meeting way out here and in the middle of the night? Because they like mud? We've got to skin out of here fast, and without bumping into Reverend Bowers and his goons."

But it was already too late for that. Several pairs of feet could be heard clopping through the mud not more than thirty yards up the beach.

"Van Ness!" Someone called. "It's me, Reverend Bowers."

I clapped a hand over Van Ness's mouth

before he could reply. "Don't make a sound," I whispered, putting my mouth up against his ear. "When I say so, drop face down in the mud and flatten out. I'll start running along the beach and draw them off. They're expecting just one man, so they'll all follow me. When we're far enough away, clear out. Don't even go into Skagway. Head south for Dyea and make your way to the mountie post at the top of Chilkoot."

Van Ness pulled my hand off his mouth. "I can't let you do that," he whispered back. "This is all my fault. I'll draw them off from you."

I didn't bother to tell him that he wouldn't stand a chance against Reverend Bowers and his friends. It was simpler and faster to kick his legs out from under him and push him face down in the mud. Before he could rise from the muck I started running along the beach, making plenty of noise.

"There he goes!" Someone yelled. I thought I recognized Slim Jim Foster's voice.

Before me lay two choices: trying to work my way back to Skagway or heading up into the hills south of the town. A glance over my shoulder confirmed that more than two dark forms pursued me. Three at least.

One fired a pistol. The flash revealed three men about fifty yards behind me, charging up off the mud flats and staying right with the sound of my feet. It was the foothills then. No other choice. Putting myself between them and the lights of Skagway might silhouette me as a target.

Running is something I like to do, a hobby from boyhood. I can jog along beside my dog team for fifteen miles without a rest. But the fun sort of disappears when you're running with three killers at your back. The mud flats fell away and the footing became easier as the ground rose. Cold air seared my lungs but I knew that a good second wind would soon fill them and give me the strength to pull away.

The three behind me were not bad on their feet, either. One of them fired again and I looked back to find they were still fifty yards behind. I hadn't gained an inch on them. Their shots didn't bother me at that point. If they fired while they ran they'd hit me only by a million-to-one chance, and if they stopped to fire I'd gain ground on them. I hoped Van Ness would follow my instructions exactly and head for the Chilkoot.

"He's cutting right!" Reverend Bowers

yelled, his voice showing no sign of fading wind.

"I see him."

The third voice was unknown to me. It wasn't Blue Jay and that cheered me. Young kids like Blue Jay can run forever.

The grade became steeper and I had to lean forward as I ran. Snow and ice would become a problem the higher I traveled, making the footing difficult. I slipped once or twice and banged my knees on the rocks. Behind me there was cursing as my three shadows had the same trouble. Grinning, I drew my Enfield and halted. If I had a chance to beat them in a shooting match, this would be it. They were framed by patches of snow behind them. I straightened my arm, cocked the weapon, and fired at the man in the lead.

They dropped to the ground and began returning my fire. Bullets ricocheted off rocks all around. None of the shots came closer to me than twenty yards.

"Stop shooting!" Slim Jim yelled. "He can see us by the flashes."

How right Slim Jim was. I'd just lined up my sights on him when he issued his cease fire. The slope below went black and I lost my target. I turned to continue up the slope and my right foot hit an icy spot. My leg went out from under me, sending me pitching forward. I hit the ground on my right shoulder. A numbing pain shot up that arm and my hand opened in a spasm. The Enfield pistol fell, clattering off the rocks and bouncing into some dark crevice. Pausing to look for it would have been suicide. I could only regain my feet and continue the climb, hoping my friends to the rear wouldn't realize I'd lost my weapon.

We climbed higher. I could hear them gasping for breath behind me and calling encouragements to each other. Here and there I stopped to look for a hiding place between the boulders and crevices or a side trail that might lead me down out of the hills. Some of the cuts to the sides looked tempting, but I couldn't tell whether they led to freedom or into natural stone boxes. The wrong turn would mean death, so I kept on climbing.

Gradually my quick searches for escape routes gave Reverend Bowers and his friends a chance to close the gap between us. I glanced back, hearing their wheezing voices, and found them no farther away than twenty-five yards. If they'd known my gun lay in the rocks down the hill they could have dropped me right then. They held their fire in fear of giving me enough light to pick off one of them. Soon, though, they'd be close enough to shoot without fear of missing.

Again my choices were dictated to me. A flat piece of ground led off to the left. It might be a trail or just a ledge that ended nowhere. I pushed aside my doubts and charged off in that direction.

"He's trying to cut across the mountainside," Reverend Bowers warned the others.

"I see him," Slim Jim called. "Hell, that ain't the guy we're after. He's too big!"

They halted. This new element in the chase caused some confusion that worked to my advantage. For a few precious seconds they wondered why they were chasing someone other than Van Ness. Where was the profit in it? Van Ness was the one they wanted. In those seconds I found myself blocked on the trail by a large boulder, a rock almost as tall and twice as wide as myself. I leaped into the V-shaped opening where the rock and the side of the mountain joined, intending to go around the rock and continue up the trail. But it occurred to me that a big rock on a mountainside made a good weapon.

Bracing my back against the side of the hill and putting my feet against the rock, I began to push. The boulder was reluctant to move. It had probably been sitting there for a hundred years and felt at home. I pushed harder, feeling my gut tighten and the tendons in my legs quiver. Still the damned thing wouldn't move. No sense of adventure, that's the trouble with rocks.

My three pursuers began to move again, convinced that even if I wasn't Van Ness I must be another spy working in cahoots with him.

My legs gave out and I lay back against the mountain to gather the strength for one more try.

"There he is!"

"By damn, that's Brian Bonner!"

I pushed with all my fury. A shot banged out and a bullet hit the dirt not three inches above my head. That did it. That gave me the extra strength I needed. The boulder moved ever so slightly. Another bullet hit the boulder itself, the sparks dazzling my eyes. And at last the boulder actually began to roll. Once started, it came to life. The boulder rolled away from me and I slid down on the trail to use its moving bulk as a shield.

"Look out!"

All three scrambled for safety as the boulder descended towards them with a surprising quietness. It carried no other masses of rock or earth with it. The boulder became a huge moving juggernaut that made noise only when it bounced. Once moving, it seemed to fly rather than roll down the slope. So softly did it travel that I was almost unaware when it picked up one of the three men and carried him down the mountainside. There was no cry of pain, no appeal for help. The victim simply blended into the great falling piece of granite and took the long trip to the foot of the hill with it. The dozen seconds of silence ended as the boulder crashed and splintered below.

"Jim!" Reverend Bowers called. "Big Ed is gone. The rock . . . it hit him . . . he's gone down there."

So the third man had been Big Ed Burns, the cigar eater from Colorado. Soapy would need one new bodyguard.

With the boulder gone the trail was open. I ran along the mountainside as quickly as the slippery footing would allow. My fears that the trail would end abruptly faded as I rounded a sharp turn and emerged onto a plateau surrounded by still higher hills.

I picked a direction at random and continued climbing. The death of Big Ed Burns had given me some breathing room. Bowers and Slim Jim were following more cautiously and staying well behind me. Thank God I wore heavy gloves. The higher I went, the more icy everything became. I was forced to scramble up the steepest parts of the hill using both hands and feet for traction.

At the top of another cut I paused to see how much of a lead I had. Reverend Bowers and Slim Jim were perhaps a hundred yards down the mountainside and keeping a twenty-yard gap between them in case I tried to roll another boulder their way. That would have been a good idea, but no other boulders came to hand. The mountain had become a jagged hunk of solid granite and slate that yawned and tilted in all directions.

The slope began to rise to my right and left. Soon I found myself climbing up a funnel toward a small opening that evidently led to still another high mesa. I had climbed into what was almost a natural stone chimney. The opening to the funnel was barely large enough for me. I strained and forced my shoulders through one at a time. It took a full minute to wriggle through the chimney, enough time to bring Reverend Bowers and Slim Jim into pistol range. They began firing and I could hear bullets whacking off the granite around my legs.

One of the rounds found its mark. I felt a bullet tear along my right thigh. It was like being branded with a hot iron. I gritted my teeth and dragged the leg through the opening. When I rolled over I saw that I'd reached a long, flat crest. The top of this particular peak. Other peaks jutted up around me, but to reach them I'd have to make my way down the opposite side of this one.

I examined my leg and found the bullet had not lodged in the flesh but only gouged a deep hunk out of my thigh. Desperately I searched the darkness for a hiding place. There was none. The crest of this hill appeared flat and devoid of vegetation or large rocks. My luck had deserted me at last.

I could hear Reverend Bowers and Slim Jim making their way slowly up the funnel toward the chimney I had used to reach the crest. That gave me some hope. The opening was too small for both men to come through at once. On the other hand, neither of them was my size. Slim Jim was well named. He'd pop through that small hole like a weasel.

I lay at the edge of the hole listening to them draw closer. Their breathing came labored and harsh. When they paused just beneath the hole for a conference I could hear their voices perfectly. They weren't five feet away from me.

"Look at that damned hole," Slim Jim said. "We can't go through it together."

"So what?" Bowers answered, panting.

"He could lay back and pick us off."

"I don't think he's armed. I think he lost his pistol on the climb. Otherwise why hasn't he shot at us again?"

"I don't know."

They were silent for a while, considering the possibilities and giving themselves a rest.

"We could slide back down this chimney and find another way up," Slim Jim suggested.

"That'd give him time to skin out. He'd be miles away before we could work our way up from another direction."

Obviously they didn't realize one of their shots had hit me.

"Okay," Bowers said. "You're the smallest

around the waist. You go through that hole first."

"Blessed are the meek," Slim Jim sneered.

I didn't blame the man. Bowers wasn't doing him any favors sending him through first. If I were still armed he'd be a dead man one second after his head popped through the hole. But I wasn't armed, and instead I'd be the one who would probably die.

Somehow I had to steal the advantage. I strained my eyes looking for an escape route. There wasn't any, not one I could use with a bad leg. But a thin ridge of granite about six inches high near the opening to the funnel caught my attention. If I held on to that ridge I might lower myself over the side of the peak just opposite the funnel opening. Anyone coming up through the funnel could easily miss seeing my fingers gripping the ridge.

The time for planning had expired. Slim Jim was scrambling up the funnel. I swung my legs over the side and lowered myself as far as I dared. Disregarding all the mountaineering advice I'd ever heard, I looked down. It was a straight five-hundred-foot drop into the same darkness that had claimed the life of Big Ed Burns. I tightened my grip on the narrow ridge above and waited.

Slim Jim came up out of the funnel. I pictured him doing that. The funnel opening resembled an overlarge rabbit hole located about six feet from the south edge of the crest of the hill. I could picture his head coming up first, swiveling for a good look around, and then his arms and shoulders emerging as he swept the area with his pistol in front of him.

"No one up here!" he yelled.

"That can't be," Reverend Bowers answered. "We saw him go up through this hole."

"Come up and see for yourself, preacher."

I counted five seconds. That would give Slim Jim time to come completely out of the hole, turn around, and reach down to give the good pastor a helping hand. The chance was fifty-fifty his back would be to me. Only a banker would want better odds than that.

My right leg went over first. Then I pulled the rest of my body upwards and rolled over the side onto the crest. Slim Jim was four feet away and I'd won my bet. His back was to me, his right hand stuck down the chimney to help Reverend Bowers. He sat on his knees and his pistol lay next to him while he braced himself with his left hand. I went for him as quietly as I could. I almost reached him when he heard me coming and snatched up his pistol. His face was a blur in the moonlight as I kicked him hard in the chest with my bad right leg. The jolt of pain that traveled up my leg went straight through the top of my skull. For a moment I feared I'd pass out before I could deal with Reverend Bowers.

Slim Jim went "Uufff!" and stumbled backwards. He went about two feet too far for his health. The night opened up and swallowed him. The profanity that he shrieked out all the way down the mountain kept me from passing out. It was a service I'm sure Slim Jim hadn't meant to provide.

At least I was conscious and halfway ready for Reverend Bowers when he scurried up from the funnel. There was no gun in his hand. He couldn't have held onto one and pulled himself through the hole. I lunged into him and we fell together in a tangle of arms and legs.

I'll be damned if a knife didn't appear in his hand. He didn't draw it. It must have been concealed in the sleeve of his parson's black coat and delivered into his hand by a spring. I've seen those contraptions before, but never in the sleeve of a preacher. "*He giveth His beloved sleep*," Bowers said as he came for me.

"Not yet, parson."

The knife came at my chest with great speed. I moved quickly and the blade swept past by a fraction of an inch. My right hand locked onto his wrist and I tried to turn it inward to break his arm with one movement. Reverend Bowers checked me with a thrust of opposite force. He had strength to spare under his parson's clothes.

We rolled over and over, each grappling for a better purchase and a clear blow with a free hand. Meanwhile he worked his knee, trying to cripple me between the legs. If I had had any compunction about fighting dirty, which I didn't, that would have freed me to act as I did. I sank my teeth into his knife hand and held on tight. Bowers swore and arched his back. Watching my dogs fight had taught me the value of holding on. I kept my teeth in his hand, tightening my bite slowly but surely.

My teeth gradually defeated Reverend Bowers. First his knife slipped out of his hand. Then his strength began to ebb. It seemed to flow out of the wound my teeth were making in his hand. Blood spurted into my mouth, sticky and tasting of salt. I let go of him with my left hand and patted the ground. My fingers closed around the hilt of his knife. I picked it up and drove it straight up through his throat. The knife was one of those thin twelve-inch blades they call an "Arkansas toothpick." It entered Reverend Bowers's neck just under his chin and continued up into his brain. He died with a single grunt and slumped down. I know a little scripture myself, and a phrase came to me: *Man goeth to his long home, and the mourners go about the streets.* It could have been from Ecclesiastes, but I wouldn't bet on it.

At three A.M. I was scratching on Hannah's door at the Mondam Hotel.

"Who is it?"

Muting my voice, "Brian."

"Go away."

"I need some doctoring."

She admitted me immediately with her mackinaw coat thrown over a new night-gown. "What happened? You look half frozen."

"Hole in my leg." I lowered myself into her bed. "Ahhh, that's it. Never thought I'd find myself here. Feels good."

"This is the *only* way you'd get into my bed. Let me see your leg." She took the knife off my belt and cut away part of my pants leg to get at the wound. "That's a bullet hole."

"So it is."

Hannah hadn't brought her full medical kit, but she did have an emergency kit with some bandages, tincture of iodine, cod liver oil, and salve. While she cleaned and dressed the wound I told her what had happened over the last few hours. She was horrified at my close brush with death. Anyone would be. In relating the story I doubled the amount of danger I'd been in and made more complaints about the bullet wound than it deserved.

"I met Reverend Bowers just tonight. He seemed such a nice man." She sighed. "To think you had to kill a pastor of a church. Brian, that's awful!"

"He was no more a preacher than I am. Where did you see him?"

Under the circumstances she was reluctant to tell me. "At Jeff's . . . at Soapy Smith's oyster house. I told you I was having dinner there again. Reverend Bowers came in about ten o'clock. Jeff . . . Soapy . . . introduced him to me, then they stepped away from the table. Reverend Bowers left just before midnight with two other men who were having dinner and drinks there, a great brute who smelled of tobacco and a very thin fellow with gentlemanly airs."

"Big Ed Burns and Slim Jim Foster. They were on their way to ambush Van Ness." I stood and tested my leg. It felt much better with a bandage for support, but for Hannah's benefit I limped around the room pretending to be in pain.

She looked properly concerned. "You'd better find your room and bed. You look exhausted."

"I'll be all right." I had hoped she'd insist I'd stay right there in her bed for the night. Instead she put her arm around me and helped me down the hall to my own room. That wasn't what I was after, but it was better than nothing.

I awoke the next morning with a sore leg and a tremendous hunger. Nothing mattered except food. I didn't even want a drink.

Hannah was waiting for me in the dining room. After bounding down the stairs, I slowed and went into my limp as I approached her table. She was again solicitous, going so far as to put sugar in my coffee for me. Two lumps, when I only asked for one.

Over breakfast I told her what I'd learned

about Reliable Packers and Equipment Brokers. She exploded, demanding that I accompany her there to give Mr. Raymond Ross a good beating.

"His name isn't Ross," I informed her, enjoying the sport of letting her know in dribs and drabs how she'd been outfoxed. "That's part of his swindle. His real name is Bascomb. When someone produces a receipt with the name of Ross on it, he simply denies it's his signature. Marshal Taylor backs him and there's nothing anyone can do."

"There's something *I* can do." Hannah started to rise.

"Sit yourself down and finish breakfast." I ordered another cup of coffee for her and explained why she had nothing to worry about. "When I learned about Reliable Packers' business methods yesterday, I contacted a drayman from Dyea named Whitley. He's an honest man with a good reputation. He'll charge four thousand dollars to pack that dredge over Chilkoot Pass and ship it to Dawson when the river is clear."

"Four thousand! That's too much."

"No, it isn't. Reliable Packers gave us a good price because they didn't plan to do anything. Whitley's prices are higher because the man follows through. He'll be at the Reliable equipment yard this morning at eleven to take the dredge apart and haul it over the Chilkoot."

"Where will we get the money to pay Reliable for the dredge and to pay Whitley, too?"

"That's simple. We won't pay for the dredge. We'll just take it. We'll recover the twenty-five-hundred-dollar deposit you gave Bascomb besides. He stole the dredge from someone else, didn't he? Let's give him a taste of his own methods."

Hannah liked my plan except for one thing. "If Soapy owns Reliable Packers he won't let you get away with robbing him."

"Soapy will have his boys out this morning trying to discover what became of three of his prime gunhands. I've got all the information on his people Steele needs. We'll leave town with Whitley and the dredge."

We finished breakfast and arrived at Reliable Packers shortly before eleven A.M. A clerk informed us that his boss was not available. Hannah showed him the receipt and said she wanted to see Mr. Ross about changing the arrangements for shipping our dredge to Dawson. The clerk scratched his head and said there was no Mr. Ross connected with Reliable Packers.

"That's his name on this receipt, and the receipt is from Reliable Packers. You saw me in here yesterday yourself."

The clerk smiled. "I'm sorry, ma'am. Our receipts have Reliable Packers printed right on them. This is just a blank piece of paper. There's some confusion here or . . ."

"Or what?" Hannah asked, feigning innocence.

"Or you've been swindled by someone," the clerk supplied. "Not by Reliable Packers." he hastily added.

"Well now," I began in my most reasonable voice. "How are we going to settle this?"

"I think you should see Marshal Taylor," the clerk suggested.

"I'd rather see your manager, Mr. Ross."

"His name is Bascomb," the clerk said, getting feisty. "And I've told you he's busy. You'll have to leave now."

"I don't believe I will." I walked around the counter and opened the door leading to the manager's office. Bascomb looked up, startled. He was reading *The Police Gazette* at his desk.

"What do you want?" He stood and threw down his *Gazette* on the desk.

Hannah brushed past me. "I want a refund on that deposit you took, Mr. Ross . . . or Mr. Bascomb. Whatever your name is, you have twenty-five hundred dollars of my money."

Bascomb had played this scene many times. He may have been a former actor, he had the oily manner and chin-up bearing. "I'm sorry, I've never seen either of you before. And I certainly don't have any money that belongs to you."

I drew my new pistol, the one I had taken from Reverend Bowers' body. It was a very fine double-action Colt .44 with a bone grip and I'd been itching to try it out. I aimed at Bascomb's leg just above the kneecap and pulled the trigger. My bullet went exactly where I intended. Bascomb fell against his desk, gripping it with both hands to keep from slipping to the floor.

The clerk made a move behind me. I wheeled, snatched him by the hair, and threw him across the room. "You're crazy!" he yelled. "Soapy Smith owns this company."

"Where do you keep your money?"

"There." Bascomb pointed at a rubber plant in one corner. "Under the plant." The effort cost him his slim hold on the desk. He slid to the floor unconscious.

Hannah pulled up the rubber plant and tossed it aside. At the bottom of the pot she found a cache of money wrapped in a copy of the *Alaskan*. She quickly counted out twenty-five hundred dollars and was about to return the balance of the funds to the pot when I said, "Take an even three thousand. They owe us some interest."

She grinned and did as I said. It was a heady experience giving orders to Hannah.

We backed out of there fast and headed straight for Reliable's equipment yard two blocks away. Mr. Whitley had already arrived with five mules and three helpers. They were busy taking apart the dredge and loading the various parts of it onto the mules. His business was located in Dyea, a town about ten miles northwest at the foot of Chilkoot Pass. He was as anxious to load the dredge and get out of Soapy Smith's territory as we were. Hannah paid him his four thousand dollars in advance.

"I'll start hauling your dredge up Chilkoot this morning," he promised. "If you're standing up to Reliable Packers you'll be having trouble with Soapy Smith. I don't want to be around when that happens."

Hannah said we'd meet him on the trail as soon as we collected our clothes from the hotel. She'd also purchased the mercury and copper plates. That, too, was in her hotel room. We packed quickly, but when we went to collect our horses at the livery stable Soapy and Marshal Taylor were waiting for us. "Hello, Soapy."

He lifted his hat with his customary flourish. "Morning, Brian. Miss Hannah, you're looking especially beautiful today."

"And you look as crooked as usual," she retorted.

"It pains me to hear you say that. I thought our relationship was flourishing."

"That's what I wanted you to think." Hannah boldly walked past him and grabbed the reins of her horse.

"I see." Soapy looked from Hannah to me. "You were keeping me entertained while Brian did whatever it is he came here for. And I've got a hunch you two didn't come to Skagway alone. Was there another mountie with you? A man named Van Ness?"

I tossed my knapsack across my horse's

back. "Yes, he was with us. He left town last night."

Soapy glanced at the Colt on my belt. "And it seems you've come across Reverend Bowers. I recognize that bone grip. Tell me, has the reverend gone to his reward?"

"Yep. Along with Slim Jim and Big Ed. They're in the hills near the mud flats, in case you want to rob their bodies."

Marshal Taylor gasped and inched his hand toward his pistol.

"I never shot a U.S. marshal before," I warned him. "You'd be the first."

Under Soapy's eyes Taylor felt forced to take some kind of action. "I'm arresting you for shooting Tim Bascomb, manager of Reliable Packers, and for stealing three thousand dollars from his office."

Hannah mounted her horse. I handed the reins to her and flipped a ten dollar gold piece to the livery boy who had saddled our horses for us. He caught the coin and dived for cover.

"Bascomb may lose his leg," Taylor said.

A piece of cordwood lay nearby. I picked it up and tossed it to Marshal Taylor, who caught it gingerly. "Give him this to stump around on. And tell him to think twice the next time he wants to cheat the Young and Bonner Mining Company."

I had tossed Marshal Taylor the piece of wood to give him something to do with his hands. Otherwise he might have felt obliged to prove himself to Soapy by drawing his pistol and trying to arrest me. I'd never be able to explain the killing of a deputy U.S. marshal to Colonel Steele. Taylor turned the cordwood over and over in his hands while I mounted my own horse.

"See you again, Soapy. Thanks for the oysters."

Soapy took out a cigar. "Glad you enjoyed them, Brian. You're lucky my boys are out of town looking for Bowers and the others. You won't be so fortunate next time. Miss Hannah, if I'd known Bascomb had made a deal with you, I'd have told him to make it good. That's the truth. Please don't think too badly of me over this."

"You needn't worry. I won't be thinking of you at all."

And with that parting remark Hannah dug her heels into the horse's flanks and moved down Broadway with me close behind. Soapy scowled at Hannah's rude reply, but neither he nor Marshal Taylor tried to stop us.

10

I'VE told you about the horrors of White Pass. The Chilkoot had its own dangers, which Hannah and I were about to face. Both passes lead to Lake Bennett. The Chilkoot is closer to Lake Bennett, but it's also steeper. At the foot of Chilkoot is the town of Dyea. A small army detachment was bivouacked at Dyea, which is why Soapy steered clear of the town.

From the foot of Chilkoot to Lake Bennett is a distance of only twenty-eight miles, but crossing the Chilkoot requires a steep four-thousand-foot climb. Near the base stood Sheep Camp, where we caught up with Mr. Whitley and his mules. Sheep Camp was the last place on the trail where you could find firewood. From there up the Chilkoot became a solid wall of snow, ice, and granite.

From Sheep Camp Mr. Whitley planned to carry the dredge in sections by mule about six miles to a place called the Scales, the last piece of flat ground until you got over the summit. Animals could go no farther than the

Scales. From there the sections of the dredge would be transferred to the backs of Chilkoot packers.

A series of steps had been cut into the snow from the Scales to the summit. Someone had dubbed them the Golden Stairs, and climbing them could take most of a day. The trail rose at close to thirty degrees in that four-mile stretch, which meant that climbers had to ascend the steps on hands and feet in an almost upright position. Often the single file of climbers would be forced to halt for an hour or more when some problem occurred at the summit. Each climber carried at least a hundred pounds on his back, and the trip had to be made over and over to bring a ton of supplies through the pass. Coming back down was much easier, almost fun. You could slide partway on the seat of your pants and have the thrill of a fast, easy trip from the summit to the Scales.

We moved as high as the Scales that day. Mr. Whitley hired seven Chilkoot Indians to take the parts of the dredge the rest of the way over the Chilkoot and sent his mules and their drivers back down the mountain. Our horses were also taken down the mountain. We slept on that windy ledge overnight, huddled together for warmth and eager for the coming day to begin so that we could get up the Chilkoot to the mountie post at the summit.

That night another fall of fresh snow was added to the heavy folds covering the granite face of the Chilkoot. During the night you could hear occasional rumbles along the slopes. I don't know if anyone else slept well. Probably the Chilkoot Packers did. No amount of bad weather could change the expressions on their emotionless faces. But I didn't like the sound of those moving masses of snow.

We survived the night, however. And early in the morning Mr. Whitley helped the Indians load and adjust their back-packs. Each of the Chilkoot Indians could carry packs weighing up to two hundred pounds. I carried two of the dredge buckets on my own back. Mr. Whitley took one. We waited some time to take our turn on the Golden Stairs. At last we started up, Whitley in the lead, Hannah behind him, the seven Chilkoots next, with me bringing up the rear.

The morning had become clear and cold, revealing no sign of the storm that had battered the mountain during the night except in the form of fresh snowfall. The first climbers up the Golden Stairs that morning found the going difficult. They had to stamp down the new snow to find their footing on the icy steps.

We had been climbing the steps for about half an hour when the mountain made a fearful cracking sound. In another place you might have thought the sound to be a clap of thunder. On the Chilkoot such a sound meant only one thing: Avalanche!

Hannah was the first to voice the word. She turned on the steps and called a warning. "Avalanche! Everyone go back to the Scales! Hurry!"

I shrugged off my backpack and heaved it away. The last thing I needed in an avalanche was the weight of two heavy dredge buckets dragging me beneath the snow. I leaped into the drift at the side of the Golden Stairs, hoping to slide down the slope ahead of the falling tons of snow. For a few moments the tactic worked. I found myself whizzing down the mountainside past a hundred or more climbers who stood dumbfounded on the Golden Stairs with their faces turned up toward the avalanche. A quick glance behind relieved my mind about Hannah. She had also jumped into the snow and was careening down the mountainside with her arms churning. Whitley and his Chilkoot packers hadn't moved as fast. A moving wall of snow swept over them.

"Brian!"

Hannah yelled my name as the avalanche broke around us. We were picked up and hurled into the air as everything underneath us rose, pushed ahead by the first tide of snow. The noise was incredible. It drowned the screams of the hundreds of people trying desperately to avoid the crushing snowfall. A face flashed past mine, mouth open and twisted in terror. Then I was swallowed up in the torrent, my body squeezed and pounded under the pressure of the snow. I felt myself plunging deeper into the morass. Snow plugged my mouth, my eyes burned with gritty particles. Deeper still I went. All the breath in my lungs became spent and I gasped for air. I'd become part of the mountain, a pebble in its frozen interior. The crushing continued until I thought my back had been broken and my arms torn out of their sockets.

Suddenly I popped to the surface. I managed to clear my throat and take several gulps of air before the avalanche bore me under again.

Something cracked my skull. Snow packed my mouth and nostrils. With great effort, I pushed the plug of snow out of my mouth with my tongue. I seemed to be moving slower, or else my senses were failing. At last I stopped tumbling as the snow around me ground to a halt. The avalanche continued, however. It passed over me with the rumbling sound of a freight train, heading down the mountain toward the Scales.

I had come to a stop buried in snow. If you've ever seen a strawberry in a gelatin salad you'll understand my position. The avalanche had spared my life but sealed me in the snow. I had no idea whether I was two feet from the surface or twenty feet. For that matter I had no idea in which direction the surface might be. My eyes opened, revealing a stark white universe. I couldn't move my head, arms, or legs. Strangely, I had no trouble breathing. The snow was porous enough to provide some air, but so tightly packed as to prevent me from making any movement. I faced the possibility that perhaps I couldn't move because my back was broken. A stabbing pain across the middle of my back had become intense. Any small attempt at movement caused pain to radiate out to all parts of my body.

Voices began to come through to me, muffled calls for help from others trapped beneath the snow. We made a world of our own down there. I didn't call out for help myself. If I had started yelling, I might have been gripped by panic. Instead I relaxed as much as possible and began testing my body with slight movements. First I tried to move my toes. They responded, which gave me hope that my spine remained intact. My fingers would move, too. Another good sign. Slowly I tried to turn my head. No luck there. The snow gripped it like a vise.

Gradually I became aware of blood draining from my feet and legs toward my head. I could feel its pressure in my neck and ears. That meant the snow held me suspended upside down. The world was up there somewhere above my feet.

I began moving the toes of both feet in a circular motion. Round and round. Round and round. Nothing seemed to happen. But after many long minutes it seemed to become easier to move my toes.

Yes! Soon my feet were moving, pushing aside the snow. The effort totally exhausted me. I tried to rest, afraid to pause too long because the cavity around my feet might collapse and seal me even tighter into the snow.

When I started again I could also move my legs slightly. I concentrated on my knees, trying to bend them while my legs expanded their circular motions in the snow. My back cracked. It seemed to snap like a stick. A single jolt of pain jarred me and the pain disappeared altogether. Whatever happened in my back saved my life. I had new strength and mobility. Soon after that I was able to kick out a cavity in the snow large enough to permit me to wiggle myself into an upright position.

With my blood flowing naturally again, I felt almost human. Very gently, then with increasing impatience, I began burrowing upwards with my hands. It was a treat just to move. At one point the snow above collapsed into the hole I was digging and I slid several feet backwards. For several minutes I was too terrified to move. But not moving would bring death certainly, if not swiftly, so I redoubled my efforts to dig my way out.

This time I moved upward at a steady pace until one hand broke through. I had reached the top of the drift! In my impatience I moved carelessly, bringing a heavy load of snow directly down on my head and reburying myself five or six feet below the surface.

I didn't repeat the mistake. The mole in me took over. When I began climbing again I moved my hands and feet very slowly. Safe inches were better than dangerous feet. Once more I broke through to the surface, very carefully pushing back the snow until I could see blue sky through a hole at least a foot wide. And like a mole I sniffed my way out cautiously, expecting danger at every turn.

When I reached the surface I collapsed onto my back, spreadeagled to the heavens. The clean air tasted as sweet as old whiskey. Later I estimated that I'd spent about thirty minutes buried under the snow. At the time it seemed a century.

My thoughts soon turned to Hannah. I struggled to my feet and stared around. A section of the mountainside measuring perhaps twenty acres had fallen about a half mile onto the Scales. Other men were picking themselves up, examining their arms and legs, mumbling thanks to God for being alive. Shattered pieces of equipment littered the area. Nearby a leg stuck up out of the snow. I reached over and yanked it, dislodging the body of a dead man. His head lay at an odd angle, a broken neck case for sure. I dropped the man's leg and stumbled away.

During the time I'd been buried word of the avalanche must have spread to Dyea and Skagway. Rescue parties had already arrived on the scene, the half-dozen army troopers from Dyea and twenty or thirty citizens. Skagway wasn't yet represented in the rescue efforts. Some prospectors had turned-to with shovels to dig for victims buried but still alive. As you might expect, many of the stampeders didn't pause to help anyone. Gold was their goal and they would not be diverted from it. Most of those above the snow slide continued over the pass. Many below turned away from the avalanche and headed for White Pass. A good number who remained at the avalanche site did so only to sightsee, not to work.

I walked down the mountain on rubbery legs, determined to put my hands on a shovel and find Hannah. She had to be alive somewhere under the snow. She had to be!

I was temporarily detoured from my purpose by a voice calling for help from directly below my feet. The voice rose from the depths of the snow like a ghostly echo.

"Hello. Where are you?" My question was meant to tell the entombed victim that someone had heard him.

"I'm trapped in here. Please help me!"

The voice didn't come from directly under my feet after all, but from a few yards to the left. I dropped to my knees and began digging at the spot like a dog going after a bone. A minute of that convinced me I was wasting my time. I needed a shovel to do the man any good. "I can't dig with my hands," I said loudly. "I'm leaving to find a shovel. I'll come back soon."

"No!" The voice rang with panic. *"Don't leave, please. You'll never find me again."*

"I will, damn it! Just hold on. Don't give up."

"No, I'm dying. I know it."

"Stop thinking like that."

"My name is Ted Johnson. I'm from Springfield, Illinois. My wife and family live on Herkimer Street." The words came through the snow riding on sobs. *"Tell my wife how I died. Tell her that I loved her and that I have gone to meet Jesus Christ, our Lord. Tell her to pray for me and to raise our sons in God's glory."* The words trailed off into more hysterical sobbing and moaning.

"I'll be back," I promised.

I raced down the mountain, paying no heed to other voices rising from the snow. God only knew how many people were trapped down there. I could help only so many myself. First Ted Johnson of Springfield, Illinois, because I'd rashly promised to return, then Hannah.

Part of the Scales had been covered by the avalanche but a large area remained untouched. The rescue effort was organizing there. Someone with good sense had started people foraging for tools from among the debris littering the mountainside. A wagonload of shovels was said to be on the way from the general store in Skagway. As people were located from their calls for help, the spots were marked with anything that came to hand. Some shovels and picks had been found, but not enough to provide tools for everyone willing to help.

I was one of those who arrived too late at the Scales to grab a spare shovel. Dozens of us milled around on that high flat piece of granite while we waited for more shovels to arrive. One young fellow was crying. "My partner's down there. I can hear his voice, but

I can't do anything to help him. I'm going crazy up here."

"You won't do your partner any good by cracking up," I told him. "The tools are on the way, you've heard that. Try to relax."

"But how long can my partner live down there?"

"Long enough." I hoped I was right. Nobody on the Scales could say just how long a person might live under ten or twenty feet of snow. Different estimates were passed around. All of them sounded too optimistic. I guessed that if Hannah conserved her air and energy she might last three or four hours under the snow, depending on how deep she was buried.

Before long a wagon pulled by six mules came laboring up the incline onto the Scales. Stacks of shovels could be seen bouncing around in the wagonbed. I cheered along with the others until I noticed who was driving the wagon. Jules Pelletier! It amazed me that Pelletier would take part in anything as unselfish as a rescue party. I was willing at that moment to forgive him all his murders in exchange for one stout shovel. I should have known that Pelletier hadn't been transformed overnight into the Good Samaritan.

Before the wagon could come to a full stop, forty or fifty of us crowded around it with our hands outstreched for the precious shovels. Next to Pelletier on the wagonboard sat Yank Fewclothes, the tattered trail beggar who also belonged to Soapy's gang. He jumped to his feet and waved a heavy shotgun in our direction. "Hold it!" he shouted.

"We need those shovels," someone said.

"You can have them," Yank Fewclothes answered, "at two hundred dollars a shovel."

"My wife's buried under a ton of snow," one man thundered. He was shaking with grief and fear.

Jules Pelletier loomed up next to Yank Fewclothes. He, too, held a shotgun pointed into the crowd. "You can have a shovel for two hundred dollars," Pelletier snapped. "Not a cent less."

A roar of anger went up, but no one seemed inclined to rush into those shotguns. Between them, Pelletier and Fewclothes could mash half the crowd with two well-placed blasts.

"Please let me have a shovel," begged the youth who had approached me earlier. "My partner's buried and he's holding our money. I'll pay you later. Please!"

"Not a chance," Yank Fewclothes laughed.

"Two hundred in silver, gold, or greenbacks, on the nailhead."

To back up their demands they both cocked their shotguns. The menacing clicks of those hammers and the knowledge of what two shotgun blasts could do in a crowd was enough to convince most people. Hands reached up to thrust greenbacks and silver at the two gunmen. Pelletier collected the money while Yank Fewclothes passed out shovels. Those without funds or who had volunteered out of duty rather than to save a partner or friend, backed off not knowing what to do.

I didn't have two hundred dollars with me and wouldn't have paid their filthy ransom if I had. Pelletier spotted my face and grinned wolfishly. "Hey, Bonner, is your woman down there? Ha! You can forget about a shovel. I wouldn't sell you lemonade in hell. Soapy says you're fair game from now on."

He could have killed me with his shotgun. No doubt he wanted to. Soapy would have paid him a bonus. But the blast would have carried away half his customers and started a riot besides.

I turned and walked away from the wagon. "What's the matter, Bonner? Afraid of a couple of shotguns?" Pelletier laughed delightedly.

I counted my paces. The young man with the buried partner grabbed my wrist, pleading with me to help him overpower Pelletier and Fewclothes. I pulled away and continued walking and counting. Pelletier shouted insults at my back while he collected money from those desperate enough to pay.

When I'd counted off one hundred paces I turned and drew my newly acquired Colt .44. The shotguns carried by Yank Fewclothes and Jules Pelletier had barrels no longer than twenty inches. They couldn't do me much damage at a hundred yards.

Yank Fewclothes saw me draw the weapon. He yelled something to Pelletier and both men threw down on me. I wanted to shoot Pelletier first, but several people stood in the way pressing money on him, so I gave Yank Fewclothes my immediate attention. I shot him through the center of his tattered jacket. The bullet tore his chest apart and dumped him backwards into the wagonbed. Pelletier's shotgun went off, spraying heavy buckshot all around me. One piece of shot nicked my ear. Before I could kill Pelletier he jumped to the ground and began running down the mountain in the direction of Sheep Camp using the wagon for cover.

I followed him as far as the wagon and tried one shot. Pelletier led a charmed life. My bullet kicked up the snow near his ankles and he kept on running, his gigantic ear jiggling crazily. Ordinarily I would have pursued and finished him. Not that day, though. Finding Hannah came first.

The shovels were going fast. I grabbed one from the wagon and joined the rescue party heading uphill into the avalanche area.

Several people had already been pulled from the snow, some dead and others alive. My plan was to fulfill my pledge to Ted Johnson as quickly as possible and then look for Hannah. Johnson had sounded fairly close to the surface. If I didn't find him in ten minutes I'd break off my search until after I found Hannah.

I didn't have to dig for Johnson after all. Someone else had already scooped him out. At least there was a man sitting near a hole in the snow by the marker I had left. "Johnson?"

He looked at me from under swollen eyelids. "Yes, I'm Ted Johnson."

"I'm the one who promised to come back

for you. I see someone else found you first."

"Thank you. Thanks for coming back. It's a miracle I'm alive."

"Good luck to you." I started away.

He clutched at my sleeve. "It's a miracle. Will you pray with me?"

"I can't. There are others still under the snow."

"But this is a miracle! Don't you see? We must pray."

He wouldn't let go. I slapped his hand away and stamped off through the snow.

The size of my task began to frighten me. The farther I walked into the avalanche area, the more impossible it seemed. The twenty acres of fallen snow amounted to millions of pounds of the stuff. I didn't know where to begin. My best hope seemed to be in determining at the start the most likely area where Hannah might be found. Hannah had been within twenty yards of me when the avalanche hit. Anything could have happened after that. She might have been swept off in another direction entirely. But my best bet was to search the area I had ended up at.

I found the hole I had dug myself out of. Starting there I began walking slowly in a tight spiral pattern, gradually expanding the size of the circle. As I walked I punched the snow with the shovel and called Hannah's name.

It took almost an hour to cover two acres thoroughly. At every step I was tempted to break my pattern and charge aimlessly around the mountain screaming Hannah's name at the snow. The discipline of my search pattern was almost too much to bear, especially when I saw others pull friends from the snow as a result of helter-skelter searches. It wasn't fair. I was being penalized for my discipline. Worse yet, Hannah might be the one to lose out because of my rigid search system. I gave myself another ten minutes of searching in a spiral pattern.

The ten minutes passed with no results. I shouldn't say *no* results. Someone else . . . a man . . . did answer my calls. I quickly grabbed one of the others in the search party and set him to work digging. But why couldn't it have been Hannah? I had just about decided to abandon my system when it paid off.

"*Brian.*"

Hannah's voice came from behind me. I had passed right over her. Another three feet away and the sound of her voice would have been lost to me. "Hannah? I hear you. Keep talking."

Her voice came from very far down. "*Brian, here I am.*"

"All right, I hear you. Don't move. And don't waste your air."

I plunged my shovel into the snow and swept away a huge mound of the heavy stuff, my arms working like pistons. The shoveling was tough work. For every cubic yard of snow I tossed aside, half a yard dribbled back into the cavity from along the sides. I dug as fast as possible, often catching the collapsing sections of my excavation on the shovel and tossing them out before they could begin refilling the hole. The first six feet took forever because of that. But once I learned how to pack the sides of my pit to keep it from collapsing, I made better time.

"*Brian,*" Hannah called again, and I took heart because she sounded closer.

"I told you not to talk."

"*I love you, Brian . . . wanted you to know . . . love you.*"

The statement was so astounding that I paused for a split second, then plunged back into my digging. "Shut up! You're using air."

It took more than an hour to reach a depth of fifteen feet. Once down that far, the big problem became getting the snow up out of the hole. I had to lift loads of snow weighing as much as thirty pounds and toss them high enough so they wouldn't fall back into the shaft. Every inch of my body ached from the effort. I called for help a few times, but those above had their work cut out rescuing others.

Finally I could shovel no more. My strength was still low from the struggle to dig myself out of the avalanche. I threw myself down long enough to collect a second wind, then went back to the job.

After five more feet I needed another rest. As I lay in the bottom of the pit I began to wonder if my tunnel could have passed her by. "Hannah! Say something. I need to know exactly where you are."

"*I love you.*"

At that point the meaning of her words hardly mattered. What did count was the direction they came from. I hadn't missed her. She was still below me and quite close.

I resumed the digging. Almost immediately the snow gave way beneath me and I fell through the floor of my shaft directly onto Hannah. She had cleared away a small cavern around her and lay huddled in one corner with her knees up against her chest.

Her eyes opened as I turned her over. There was a cut on her forehead.

"Hannah?"

She stirred and her fingers closed around my wrist with surprising strength. "I was afraid you wouldn't find me."

"Nothing to it. Just a matter of digging up half the Chilkoot."

Hannah attempted a smile.

"Hold onto me now." I lifted her and it hit me that I'd dug a fine grave for both of us. We were twenty feet down in the bottom of a shaft with no way out. "Hello up there! Somebody throw us a goddam rope!"

In my impatience I envisioned us stranded at the bottom of the hole for hours. But a head soon appeared at the top of the tunnel, a prospector with a wizened face and no hair.

"You all right, mate?"

I had to laugh at that. "Sure, we're all right. Just waiting for the ferry to Victoria."

"Don't get up on your 'arse, mate, or I'll leave you down there." The prospector with the cockney accent went off to find a rope and returned presently with two more men, both of them cockney, too. They dropped the end of the rope. I tied it under Hannah's arms and told the Englishmen to haul away. They took Hannah up. When she was safe the bald cockney looked down at me. "By the by, weren't you the lad what shot Yank Fewclothes off his wagon?"

I didn't like the familiarity the cockney implied to Yank Fewclothes. He could be a friend of that thug, or perhaps even another member of Soapy's gang. There was no point in lying so I answered, "Yes, I am. And I'm only sorry I missed the man who was with him."

The cockney grinned. "So am I, mate. They were a ripe pair. Two hundred dollars a shovel, b'God!" He tossed the rope down and, with his friends' help, pulled me up.

They had brought blankets with them. I wrapped Hannah in one and carried her down the slope. She didn't resist my command to lay back in my arms and be quiet, as she would have in other circumstances. Nor did she seem to mind when, caught up with relief and tiredness, I impulsively raised her face and kissed her. She only smiled and closed her eyes.

Sheep Camp had become a center for medical aid. The survivors of the avalanche, as well as the bodies of the dead, were being brought down to Sheep Camp from the Scales. Medical tents were set up and two doctors from the area, one a resident of Dyea and the other a ship's doctor off a vessel tied up at the Skagway dock, did their best to bring order to the Chilkoot.

We remained at Sheep Camp the rest of the day, Hannah lying on a cot in one of the tents sipping at hot soup while I returned to the slopes to help in whatever way I could. Hannah's words . . . *I love you, Brian* . . . returned to me occasionally as I worked. I didn't take them seriously. She had been pushed to the edge of hysteria when she called that message to me. A person buried alive might say anything to spur on a rescuer.

It was a grisly day's work on the Chilkoot. Bodies were uncovered all along the Golden Stairs. Some lay in twenty feet of snow, others just a few feet from the surface. Many died thinking themselves far under the avalanche when they were actually less than three feet from freedom. I found Mr. Whitley's body myself. He lay on his belly under ten feet of snow, pinned by the dredge bucket on his back. Most of our Chilkoot packers died as well. In all, sixty-five bodies were found that day. Others, unfound, are resting under the snowdrifts yet.

There were many successful rescues. I took part in one myself, unearthing a young man who had just about reached the end of his rope. In fact I judged him a corpse as I dragged him from the snow. I saw no evidence of breathing and I couldn't find a pulse in his neck. But I was stopped from adding him to the rows of dead at Sheep Camp by the young man who had wanted to help me overpower Jules Pelletier and Yank Fewclothes.

"You've found him!" He rushed up and threw his arms around his friend.

"I think he's dead."

"He's not! Sam couldn't be dead."

"There's no pulse."

The young man looked at me as if he'd never heard of a pulse. "I'll breathe life into him, that's what I'll do." And he put his mouth over his friend's and began breathing in and out rhythmically.

It's no use, I thought. But since the young prospector couldn't do the corpse any harm, I let him continue. And I'll be damned if the corpse didn't begin breathing! Within five minutes the corpse sat up, opened his eyes, retched out the contents of his stomach, and began to speak.

"Jimmy," he mumbled.

"Yes, Sam," his friend answered eagerly.

"Jimmy, am I alive?"

"You are, thanks to this man who found you."

The former corpse looked at me.

"Hey," I said. "I was ready to give you up for dead. Your friend Jimmy wouldn't have it. He breathed the spark of life into you with his own lungs."

The boy Sam began to weep and hug his friend.

"It's all right," Jimmy said, comforting him. "I owed you one, didn't I?" He explained to me. "Sam saved my life when we were twelve, pulled me out of the old swimming hole when my stomach cramped and I started to drown."

I left the boys to their reunion, glad to see one joyful sight on that cursed mountain. Their affection for each other somewhat softened my attitude toward the gold hunters. Some were scum, but just as many would carry God to the Yukon, like Ted Johnson of Springfield, Illinois, or bring solid friend-ships with them, like young Sam and Jimmy.

There was hope for the Yukon yet with people like them among the stampeders.

One rescue that afternoon made me laugh. An ox was discovered under twenty feet of snow near the Scales. When uncovered he was standing exactly where he'd been when the avalanche struck. The stubborn beast had refused to be budged by the avalanche. The whole event left him so unruffled that he avoided asphyxiation by standing at peace with himself, chewing his cud. Sometimes you can survive disaster through sheer dumb power, the ox and I were proof of that.

By late afternoon the pass had been opened and the gold hunters began climbing again. Hannah insisted she had the strength to join them. She couldn't bear to spend another night on the Scales or at Sheep Camp. We climbed without words. Just being alive and on the move gave us pleasure.

It worked out that we left Sheep Camp just in time. That evening Soapy arrived there with most of his gang. He had hit upon a new swindle. Marshal Taylor had appointed him "coroner" for the territory so that Soapy and his men could take charge of the bodies. Before the day was finished they had stripped the bodies clean of all possessions, supposedly "to be held in trust for the relatives of the deceased." The proceeds of course, went into the pockets of Soapy and his gang.

I looked forward to my next meeting with Soapy, when I would make a point to settle accounts for the widows of the Chilkoot dead.

Colonel Steele greeted our return to White Pass with relief. Van Ness had manfully informed Steele of his blunder in taking Reverend Bowers into his confidence in Skagway, and of the ambush on the mud flats. Then, just before Hannah and I appeared at White Pass, Steele received word that a warrant had been issued for my arrest by the deputy U.S. marshal in Skagway. The charges: armed robbery of Reliable Packers and Equipment Brokers and the attempted murder of Timothy Bascomb, general manager.

"I didn't know whether to curse or cheer when I heard about the warrant," Colonel Steele said. "It indicated you were still alive, but that you'd gone far beyond your brief in scouting Soapy Smith's gang."

"The warrant is a piece of spitework," I said, and explained the circumstances of our encounter with Reliable Packers. I went on to

341

describe my tangle with Soapy's three killers, the Chilkoot avalanche, and the short but satisfying gunfight with Yank Fewclothes and Jules Pelletier.

Steele punctuated my story with a groan. "So in two short days you killed four men, shot another through the leg, and lifted three thousand dollars in disputed funds from a potted plant. I don't know how I'm going to explain this to Ottawa. Officially, you weren't even supposed to *be* in Alaska."

"I'm sorry, sir."

The colonel fussed with the copy of the warrant he had been sent. "It's a pity you missed Pelletier with that second shot. I wouldn't half mind the trouble I'll have with the High Commissioner if you'd put that bastard in his grave."

"I tried, sir."

"I know you did. Constable Van Ness threw you in the soup and you had to get out as best you could. Van Ness is a game young man, but terribly green. He's very grateful to you for taking those three killers off his back."

"Doesn't matter."

"Yes, it does. You'll need strong supporters. I'm afraid your reputation is going to suffer as a result of this damned warrant. Marshal Taylor may be a crook, but he's an official of the United States government. This whole affair is going to look bad on your record and I feel partly responsible."

"My record already has a few holes in it," I pointed out.

"Yes," he admitted frankly, "it has. Now give me the best descriptions you can of the members of Smith's gang. I don't want a single one of those vermin slipping past our check-points."

He wrote down everything I told him in a careful hand, noting every physical detail of the gang members and their special lines of larceny. Now and then he'd shake his head and mutter to himself. When I told him what I'd heard of Fatty Green he mumbled, "Dear God, we must keep that fat fox out of our henhouse." And when I told him that Jules Pelletier would now be easy to spot because of his ear, and described the ear, Steele laughed and said, "I hope it swells up another six inches. It'll give the children a good target for their slingshots."

We spent a lengthy afternoon talking about Soapy's men. Steele was intrigued with Soapy's remark that he needed to make a big killing. "What do you suppose he meant by that, Brian?"

"Hard to say. It confirms to me that he's got a plan for putting his hands on a large part of the gold that will be coming out of the Yukon this summer. But as to whether he plans to set up his activities in Alaska or take his men into the Yukon, I'm damned if I know. Whatever Soapy tries will be ambitious, that's all you can count on."

Steele dismissed me, suggesting that I look in on Hannah. She was resting in the colonel's cabin and would be spending the night there. "You can bunk with Freddy Loomis or . . . er . . . make your own arrangements."

The colonel's stammer resulted from his observation that something had changed between Hannah and me. He didn't quite understand what that change meant. For that matter, neither did I. All either of us knew was that Hannah now looked at me in a new way.

"All right, sir. I think I'll do that. We'll probably be leaving for Dawson tomorrow morning."

"Very well. I'll tell Van Ness to be ready. I'll be glad to hand your dogteam back to you, too. They're the nastiest brutes I've ever seen."

On my way to the cabin Freddy Loomis stopped me. "Brian, look at this. Real whiskey from Scotland! Not that boot polish you usually drink. Come on over to my barracks, I don't go on duty for two hours."

"Not right now, Freddy."

Freddy almost dropped the bottle. "Brian Bonner refusing a drink? Has the whole world gone mad then?"

"Just save me the dregs."

I found Hannah up and around, sewing new buttons on her mackinaw. Her hair was freshly washed and more abundantly tangled than ever.

"You're finished with the colonel for today?"

"I may be finished for good. The colonel's upset with me for spilling so much blood in Alaska. That crook Marshal Taylor has sworn out a warrant against me."

"Pah! Who cares what he did. In a month you'll be rich enough to buy Alaska if you want it." She had recovered much of her old zip. "Come here and dry my hair."

Hannah gave me a towel and I followed her to a chair. She sat down, put a mirror on the table in front of her, and shook out her hair until the curls bounced at full length. I began rubbing her hair between the folds of the towel. She watched me in the mirror with a bright sparkle in her green eyes. After a while she raised her hand and softly touched my arm.

Her touch made me jump.

"What's wrong?" she asked.

"I guess I'm a little spooked around you because of . . . you know . . . what you said back at Chilkoot."

"When I was under the snow? When I said I loved you?"

At least she remembered saying it. "Yeah, that's it. I know you were scared and everything, so don't worry. I didn't take it seriously. We're business partners only, like you've always insisted."

I continued drying Hannah's hair, waiting for her to contradict me, to tell me she really did mean it. But she said nothing. She just watched me in the mirror, the amused smile growing wider. Yeah, it was stupid to believe she could actually love me.

"What makes you think I didn't mean what I said?" she said at last.

"Well, the only time I ever tried to kiss

you, I wound up with a knot on my head the size of a darning egg. That's one clue. For another, you haven't let me get close to you since then, not even when I was grievously wounded above the Skagway mud flats."

She laughed at that. "*Grievously wounded.* You had a little hole in your leg."

"A little hole!" I stopped drying her hair and threw the towel on the floor. "That's just like you, Hannah. I could have died from gangrene for all you seem to care. I've let you twist me around your finger . . . I've gone into debt, dug up mountains, sipped apple juice, let people laugh at me behind my back . . . all because I love you! There, now I've said it. Though you must know, because I've shown you that every damned chance I could find. But the Chilkoot had to fall on your back before you'd say one kind word to me. And now that you're free and kicking again, you're taking back your statement. That's mean treatment, Hannah."

She jumped up and faced me. "Who said I was taking it back? I do love you, Brian, even though you're hopeless. You've got no ambition and you'll never fit into the kind of house I intend to own on Nob Hill, but I can't help myself. I love you. Get it through your thick head. When I want something, I say so. And I want you, God help me."

"You do?"

I was as surprised as I'd been the first time she said it. But at least I wasn't separated from her by several feet of snow now.

The colonel's cabin was small and neat, a typical military man's quarters. Beside the chair and table there was only a bed and one lamp. I don't know what gave me the courage to lift Hannah and carry her to the bed. I was still half convinced she'd bust me over the head with a kettle again. But she didn't resist me. Instead she loosened her shirt and brought my face down against her breasts. I kissed them and helped her slip out of the shirt. I removed her coarse work pants as well. Her skin had a golden glow. I held her so tightly that she drew in her breath between her teeth.

"Turn out the lamp," she whispered.

As usual, I did as Hannah asked.

11

THE next few weeks went faster than any other time of my life. When we returned to Dawson, Hannah went back to the job of making our claims a success. Inspector Constantine had piled up plenty of work for me, too. But Hannah and I made time to be with each other, sharing dinner in her cabin most evenings and on other nights cutting holes in the ice of the river to fish. We didn't catch many fish, but we enjoyed sitting over the hole watching for movement on the line in the flickering light of a fire. We laughed a good deal and I taught Hannah to appreciate the straightforward taste of Perry Davis Painkiller.

By mid-April the long days of darkness were ending. As the sun appeared for increasing periods of time each day it brought a new mood to Dawson. Men who had been hardened enemies all winter shook hands and stood drinks for each other. Moose and caribou came down from the high country anticipating fresh grass. Some bright mornings Hannah and I would climb to the top of Midnight Dome, the great hill overlooking Dawson, and watch the scurrying activity along the creeks.

Don't misunderstand, Hannah could be as vexing as ever. The coming of spring generated even bolder plans in her mind. She began buying, trading, and selling properties again, often just to test her opposition's character; to see if he could be beaten down another ten thousand if she was buying or if the price could be jacked up another ten thousand when she was selling.

At one time we controlled, through outright ownership, leasing, or on mortgage, twenty-two claims. At other times we controlled only ten or twelve. Hannah bought and sold as many as ten properties a week. I recall walking up Front Street with Hannah one evening and meeting Antone Stander coming out of the Bank.

"Antone, when are you going to sell me Eighteen Above on Bonanza?" Hannah asked. "I've made my best offer, so you needn't hold out for a higher price."

The question drew a laugh from Antone. "Why Hannah, I sold you that claim three weeks ago. You turned around and traded it to Charles Berry a few days later for two other properties."

"I did?" Hannah scratched her head. "That's right, I did." She shook her finger in Antone's face. "And now that I think about it, you overcharged me for that piece of dirt! I went down in the shafts and tested out every foot. That claim isn't a skunk, but it's not worth what you charged me. I was lucky to trade it off at any price. I've a good mind never to do business with you again."

Stander's face reddened. "Who the hell wants your business? Not me! You came to me about that claim, Hannah. Practically twisted my arm until I sold it just to shut off your talk, and for a damned decent price." He stamped off cussing in a loud voice about the feeble-mindedness of women in general and Hannah in particular.

In those hectic weeks of trading I didn't argue with Hannah about any of her business decisions. I simply signed whatever papers she and Joe Rudolph waved in front of me. I didn't give a damn for the gold. If Hannah enjoyed the game of scrambling for it, that was good enough. Whether we came through the summer broke or rich was a matter of indifference to me. My nights with Hannah were my idea of riches.

Her business affairs caused me problems, though. One night while making my rounds I heard a pair of footsteps dogging me from the rear. Someone was staying about fifty yards behind me, stopping whenever I stopped and turning down the same dark alleys that I did.

My first thought was of Soapy Smith. He wouldn't forget the trouble I'd caused him, and his style would be to send a thug to take me from behind. I slipped out my pistol and continued walking. My rounds had taken me into Paradise Alley. Music and coarse laughter came from the cribs. Staying to the shadows, I strolled through the district until I came to a spot where a crib had burned down. Instead of going past I stepped into the burnt-out wreckage and waited. Whoever was following me also paused, then came along quickly to find out where I'd gone. As he passed I jumped out behind him and put my pistol in his ribs.

"Stand right there," I commanded. "Make one hasty move and I'll put a bullet through your spine."

The dark figure's hands flew above his

head. "Don't shoot me! Please! For God's sake it's me, Waterfront Brown."

"Step into the light."

The man went forward until the light from a window fell across his face.

"Damn it!" I lowered the hammer on my revolver and holstered it. "Waterfront, what the hell do you think you're doing footpadding after me?"

Waterfront Brown was Dawson's resident bill collector. He haunted the waterfront watching for people trying to slip out of town without paying their bills. Sometimes he hired out to a merchant, watching a particular deadbeat who might be likely to bolt. For years Waterfront Brown had been a deadbeat himself, skipping out on dozens of towns and three wives in the United States. He had left an impressive trail of unpaid bills behind. That's what made him such a good bill collector; he knew every trick.

The little man trembled in my grip. "Jesus, Brian. I didn't mean to scare you."

"You didn't scare me, you little ferret. You made me mad. That's worse." I picked him up until his feet dangled above the ground. "Now why are you following me?"

Between gasps for breath, he explained.

"Pat Galvin and Alex McDonald hired me to keep an eye on you and Hannah . . . They're afraid . . . Brian, I can't breathe . . . my throat . . ."

I dropped him. "Why should Galvin and McDonald care about me?"

"You and Hannah owe them four hundred thousand dollars."

"The hell we do! They loaned us three hundred thousand and we paid them back two weeks ago when Hannah sold off some claims."

"Then you turned around and borrowed another four hundred thousand last week to buy some others. Don't you read what you sign?"

"Of course I do." Of course I didn't. Joe Rudolph's handwriting became harder to read every day. "But why do they think we'd bolt?"

"It's no secret Hannah's in over her head again." Waterfront Brown probed the spots on his neck where I had held him. "And it's a favorite dodge of debt skippers to bolt during the middle of the workday. I've done so myself many times."

"Listen, go tell Galvin and McDonald to leave us alone. Hannah and I will be here through the summer. Tell them that if I see your head bobbing up behind me again . . . or theirs . . . I'll start shooting. Understand?"

"Sure, Brian. I'll tell 'em. Count on me." Waterfront Brown scampered off into the night.

That incident convinced me I'd been too cavalier about our finances. I didn't mind going broke. What I did mind was having weasels like Galvin and McDonald sniffing around me. Talking about money with Hannah always gave me a headache, so I prepared myself for the ordeal by drinking half a bottle of Perry Davis.

Hannah didn't mention the smell of my breath when I came into her cabin later that evening. She no longer ragged me about my drinking. There are very few women who'll take a man as he is, warts and blemishes in place. Hannah seemed prepared to do so. She kissed me warmly and started telling me about a promising test on one of the new claims.

"Hannah, that's what I want to talk about, the claims. Waterfront Brown came sneaking around me tonight. Galvin and McDonald hired him because we seem to owe them four hundred thousand dollars. Hannah, I didn't know we'd gone into debt with those two again. Why didn't you tell me?"

"You signed the notes, Brian."

"You know I don't bother to read what I sign anymore. I trusted you to keep us afloat and look what's happened—Waterfront Brown!"

She nodded. "He came snooping around here, too. I ran him off. Brian, we're within an ace of making millions of dollars. Millions! All we have to do is keep up the interest payments on all our loans for another month, until the end of May. Then the ice will be gone and we can start washing dirt."

I had heard that refrain too many times. "Hannah, can we make our interest payments? Give me the facts."

"All right." In her brisk businesslike way she set out her ledger and began showing me the facts. "Our notes come due on July fifteenth. Our various mortgages right now come to five hundred and twenty-two thousand dollars . . ."

"Oh my God!"

"That's not as bad as it sounds. When the rivers are free of ice we'll wash that much out of our dumps in a month. The problem is paying the interest until then. Galvin and

McDonald didn't hire Waterfront Brown to spy on us because they think we might run out on them. They want to know whether we'll be able to keep up our interest. If not, they can legally take over most of our claims. I'm sure they wish we *would* bolt."

So that was it. "Okay, how much interest do we have to come up with between now and June first?"

"Fifty-six thousand," Hannah answered promptly.

"Can we do it?"

A canny look came into Hannah's eyes. "Yes, if you'll go along with a plan I have."

I threw my hat on the dirt floor. "Dammit Hannah, no! Whatever it is, no!"

The witch grabbed my face and gave me a big kiss on the lips, the kind that in those days was called a "buss."

"Brian, this is the best idea I've ever had. We're about fifteen thousand short on the interest and I know a way to pick up a very fast twenty thousand dollars and have a lot of fun doing it."

"I don't like the sound of that. What's your idea?"

"We're going to win the lottery!"

There was only one lottery going on in

Dawson, but the idea we might win it was crazy. I had presented Hannah with a one-dollar ticket the week before as a joke. I told her the ticket would be my contribution to making us rich. Joe Ladue had started the lottery a couple of years before and it had become Dawson's one annual tradition. Tickets were on sale at Ladue's saloon, 20,160 of them. Each ticket represented a different one minute period between May first and May fourteenth. That's the two-week period during which the ice tradition-ally cracks on the Yukon River with a great shuddering roar. Then within a few days the ice begins breaking up and flowing downriver toward the Bering Sea in great chunks.

Joe Ladue had rigged up an old steamboat pressure gauge on the Yukon River ice at a spot just opposite Dawson. A thin steel cable ran from the pressure gauge to a clock fixed above Ladue's bar. When the ice finally cracked, the pressure gauge would set off the alarm on the clock and automatically register the time of day. Whoever held the ticket for the exact minute the ice cracked on the Yukon would win slightly more than twenty thousand dollars. "Hannah there are 20,160 tickets outstanding. What makes you think we'll be the lucky winners?"

"Because we won't trust to luck. Look at this ticket you bought for me. It's for 3.23 A.M., May sixth, the dark of night."

"So what?"

Hannah went into the corner of the cabin and pulled a tarpaulin off what looked to me like ten sticks of dynamite. "Here's my plan: You'll take this dynamite upriver about two miles. You'll take this watch, too. We'll synchronize it with the clock in Joe Ladue's saloon. At exactly 3.23 A.M. on May sixth you'll explode the dynamite. You can bury it in a shallow hole in the river ice. That should set off the pressure gauge and ring the alarm clock in Joe's saloon. And we'll win twenty thousand dollars!"

I didn't even know where to begin explaining how insane her idea was. So instead I focused on a side issue, the dynamite. "We had a report today that ten sticks of dynamite had been stolen from the A.C.C. warehouse. Was that your work?"

"Of course. I couldn't very well go out and buy dynamite. Someone might connect that with our winning the lottery afterwards."

"Hannah . . . I don't know how to tell you

this . . . you're crazy. . . . I guess that's the best way. . . . Why avoid the subject. . . . *You're crazy!*"

"Why?"

"Why? . . . Well, it's just . . . everyone would hear the damned dynamite explode, that's why! They'd know the ice hadn't cracked by itself, damn it!"

Hannah disagreed with her placid smile. "Last year was my first in the Yukon. When the ice cracked it sounded like a clap of thunder, the same kind of sound ten sticks of exploding dynamite would make. It scared the hell out of me. I thought the world was ending. Now if I can't tell the difference between dynamite exploding and the ice cracking, no one else will either."

A hundred other objections went through my mind. "Someone would see me."

"At 3.23 A.M.? I don't think so."

"People will ask questions. I only bought one ticket. Others have bought twenty or thirty tickets. It'd look pretty suspicious if we won the lottery with just one ticket."

"You're right. That's why I went out and bought forty more tickets this afternoon." Hannah looked pleased with herself for anticipating that objection.

I quickly selected another objection. "What if something goes wrong with the timing? Fuses are tricky things. If we miss by one minute, we lose."

Hannah chuckled. "Among the other tickets I bought this afternoon were the ones for 3.22 and 3.24 A.M. on the sixth. You've got a minute leeway on either side of your target."

I moved on to my next objection. "Hannah, I don't know that much about handling dynamite. I could blow myself to pieces. One little mistake with a blasting cap, a slip on the ice, that's all it would take."

"Please Brian, be *very* careful handling the dynamite. I couldn't bear to lose you now, after discovering how I feel about you. God, that would be terrible." She threw her arms around me, trembling in fear for my life.

I'd never understand her. She did love me, she had shown that in a hundred different ways since the Chilkoot avalanche. We spent almost every night together in her cabin, with me making my way back to the barracks at dawn. She talked constantly of the life we'd have together after we became rich. She knew I hated cities, so she wanted me to open my distillery in the wilds of Mendocino County in California. That would be far enough out in the wilderness to satisfy me and close enough to San Francisco to satisfy Hannah. We'd buy houses in both places, moving back and forth as the mood struck us.

Yet despite all our plans she was perfectly willing to plunge me into an adventure that was highly dangerous . . . not to mention illegal . . . at the same time trembling at the thought I might be killed. How do you handle a woman like her?

For the next hour I argued, throwing up objections and pointing out weaknesses in her plan. It did me no good. She kept insisting that her plan had to work because it was so simple.

You know the result. In the end I agreed to blow a hole in the Yukon ice so that Hannah could win the lottery.

The following morning Inspector Constantine called me into his office for a "chat." We'd been having regular "chats" ever since my return from Skagway. Previously such conferences had concerned themselves with my drinking habits and lack of military grooming. These days Evan Van Ness was the subject of our meetings.

"I don't know what to do about Evan," Constantine complained. "Until recently he was a model constable. Now . . . I don't know . . . I've both reprimanded and counseled him. Neither has done any good. Will you talk to him, Brian? You're the only one he seems to listen to these days."

"I will, if you think it would do any good. Is there a particular problem this time?"

"Yes. Last night at the Aurora Evan knocked Axel Anderson down. I don't know what the argument was about. I don't care really. It's all the changes in Evan in total that bother me. See what you can do to straighten him out, will you?"

"I'll try, sir."

You can imagine how desperate Inspector Constantine must have been to ask my help in improving another mountie's discipline. His remark about me being the only person Van Ness would listen to was true, believe it or not. Ever since I saved Van Ness's life on the Skagway mud flats he had been treating me with respect. Actually, hero worship would better describe his new attitude toward me.

All the way back from White Pass to Dawson he had pestered me with questions.

How did I keep my dogteam under such good control? Why did I usually carry an Enfield pistol instead of an Adams? Why did I wear an elkskin parka instead of a heavier fur? His questions amused Hannah and drove me mad.

I discovered the reasons for his questions when we reached Dawson. The damned fool planned to pattern his life after mine! He traded his fur parka for an elkskin, his Adams for an Enfield, and took up drinking and whoring on a grand scale. To finance his new vices he started gambling. To everyone's surprise Van Ness possessed great talents in that direction. Most evenings he'd walk away from the gaming tables with two or three hundred dollars above his original table stakes.

I left Constantine's office and made for the Aurora, where Van Ness had last been seen, wondering what I would say to him. I couldn't advise him to ease up on his drinking, not with last night's Perry Davis Painkiller on my breath. It would be useless also to tell a man on a hot winning streak to quit gambling. And there would certainly be no purpose in trying to keep Van Ness away from Paradise Alley when everyone knew I'd been a prime customer of the district until Hannah entered my life.

Van Ness was in the Aurora at a back table with Swiftwater Bill Gates and a woman I didn't immediately recognize. Bill and Van Ness were playing Acey Deucey while the woman watched.

"Brian!" Van Ness waved as soon as he saw me. "Over here! How about a hand of cards?" He jumped up and offered me his seat.

"No thanks, Evan. Hello, Bill. How come you aren't out at your diggings?"

"My shafts're starting to fill with seepage. Looks like spring is about here. My guess is the ice'll crack on May tenth. That's what my lottery ticket says, anyhow."

I could have told him when the ice would crack to the exact minute, but I held my tongue.

"You didn't say hello to me," the woman with Bill complained in a whiny manner. "Nobody says hello to me any more. You'd think I was a piece of furniture."

I took a good look and realized the woman was Gussie Lamore. She had put on at least seventy pounds. "Oh. Hi there, Gussie. I see you're still working on the potatoes."

"Sometimes I think it's not worth it," Gussie pouted. "No one ever talks to me and I haven't danced for ages. I don't even know if I *can* dance anymore."

"Sure you can, honey." Swiftwater Bill put his arm around her as far as it would go and kissed her on the cheek. "And as soon as we're married and you've got your dowry, you can stop eatin' potatoes and start dancin' again. Meanwhile, I think you're still the prettiest gal in Dawson."

"I won't even be able to find a wedding dress to fit me."

The bartender sat a glass in front of me and Van Ness poured a drink for me from his own bottle. He now drank Perry Davis Painkiller, and plenty of it. We drank together and Van Ness smacked his lips, remarking on how much he preferred Perry Davis to Juice of the Snake or Chilkoot Dynamite. He hadn't shaved in a day or two and his boots were as scuffed as my own. Soup stains spotted the front of his tunic.

"I hear you coldcocked Axel last night, Evan. What was that all about?"

"Nothing," Van Ness said, avoiding my eyes.

"I saw it," Swiftwater Bill said. "And

heard it. Axel was going on about that warrant issued against you in Alaska. You know Axel, he has a bad word about everybody. Said you were guilty of the charges and afraid to face the music. That's when Evan lit into him. Damned good punch the youngster has, too."

"I don't need you to fight my battles," I told Van Ness.

"I couldn't stand by and let Axel . . ."

"Yes you could. And you will. Now get out of here. Clean yourself up at the barracks. Then go on about your rounds. Constantine wants you on patrol tonight, there's a pack of wolves threatening some prospectors at Carmack's Fork."

"Awww . . ." Van Ness sullenly picked up his deck of cards and stuffed them into a pocket. He also took the bottle of hooch. "I'd better have something to fight the chill," he said with a wink.

"Get out of here!"

When he was gone Swiftwater Bill burst out laughing. "By God, he's you right down to the soup stains, Brian. How'd you do it?"

"I didn't do anything! The idiot got it into his head that he wants to be just like me. I liked him better when he was Constantine's toady. He didn't bother me then. Now he goes everywhere I go and says everything I say. It's like having one of those what-doyoucallits around . . ."

"*Doppleganger*," Gussie supplied. "Someone who looks just like you. We did a skit about that when I danced in a revue in Kansas City. I was beautiful then," she said wistfully.

"Right," I said, "a *doppleganger*."

"It's sort of a compliment, though," Swiftwater Bill said. "No one ever wanted to be like me, except to have my claims."

"No one wants to be like me either," Gussie sighed. "Not anymore."

Swiftwater Bill did his best to comfort her. "They will, honey, when you're worth your weight in gold."

At 3.05 A.M. on May sixth I found myself creeping along the east bank of the Yukon River carrying ten sticks of dynamite, a trainman's watch, a pocketful of blasting caps and fuses, and an ice axe. The night was black and windy but not very cold. The ice would be breaking any day without my help. But Hannah wanted it to crack at 3.23 A.M. so that's when it would happen.

I found a likely spot and walked out across the ice. The river was about a hundred yards wide at that point, which was about two miles above Dawson. After lowering the dynamite carefully onto the ice, I took my axe and began chopping into the hard gray surface of the river.

The ice was still at least three feet thick. I planned to cut down about two feet below the surface, set in the dynamite, and then cover it with snow and ice to force the explosion down and out as much as possible. It took less than five minutes to chop out the hole and set the dynamite in place.

Each stick was wrapped in slick wax paper. It took me more time than I had allowed to peel the wax paper off the end of one stick. I held the watch up to within an inch of my eye in order to read the time in the dark: 3.15 A.M. Eight minutes to go.

There were three blasting caps in my pocket, each heavily wrapped in cotton. One wrong nudge and they would explode. I stripped the cotton away from one cap and inserted the cap into the stick of dynamite. Then I took a two-foot fuse from my other pocket, bit through its jute wrapping until I tasted the black powder inside, inserted the fuse into the blasting cap, and put the stick of dynamite back with the others.

Before I could consult my watch for the last time, I had one bad scare. I could hear the sound of a dogteam mushing downriver, closing on me fast. I dropped flat on the ice and kept my face down. A few seconds later the dogteam whooshed past in the darkness, perhaps twenty yards to my left.

When the sound of the dogs and sled faded, I stood up and breathed easier. Suddenly I plunged my hand into my pocket and felt for the other two blasting caps. In my haste to hide myself I had fallen right on the caps. It was a miracle they hadn't exploded under me. One less wrapping of cotton and they might have done just that.

My hand shook as I placed the two spare blasting caps on top of the dynamite and checked my watch once more. The time was 3.20.

The two foot length of fuse was supposed to take one minute to burn down. I prayed that the manufacturer's directions would prove accurate as I took out my matches and prepared to light the fuse at exactly 3.22.

At ten seconds before 3.22 I struck a match and cupped my hands around it to make sure it wouldn't go out. It went out anyway. I stuck another match. That one didn't go out. It was a shade past 3.22 when I put the flame to the fuse. It sparked and began to burn. In fact the fuse began burning along its two-foot length at a crackling speed. At that rate it would explode the dynamite in about thirty seconds.

"One minute fuse hell!" I began running for the riverbank. I took a dozen steps and my legs slid out from under me. I fell with a jarring force, jumped up and raced for safety. I almost made it. I was within six feet of the bank when the dynamite exploded.

The ice under my feet heaved and I shot up in the air. God knows how high the erupting slabs catapulted me. I seemed to ascend forever, then fall back into the turmoil in less than a second. The ice-covered river was boiling and buckling when I hit it, landing hard on my left shoulder. Before I could stand the ice buckled again in a whiplash motion, sending me skidding along on my back.

Heavy chunks of ice the size of canonballs began falling all around. One hit me a glancing blow off the hip; if it had fallen on my head I'd have been killed outright. Instead it seemed my fate to drown, for as the ice tilted and broke up I couldn't stop myself from sliding off my slab of ice and into the river itself.

I plunged in headfirst, the freezing water robbing my breath and draining me of strength. It was Chilkoot all over again. Somehow I managed to surface and throw my arms around a floating chunk of ice about the size of a beer barrel. It was impossible to tell in the churning confusion how far I might be from the riverbank. My only hope lay in climbing back up onto a larger base of ice and trying to jump from one ice floe to another until I reached shore.

Just then the water swelled and two huge sections of ice closed together on me. The smaller piece I'd been clinging to shattered under the pressure of the two larger blocks. I let go as it disintegrated and tried to scramble onto the larger slab. My hands were too numb to get a decent grip and I found myself trapped as the mountains of ice slid slowly together. Each piece weighed several tons. They would have crushed me to jelly. At the last moment I pushed myself under the water and let the two sections slam together above me.

I had inhaled enough air to last me a

minute, no more. In that allotted time I groped desperately along the underside of the ice looking for an opening above. I couldn't see a thing. The world beneath the ice was as dark as it was cold. At last my hands slipped off the ice and I felt myself rising. I popped to the surface and shook my head to clear my eyes of water. Another large block of ice bobbed near me, close enough to touch. My hands were useless so I threw my arms up on it, shoved my head and shoulders onto the ice, and tried to roll my legs over the side. Somehow I managed to slide, seal-like, onto the float.

The motion of the river had eased, so that I was in less danger of slipping off my perch. Up and down the Yukon fierce snapping sounds could be heard as the violent seizures of ice created gigantic cracks in the river's frozen surface. I felt certain my mission of setting off the alarm clock bell in Joe Ladue's saloon had been a success. The question was whether I'd live to enjoy the benefits of my night's work.

On all sides the ice had broken into blocks of various shapes and sizes, some small and others as large as buildings. The nearest shore was less than thirty yards away. There were no pieces nearby large enough for me to scramble across, so I decided to plunge back into the water and swim for shore. I couldn't get much colder or wetter than I was.

I dived in and began thrashing away. My parka and boots held me back, but somehow I made it to shore. I dragged myself up on the snowy bank and collapsed for a minute's rest, all I could afford. If I didn't reach my barracks within thirty minutes at the most I'd certainly freeze to death.

I'll never forget the cold misery of that walk back to Dawson. I stumbled along half dead, my hands and feet numb except for occasional flashes of pain. My teeth chattered so hard that a piece chipped off one of my back molars. And I'm not stretching the truth when I say I feared losing both my hands and feet.

At last I did reach the barracks room. Fortunately it was empty. Inspector Constantine slept in his own quarters. Captain Scarth lived in the barracks, but he had gone on patrol downriver and Van Ness was out imitating me by whoring and drinking all night.

It took a painful half hour just to separate myself from my clothes. They were frozen to my body in places so that patches of skin tore off as I removed them. Bundled in wool blankets, I sat on my bunk and began rubbing my hands and feet as vigorously as I could. For a long time they failed to respond. Then at last they began to feel all prickly and hot as the blood started to circulate again. I helped along the circulation with liberal doses of Perry Davis Painkiller, taken internally as the prescription directs.

By dawn I felt half human. About that time Van Ness staggered into the barracks room reeking of whiskey and chuckling to himself. He began emptying his pockets of poker chips from Joe Ladue's saloon and dropping them on his bunk by the handful. "I had a hell of a night. You should have joined me, Brian. Too much sleep is bad for a man."

He apparently thought I was just rising from my bunk after a quiet night of rest. "I have to sleep once in a while, Evan."

"Sure." Van Ness stopped taking chips out of his pockets. "Hey, I'll bet you haven't heard! Hannah won the lottery."

"The lottery?"

"She held the ticket for 3.23 A.M. this morning and that's just when the ice cracked. Didn't you hear it? Made a hell of a noise. You must sleep like Lazarus."

"That's great," I said weakly. "Did anyone tell her yet?"

"Joe Ladue and a bunch from the saloon took her winnings out to her. I wanted to go with them but I was on a winning streak of my own. Joe woke her up to give her the good news and she invited everyone into her cabin for a drink." Van Ness winked broadly. "They were surprised not to find you there. I told them Constantine had you on patrol; I forgot it's Captain Scarth who's downriver. How come you weren't with Hannah? It's strange to find you in the barracks these days."

I coughed and thumped my chest. "Not feeling good. Fever. Chills. Coughing. Didn't want to give it to Hannah."

"You do look terrible. Want me to take town patrol? I don't have the duty until this afternoon."

For the first time Van Ness's new friendship was welcome. "Would you? I'd appreciate it."

"Glad to, Brian."

"Thanks. Wake me when you come back." I bundled myself in blankets and crawled into my bunk.

I slept straight through until four that afternoon when Van Ness awoke me as I'd asked. Aside from the raw red areas where the skin had been torn, I felt pretty good. Nevertheless I took my time dressing and walking out to Hannah's cabin.

She was standing above one of the shafts peering into it when I arrived. Seepage had filled the shaft as the temperature rose and the frozen moisture in the ground began to thaw. Three-Inch White and two other workmen were with her. "Hi, Brian," she said. "Did you hear the news? I won the lottery."

"Van Ness told me. Congratulations, this is your lucky year."

"Them that has, gets," Three-Inch White muttered.

"Boys, I'm afraid we're out of business," Hannah said. "I won't have any more work for you until the rivers are clear. Then I'll start washing dirt and you'll be the first I hire."

"I'll be working my own claim," one of the men said. "And I'm hoping for just half your luck, Hannah."

She shook his hand. "Good luck to you, Ben. Let me know if I can do anything to help."

"Thanks, Hannah."

She paid them off for their week's labor and as they departed Hannah grabbed me by the arm and drew me into the cabin. Inside she jumped on me and threw her arms around my neck. "We did it! I knew it would work. Everything went just right. You should have seen Joe Ladue, he didn't suspect a thing! Neither did anyone else."

I removed her arms from around my neck. "For your information everything didn't go 'just right.' That fuse you gave me burned like one of Satan's cigarettes. I couldn't get off the ice before the dynamite blew. When the ice broke up I went into the water and damn near drowned. Then to top off the evening I almost froze to death getting back to the barracks. This is the *last time* you involve me in any of your crazy schemes, Hannah. Get that through your head."

"Whatever you say, Brian." Her mouth pouted prettily. "You needn't get all nasty and noisy about it."

"Look at this." I raised my shirt and showed her a place where a chunk of skin the size of a small steak had been ripped out. "Wouldn't that make you nasty and noisy?"

"Oh my." Hannah ran her fingers along

my ribs and began pushing my shirt higher. "Let's get your clothes off so I can take care of those bruises."

The touch of her hands did wonders for my health. Most of the aches and pains melted away under her fingers. "Well, they don't hurt much anymore."

She smiled and put her tongue in my ear. "Let's get your clothes off anyway."

12

THE next three weeks were like a holiday. Most work came to a halt on the creeks in the Klondike Gold District. Every shaft filled with seepage and the miners sat around waiting for the ice to disappear completely. The only task that could be done during the last weeks of May was to cut timber and build sluice boxes. Hannah had several sluice boxes left from the previous summer. She brought them out of storage and recaulked the spaces between the planks with oakum. That took only a couple of days.

The ice began breaking up on the Yukon in earnest. All day and night the air rang with booms and snaps as the ice convulsed. It sounded like a gunfight between giants. The river overflowed until Front Street lay under several feet of water. That wasn't unusual. The flooding would continue until the ice broke up all the way downriver and began flowing into the sea.

The flooding became so bad that the floors

of all the saloons in Dawson were awash. I complained to Sam Bonnifield that minor catastrophes like floods and wars shouldn't be allowed to interfere with saloon service. He replied that he was doing his best. Most people weren't overly inconvenienced. I recall wading through the doors of the Aurora one evening to find scores of customers lined up at the bar as if there was nothing unusual about standing knee-deep in water to buy a drink. It was an inspiring sight. Deephole Johnson added a note of humor to the scene by spitting a stream of tobacco juice into a cuspidor that floated past him.

The warm Chinook winds came blowing up the valley during the second week of May and the ice began to move on the Yukon. For three days blocks of ice flowed past Dawson like silent white boxcars. When the river was at last free of moving ice the flooding subsided and a strange warm peacefulness descended on the town. Coats and jackets were put away until September. People played harmonicas on the street. Lettuce, radishes, and carrots began to grow in the little vegetable gardens planted on the sod-roofed shacks throughout the Klondike.

Inspector Constantine called a meeting of

all the mounties between Fort Cudahy and the Stewart. There were only fifteen of us, which prompted Constantine to advise everyone to get plenty of rest in the next few days. "The river is open in both directions now. People will begin arriving by boat from Lake Bennett by the first week in June. Then the stern-wheelers will start coming in from the other direction carrying prospectors who have shipped out from Seattle and Nome by way of the Bering Sea. We'll be busy twenty-four hours a day."

By the last week in May Hannah was working around the clock herself. The sun now stayed out for almost the full twenty-four hours each day and the miners were making the most of the light and the clear streams. Hannah quickly set up four sluice boxes and began washing her dumps. Instead of spreading the boxes around our various properties, she planned to wash all the dumps on one claim and then move the boxes to the next. She reasoned that all the gold passing through the workmen's hands wouldn't end up in our pockets unless she could personally oversee each sluice box.

Between May twenty-fifth and June seventh Hannah washed out more than one hundred thousand dollars in gold from three of our claims. Others among the prospectors did as well. Antone Stander and Axel Anderson made big strikes on some of their new properties. Deephole Johnson's dumps were disappointing to him, but he planned to recoup by selling three claims to the stampeders. His asking price would be seventy-five thousand dollars per claim. Swiftwater Bill was losing twice as much money every evening and throwing nuggets by the handful down Paradise Alley.

One evening I dragged Hannah away from her work long enough for a picnic on Midnight Dome. It was two o'clock in the morning, a strange hour for a picnic except it could have been high noon, the sun was that bright. We spread out a blanket and enjoyed the bright red fireweed covering the hills on both sides of the river. Ladyslippers were out too. The food situation had improved with the arrival of arctic greyling, pike, and dolly varden. We cooked fish over an open fire.

I found the nerve to ask Hannah a question that had been in my mind since the Chilkoot. "When did you start loving me? And why for God's sake? You used to think I was a clown."

She put her head in my lap. "Oh, it was a gradual thing. You snuck up on me. Just being with you started to give me tingles because literally anything can happen when you're around. You're a mountain, Brian. You make other men look puny by comparison, even Coatless Curly Munro." She smiled and rubbed her palm over my chin. "And other times you're such a sweet, tender baby. Don't shake your head, you are."

She lifted her face so that I could kiss her.

On the morning of June eighth boats began arriving in Dawson from the outside world. I was walking up Front Street when the first one came into sight, a big raft loaded with supplies and manned by two bearded gents who were poling hard to bring the raft into shore.

A shout went up and people came running from the saloons. Someone threw a rope and one of the men on the raft grabbed it. The raft was pulled ashore and they jumped to the ground. "We made it!" the first one laughed. "I said we'd be first into Dawson and we are."

The second took himself more seriously. "Are you a mountie?" he asked me.

"I am. Welcome to . . ."

"Where do we file claims?"

"Right over there at the recorder's office. They've got a map with all the unclaimed properties marked. You can . . ."

"We can each file one claim, is that it?"

"That's right. A claim runs five hundred feet along . . ."

"We know all that." He turned to his partner. "I'll go file a claim on Bonanza Creek right away. You watch the stuff. Don't trust anyone. When I come back you can go file on the piece of ground next to mine." He hurried away.

Before I could pass a testy remark to the first gent about his partner's manners, four more boats came into view. They were followed in quick succession by dozens more. There was no similarity among any of the craft. Some were rafts, others full-fledged boats with rudders and cabins. Some looked painted, some not. Some were big enough to carry four or five people and their goods, others built to carry one man. There were stout peterborough canoes purchased from the Indians and tiny little kayaks made from flattened coal oil drums.

Within three hours hundreds of boats

arrived, creating a floating city along the Dawson waterfront. I gathered from the conversations of the stampeders that hundreds more were just behind, although a number of people had stopped at the Stewart and Indian Rivers to stake claims in that area. Most of the arriving prospectors had little time for small talk. They were anxious to stake a claim on one of the major creeks where gold had already been found. The line of people waiting to get into the recorder's office grew to a mile long and Commissioner Fawcett agreed to keep it open sixteen hours a day.

The first stern-wheeler arrived from the Bering Sea on the same day, the old *Mary Ann*. As she pulled into the small Dawson dock with her steam whistle tooting merrily, people began jumping down to shore from every deck and rushing toward the recorder's office. I shouted a hello to the captain up in the wheelhouse. "Did you bring any cargo, or just people?" I called.

"Damned right I brought cargo," he yelled back. What he said next was lost in the sound of his steam whistle.

"What did you bring?"

The captain cupped his hands around his

mouth and relayed the information down to me more slowly. "ONE . . . HUNDRED . . . BARRELS . . . OF . . . AGED . . . WHISKEY!"

My vision blurred. I felt like a kid on Christmas morning. For two weeks the saloons in Dawson had been selling the dregs from the bottom of their kegs of hooch, stuff so bad that even I sometimes choked on it. A hundred barrels of whiskey sounded just about right, fifty for me and fifty for the rest of Dawson. "God bless you! And take care in unloading your cargo!"

It didn't take long for that news to reach Dawson's saloon owners. Tom Chisolm, Diamond Tooth Gertie, and Silent Sam Bonnifield boarded the *Mary Ann* and began bidding on the shipment.

My bliss evaporated as people began shouting and running toward the river. They were pointing to a man's body floating face down, moving with the current. He looked dead. I handed off my pistol and boots to someone and dived into the water. I swim with awkward chopping strokes, but they get me where I'm going. The man wasn't very far out in the river, not more than thirty yards from shore. I reached him and got hold of his hair. I turned his face up in case he did have some breath left in him. Paddling for shore with his chin wedged under the crook of my arm was a hell of a job. I might have been working at it yet if Three-Inch White hadn't thrown me a line. All my effort was wasted, though. When I dragged the man onto shore and laid him out it was obvious he'd been dead for several days. He was twenty-five to thirty years of age, clean shaven, and had a purple bruise on his forehead.

"What happened to him?" Three-Inch White asked. "Was he murdered or what?"

"No, he drowned somewhere upriver. He must have been in the water a couple of days, look how bloated he is."

Three-Inch shivered. "I see what you mean."

Constantine hired Three-Inch to dig a grave for the corpse. On further thought he commissioned a dozen more graves out behind the kennels. He guessed that additional corpses would be found in the river before the summer ended. The five-hundred-mile stretch of the river between Lake Bennett and Dawson includes some dangerous spots. Miles Canyon, for instance, where the wide Yukon narrows to just fifty feet and the water rams past the black basalt walls like an express train. Besides the fast water and high walls, an eerie perpetual whirl-pool exists in the center of the canyon. Many small craft have been caught in the whirlpool and pulled in. Very few people have emerged from that experience alive. Then there's Squaw Rapids, another rushing length of water that hides a gamut of sharp rocks just below the surface. Plenty of boats have torn out their hulls on those rocks. The deadliest spot on the river may be Whitehorse Rapids, named by the Chilkoot Indians who say the crashing plumes of foam are the spirits of white stallions.

The inspector's prediction proved conservative. Within a week he called Three-Inch back to dig more graves. In the first weeks of the gold rush a total of twenty-two bodies washed down as far as Dawson. When you consider that less than ten per cent of the people drowned upriver would float all the way to Dawson, you know that at least two hundred stampeders lost their lives on the river in the first two weeks of the rush.

I've never seen a town grow as fast as Dawson did in June of 1898. By the end of the month the Klondike Gold District had a population of twenty-five thousand, compared to the five thousand souls who had lived and worked there during the winter. The countryside was stripped of timber for five miles in every direction to build shacks to house the newcomers. The Crown began selling waterfront lots on Front Street. Those who bought the lots beached boats on them and turned them into gambling houses and other business enterprises.

Paradise Alley outgrew itself and a second brothel area was established across the river from Dawson. The new section was soon given the name Lousetown, owing to the fact that the new whores weren't as clean as the established girls on Paradise Alley. The town of Dawson spread out, too. Soon you could no longer go picnicking on Midnight Dome because the majestic hill became the site of several hundred hastily built shacks.

The mounties' days were spent directing newly arrived *cheechakos* to the gold fields, breaking up fights, and enforcing the law banning handguns in the town of Dawson. That last duty gave all of us some edgy moments.

Many of the *cheechakos* were hardcase types accustomed to carrying guns wherever they went. They could be downright hostile when told to leave their guns at their claims. Van Ness asked my advice on how to handle that situation, as he sought my advice on just about everything.

"Don't argue with them, that's rule number one," I counseled. "People who carry guns think that a man who talks a lot won't fight." We were walking up Front Street as I passed on that little gem. Just then a *cheechako* packing a gun on his hip came out of the N.A.T. & T. store with a load of supplies. "I'll show you what I mean."

The man carrying the gun was very tall. He wore a Western hat with a big brim and walked with a cowboy's rolling gait.

"Excuse me, I'm Constable Brian Bonner. I guess you haven't seen the notice posted around town about guns."

"I saw it." The *cheechako* bit off his words as if I'd angered him just by raising the subject.

"The law is plain," I continued. "No sidearms or handguns of any kind are allowed in Dawson. You'll have to leave that gun at your claim next time you come to town."

"And what if I don't?"

"If you don't, I'll take it away from you and

keep it until you leave the Klondike Gold District for good."

The *cheechako* dropped his supplies at his feet. "Listen mountie, that pretty red jacket don't mean spit to me. I'm Joe Tom Turner from Big Springs, Texas and I carry my gun wherever I go. Why, I packed this weapon to church the day I got married! I've worn it to work, worn it to bed, worn it to my dear old dad's funeral, worn it to Elks Hall in Big Springs, and worn it to the bank to make a loan to come up to this damned stupid country. Now if I wore it to all them places, I sure ain't gonna take it off for no 'mountie' in Dawson. I'll go you one better, I think 'mountie' is a damned silly word. What do ya think of that?"

I pointed at Van Ness. "Don't tell me your troubles, tell him."

When Joe Tom turned his head to give Van Ness a few additional words of warning I whipped out my own pistol and whacked him on the skull with the barrel. Joe Tom's long legs buckled and he toppled directly into Van Ness's arms. "You see what I mean, Evan? I hardly had to say a word."

Since Van Ness already held Joe Tom Turner under the arms, I grabbed his legs and we carried him off to the lockup. Joe Tom wouldn't stay there long, it was too small to hold all the minor offenders. After he woke up, got mad, then calmed down, he would be free to go. Without his revolver, of course. Anyone who caused trouble more than once was given a blue ticket out of the territory and put forcibly aboard the next stern-wheeler for the outside world.

Van Ness quickly picked up my gun control technique, adding a refinement of his own. If he spotted someone carrying a gun, Evan would simply step behind the man and without prior warning bash him with his pistol butt. Constantine didn't approve of that. Neither did he order Van Ness to stop doing it. His main concern was to keep guns out of Dawson, where most of the drinking and gambling was done. If we cracked some heads to accomplish that, it was all right. And our efforts bore fruit. The word soon spread that a man could wake up with a very bad headache if he took his gun into Dawson.

As Dawson grew the "no guns" law was also applied to Grand Forks, a town which sprang up at the junction of Bonanza and Eldorado Creeks. By mid-summer Grand

Forks became as big as Dawson had been the previous year.

Three more mounties finally arrived at Dawson to reinforce us near the end of June. They came with a message from Colonel Steele, who was still at White Pass. He reported that things were chaotic up there. So many people were drowning in the river that he'd been forced to establish a new checkpoint where all boats and rafts could be certified as safe. No unsafe craft were allowed to go through the rapids. There were fights and a few killings on the river and at Lake Bennett. None were attributed to Soapy Smith or his gang, however. Smith hadn't made his move yet. Steele was convinced it was only a matter of time. That's why he would release only three mounties to Constantine. He said he knew Constantine would understand and wished him luck.

Steele also said he'd been receiving good reports about our work except for some complaints that Van Ness and Bonner were too quick to "cosh" people. I liked the word "cosh." It's a nice soft word, makes it sound as if you've hardly touched your victim. He suggested that if Bonner and Van Ness liked to "cosh" people, one of us should be sent to the Pelly. There were plenty of trouble-makers at the Pelly who needed to be "coshed."

I was detailed to make a quick trip to the Pelly to see what Steele meant. The next morning I left on a boat going that far upriver. The rapids on the Yukon end before the Pelly and small paddlewheel boats made one-day trips between the Pelly and Dawson bringing in stampeders who could afford the high steamship rates.

When I arrived at the Pelly that evening I saw what Steele was talking about. At the mouth of the Pelly is an island which the stampeders had named "Split-Up Island." Having made it safely through the rapids, many travelers stopped there to break up partnerships. Not all the split-ups were happy ones. Many were like nasty divorces in which both parties argue over possessions. Going through a rapids could be a hard, nerve-wracking experience. Tempers frayed and when valuable supplies were lost overboard one partner would often blame the other. The *cheechakos* weren't accustomed to the fact that in the wilderness you can easily lose all you own in one stroke through capsizing, fire, flood, robbery, or whatever. They were like kids arguing over the last unbroken toys.

"That's my pair of boots!" one would yell.

"No t'isn't! I bought those boots in Skagway," his partner would claim.

"Well, they fit me and I'm takin' 'em!"

"No you ain't!"

And the fight would start.

At first I tried to break up those fights. That was impossible. There were too many fights and no handy jail to throw people into. Many of the broken partnerships were short-lived anyhow, the partners had been together only since Skagway or Dyea. But some split-ups occurred between friends who had come a long way together.

I looked around at all the bitter arguments taking place and jumped back on the paddle-wheel boat as it pulled out for the return trip to Dawson. Nothing I could do would help those people. The gold rush had crippled them. I hoped that they all killed each other before they reached Dawson.

The return trip was the only rest I had that week. As I stepped off the boat at Dawson the next morning an excited stranger rushed up to me. "Mountie, you'd better come quick, someone's beating up one of the girls on Paradise Alley."

I ran with him down Front Street and cut over into Paradise Alley.

"I was with . . . one of the girls," he panted as we ran. "Heard screaming . . . next door . . . guy beating her."

We found the narrow alleyway filled with people in front of the crib where the screaming had been going on. Girls from nearby cribs had come out in flowered silk robes and some of the men hadn't yet buttoned up their clothes.

"What's happening in there?"

Sally, a girl I had once given my patronage, spoke up first. "We heard Annie Loon crying that she was being killed. A john started shouting too, and then everything went quiet. I tried the door but it's locked."

Van Ness arrived. "Brian, I didn't know you were back. What's going on?"

"Some gent's been getting rough with Annie Loon."

"Is he still in there?"

"Must be. The door is locked from inside."

We both drew our revolvers and the crowd backed away.

"I'll go in first," Van Ness said. "You cover me."

"Okay."

I lifted my right leg and kicked the door with the sole of my boot. The flimsy wood splintered and the door collapsed away from its hinges. Van Ness dived through the door with his gun held well out ahead of him. I went in next standing up. It took a second for our eyes to adjust to the darkened room.

"Dear Jesus," Van Ness whispered.

People tried to crowd in behind us to see what had happened.

"Get out!" I picked up the door and set it into place to spoil their view.

Van Ness pulled a heavy red curtain off the one window in the room and spread it over Annie Loon's body. She lay across her narrow bed under a crucifix, the room's only decoration. The killer had sliced her torso twenty or more times with a heavy clasp knife that now lay on the floor. That corner of the room was soaked in blood.

The killer himself was sprawled on the floor next to the bed. After torturing Annie Loon to death he had evidently stabbed himself in the stomach just under his rib cage.

"How do you think it happened?" Van Ness asked.

"Who knows? Maybe he paid her to let him do something a little ugly. Maybe it went too far, farther than he intended. When he had done it, killed her I mean, he must have been sickened and scared for himself. So he put the knife into his belly."

"Do you know him? I don't."

I stepped closer to the man. He lay on his back naked from the waist down. "I know him. His name was Ted Johnson and he came from Springfield Illinois. He lived on Herkimer Street. He was trapped under the snow near me at Chilkoot. I talked to him before someone else dug him out and he asked me to pray for him and tell his wife to raise their sons for God's glory. What a waste."

Van Ness put a blanket over Johnson. "At least we know where to send his goods. This country does crazy things to people. While you were down on the Pelly a *cheechako* hanged himself because his claim was a skunk."

"It's not the country, it's the gold. People who find it go crazy and those who don't go crazier. I'd be willing to bet Ted Johnson's claim was a skunk, too. Poor dumb bastard."

I wrote the letter to his wife myself.

Naturally I didn't tell her what really happened. Instead I made up a yarn about a mine cave-in. I was right about the gold, too. He didn't have any among his belongings. The claim he staked on Quartz Creek had turned out a skunk, all right.

Others did better than Ted Johnson, especially those who came to Dawson to trade goods rather than dig for gold. Mr. Harry Miller managed to get the first cow into Dawson at the end of June and sold the milk from it at thirty dollars a gallon. People were willing to pay almost as much for milk as for whiskey; there's no accounting for taste.

The merchants began arriving with every possible kind of goods. From a town where you couldn't find an egg because one man had bought up the entire supply, Dawson became a town where any luxury could be purchased. You could buy champagne as well as whiskey in the saloons and the A.C.C. store now stocked Paris fashions as well as mackinaw coats and wool shirts. Food was no longer a problem. You could buy anything from steak to smoked oysters, for a big price. One man came to Dawson to make his fortune with only seven live hens and a rooster, and did it. He charged onlookers a dollar apiece to watch the first egg being laid in Dawson.

The sandbar in the river in front of Dawson was broken up into building lots to be sold by the Crown and new saloons opened every day—the Pioneer, the Domino Club, the Pavilion, the Keno Palace, and others. Women followed the men into Dawson. Mostly they were whores, but a few had other talents. They opened boarding houses at Grand Fork or in Dawson and set up laundries and restaurants. A pair of twin sisters won Dawson's heart. They called themselves the Singing Oately Sisters and Antone Stander fell in love with one of them. Both sang off key and neither could match Hannah in looks, but they were showered with gold. An actress named Violet Raymond arrived and Antone fell in love with her, too.

People hungered for word from the outside world. Old Man Hunker bought a weeks-old copy of the *Seattle Post-Intelligencer* from a *cheechako* for fifty dollars and hired an out-of-work politician with a booming voice to read it aloud on Front Street. Everyone cheered when they learned that Dewey had whipped the Spanish fleet in Manila Bay. Two local newspapers began publication, the *Klondike*

Nugget and the *Dawson Midnight Sun*. Competition leaped up in every business. The bankers went at each other fiercely, with both the Canadian Bank of Commerce and the Bank of British North America offering to buy gold at eighty-five percent of value in exchange for notes that could be redeemed in Vancouver or Edmonton. Many miners turned in their gold for banknotes because they were easier to carry. Not Hannah, though.

"Why should we give some bank fifteen percent of our profits?" she snorted when I suggested it.

"For convenience. What good is the gold if it just sits here in Dawson?"

"We won't let our gold sit here," she said. "I'm taking it down to San Francisco myself at the end of July to deposit it with Wells Fargo. We might as well draw interest until we're ready to leave the Yukon for good."

That was the first time Hannah mentioned leaving Dawson. She could see the idea upset me. "I'll be gone only six weeks," she promised. "Just long enough to deposit the gold in San Francisco and buy a few things we both need. Why don't you come with me?"

"We're too busy here."

"Quit the mounties. We have plenty of money."

We had talked that over before. "You know I want to serve out my five years to get those hundred and sixty acres from the Crown."

"Why? We can buy all the land we want in California."

"I'm all for that, Hannah. But I've almost earned my hundred and sixty Canadian acres and I want 'em. It's important to me. I promise you, when my five years are up in November I'll resign."

"All right. 'Till November," she agreed.

"We'll get married then, too," I said. It was the first time the subject had been mentioned between us and I didn't know how she'd react.

"Married? Brian, I didn't know you wanted to marry me. You were always so . . ." She started smoothing her hair. "It's something so . . . Are you sure you want to?"

"I'm sure. How do you feel about it?"

And I'll be damned if Hannah Young didn't blush like a schoolgirl. "Yes," she said softly. "I want to. I won't be much good to you as a housewife, though. You're a better cook than I am, and whenever I try to sew anything I stab my own fingers."

"Listen, I can sew, too. Wait'll you see my double stitching."

So it was settled. Hannah would go to San Francisco early in August, deposit our growing hoard of gold, buy a wedding dress and return before the snow and ice closed the river in September. She'd be transporting close to half a million dollars worth of gold after all our mortgages were paid. Everything was working out perfectly for us.

13

IN mid-July a piece of news reached Dawson that gave every mountie in the Yukon cause to smile. Soapy Smith was dead! He had been killed on the night of July eighth by Frank Reid, the man who had faced down Soapy in his restaurant on my first night in Skagway.

It seemed that one of Soapy's men broke a cardinal rule: he cheated and killed a local citizen. That set off a storm of fear and protest among the permanent residents of Dawson, giving Frank Reid the opportunity to rally people against Soapy for the first time.

Reid finally cornered Soapy on one of the Skagway wharfs. Gunshots were exchanged and Soapy fell dead. Frank Reid was also hit. He lingered in pain for several days, then died. The citizens of Skagway gave Reid a handsome sendoff, erecting a tombstone bearing the legend, *He gave his life for the honor of Skagway*. The damned hypocrites.

On hearing the news Inspector Constantine

called another conference of all mounties between Fort Selkirk and Fort Cudahy. He had decided to shift his forces around, moving additional men into the Klondike Gold District from the outlying posts.

At the meeting he explained his reasons. "First, the greatest part of the rush is over. Colonel Steele reports that there are no more big camps of people on Lake Bennett. He's staying up on White Pass for a while yet because a boundary dispute has developed there with the United States. My second reason for shifting personnel is pretty obvious. Soapy Smith's death takes a lot of pressure off us. Now that we don't have to patrol the borders against Smith and his gang we can concentrate on the petty theft cases and complaints about bunco games. I think every small-time confidence man in the western hemisphere had found his way to the Yukon."

He began discussing the transfers with the officers commanding Fort Selkirk and Fort Cudahy. It was quickly decided that Sergeant Mahafey and Constable Jim Carney would come to Dawson in exchange for the three new men now attached to the Dawson barracks.

"Brian, what's the matter?" Constantine had noticed my preoccupation. "Speak up."

"I'm just wondering if we can really forget about Soapy Smith's gang that easily."

Captain Scarth laughed. "You think his bloody ghost will come back to sell cakes of soap on Front Street?"

Constantine took my doubts more seriously. "I think I know what's bothering Brian. I was doubtful myself at first. How could a man as careful as Soapy Smith be killed so easily? I thought perhaps the story was a ruse, an elaborate trick designed to put us off our guard. Colonel Steele had the same thought. He sent a man into Skagway for Smith's funeral." Constantine smiled with satisfaction. "The corpse was Soapy, no doubt about that at all."

"That's not what I had on my mind, Inspector. I'm wondering where Soapy's gang was when Frank Reid killed him."

"I don't see your point. What difference does it make where his gang was?" Constantine was impatient to get on with reorganizing his roster.

I said, "My point is that Soapy always had some of his boys nearby for protection. Where were Yea Mow Hopkins, Blue Jay,

Marshal Taylor, Jules Pelletier? I'm wondering if Soapy had already started his operation, whatever it is. Maybe his gang is somewhere in the Yukon right now."

"They didn't get past Fort Selkirk," Sergeant Mahafey said. "I'd swear on it."

Captain Scarth had his own opinion. "I don't think we have anything to worry about from Soapy's gang, Brian. Without Smith they're nothing."

With his newfound loyalty to me, Van Ness couldn't let Scarth's comment stand. "Brian could be right, you know. From what I've seen Smith was an organizer. He might not even become physically involved in whatever he had planned."

I pressed the point. "That's just what I'm saying. Soapy always liked to put someone else between himself and the rough stuff. He was a con man, not a gunman. Besides, he liked people to think well of him and he wanted a commission in the U.S. Army. He'd stay in the background. That's why I can't get it out of my head that Soapy's gang is still intact and on the move."

Constantine gave me the benefit of a long minute of consideration before responding. "Brian," he said at last, "I respect your instincts. But this time I believe you're wrong. When things got hot for Smith, his men deserted him. That's why he had to meet Frank Reid alone on that dock. Smith's gang was made up of scum, their kind has no loyalty to anyone."

Everything the inspector said was logical, but I still found myself worrying that the gang was intact. However, my mind was put at ease as time went by and nothing more was heard of the gang or its members. As July wore into August I came to be convinced, along with everyone else, that Soapy's gang had broken up and fled after his death. I had plenty of other problems to occupy my time: shootings, arguments over claim markers, stabbings, card cheats. We shipped about fifty troublemakers a week out of Dawson on riverboats headed for Alaska. After a month I managed to put Soapy's gang pretty much out of my mind.

Back in the winter months Swiftwater Bill had booked the entire upper deck of the river steamer *Northern Queen*, a two-hundred-foot stern-wheeler with a speed of almost twenty knots and a draught of only eighteen inches. It was the best ship on the Yukon River.

Swiftwater Bill would settle for nothing less for himself and his friends. Hannah, Axel Anderson, Antone Stander, Deephole Johnson, Coatless Curly Munro, Charles Berry, and Thomas Lippy were invited by Bill to join him on the first leg of a trip to San Francisco. The *Northern Queen* could make the run from Dawson to the village of St. Michael on the Bering Sea in only eleven days. From there the miners could board coastal steamers for San Francisco, Portland, or Seattle.

The ship was scheduled to leave Dawson on August fourth, giving the miners just enough time to reach the outside world with a substantial part of their wealth, do their business, and return before the ice sealed the river at the end of September.

On the day of departure I helped Hannah move our gold onto the *Northern Queen*. The dust and nuggets had been packed in twenty specially made moosehide sacks, each weighing one hundred pounds. Hannah was taking out two thousand pounds of gold worth about five hundred thousand dollars at that year's market price of sixteen dollars per ounce. The *Northern Queen*'s management had been preparing for this trip since January.

A special strongroom had been constructed on the ship to hold all the gold going out of the territory and twelve armed guards had been hired. They were bonded jointly by the Canadian Bank of Commerce and the Bank of British North America. Each bank had more than one million dollars in gold in the strongroom. In total the *Northern Queen* was carrying five million dollars in gold to the outside world, about twenty thousand pounds of the yellow metal. Each bag of gold in the strongroom carried a red tag with the name of the owner, and we'd been given receipts for the gold by the steamship line.

I don't want to give the impression that the *Northern Queen* was nothing but a glorified freightboat. Far from it. As I went on board to say goodbye to Hannah, a glass of champagne was thrust into my hand by a steward in a white jacket and three strolling musicians began playing fiddles in my ear.

"Let's get away from these damned gypsies!" I hollered. Hannah and I went into the grand salon, which was carpeted in red velvet and paneled with burnished mahogany. A table set up along one side of the grand salon was weighted down with beverages in shining crystal glasses. I disposed of the sour champagne, exchanging it for a glass of honest whiskey.

"Hello, Hannah. Good morning, Brian." Axel Anderson brandished a champagne goblet like an opera goer. "Well, we did it. We made our mark. Now that we're all rich, why don't we put aside our past disputes and drink a toast to the voyage."

"That suits me," Hannah agreed.

Axel held out his glass. We clinked ours against his and drank deeply. Axel waved his glass. "Say, look at Swiftwater Bill!"

Bill had jumped onto the beverage table and was dancing a jig to the music of the strolling musicians. The fact that they were playing some kind of Hungarian waltz didn't stop Bill from dancing Turkey-in-the-Straw. He was so happy to be heading for San Francisco, where Gussie Lamore had already gone to buy her trousseau, that I thought he just might dance all the way to St. Michael.

There were a number of old friends on board. Dolly Morgan was traveling to San Francisco with Deephole Johnson. They had enjoyed their unofficial "marriage" so much that they had decided to make it permanent and legal in San Francisco. Johnson carried a hundred thousand dollars in the strongroom for the honeymoon. Antone Stander had deposited seven bags of gold in the strong-room. Axel Anderson was also taking a good deal of gold out of the territory.

"Come on," Hannah said. "I want to look at the ship."

We introduced ourselves to Captain Dol-guard, a gracious old veteran of the Missis-sippi River trade, who was delighted to show off his vessel to us.

"This ship was built in Seattle fifteen years ago, and she's as sound today as she was then," he boasted. "You see, triple galvan-ized hull." He bent and clanged his knuckles against a place where the hull joined the wooden deck.

He showed us that most of the first deck was occupied by the *Northern Queen*'s boilers, furnaces, and coal holds. The open part of the deck could be used to carry cargo and second-class passengers willing to buy deck space. The *Northern Queen* would be picking up deck passengers at the settlements along the river between Dawson and St. Michael.

"Now a riverboat is nothing but an engine on a raft," Captain Dolguard explained, "With hardly anything below the waterline at all. Believe me, with all the snags and sand-bars you just can't afford a draught of more than eighteen inches on any river, especially the Yukon."

The boiler deck also contained the kitchens and living space for the cooks and stewards. The next deck up was the main deck and held staterooms, a men's bar, the grand salon, where meals were served, and the ship's office. A promenade ran all around the main deck. A third level called the "hurricane deck" provided more staterooms.

"I think I just made a discovery," Hannah announced. "All the staterooms have names on the doors. Illinois, Virginia, Kentucky. Is that where the term stateroom comes from?"

Captain Dolguard bowed. "You're an observant young woman. Yes, the practice of giving first-class cabins the names of states originated on the Mississippi riverboats."

As we climbed to the fourth deck of cabins Captain Dolguard said, "This deck is called the texas. When riverboats were first built this deck didn't exist. It was added onto most Western riverboats built after the 1840s, just like the state of Texas was added onto the union in 1845."

The pilothouse was located on top of the

texas and offered the best view. Dawson and the countryside for miles around lay spread out for our inspection. Hannah pointed out to Captain Dolguard the different creeks and told him which were skunks and which had good dirt. The captain was totally charmed by Hannah. They were having such a good time I hated to inject a contrary note.

"I've noticed that except for its bottom this ship is all wood," I said. "Mighty thin wood at that. All those gingerbread designs along the rails may look pretty, but they're tinder-wood. A fire would consume this boat in minutes. Don't you ever worry about that?"

The captain took my criticism in good humor. "Alas, sir, you're correct. Like any beautiful woman," he paused to kiss Hannah's hand, a damned impertinence, "the *Northern Queen* has her faults. In order to achieve a shallow draught the structure on top of the hull must be as light as possible. Riverboats can burn to the waterline very quickly, but we'll endeavor to avoid that fate on this trip, as we've avoided it for the past fifteen years."

By the time we returned to the grand salon a full-fledged party was underway. Swift-water Bill had come down from the table and the three musicians had been hauled up there instead. A half dozen of Dawson's best whores, hired by Swiftwater Bill as "hostesses" for the trip, were dancing with each man in turn. Trays of food had been added to the beverage table, along with a keg of beer.

The steam whistle began tooting and stewards went around asking visitors to leave the ship. The *Northern Queen* was preparing to embark. I kissed Hannah goodbye kind of roughly. "I hate to see you go."

"I know." She moved against me in a comforting way. "I'll be back in six weeks, don't worry. And I'll miss you every day I'm gone."

"I'll miss you too, partner."

She jabbed my ribs. "You'd better stay out of Paradise Alley and Lousetown. I'll hear about it if you don't."

"Hannah! I haven't been there in months, except to make my town patrol."

"Be sure that's all you make in Paradise Alley."

It tickled me to know that Hannah could be jealous, too. She didn't know that I'd come within an ace of picking up Captain Dolguard and tossing his refined Southern ass off the pilot-house when he lingered over his hand-kissing. "Don't you get too friendly with Captain Dolguard on the trip. I don't trust him."

"Brian, he's sixty if he's a day."

"Those old Southern gentlemen can be mighty spry. Some are nothing but sex fiends. I've heard all about them."

"You're a fool." And she kissed me once more before I had to leave the boat.

Later I wandered into the Bank feeling lost and depressed. Six weeks stretched ahead like a century. I regretted my stubborness. What was one hundred and sixty acres of Canadian soil compared to six weeks' separation from Hannah? I should have resigned from the mounties and gone with her. My depression was so complete that when the bartender put a glass in front of me I just stood there staring at it, I didn't even feel like drinking.

I looked around for entertainment. A good fight might help, but I didn't see any genuine enemies in the room. Even Axel and Antone were gone, enjoying Hannah's company on the *Northern Queen* while I rotted in Dawson. It wasn't fair.

One man in the room did catch my attention. Silent Sam had recently hired a new janitor to sweep up and stack glasses. He was an elderly citizen, his hair snow white and face ravaged into collapsing seams. The janitor seemed not quite right in the head. His face twitched and every so often his whole body went into a spasm as if touched by an electric current.

I called Sam Bonnifield over. "Your new janitor, what's his name? I know him from somewhere."

"His name is Anson Black."

"Anson Black." The name was familiar. "Sure, I remember him now. I ran into him at White Pass. He was beating a mule to death and I had to educate him out of it. He was a big strapping gent then. What happened to him?"

"Black had a bad experience coming down-river," Sam explained. "You know that whirlpool in Miles Canyon. Black's raft got caught in it. The whirlpool didn't drag him in, though. His raft just went around and around on the edge of the whirlpool. It was seven hours before the raft floated loose. Hanging on like that, waiting to be sucked in and drowned, did something to Black's mind. When he came out of the canyon his hair had turned white and he couldn't remember his name. Someone found it in his papers. I don't think he'll ever be sound in the head again."

We were agreeing with each other that the Yukon had ruined more men than all the whores in Seattle when Captain Scarth came into the Bank and told me to report to the barracks. I went there at once to find every mountie in Dawson assembled and Inspector Constantine issuing shotguns and rifles. He greeted me with a sheepish frown.

"Brian, you were right. Smith's men are loose in the Yukon. We've just had word that several miners taking their pokes out by mule have been robbed between here and Indian River."

"How do you know it's Soapy's crew?"

"They bragged to one of the men they robbed that they were the Soapy Smith gang."

"And left him alive?"

"Yes. Brian . . . Evan . . . I'm leaving the two of you here in Dawson."

We both raised objections but Constantine cut us off. "I don't have time to argue. Someone has to handle town patrol. You two know Dawson best so you're elected. I understand how much you want Jules Pelletier, Brian. We'll try to bring him in for you."

A small river steamer was waiting to take Constantine, Captain Scarth, Sergeant Mahafey, and Constable Jim Carney to the Indian River country. Van Ness and I stood on the riverbank and watched them leave.

"What do you think, Brian? Is it really Smith's gang, or just someone bragging that they're his men?"

"How the hell should I know? I'll tell you this, though. I can't see Soapy's boys telling a victim who they are and then leaving him alive to repeat it to the law."

"Huh. That sounded odd to me, too. What'll we do about it?"

I didn't know what to do. Constantine had taken us out of the game. "I'm going back to the Bank and finish my drink."

"I'll join you." Van Ness fell into step with me.

A few months earlier I'd have been annoyed with Van Ness for forcing his company on me. However, in the past weeks I'd grown accustomed to his new personality and I now found him an agreeable drinking companion. How could I feel otherwise? Shunning his company would be the same as trying to avoid my own.

Van Ness had become intrigued with my

experiences in the whiskey trade. As we drank together in the Bank he questioned me about the art of smuggling whiskey; the differences between Canadian and U.S. duties, the safest border crossings, the most profitable-sized loads to smuggle, and a host of other technical questions. I enjoyed the role of guest lecturer and was delivering a lengthy answer to a question when a remark passed by a nearby patron caught my attention.

". . . had an ear the size of a head of lettuce. Biggest thing I've ever seen attached to a man's scalp."

"What was that mister? I heard you mention something about a man with an oversized ear."

The *cheechako* was at first annoyed by my interruption, then became eager to cooperate when he realized he was talking to the Northwest Mounted Police. "Why . . . yes. I was just telling these fellas about him."

"About who? Where did you see this man?"

"Well, I arrived on the *Titus J. Murphy* an hour ago. I saw that fella . . . the one with the swollen ear . . . over t' Circle City across the border in Alaska."

"When was that?"

"Yesterday. The boat stopped at Circle City. There was a fella on the dock wearing a big floppy hat with a wide brim. The hat was so big it pretty much hid his face. He was standing around with some other fellas and one kinda teased him, grabbing at his hat. It fell off and I saw why he was so anxious to keep his head covered. His ear was the size of a head of lettuce, like I said, and all puckered with red and blue lines. Made me sick. He grabbed up the hat, slammed it back on his head, and gave the fella who teased him a crack that sent him reeling. I don't blame the poor guy; it's bad enough to suffer an affliction without having some joker embarrass you about it."

"Who was the man with him? Describe him."

"Let's see. A young kid. Eighteen or twenty, I'd say. Wore a red jacket. That's all I remember about him."

Blue Jay! I recalled Soapy telling the kid to get rid of that red jacket and buy something that blended into the background. "Who else was with them?"

"I'm sorry, mountie, I wasn't paying that much attention."

"This is important."

The *cheechako* gritted his teeth. "Damn. There was someone else, but I just can't . . ." His eyes rolled. "Sure! How could I forget. There were two others, a huge fat man and another who looked part Chinese, a big gent with a shaved head. I remarked to someone that you see all kinds up here in the Yukon."

"Anyone else?"

"That's all I can remember. What's so important about those folks?"

"They're old friends." I latched onto Van Ness and steered him for the door. "The four men that *cheechako* saw yesterday at Circle City were Jules Pelletier, Yea Mow Hopkins, Blue Jay, and Fatty Green."

"Soapy's men!"

"That's right, and you can bet there were more of the gang around, too."

Van Ness saw what that meant. "Then Soapy's bunch aren't upriver robbing miners. Those robberies on the Indian River must have been a decoy to draw mounties from Dawson and Fort Cudahy in that direction. But why?"

"They're going to hit the *Northern Queen*, that's why. Soapy knew all along there would be at least one huge shipment of gold coming out of the Yukon. Swiftwater Bill chartered the top deck for his friends months ago, and Soapy must have learned about the strong-room being built into the riverboat. That's what he was waiting for. His gang was already on the way to Circle City when Soapy was killed in Skagway, with a few of them detailed to stir up trouble on the Indian the day before the *Northern Queen* was scheduled to leave Dawson. Very slick."

I was headed for the barracks to pick up a rifle and plenty of ammunition, my mind racing with plans.

"I don't see how they can take the *Northern Queen*, Brian. The banks have twelve armed guards on board that steamboat. None of them have ever been connected with Soapy, the banks checked them out carefully before they bonded them."

"Soapy had a plan, you can bet on that. And that Jules Pelletier will carry it out. The only difference is that Soapy won't be around to take the lion's share of the loot."

At the barracks I took half a dozen Winchesters out of the gun rack and a like amount of Enfield pistols. Somewhere along the way I'd have to find help. I pressed the rifles into Van Ness's arms. "Evan, go down to the dock. That *cheechako* came in on the *Titus J.*

Murphy. Grab hold of Captain Murphy and don't let him shove off again until I get there. I'm going to follow the *Northern Queen* downriver. You'll have to keep order in Dawson alone until Constantine gets back."

"But the *Northern Queen* will be in Alaska before you can reach it. We don't have jurisdiction over there."

"My jurisdiction is whatever comes within range of my Winchester. Now get down to the waterfront and stop that launch from pulling out."

Van Ness went running for the river while I gathered up the pistols and twenty rounds of ammunition for each of the six rifles and handguns. I packed everything into one ammunition crate, threw in some cans of tinned food, and followed Van Ness to the dock.

I found him involved in a loud argument with Titus Murphy, the captain of the small river launch bearing his name, and the dozen or so passengers who had purchased tickets to Circle City.

The *Titus J. Murphy* and the *Northern Queen* were both called riverboats, but that's where the comparison ended. The *Northern Queen* was sleek, clean, and beautifully appointed, the *Titus J. Murphy* as small, dirty, and disorganized as its owner and namesake. Years ago the *Titus J. Murphy* had probably been painted red, but most of the paint had long since peeled from its boards or been covered over with layers of soot. It was only twenty feet long and a good part of its rear deck was used to store the firewood that fueled its cranky furnace. Captain Murphy was a living complement to his ship, a small and untidy New Englander who had been chased off the eatern seaboard for a variety of marine crimes ranging from barratry to criminal negligence. He considered every dock on the Yukon River unsafe because they frequently splintered and collapsed when he rammed into them, which was his own peculiar method of docking a boat.

I knew he'd give me trouble so I decided to take a hard line immediately. "Captain Murphy, I'm commandeering this craft in the name of the Crown. Please disembark your passengers right now."

The little man cackled like a bantam rooster. "Brian, the only thing you've ever 'commandeered' is a whiskey bottle. You ain't starting something new with my boat."

A merchant from Circle City spoke up in protest. "Look here, mountie, I have business in Circle City and you have no right stopping me from going there. I paid good money for passage on this boat, such as it is, and I'll thank you to step off so the captain can get underway."

I hauled the merchant to his feet, turned him around, and booted him hard. He flew forward and fell overboard into the water. The example worked wonders. There was a general scramble and the boat was evacuated in seconds.

"Now we can get underway," I told Captain Murphy.

The captain pushed his seacap over one eye, scratched himself, and said to Van Ness, "Cast off that line. Folks, I'm sorry that I can't issue refunds on your tickets. The money has already been spent on necessary supplies. You may rest assured I will make good your loss at some future date."

The *Titus J. Murphy*'s engine kicked over . . . failed . . . kicked over again . . . failed again . . . and finally sputtered to life. We pulled out of Dawson to a chorus of angry complaints and headed downriver in pursuit of the *Northern Queen*.

Three hours later we crossed into Alaska,

moving swiftly with the current and only occasionally bouncing against the sandbars concealed just under the surface of the river. Captain Murphy seemed totally unconcerned about the snags. His attention centered on the bottle of gin at his side. Soon after leaving Dawson he produced the gin from a fresh case stored in the wheelhouse locker. The bottles of gin were the "necessary supplies" on which Captain Murphy had spent the passage money. Ordinarily I'd be the last man to quarrel with a man's drinking habits. In this case I didn't want our voyage interrupted by collisions with sandbars or other navigational hazards.

"Captain Murphy, could you take it kind of easy on that bottle? We'll have a tough enough time catching the *Northern Queen* without fetching up on a sandbar."

"A sandbar? Is that what worries you, Constable Bonner? Sir?" Captain Murphy cackled and took another long slug of gin by way of defiance. "What should worry you is the fact that the *Northern Queen* cruises at a speed of twenty knots while the *Titus J. Murphy*, the finest riverboat on the Yukon in most respects, can make fourteen knots tops. And just why are you so damned anxious to catch the *Northern Queen* anyhow?"

"Because it's carrying my woman plus five million dollars in gold and Soapy Smith's gang is out to grab it, that's why."

"Jehosophat! That fries it." He cut the engine switch, slowing us to the speed of the river. "I'm not going anywhere near that crew, not for all the yellowlegs in the territory." Captain Murphy took a firm grip on his gin bottle. "And don't threaten me or I'll christen you with this bottle and go over the side."

I couldn't do without the captain. Running a boat is simple enough, especially one as small as the *Titus J. Murphy*, but he knew the river. "Relax, captain. I'm not going to force you to do anything. But I will pay you to follow the *Northern Queen* and help me board her."

Murphy spit over the side. "What are you going to pay me with, half of the two dollars a day the Crown owes you?"

"You know I'm partners with Hannah Young. We've got half a million dollars on the *Northern Queen*. I'll pay you half that, a quarter million dollars, for your boat and your help in overtaking the *Northern Queen*.

You'll never have another chance like this, captain. What do you say?"

He must have been surprised, for he put down his gin. "You've got half a million? It don't seem possible."

"Damn it, captain, you must have heard that Hannah struck it big!"

"Yes," he said slowly, "but how do I know any of that gold really belongs to you?"

Before She left Hannah had given me a copy of the receipt for our gold that the steamship company had provided, for safekeeping. I dug it out and showed it to Captain Murphy. He looked it over carefully, pushed his sea-cap over one eye, and scratched himself, a sequence of events that seemed to precede any major decision.

"All right," he said. "The boat is yours for a quarter million, but that gold better be on the *Northern Queen*."

"It is. Now get this thing going."

Captain Murphy restarted the boat and we were once again on our way.

As we steamed closer to Circle City, I turned my thoughts to how Soapy might have planned for his men to grab the gold on board the *Northern Queen*. He wouldn't have tried a direct assault on the steamboat, that just wasn't his style. The chances are he'd place someone on board the ship first, someone who could put those twelve armed guards out of action. But who? And how could Soapy's men possibly get the upper hand over all the people on that steamboat? Damn Soapy! He was as much trouble dead as he had been alive.

14

CIRCLE CITY is about a hundred miles inside the Alaska border on the Yukon. It's the river settlement closest to the arctic circle, which is where it gets its name. Before gold was discovered near Dawson most of the action on the river centered around Circle City. The town now existed on the overflow business from Dawson. When we pulled into Circle City at about eleven o'clock that evening the sun still shone brightly. Captain Murphy docked his boat in the usual way, cutting his engine at the last minute and letting the bow of the *Titus J. Murphy* ram the dock and splinter several timbers.

"I'll take on some firewood," he said.

"Don't take long. I'll be right back." I jumped to the dock and hurried across the main street into the handiest saloon. "How long since the *Northern Queen* left?" I asked the bartender.

"About four hours."

"Was everything all right on board?"

The bartender paused in his ritual bar polishing. "Sure, why shouldn't it be?"

"Have you seen a gent with an oversized ear? You couldn't miss him. His left ear is swollen up like a balloon."

"I know who you mean. He was here all week but I haven't seen him today. I think he bought deck space on the *Northern Queen*. Say, what's a mountie doing this side of the border anyhow? And aren't you Brian Bonner? Goddamit, you *are* Brian Bonner. Get the hell out of here! The last time you came to Circle City you practically ruined poor Tommy Noonan's place." He took a stout club from behind the bar. "Come to think of it, you're wanted on charges here in Alaska. You could be shot out of hand, and there's plenty here who would take pleasure in it. Beat it! And don't come back."

You can see why I didn't try to recruit help in Circle City. Two years before I had visited the town on leave. It was not an altogether pleasant holiday. A card cheat in Tom Noonan's saloon tried to deal seconds to me. I also caught him daubing the deck and wearing a shiner, a reflecting ring that showed him what cards he was dealing. My response to that outrage was to throw the card cheat through Tom Noonan's window, which at the time was the only genuine plate glass window in the Yukon. Noonan had shipped it into Alaska at an expense of three thousand dollars. I further expressed my displeasure by smashing as much furniture as possible before Noonan and his staff could forcibly evict me. Since then I haven't been especially welcome in Circle City.

Captain Murphy had replaced most of his firewood fuel by the time I returned to his boat. "Let's go. Soapy's boys are on the *Northern Queen*, no doubt about it. They bought deck passage."

"Wouldn't somebody know them?"

"There are two hundred and fifty passengers on that boat. No one's going to pay attention to them, unless someone spots Pelletier's ear, and he's wearing a big floppy hat to hide it."

As soon as a head of steam built up in the boiler, Captain Murphy shoved off from Circle City. He opened his fourth quart of gin since our departure from Dawson and seemed to take an interest in the river for a change. "You were talking about sandbars, Brian. I'll be showing you sandbars."

"The Yukon Flats?"

Captain Murphy nodded.

I'd been up and down the river enough times to know the Yukon Flats. Below Circle City the river begins to expand until it's between one and three miles wide, almost a lake. There were many shallows along the Yukon Flats with constantly shifting bottoms that defied charting. It was common for a riverboat to hang up so solidly on a snag that it would have to wait for a passing boat to tow it off. If the *Titus J. Murphy* foundered in the Yukon Flats we might never catch up with the *Northern Queen*.

The sandbars began very soon. I was agreeably surprised by Captain Murphy's ability to avoid them. He seemed to have a sixth sense. We'd be traveling down the center of the river when, for no reason that I could see, he would suddenly shift his wheel a few degrees. Moments later the telltale surface ripples indicating a submerged sandbar would loom next to us and we'd glide past the hazard by a few feet.

The navigational dangers didn't stop Captain Murphy from punishing his bottle. In fact his gin consumption increased with the number of sandbars and floating logs we avoided.

"Look there!"

We were about forty miles past Circle City when we came around a curve in the river and Captain Murphy pointed ahead. Scores of people were milling around on the riverbank ahead as if waiting for a ferry. Others lay on the grassy embankment above the river or sat on rocks a little way out from shore with their feet dangling in the water.

As we came into view they began waving and jumping up and down. Shouts of help went up, even though we could scarcely miss seeing more than two hundred people gathered in front of us. The only ones who didn't cheer our arrival were a half dozen corpses laid out neatly under a tree somewhat apart from the crowd.

I strained my eyes in vain looking for Hannah. There were only a few women in the crowd and she wasn't among them. Captain Murphy put the launch against the embankment and willing hands grabbed the bow and stern ropes to help secure us to shore.

People surrounded me when I jumped down from the launch, each eagerly telling his story in his own way. As a result I couldn't understand anything that was being said. "Quiet! I'll never find out what happened this way. Where's Swiftwater Bill? Come here, Bill. Tell me and make it quick."

Swiftwater Bill was so puffed with anger he could barely speak. "Those goddam . . . the dirty . . . Brian, it was Jules Pelletier and his friends from Skagway!"

"How did they get on the boat?"

Axel Anderson wouldn't let Bill finish. "They must have all come on at Circle City among the deck passengers. And then, as we were about to pull out of the Circle City dock, a doctor came running up and jumped on the boat. At least he claimed to be a doctor. Dr. John Malone from St. Michael is what he called himself. He told us he'd just come in from St. Michael to warn people about the 'cholera epidemic' there and to 'issue medication' to everyone heading in that direction. Dr. Malone told the captain to continue downriver, he'd give us the medication right on the boat and get off at Fort Yukon to care for the people there."

I knew immediately who Dr. Malone was, one of Soapy's men who robbed people after feeding them medication containing a powerful drug. "Knockout drops," I said. "He gave everyone on board the *Northern Queen* knockout drops!" It was so bizarre I almost laughed. Just the kind of stroke Soapy would hit on.

Swiftwater Bill recaptured the explanation. "That's right! The bastard looked like a saint with his black suit and little black bag. Who would have guessed he wasn't a doctor? He said the governor of the territory had sent him upriver and that no one would be allowed to pass through St. Michael without a 'certificate of cholera medication'."

Only Soapy Smith could have dreamed up that phrase. I could picture him sitting at his rolltop desk, toying with different words for his fake doctor to use and chuckling when he hit upon the ploy of forcing everyone on the riverboat to take his knockout drops in order to acquire a 'certificate of cholera medication.'

"Didn't anyone question him?"

"No," Bill said. "Who questions a doctor? Doctors don't answer questions anyway, they give orders. And besides, there was a cholera epidemic at St. Michael last year. Everyone knew that and we weren't surprised it had broken out again. We should have guessed at something when he started his 'medication' with the strongroom guards."

"Didn't anyone fight?" I asked.

Axel pointed at the corpses under the tree.

"They did. The rest of us were passed out by then. We were still groggy or unconscious when Pelletier and his men tossed us off the boat on this shore. That was about four hours ago. Yours is the first boat to come by."

John Tanner forced his way through the crowd. He was the Bank of British North America agent for the Yukon, a lean Englishman with flinty eyes and a red face that advertised his perpetual sour humor. "Bonner, there's five million in gold aboard the *Northern Queen*, as you well know. We must stop those river pirates before they reach St. Michael. They certainly have an ocean steamer waiting. If they make it to sea no one will ever catch them."

"Never mind the gold!" Deephole Johnson thundered. "They've got my woman on board. Brian, they've got *Dolly*."

"What about Hannah?" I asked. "Does anyone know what happened to her?"

"We've taken count," Tanner said. "Nine people are missing. Captain Dolguard, the first mate, the engineer, a helmsman, a stoker, two of the Dawson whores, plus Dolly and Hannah. Obviously they needed men to run the steamboat. You can guess for yourself why they wanted the women."

439

"I'm going after them. Who's coming with me?"

"I am," Tanner said. "Those bastards have a million dollars of my bank's gold."

"I've got some medicine of my own for that so-called *doctor*," Swiftwater Bill declared. "Count me in."

"You're not leaving without me," Johnson called.

"I'll go," Antone Stander volunteered. "They've got a big chunk of my gold, too."

"Same for me," said Axel.

Little Rollo Moon, the handyman defended by Hannah against a murder charge in Dawson, pushed through the crowd. "Hannah saved my life. I'll do what I can to save hers."

"What are you doing here, Rollo?"

"Captain Dolguard gave me a job in the furnace room of the *Northern Queen*. That's another reason I want to come along. He's been good to me."

"All right, Rollo. You're in. And I hope you have a chance to give Pelletier and his men some of what you gave Mike Lynch."

"I'm coming along." Coatless Curly Munro stepped forward.

And those were all the volunteers. Seven

men. A disappointing response. There were several reasons why so few people were willing to join me. First, no one with any sense wanted to go up against Soapy's gang after having met them once. The bodies of those who had been only mildly affected by the knockout drops and were killed trying to fight back made a powerful deterrent to a posse. For another reason, many of the passengers still suffered from stomach cramps, nausea, and other ill effects of the knockout drops. But most important was the fact that so many prospectors had discounted their gold to either Tanner's Bank of British North America or the Canadian Bank of Commerce. They could still collect on their banknotes in Vancouver, so they had suffered no real loss at all and had no personal reason for pursuing the killers. None of the twelve armed guards hired by the banks volunteered to join me. They argued that I'd never catch up with the *Northern Queen* anyway. That's the trouble with hired guns, they scare too easy.

Despite our small numbers I felt we could give Pelletier and his boys a good fight, if we could only catch up with them.

The worst place to be when you are in a

hurry is a boat. Boats are made for leisurely travel. There are no sudden surges of power or sounds of strain. You glide through the water with little evidence of effort. It can be a restful feeling under the right circumstances, but when you're trying to catch up with a pack of killers it can be pure hell. A dozen times I wanted to jump overboard and swim for it. My mind was in such turmoil that I was half convinced I could outdistance the old *Titus J. Murphy*.

We had steamed about thirty miles since coming across the stranded passengers when Captain Murphy cut back his engine and began edging his boat toward the riverbank.

"What's wrong? Why are you stopping?"

He answered my questions by pointing out a pair of bodies lying half on the riverbank and half in the water. And one was a woman!

Murphy could be gentle with his boat when he wanted. He beached it expertly on the sandy shore while Deephole Johnson and I both jumped into the water and waded to the bodies. I reached them first and turned over the woman. It was Dolly Morgan. At first I thought Dolly was still alive and smiling at me with her wide painted mouth. What I confused for smiling red lips were the two bloody edges of a long cut. Someone had slit Dolly's throat from ear to ear. She was naked and bruised as well. It looked like the work of Fatty Green.

"Dear God," Johnson wept.

I stood back while he moved her up to a grassy spot and laid her out carefully in the shade. He knelt at her side, crying quietly and smoothing her hair. The others in the boat respected his grief by turning their eyes away from Dolly's nakedness and concentrating on the second corpse.

Captain Dolguard lay fully dressed with his legs on the shore and his torso in the water. When I pulled him up on the sand we could see he'd been shot a number of times through the chest.

"They made a mistake killing Dolguard," Murphy said. "He was the best pilot on the Yukon River. Without him they'll play hell getting that big steamboat through the Yukon Flats. The *Northern Queen* may not draw much water, but she's a wide old bitch."

"Let's push on then. If they do run the *Northern Queen* aground we might have a chance to catch up with them." I went over to Deephole Johnson. "We have to move out. I'm sorry, but there isn't time to bury Dolly.

Maybe we can come back, if things work out."

"I understand," Johnson said.

"You can stay here with her, if you'd rather."

"No, I want to get my hands on that bunch even more than you do." He looked up at me. "The funny thing is, after a while Dolly didn't even care about the money. All she ever really wanted was a good husband." He rose and we climbed back into the launch.

As we continued downriver my mind was in a greater frenzy than ever. If they'd done that to Dolly, what had become of Hannah? Was she already dead somewhere along the shore, her body washed up on some side creek, or still floating in the river? Even if she was alive, could we overtake Soapy Smith's gang?

It occurred to me that I was making a serious mistake in thinking about the killers as "Soapy Smith's gang." They weren't his gang anymore. They had a new leader, Jules Pelletier. Although Pelletier was the smartest of the gang he came nowhere close to having Soapy's abilities. He'd proved that by killing Captain Dolguard instead of forcing him to pilot the boat. Soapy would have made full use of the captain. Now that Pelletier had successfully carried out Soapy's plan for a five-million-dollar robbery, he'd be anxious to establish himself as leader. He'd start giving orders and some would be mistakes.

We ran on down the river without encountering any problems. My watch read two A.M. but the sun continued to shine low on the horizon, casting long shadows. Occasionally we saw a lone moose or a small herd of caribou grazing on the hills.

I studied the horizon for some sign of smoke from the *Northern Queen*'s two big stacks. The sky gave me no comfort; it remained clear and flawlessly blue all through the night.

15

WE could tell when morning came only because the sun rose higher in the sky. There was still no sign of the *Northern Queen* and I was beginning to have private doubts that we'd ever catch up with her. Then our fortunes changed.

"Smoke!" Captain Murphy called.

And there it was, a plume of black smoke drifting above the river in the distance.

"How far away?" I asked.

"Ten miles mebbe."

"How did we catch up to 'em?" Swiftwater Bill wondered. "They were four hours ahead of us."

Captain Murphy took a slug of gin while he considered the question. "Anyone know the first mate's name?"

"I do," Rollo Moon said. "It's Tim Prentiss."

"Tim Prentiss!" Murphy laughed harshly. "Well there you are, Prentiss couldn't pilot his way to an outhouse."

"That's true," Rollo said. "Captain

Dolguard always piloted the boat himself when we were going through a hazardous stretch of river like the Flats."

"They probably hung up on a sandbar and spent a couple of hours getting off," Captain Murphy suggested. "After that they slowed to fifteen knots to avoid more problems. They think no one's after them, so why shouldn't they slow up. They'll go back to top speed when they see our smoke."

Tanner asked how long it would be before that happened.

"Don't know," Captain Murphy answered. "Depends if they've posted a lookout on the texas, which I doubt. And whether they think another boat could catch them, which I doubt. And whether they can see the little bit of smoke the *Titus J. Murphy* makes, which I also doubt."

Tanner persisted. "So we might be able to close to within a mile or two of the *Northern Queen* before they spot us."

"Unless they suddenly speed up to twenty knots," Captain Murphy replied. "Which I doubt."

One thing worried me about closing in on the *Northern Queen*. "If we do manage to overtake that steamboat and try to board her,

Pelletier may do something crazy like killing Hannah just for spite."

"We don't even know that Hannah is still alive," Antone said.

"We don't know that she isn't. And there are others on that boat besides Hannah. Pelletier might hold them hostage. All I'm saying is now that we've come so close, we'd better be damned careful about what we do."

"No one wants to see innocent people hurt," Axel said. "I'll be honest with you though, my gold comes first. I want my gold back. If you've got another way to do that besides catching up with the *Northern Queen* and trying to board her, let's hear it."

I didn't have another way. Any other solution would have to involve a miracle.

A minute later Captain Murphy handed us that miracle. "I've got one idea," he said slowly. "It's a wild one, though."

"Let's hear it," Curly Munro demanded.

Murphy tickled his imagination with another sip of gin. "In just about five minutes the *Northern Queen* will go around a pretty sharp bend in the river. It's a hairpin, in fact. Then the river runs straight for two miles before meandering back to its original course."

"So?" Tanner said.

"What I'm saying," Captain Murphy explained, "is that for a few minutes the Yukon river will be right over there." He pointed to our left.

"How far?" Swiftwater Bill said quickly.

"About a mile," the captain answered. "Hell of a mile, though. Uphill and down, I expect."

"What you're saying," I prompted, "is that if some of us went ashore right here we could cut across that hairpin and come out on the river ahead of the *Northern Queen*."

"Mebbe," Captain Murphy said.

"Let's do it!" Johnson yelled.

Not everyone was as convinced the idea would work. Tanner, for one. "Suppose we do come out ahead of the *Northern Queen*," he said. "How do we board her from shore?"

"I was getting around to that," Captain Murphy rasped. "There's a hill crowned by a big flat rock where the river turns back to the southwest. The crown is high up, about sixty feet above the river, and it hangs out a few feet over the water. Now to maneuver the last turn in the hairpin the *Northern Queen* has to slow to five knots and make a wide turn. She'll come within mebbe thirty feet of the shore. A few men with nerve and luck might be able to jump from that big flat rock onto the riverboat. I'd try to land on the texas or the hurricane deck myself. Those're the highest decks. Wouldn't be more than a twenty-foot fall that way."

"It's worth a try," I decided. "If we don't make it across the hills in time, we won't have lost anything. Captain Murphy can always pick us up when he comes around the river-bend."

"I'm game," Curly Munro said.

"This could be our only chance," Tanner agreed. "Once we reach the Yukon Flats they'll know they're being chased. You can see for miles on the Flats."

Everyone agreed to the plan. I suggested we leave the rifles on board and each take a pistol. Carrying rifles would just slow us down, and they wouldn't be as good as pistols for close-in fighting on the riverboat. While each man was loading his pistol I drew Swift-water Bill aside. "Bill, I want you to stay on board."

He objected until I explained my reasons in a quiet voice. "Whatever happens to me or Hannah or the others, I don't want Pelletier to escape. If we're killed on this try I want you to set fire to this launch and ram it into the *Northern Queen*. That steamboat is a floating tinderbox. I noticed a bucket of coal oil in the stern locker, that ought to do the trick. You'll have to deal with Captain Murphy, he's attached to this old tub. I'm depending on you, Bill."

"I won't let you down."

I told the others that Bill would stay on board the launch without going into the real reason. Instead I explained that we needed a man in the launch when Captain Murphy got within rifle range of the *Northern Queen*. "Bill's a good rifle shot," I said. "He could pick off anyone on deck and we'll need the cover."

"There she goes," Captain Murphy announced. "You can see from her smoke that she's turning left into the hairpin." He glanced at the shore. "If you head due west from here you should hit the spot where the river doubles back." He nudged the boat into the riverbank.

We clambered off in a bunch, sinking waist deep in water with our pistols raised above our heads, and waded up into the wooded slopes.

"This way." I took the lead, starting uphill

as fast as I could travel. The others fell in behind me.

A mile doesn't sound very far, but in the Yukon it can seem like ten miles. The Yukon in summer is a giant tundra. The snow melts and runs off from the mountains into the streams and rivers. What water doesn't reach the rivers collects in huge swampy areas because it can't all percolate down through the permafrost. In turn the wetlands produce mosquitoes by the tens of billions.

We hit a swampy area right away, a hilly marsh full of overgrown shrubbery and fallen trees. The mosquitoes closed in with a vengeance, covering our faces and flying into our open eyes and mouths. They'd been relatively scarce on the fast moving river. The pools of standing water we splashed through bred insect life of every kind and we were fresh blood to them.

I heard the others slapping at themselves as they ran. They were only wasting energy and slowing themselves down. There was no use trying to tell them that, I'd only waste my own breath.

As we came out of the marsh the ground under our feet hardened and became rocky. The mosquitoes thinned. I guessed we'd come about a quarter of a mile. Another hill loomed in front of us and we scrambled up the incline on hands and knees. Our breathing was very labored by then, and with every deep breath we sucked a variety of mosquitoes and flying gnats into our lungs.

"Hey! Help me!" The plea came from Rollo. "I hurt my ankle."

Tanner looked at the little man with disgust. "That's all we need." And addressing the rest of us, "We'll have to leave him."

"No!" Rollo managed to stand, but he couldn't put his full weight on his left foot. "It's just a sprain. Someone help me, let me work out the sprain. I'll be all right."

I grabbed him under one arm. "Curly, take his other side."

"That's all we need," Tanner repeated.

The others went ahead. Curly and I half carried Rollo as he tried to put increasing pressure on his left foot.

"How's it feel?" Curly asked.

"Better . . . better."

We traveled another quarter mile with Rollo hanging onto us. I was about to agree that Rollo would have to make his own way to the river when he said, "You can let go of me now. I'll be all right."

We removed our support and he winced in pain. "You go ahead, I'll catch up."

The terrain was sloping down now, improving our progress. The river could be seen through the trees. We emerged onto a very high embankment above the river. The embankment was almost a cliff, mostly limestone covered with moss and scrub brush.

"That must be it." Axel pointed out a large granite outcropping that hung over the river. The big sheet of rock was located just opposite the final turn in the hairpin, as Captain Murphy had indicated. It slanted up from its base. A few men crouched behind it couldn't be seen by anyone on the deck of an approaching riverboat.

"By God, it might work!" I said. "Let's get up there before the *Northern Queen* pulls by."

We could see the smoke of the riverboat approaching this last bend at a slow speed.

Rollo caught up with us as we slid down behind the rock.

"Get out of sight," Axel commanded.

"And try not to blow any of us apart with that thing," I added.

Rollo had pulled out his pistol and was fiddling nervously with the hammer. "I won't," he promised.

"Will your ankle take the jump?"

"I'm *all right!*"

He wasn't all right. The little streetcar conductor from Seattle was scared as hell and I didn't blame him. He kept cocking and uncocking his revolver. "Don't do that. It might go off and warn Pelletier's boys that we're here."

Rollo blushed. "I'm sorry. I guess I'm nervous."

"We all are."

That was no understatement. Antone's face had gone chalk white and his hands were trembling. Axel sat on his haunches repeating a prayer over and over in a whisper. Next to me Coatless Curly Munro kept wiping the sweat from his face with the back of his hand, and the sweat wasn't completely caused by the mile run and hot weather. Even Tanner looked as if he'd had second thoughts. We all had tight stomachs except for Deephole Johnson, who looked cool and expectant.

"There she is," Axel whispered.

The *Northern Queen* churned down the river at a steady ten knots. I was accustomed to seeing noisy groups of passengers lounging on the decks and leaning out the windows of the grand salon with champagne glasses in their hands. Today the steamboat was deserted, a ghost ship except for a few unfriendly figures.

I spotted Yea Mow Hopkins leaning against one of the cabin doors on the hurricane deck and staring moodily at the hills. Obviously no one on the riverboat had seen the smoke of the *Titus J. Murphy* or Hopkins wouldn't have been so relaxed. Our luck was holding.

Just then Jules Pelletier came out of the grand salon. He had removed his big floppy hat and his huge left ear jiggled merrily as he strode along the promenade with an air of ownership. He stopped to look over the side and spit down into the river. I could have picked him off then, but that would have warned the others.

The third gang member in evidence was the kid they called Blue Jay. I couldn't see his face, but that red jacket of his stood out. He was pacing inside the pilothouse behind the helmsman. The helmsman's face was clear enough. He was a middle-aged man who looked plenty scared and very tired. There was a gash on his cheek, probably from a punishment blow for running the *Northern Queen* onto a sandbar earlier.

The helmsman wasn't going to make that same mistake twice. As the steamboat approached the sharp turn it slowed to about five knots. The helmsman moved the wheel slightly and began bringing the steamboat closer to our side of the river in preparation for the wide turn.

"The damned boat's not going to come close enough!" Antone whispered.

The *Northern Queen* was now fifty yards upstream and within twenty-five yards of the riverbank. It would have to draw another ten yards closer to give us a chance to board her.

"That's as close as she's coming," Johnson said.

"What'll we do?" someone else whispered.

"We've got to go!" Johnson insisted.

"Not me," said Antone. "Unless that boat comes closer to the shoreline I'm not jumping. I just decided I'd rather be poor than dead."

"You'll jump," said Axel. he turned the barrel of his revolver toward Antone. "You'll jump or I'll blow your guts out."

I pushed Axel's pistol away. "This isn't Split-Up Island. Anyone who wants to come along is welcome. When we get on board, try to take the pilothouse and swing the wheel around until the *Northern Queen* runs up on the beach."

"It's coming closer to the shore," Curly said.

The *Northern Queen* had drawn nearer to us. It would still be a hell of a jump, but at least Antone seemed ready to follow the rest of us.

"Don't stick your revolver in your belt," I suggested. "You're liable to lose it when you hit the deck."

That was the last piece of advice I had time to give. The *Northern Queen* came steaming up to our position, its two big stacks visible above the level of our hiding place.

"Here I go!" Deephole Johnson stood and took a running jump off the rock.

"Not yet!" My warning was too late to stop him. Despite our need to stay out of sight, I leaned out to watch him. What I saw sickened me. He'd jumped a few seconds too soon, while the steamboat was still completing its turn near our hiding place. He missed the upper decks by several feet and his head cracked against the hull as he fell into the water.

"What happened?" Curly asked.

The truth would have paralyzed them so I said, "He made it."

The upper decks suddenly came nearer. I went into a crouch and pushed off into the air. My jump seemed pitifully short, but fortunately the steamboat was moving in my direction as I fell.

I hit the roof of the texas with a splintering crash going right through the flimsy wood and landing in one of the oppulent first-class cabins. As I struggled to my feet I heard the others landing on the steamboat. Any idea I might have had about making silent, catlike landings on the *Northern Queen* and taking Pelletier and his men by surprise was quickly put aside. We had all made a hell of a racket, but at least we were on board.

Shouting broke out all over the ship, followed quickly by the rattle of gunfire. I cocked the Colt and went out onto the promenade.

The first person I saw was Coatless Curly Munro lying on the deck with half his face missing, torn apart by at least two bullets. I didn't waste time wondering what had happened. Somebody had the promenade covered and that was all I needed to know. I vaulted over the rail as a bullet ripped into the deck where I'd just been standing. Out of the corner of my eye I saw Blue Jay firing at me from the window of the pilothouse. He fired two more shots as I dropped out of his field of fire onto the next deck.

"It's Bonner!" he yelled. "He's on the hurricane deck."

Yea Mow Hopkins and Marshal Taylor came charging up the companion from the main deck. Hopkins's shaved skull made a beautiful target. I split it open with one .44 bullet that sent the Chinese hatchetman flying backwards down the steps. Taylor had already gone into a shooting position, holding his revolver at arm's length with both hands. He got off a shot too fast and a sharp sizzling sound went past my ear. He tried again but his revolver misfired. Taylor went pale. "No, man!" he begged.

I aimed and fired at just that moment. Taylor's head snapped forward, then rolled back to reveal the bloody hole where the bullet had penetrated his neck. His body went into spasms as he collapsed on the deck.

Someone ran through the grand salon, a man in a black coat. I turned quickly and fired through the window of the salon, but he dropped to the floor. I slid along the passageway and ducked through the door to the men's bar. The bar ran all the way to the opposite promenade. It was a plush bar with a great variety of bottles in the racks and brass cuspidors on the carpet. I went through to the the other door without pausing. That was probably the first time in my life I'd ever passed through a bar without stopping for a drink.

I opened the door to the opposite deck and peeped out. The steamboat had come out of its big turn and we began heading out into the Yukon Flats. There was a lot of gunfire toward the stern, pistol shots and the roar of shotguns.

Someone came running in my direction and I ducked back inside the door. As the man went by I stepped out with the Colt cocked and leveled it at his back. I came within an ace of putting a bullet in Axel Anderson.

"Axel."

He spun around with a terrified look and I had to knock his gun aside to avoid being plugged.

"Bonner!"

"What's happening back there?"

"Rollo Moon is dead! His bad ankle broke when he landed on the deck. Pelletier just walked up and cut him in half with a shotgun blast. Rollo was too frightened to lift his pistol. He just sat there crying and let himself be killed. It was awful."

I pulled him back inside the men's bar as someone hurried along the deck above. "Keep your voice down. What about Antone and Tanner?"

"That's who they're shooting at now. They've got Antone and Tanner pinned down behind some crates on the stern. There's no way they can escape. They can't even jump overboard, the paddlewheels would grind them up."

"Let's go and give them a hand."

Axel pushed me away. His eyes were wide with fear. "Not me! I'm going over the side. This was crazy. It won't work. The gold isn't worth it. Where are Johnson and Munro? I'll bet they're dead, too." He read the answer in my stare. "I knew it!"

"Have you seen Hannah?"

"No. You do what you want. I'm getting out of here right now."

Before I could stop him he threw open the door to the men's bar, rushed across the deck, and jumped over the rail. The splash he made drew a lot of attention.

"Someone's in the water!" Pelletier called out. "There he is! Get him!" And a furious burst of gunfire let loose at poor Axel.

I decided to try reaching the pilothouse while everyone concentrated on killing Axel. The companion to the hurricane deck was clear and I took the steps two at a time. Once on the hurricane deck I paused to see how Axel was making out. I saw him swimming toward shore about twenty yards out from the steamboat. The water was pocked with tiny white splashes as bullets hit all around him. Pelletier and his boys were laughing and making bets with each other about who'd hit the target first.

Someone won. Axel's head jerked back and he stopped swimming. A red stain spread out around him and he slipped under the surface of the water.

I went on up to the promenade around the texas. There was no cover over the deck and if Blue Jay was still up in the pilothouse I'd know it soon.

Sure enough, he stuck his head out the window again and his pistol bucked in his hand as he fired three fast shots at me. I fell flat and rolled against a cabin door as the bullets whined past me.

"Bonner's back up here!" Blue Jay called to his friends in the stern.

I raised to one knee and pumped several shots into the pilothouse. I intended to kill Blue Jay and beach the *Northern Queen*. I bellied along the promenade until I came to the iron ladder that went up to the pilothouse. Before rushing the pilothouse I reloaded the chambers of the Colt and tested its action.

"Hey, Bonner," Blue Jay said. "Come on up. The view is great."

I answered, hoping to anger him into a foolish act. "Did you ever catch the view from the hills above Skagway, kid? It was the last thing your pal Slim Jim saw before I killed him. He died hard up there."

Blue Jay replied with a volley of bullets that tore up the deck a couple of feet behind me. When I heard his hammer fall on an empty chamber, I knew I'd never have a better chance at him. I scrambled up the ladder and emerged at the pilothouse door while Blue Jay was still reloading his revolver.

Behind Blue Jay was the helmsman, his face contorted with fear. His knuckles stood out white as he grasped the great wooden wheel that was taller than he. To steer it he was seated on a tall chair that raised him above the wheel to give him a commanding view of the river.

"Drop!" I told him.

The helmsman threw himself off the chair as I shot Blue Jay through the chest. The force of the bullet lifted the kid off his feet and spun him around. He hit the glass window of the pilothouse and shattered it. Blue Jay's young face was twisted with pain and surprise as he fell to the floor.

My goal was still to beach the *Northern Queen*. The steamboat was continuing down the Yukon on a straight course without the helmsman at its big wheel. The wheel was locked in position with a rope brake. If I didn't beach the boat quickly we'd be so far out into the Flats that the nearest shore would be a mile away.

The helmsman still lay on the floor, arms covering his head. I shook him roughly. "Come on, you've got work to do."

He whimpered and closed his arms tighter over his head. "Please, I'm not one of *them*. Don't kill me."

"I know you're not with them. I want you to beach this tub. Put it as far up on the shore as you can. Tear the hell out of the bottom so they can't get it moving again."

465

"No! They'll kill me. They beat me with pistols just for catching us up on a snag. If I beach her they'll kill me for sure. Leave me alone!"

The man was too scared to be of use. I was loosening the rope brake myself when someone began climbing the iron ladder I'd used to reach the pilothouse. There was a second ladder on the opposite side which another of the gang was climbing at the same time.

"Blue Jay?" one of them called. "Are you all right?"

I put my head out the pilothouse window and fired down at the speaker. It was Old Man Tripp, his white beard flowing in the wind as he came up the ladder. My bullet thwanged off the ladder and Old Man Tripp quickly fired back. His bullet crashed through the window near my head, showering my face with fragments of glass and temporarily blinding me. I wiped the glass away with my free hand, at the same time firing twice more in Old Man Tripp's direction.

I heard footsteps behind me and turned too late. My eyes cleared just in time to see Jules Pelletier swinging at me with a shotgun. The heavy barrel of the weapon caught me on the side of the head. I stumbled, dropping my

Colt, and grabbed at Pelletier. He hit me again in the same place. The pain traveled straight to my legs, which went out from under me. Pelletier hit me once more as I fell.

16

"**B**RIAN! Are you all right? Can you talk? Try to open your eyes. Please!" The words meant nothing to me but I responded to the voice. Hannah's voice. Talking to me from far away. Fuzzy at first. Clearer after a while. So familiar and welcome. But I couldn't open my eyes. When I tried to move any part of my head an enormous cloud filled my mind. I felt drugged by pain. Unable to coordinate the smallest movement. All I wanted was a peaceful place to lay myself down. I knew that. I knew I was standing and that I wanted to lay myself down. How I could stand was a mystery. No parts of my body were working, especially not my legs. They were numb. Yet I was standing.

"Please, Brian. We don't have much time. Try to open your eyes. Try!"

Gradually my eyes did open. Everything in front of me was out of focus in shades of gray and brown. A shot of Perry Davis Painkiller would have straightened out the whole problem.

"That's it, Brian. Move your head up and down."

I tried. My head did move. I couldn't keep it where I wanted it, but that was another problem. One step at a time. First my eyes. I struggled with them, focusing first on a patch of gray, then on a patch of brown. Other colors revealed themselves. Blues and reds. The reds had tangles in them.

"Hannah."

"Yes, Brian." She celebrated my survival with a single sob. "When they brought you in I thought you were dead. I thought they'd hung you up there just to torture me with your death. They'd do that."

"Hung me up? Where are we?"

Some feeling had finally worked its way into my legs. I was standing on solid footing, but for some peculiar reason I could lift both my legs without falling down. I noticed that when I did that my wrists began to ache. With great reluctance I moved my head far enough to look at one wrist. There was a steel shackle around it. The shackle was fixed to a metal pipe about twelve inches above my head. "Where the hell are we?"

"The boiler room of the *Northern Queen*."

"Whew! That explains the heat. I thought I'd died and gone to hell."

"Pelletier and his men are up on deck. I heard so much shooting that I thought . . . I hoped . . . but they won or you wouldn't be in irons."

"I didn't bring enough men," I said. "And most of those I did bring weren't good enough. They cut us up pretty bad. I'm surprised Pelletier left me alive." My head felt better. I blinked back a sharp pain behind my eyes and looked around the boiler room. There were several more pairs of handcuffs fixed to the pipes that ran between the boilers, enough to chain up at least a dozen people. "Who are those for?"

"They had the other girls chained up there, Dolly Morgan and the two from Paradise Alley. Captain Dolguard, too, until they needed him to pilot the boat. Then they took him out and I never saw him again."

"He's dead. What about the two girls?"

Hannah shivered even though the boiler room heat was stifling. "Fatty Green took them and Dolly Morgan up to the grand salon one at a time. Have you seen him? He's gross, hardly a man at all. He's a thing. His eyes are the size of raisins and he licks his fingers whenever he looks at me. He must weigh four hundred pounds and I don't think he's ever been in a bath. After he takes a girl out of here you can hear her screaming all over the boat. None of them ever came back. I'm sure they're dead."

"Dolly is dead," I confirmed. "I guessed that Fatty Green had killed her. Her throat was cut."

Hannah took that news calmly. "Fatty says he's saving me for last. That's all, just that he's *saving me*. I knew what he meant. Brian, what can we do?"

I braced my feet and began testing the pipe my irons were attached to. Unfortunately, the *Northern Queen* was a well-built ship. All the pipes were solidly connected to their boilers. The pipe wouldn't bend or pull loose from its fittings. If Hannah and I had been shackled to the same pipe, we might have had a chance to pull it loose. But we were chained on opposite sides of the compartment with eight feet of space between us.

"That's no good," Hannah said. "Captain Dolguard and the ship's engineer were hand-cuffed to that pipe at first. They both tried to break loose and couldn't."

"Where's the engineer now?"

"Fatty Green was guarding him this morning, along with the stoker and the first mate. He put all of them into the furnace room to feed coal and they wiggled out to the opposite deck through the coal chute. I guess they slipped overboard and got away. God knows where they went. Pelletier was furious for letting them escape. That's the only good thing that's happened today."

That explained why Pelletier hadn't killed me straight off. He was short of labor. He probably planned to use me as a stoker until they came within a few miles of St. Michael. He'd kill me then, and it wouldn't be an easy death. "Who else is on board?"

Hannah put her chin down and used it to scratch her shoulder. "Let's see, there's Jules Pelletier . . . Fatty Green . . . a youngster they call Blue Jay . . . an elderly man with a beard, I think they call him Tripp . . . the Chinese bodyguard I met in Skagway . . . Marshal Taylor . . . and Doc Malone. That's all, I think."

Not as bad as it might have been. "I narrowed the odds somewhat. Pelletier, Fatty Green, Old Man Tripp, and the Doc are the only ones left. How the hell did you fall for that fake doctor, Hannah? Of everyone on board, you should have spotted him for a fraud first."

"Me?" She groaned. "I was the worst of all. You know how I admire doctors. I thought Doc Malone was a wonderful man, another Father Judge. Fighting a cholera epidemic single-handed, and all that. I went through the steamboat with him and whenever someone balked at taking the 'medication' I bullied them into swallowing it. What an *idiot* I was. But Brian, he was so convincing. I could have sworn he was a real doctor."

Cool air rushed into the boiler room as Jules Pelletier opened the iron door and stepped through. He was followed by Fatty Green and Doc Malone. I had never seen Fatty or the Doc up close. Fatty Green was even more disgusting than Hannah's description. His skin hung in great folds under a loose fitting pair of trainman's overalls which were so black from filth that none of their original blue denim color could be detected. Besides being the size of raisins, Fatty Green's eyes were so close together they appeared to be one large misshapen eye in the middle of his head. He wore the perpetual smile of a nasty child. As soon as Fatty's little eyes came to rest on Hannah, he began licking his fingers.

Put Fatty Green together with Jules Pelletier and his gigantic ear and you could start your own carnival sideshow.

Doc Malone was the opposite. He was tall and dressed in a conservative dark suit. His hawkish profile commanded attention and he had the piercing eyes of a man accustomed to the respect and obedience of others. If he'd ordered me to take a spoonful of cholera medicine, I'd have opened my mouth and said "ahh" for him. It was easy to see how he had put over his act.

"So you've come around." Pelletier strutted up to me. "Good. We need you . . . for a while." He took a key from his pocket and gave it to Fatty. "Put a pair of those cuffs on Bonner's ankles. We don't want him running off from us. He might fall down a companion and hurt himself."

"Okay, Jules," Fatty said. His voice had a mincing quality that was at odds with his size.

"I'm not sure we should keep him alive," Doc Malone said. "He's too dangerous. Kill him right now." The doctor, on the other hand, spoke with just the right voice for his appearance, direct, competent sounding, and full of authority.

"That's fine with me," Pelletier agreed. "If you want to shovel coal all the way to St. Michael, go ahead. You've done damned little to earn your share as it is."

Doc Malone regarded Pelletier cooly. "I'd like to see you put two hundred people out of action in one stroke. It was my medicine that captured this steamboat, Jules, not your guns."

" 'Medicine,' he calls it." Pelletier laughed. "You should've seen the folks topple over, Bonner. Funniest sight of my life."

"What happened to the other men who came on board with me?" I asked. "The ones back by the paddlebox."

"They jumped overboard before we could finish them. I imagine they were pulled into the paddlewheels and killed." Doc Malone sounded reasonably satisfied with their fate.

"We finally spotted that little boat you used to follow us," Pelletier said. "How many men are left on it?"

"A dozen," I lied.

Doc Malone smiled. "If you had another dozen men they would have been with you. Besides, that small launch couldn't carry twenty men without running up on a snag. A poor lie, Bonner."

"You won't think so when they catch up with you."

"They aren't gonna catch us." Pelletier looked at the pressure gauge on the boilers. "As soon as we get through the Flats and onto a nice safe piece of water, we're going up to twenty knots and pull ahead of that little tin-whistle bathtub."

Fatty Green had finished locking the shackles around my ankles. "Can I have that last girl now, Jules?" he asked in his high nasal voice.

"Not yet, Fatty."

Fatty pouted. "You promised."

"You'll have her. Don't be so greedy, I gave you the other three already."

Fatty waved his pudgy fingers at Hannah, "But she's the best."

"You'll get her. Just shut up about it." Doc Malone sounded disgusted with his partners and anxious to rid himself of their company.

Pelletier gave the key to the shackles to Doc Malone. "Free his hands and put him in that furnace room to shovel coal. The pressure is starting to drop in the boilers."

"Why me?" Doc objected.

"Because I say so," Pelletier replied. "Old Man Tripp is keeping an eye on the helmsman. Fatty isn't quick or smart enough to guard Bonner, and I have to get rid of those bodies on the other decks before they start stinking up the whole ship. Don't worry, I'll take my turn watching Bonner when the furnace needs stoking." He smiled at me. "I wouldn't miss it, in fact." He put his hand on Fatty's shoulder. "Tell you what, Fatty. When we're close to St. Michael you can have your fun with the girl right in front of Bonner. How about that? Won't that be a laugh?"

"I don't want to wait 'till St. Michael!" Fatty's disappointment erupted in a scream.

"You'll have to," Pelletier said sharply. "If we gave you the girl before that, Bonner would never shovel coal for us. He'll only stoke the furnace if he thinks he has a chance to get loose and save Hannah. So Doc, keep your eyes on that mountie. Don't let him get too close to you."

Doc Malone drew out his pistol. "Never fear, he's safe enough with me."

Before leaving the boiler room Pelletier sneered at me one more time. "The Man Who Killed Almighty Voice. That Cree must have been deaf, dumb, and blind to let you nail him."

When Pelletier and Fatty were gone, Doc Malone carefully unlocked my shackles. As he did so he kept his pistol in my ribs with the hammer cocked. "One suspicious move and this gun will go off in your gut."

As soon as my hands were free, Doc stepped away from me. "Go into the furnace room."

I could take steps no longer than six inches, so it took several minutes to make my way through the door leading into the furnace room. Doc may not have known how to hold a scalpel, but he could certainly handle a gun. He kept me covered every minute that my hands were free. I had half made up my mind to try tossing a shovelful of coal in Doc's face and make a dive for him, but he scotched that plan by staying on the far side of the furnace room.

It took me fifteen minutes to build up the fire. Doc estimated I'd have to spend about fifteen minutes out of every hour stoking the fire for the next ten days until we reached the outskirts of St. Michael.

"I imagine you've got an ocean steamer

waiting there," I said, shutting the furnace cockpit with my shovel.

"That's right," Doc admitted. "A month from now I'll be in some other part of the world, rich and retired from practice." He straightened abruptly. "Put down that shovel!"

The good doctor didn't miss much. I had been moving my hand down the handle of the shovel in what I thought was a casual way, preparing to throw the heavy tool at his head. "Sorry. Didn't mean to scare you."

"The only thing that scares me is the idea of shoveling coal for the next ten days. Please don't be foolish again. Be smart so you can live until we reach St. Michael."

"You're very generous, Doc."

He shrugged. "I don't like to shovel coal. And besides, you did me a favor by killing Blue Jay, Yea Mow Hopkins, and the marshal. That automatically doubled my slice of the pie."

"That was just a small favor. Frank Reid did you a real favor."

"By killing Soapy? He certainly did. Soapy would have taken two-thirds of the loot for himself. He was a very greedy man."

"And you're not?"

"Not like Soapy. He wanted the whole world."

"I guess he'll have to take it in six-foot chunks."

Doc watched me just as carefully as I shuffled back into the boiler room. Hannah was slumped in her bonds asleep. Fatigue had finally caught up with her. Again Doc Malone kept his pistol in my ribs while he fastened the shackles to the boiler pipe above my head. It was frustrating to have such a thorough man standing guard on me.

He tested my cuffs to make sure they were tight, then put away his gun. "That should hold you. You have a good sense of humor, Bonner. It's too bad Captain Dolguard didn't have one. We didn't want to kill him. We needed him to help run the steamboat. But he made so much noise about everything, especially about Fatty's little parties in the grand salon, that Jules got fed up and shot him."

"I'll try to keep my voice down."

Doc chuckled and went to the door. "I don't understand why Jules hates you so much. See you later."

I tested the shackles again but the boiler pipe still wouldn't give. Feeling angry and exhausted, I fell into the same kind of uncomfortable sleep that had claimed Hannah.

I was awakened by the big steel door opening from the main deck. Pelletier came into the boiler room with Fatty, the two of them carrying block and tackle equipment, which they dumped into a corner.

Pelletier was in an amiable mood. "We'll use this block and tackle to move the gold onto the steamship that's waiting for us. Five million in gold. What a haul!"

"Don't spend it all in one place."

The swollen left ear bobbed up and down as Pelletier nodded his head. "Doc said you were full of jokes. You won't think everything is so funny when I turn your girl friend over to Fatty."

Hannah came awake, too. The brief rest, however uncomfortable, had restored her spirit. "The last laugh hasn't been heard yet, you freak-eared sadist." Pelletier was unlucky enough to be standing within range of Hannah's legs. She suddenly kicked high with one foot, catching Pelletier square on his bulbous left ear.

Pelletier howled and doubled over in pain, clutching the injured ear with both hands.

Tears rolled down his face. The puffed-up piece of flesh turned a crimson red. Pelletier nursed the thing like a sick baby, bawling and fondling it until the crimson faded into a less violent pink. Presently he stopped sobbing and, with a few final soothing caresses, let go of the ear.

I feared Hannah had gone too far. Pelletier turned on her in such a dark rage I thought he might kill her on the spot.

"You dirty little bitch." He slapped Hannah so hard that her head bounced off the boiler plate. "Bitch," he repeated, hitting her again. I strained to reach him, but there was nothing I could do. Fatty giggled as he watched me struggle. Pelletier slapped and punched Hannah several more times, until a smear of blood spread down from her nose and mouth. That seemed to satisfy him for the moment.

"Here." He handed Fatty the key to the handcuffs. "Shackle her feet together like Bonner's." He spat in Hannah's face. "You've just begun to pay for that."

A grinding noise interrupted Pelletier's further plans for Hannah. It began as a low distant sound, building into the heavy screech of metal binding against some large, gritty obstacle. The triple galvanized plates of the steamboat seemed to rise underfoot. Then the boat lurched and came to a stop, throwing Pelletier and Fatty against one of the boilers.

"What the hell happened this time?" Pelletier swore.

The stern paddlewheels could be heard making their endless revolutions through the water, but the steamboat wouldn't move. A strain began building up in the boilers, reflected in the rising pressure on the master gauge. "We're grounded again!"

Pelletier quickly reduced the boiler pressure by turning a valve that allowed the excess steam to escape through vents, and rushed out of the boiler room. Fatty followed like a faithful dog.

"You shouldn't have done that, Hannah."

She licked away some of the blood from around her mouth. "I'm glad I kicked him. Did you watch his ear? You've never seen a sunset that red."

"He was about to *kill* you!"

"So what! He's going to kill us anyway. I'd rather get in a few licks first, wouldn't you?"

"Hannah, it's ten days to St. Michael. Somewhere along the way Pelletier will make a mistake. Just try to keep your damned mouth shut for once and play the breaks."

The door to the main deck had been left open and we could hear some serious swearing going on outside. I gathered that the steamboat was again snagged on either a submerged tree trunk or a sandbar. Doc Malone and Pelletier were exchanging opinions about the extent of the problem at the top of their lungs. Old Man Tripp was still up in the pilothouse, and I imagined the helmsman would suffer another beating. They couldn't hurt him too badly since the steamboat was already dangerously low on crew; the helmsman was the last man they could afford to lose. Old Man Tripp would stick to him like flypaper.

There was a splash. Someone had gone into the waist-deep water of the Flats to find out exactly what the *Northern Queen* had piled into.

Fatty appeared in the doorway of the boiler room wearing a sly smile. He came in and closed the door behind him. "Jules is trying to fix the boat." His high voice had an edge to it, a tremor of excitement. "And look." He held up the key to the handcuffs. "Jules forgot to take the key back from Fatty." he tittered and came close to Hannah.

"What do you want?" Hannah said.

"Fatty likes you."

"You'd better stay away from her," I warned Fatty. "Pelletier doesn't want you to touch her yet."

Fatty's thick fingers reached out and closed around one of Hannah's breasts. They kept closing until he had her breast crushed inside his fist. He giggled again as Hannah cringed from him.

"Do you like Fatty?" he asked.

I tried once more to employ Pelletier's name. "Jules won't like this. He'll do something bad to you, Fatty."

He looked at me. "Jules won't hurt Fatty."

"It's all right," Hannah said. She'd wiped the fear and disgust from her face and replaced it with a seductive smile. "I don't mind if Fatty touches me. Go ahead, do it again."

Fatty's smile revealed a set of greenish teeth. "You *do* like Fatty."

"Yes. Go ahead. Do that again. It felt good to have you hurt me."

He seized her other breast, digging in his fingers even harder. Hannah managed a tight-lipped smile.

"Harder, Fatty! Squeeze it harder!"

Fatty was having too much fun to notice the tears forming in the corners of Hannah's eyes as she urged him on. He continued abusing her, kneading in his fingers and scratching like a cat.

"Come on, Fatty. Loosen my hands. Let me show you something you've never seen before. I'll teach you everything I know and you can hurt me as much as you want. Come on, I know more than the girls on Paradise Alley ever did. Let me show you, Fatty."

He looked at her suspiciously. "You won't tell Jules on Fatty?"

"I won't tell him. But hurry, while he's still working out there in the water."

Somehow I kept my mouth shut while Fatty ground his hammy fingers into Hannah. I couldn't argue with her purpose. If she could get her hands free, and if Fatty could be maneuvered into making a mistake . . .

Fatty was panting. "Where will we go?"

"In there." Hannah moved her head in the direction of the furnace room. "Let's go in and roll around on the coal together. We'll get dirty and do wonderful things to each other. Hurry up, Fatty."

He reached up and tried to unlock the irons. His hands shook with such excitement that he fumbled for several seconds before getting the key into the lock. He turned the key and Hannah's shackles clicked open.

I prayed she wouldn't try a hasty move and spoil her chance. Better to take her time and wait for just the right moment.

Hannah sighed and rotated her shoulders in a circular motion to work out the stiffness. Her movements were a little too sensuous to be entirely honest. She was still working on Fatty, trying to lower his guard. Her act was a success. Fatty stepped back about two paces, the better to watch Hannah move.

After all my talk about waiting and playing the breaks, I was the one who grabbed at the first chance that presented itself. I took hold of the pipe above my head, swung my legs up and out, and brought them down over Fatty's head. The handcuff chain slipped under his many chins like a noose and I clamped my legs around Fatty's neck in a stranglehold.

Fatty choked and leaned into me, grabbing desperately for my legs.

"Hannah, get the shovel from the coal pile. Hurry!"

She took one quick look at us, then rushed to the furnace room.

Fatty continued struggling and choking, his overpowering weight driving back on me. I couldn't hold him long. My aim was to pin him there until Hannah could return with the shovel and bash in his stupid head. But Fatty was too strong and heavy to be held that way for more than a few seconds. With a piercing nasal scream, he twisted out from between my legs, falling to his knees. I kicked him in the kidneys as he rolled away. He came to his feet out of range of my legs, breathing hard through his nose.

Hannah came through the furnace room door, the shovel raised like an axe.

A straight razor appeared in Fatty's hand as if by magic. He flicked the eight-inch steel blade back with his thumb. He held the razor as a barber would. The razor was flecked with the blood of Dolly Morgan and the other two girls Fatty had disposed of in the grand salon. It was obvious from the way he held the blade that Fatty could use it expertly.

"You lied to Fatty," he said, smiling primly at Hannah.

She didn't reply. The razor in Fatty's hand seemed to hypnotize her.

Fatty went forward flatfooted, the razor held out in front of him.

"Hannah, go for his head!"

She ignored my advice. Instead Hannah struck down with the shovel at Fatty's arm.

He moved nimbly, but not fast enough to escape the shovel altogether. It sliced the back of his hand open and the razor flew away into a corner.

"Ow!" Fatty clicked his tongue like a little boy. "You hurt Fatty." The prim smile fell away and Fatty's chins began to tremble. He lowered his head and ran at Hannah like a mad bull charging a helpless calf.

Except that Hannah was far from helpless. She'd shoveled tons of earth in her two winters in the Yukon. Not only could she use a shovel, but the muscles under her tawny skin were as hard as sheets of smooth rock. She swung the shovel just before Fatty reached her. It caught him flush along the jaw, sending his huge body reeling against one of the boilers. The boiler quivered under the impact. He sank to one knee and stared at the floor plates.

Hannah stepped up and hit him again, this time just under the back of his neck. Then again, on the head. And again. And again. And again. Fatty remained in a crouch for a remarkable length of time while Hannah rained blows down on him. He talked to her while she hit him, saying: "Don't hurt Fatty. . . . Please . . . Ouch . . . No . . . Stop hitting Fatty. . . . Fatty doesn't like that. . . . Stop . . . Ow . . . You're hurting Fatty. . . . It hurts too much. . . . Ow . . . No . . ."

It was like trying to kill a mountain. Gradually the words became softer and less distinct, until Fatty slumped against the boiler and stopped talking. His head was a mass of blood and flat angles.

"Stop it, Hannah! He's dead."

She dropped the shovel and leaned against a bulkhead, exhausted and trembling. "I thought he'd never quit talking. Why did he have to talk to me while I was hitting him?" She pressed her hands against her temples.

"Get his key."

"I can't touch him."

"Damn it, get the key! You can be sad and sensitive later, right now we have to get off this boat."

My words startled Hannah. She was about to spit an angry answer at me, but instead bent and slid her hand into the pocket where Fatty had put the key. She found it, unlocked the shackles on my wrists, and gave me the key so I could undo my own legs.

A lot of shouting had begun outside during the last minutes of Fatty's death. I had thought Pelletier and the others were arguing over how to get the riverboat out of its predicament. Then rifle shots broke out.

"Just a minute." I kept Hannah back as I opened the boiler room door and peeked out onto the boiler deck. More shots were fired, volley after volley. I quickly saw what all the gunfire was about.

The old *Titus J. Murphy* was approaching the *Northern Queen* from its starboard side. Swiftwater Bill was as good as his word. I'd told him to ram the *Northern Queen* and that's just what he intended to do. Already Captain Murphy's launch had come to within a hundred yards of the larger riverboat. Pelletier, Old Man Tripp, and Doc Malone kept up a heavy broadside of rifle fire at the little boat. The glass enclosing the pilothouse of the *Titus J. Murphy* was starred with bullet holes.

The gunfire wasn't entirely one-sided. Swiftwater Bill, still in his derby and Prince Albert coat, would raise up every few seconds and fire back at the *Northern Queen*, then duck behind the engine cover. I assumed Captain Murphy was huddled in the bottom of the pilothouse, steering his launch as best he could.

"What's happening?" Hannah whispered.

We were both concerned that someone would discover we were loose and unarmed.

"It's the launch we followed you in. Swiftwater Bill is trying to ram this boat with it."

"Can he do it?"

"I don't know. But he's come pretty close already, and the *Northern Queen* isn't going anywhere."

"What'll we do?"

"Let's stay put for now."

The *Titus J. Murphy* continued bearing down on the steamboat. As it drew closer I could see that Swiftwater Bill had followed my instructions and drenched the bow of the launch in coal oil. Splotches of black covered the bow and the coal oil can was lying on its side in front of the pilothouse.

As the launch came to within fifty yards of the *Northern Queen*, I could also see Captain Murphy, or I should say I could see his right hand, holding the wheel steady. The captain himself remained crouched in relative safety in the pilothouse.

These were the crucial minutes of the gamble. The *Titus J. Murphy* could easily run its bow into whatever underwater obstacle had stopped the steamboat. If that happened, Swiftwater Bill and Captain Murphy would be nothing more than target practice for the three river pirates on the upper decks. And the closer they came to the *Northern Queen*, the more risk they ran of being hit by the steady stream of bullets pouring into the launch.

That worked both ways. I saw Swiftwater Bill raise up, fire, and duck his head again. As he ducked I heard a loud scream of pain from somewhere above and a black form crashed onto the boiler deck almost in front of us. One of Swiftwater Bill's bullets had found its mark. Doc Malone lay dead at our feet with a neat red hole in the middle of his chest. Bill had paid back the Doc for his bad medicine with interest.

The Doc's rifle had fallen somewhere up on the main deck, but I could see his pistol still tucked under his coat. I nipped out of the boiler room and helped myself to Doc's revolver and a leather ammunition pouch on his belt.

The *Titus J. Murphy* was on top of us. Just before it hit, Captain Murphy reared up from the cockpit and threw a gin bottle at the bow of his launch. The gin bottle was filled with coal oil. A burning rag in the neck of the bottle served as a fuse. When the bottle broke on the oil-soaked bow, the entire forward section of the *Titus J. Murphy* went up in flames. Two seconds later the launch plowed into the *Northern Queen.*

"Look out!" I grabbed Hannah's arm and pulled her down the deck. The fire spread faster than I had believed it could. It leaped along the filigreed railings and jumped across the decks into the cabins. The wood was so dry that the spreading fire sounded like strings of firecrackers exploding.

Swiftwater Bill waved at me from the stern of the *Titus J. Murphy.* "Brian! Get off that thing before she blows! When the fire reaches the boilers and coal, she'll blow!" Bill and Captain Murphy jumped into the water. Bill began swimming for shore, but Captain Murphy elected to wade through the shallows of the Flats. His arms were filled with the remaining bottles from his case of gin.

I pushed Hannah to the rail. "Get to shore. I'll meet you there."

"The gold, Brian! What about the gold!"

"Later!" I yelled over the noise of the fire. "We'll get it later, when the fire burns out."

"I won't go without you!"

Arguing with Hannah was always useless. I took her by the seat of her pants and the collar of her shirt and pitched her out into the air. She hit the water screeching and came up thrashing her arms.

The fire had spread all the way to the texas. I ran up the companion to the main deck, hurried past the inferno of the grand salon, and climbed up to the hurricane deck. Licks of flame jumped out of the cabins. At one place I had to edge along the outside of the railing to get past a collapsed section of deck.

I was counting on the steel plates of the furnace room to keep the fire away from the boilers and coal bins until I finished with Pelletier. Whatever happened, I didn't want to be on the *Northern Queen* when she blew. The two big boilers and three hundred tons of coal would make quite an explosion. I prayed the strongroom walls would stand the blast.

An eerie form hurtled past me, a fiery ghost wailing in some alien tongue. It was Old Man Tripp, his clothes and flowing beard aflame. He fireballed from the hurricane deck and fell into the river. I don't believe he ever came up.

"Pelletier!"

He could have jumped already, but somehow I didn't think he'd leave the steamboat and all that gold. And I was right. A minute later Pelletier stumbled into view on the promenade of the texas. We spotted each other at the same second. Pelletier seemed dazed. He managed to lift his pistol and begin shooting at me. I couldn't hear his shots. The roar of the fire was too intense. But I could see the flashes from the barrel of his pistol.

I followed mountie procedure by returning his fire with three spaced shots. Each of my bullets hit Pelletier. He lurched backwards, his enlarged ear bobbing, and disappeared into the holocaust of flames eating up the cabins of the texas.

By then the full two-hundred-foot length and forty-foot beam of the *Northern Queen* had become a giant torch. I threw away the revolver and jumped from the hurricane deck into the river. The water of the Yukon Flats was less than three feet deep there, and my legs sank in mud to the knees. I pulled loose and began swimming as flaming pieces of timber fell around me. It was a half mile to shore. I'd gone about a quarter mile when the first explosion erupted on the *Northern Queen.*

17

WE might have been having a picnic. If anyone had happened by, which wasn't likely, they would have found Hannah, Swiftwater Bill, Captain Titus Murphy, the bedraggled helmsman from the *Northern Queen*, and myself sitting on the shore passing a bottle of gin back and forth.

Ordinarily I don't care for gin. It's a poor substitute for honest whiskey. But it tasted like mother's milk that day. "There she goes again," I said.

Another explosion racked the *Northern Queen*. The steamboat had gone through a series of eight explosions in the hour since the five of us found each other on the riverbank. Each succeeding explosion surprised us because it didn't seem possible that there was anything left to explode. All decks, the pilothouse, and the huge paddlebox at the stern of the steamer had burned away. Only the "triple galvanized hull" that Captain Dolguard had been so proud of remained, unable to sink because it was already derelict on the sandbar.

"Why's she keep on exploding?" the helmsman wondered. He had escaped from Old Man Tripp by leaping all the way from the pilothouse ladder into the Yukon.

"The boilers," Captain Murphy explained. "A boiler is just a bomb under control. Take away the control and it's a bomb, period. Then there's the three hundred tons of coal. That makes a nice bonfire all by itself."

"Someone's coming." Hannah pointed down the shore at a man running towards us. He was a good way off, too far to see his face. I found myself regretting having heaved away that revolver. Then the man's face became clearer. "Oh, hell. It's that noisy banker, John Tanner. I thought he was killed. Too bad they missed him."

Swiftwater Bill handed the gin to Captain Murphy. "The only thing that can kill a banker is a sudden drop in interest rates."

Tanner jogged up to us and dropped to his knees in the sand. He was out of breath and in his usual bad temper. "What the hell happened to that steamboat?"

"We set fire to it," I said.

"*You* set fire to it. You pack of idiots. What's going to happen to our gold?"

"That's a good question," I admitted. "For myself, I thought there'd be one or two explosions and the fire would burn itself out, leaving the strongroom untouched. But that damned boat wants to keep on exploding. I've never seen anything like it, and I was in Chicago once on the fourth of July. I'm afraid the gold is lost."

Tanner fumed. He looked ready to skin me alive. "Of all the stupid . . ."

His head snapped back as Hannah slapped him across the face. "Shut up! You weren't there. You jumped over the side when the going got rough. Brian and the others stayed and fought it out while you were busy saving your own hide."

"But . . ." Tanner rubbed his cheek. "What about the gold?"

"See for yourself," Hannah said. "There's nothing left but the hull. The strongroom was blown away two or three explosions ago."

"Wouldn't the gold still be there? Or down in the water? All that gold . . ."

"Is spread across the Yukon Flats," I supplied. "Sure, the gold would still be on the hull or scattered around the sandbar if it was in solid bars. But everything in the strongroom was nuggets and dust packed in moosehide sacks. The explosions have ripped those sacks apart and sent the dust and nuggets flying. You might find some of the nuggets if you worked at it long enough."

"I'm ruined!" Tanner cried. "I've lost a million dollars of my bank's gold. I can never go back."

"Don't take it so hard." I patted the poor chump on the shoulder. Even a banker deserves sympathy now and then.

"You can say that," Tanner complained. "You still own good claims in the Klondike. You can go back there and dig out more gold."

"And pay me my quarter million dollars," Captain Murphy said. He leaned over to Hannah. "Your partner here promised me half of what you had on the *Northern Queen* if I'd throw in my launch toward catching up with Soapy Smith's gang. I'm holding you to that even though the gold on the steamboat is gone. You can pay me out of your next big wash." He opened another gin and raised it in salute to the burnt-out wreckage of his boat. "Here's to the *Titus J. Murphy*, the best damned riverboat that ever sailed the Yukon River." He drank deeply, then raised the bottle in a second salute. "And to the *Titus J. Murphy II*, my next command, which will be the biggest, finest, fastest steamboat this territory has ever seen."

Swiftwater Bill smiled wistfully. "Wish I could go back to Dawson and dig out more gold. But it ain't possible."

"I don't understand," Hannah said.

"My claims're played out," Bill explained. "The seventy-five thousand I had on the *Northern Queen* was the last of it. I only washed a hundred thousand this summer; I expected ten times that. Now I'm broke." He looked sheepish. "If you want the truth, I sent Gussie ahead to San Francisco without me because I meant to jilt her. I planned to catch a freighter for Australia at St. Michael. I heard news of a big strike in Australia."

Hannah threw back her head and laughed.

"Hannah! Stop that!" I spoke sharply because Hannah's amusement at Swiftwater Bill's disaster was cruel, not like Hannah at all.

"I'm sorry, Bill. You too, Brian. It's just so funny . . ."

Hannah sat in the sand and hugged her

legs, the laughter coming on her in waves. She laughed so hard that the rest of us had to laugh along with her, not knowing why. She laughed until I wondered if the hardships of the past two days had affected her mind. I thought only a crazy person could laugh for ten minutes without taking a deep breath.

Finally she got hold of herself and wiped the tears off her cheeks. "Oh, my sides hurt . . . Brian . . . that was terrible . . . Bill . . . but I couldn't help it . . . it's so funny . . ."

"What's so funny?"

"Brian, do you remember those papers you signed about three weeks ago?"

"I remember some papers. I don't recall what they were."

"I was doing some more trading. There were four claims up on French Hill that I had a hunch about. You know how I am when I have a hunch. Well . . ." Hannah bit her lip. "The fact is those papers you signed were deeds of conveyance. I made another big trade and it didn't work out this time. Those new claims are skunks. *Terrible* skunks. I can practically smell them from here. Brian, I'm afraid . . ."

"You mean we're broke, too?"

"Right. We still own those claims, but we

couldn't sell them for much now that the *cheechakos* with money to invest are getting scarce. That's why I wanted to put that five hundred thousand dollars in a San Francisco bank, so I wouldn't be tempted to gamble with it. That gold was every cent we had."

"Broke," I repeated. "After everything we went through."

"I don't know what's wrong with me," Hannah said. "Whenever I get a hunch, I have to gamble."

"I'm the same way," Swiftwater Bill declared. "*Got a hunch? Bet a bunch.* That's my motto."

Captain Murphy took the setback philosophically. "So much for the *Titus J. Murphy II.* It was a sweet dream while it lasted."

"Are you mad at me, Brian?"

I put my arm around Hannah. "Hell, no. Wasn't I the one who got the bright idea of setting fire to the *Northern Queen?* Come right down to it, I'm the one who busted all of us."

"And I still say it was a stupid thing to do," Tanner grumbled, taking care to be out of range of Hannah's fist.

"Besides," I went on, "I never really got

used to being rich. That'll make it easier to be broke again."

"We won't be broke for long," Hannah promised. "I have plenty of ideas, Brian. Don't worry about that."

"Hannah, we don't have to be rich. In November I'll have my hundred and sixty acres. We'll open the distillery in Saskatchewan and start selling *Brian Bonner's Old Dependable Canadian Whiskey*. You'll like the whiskey business, Hannah. Gold is all right, but all you can do is look at it. Now with whiskey you've got a product you can warm to."

Hannah stood up and began pacing the beach in her restless way. "Nothing against whiskey, but there's not enough money in it. Not the kind of money I have in mind."

"I'm ruined," Tanner repeated, still trying to interest us in his problems. "My managing director will blackball me with every bank in Canada, The United States, and England." He turned to Swiftwater Bill. "Would you mind some company to Australia? Maybe I can get a new start there."

"Welcome aboard," Bill said cheerfully.

Hannah continued pacing the beach and talking about other possibilities. The lumber business. Silver in Nevada. A new kind of black gold people were talking about, oil from hundreds of feet under the ground. Cotton futures. She said she'd always wanted to run a newspaper. And then there was the freight business; fortunes were being made in shipping and railroading.

"Hannah, don't you think you might scale down your ambitions just a little. Instead of a fortune, start thinking in terms of a good living. I can make a good living for us with whiskey, I know I can."

"No!" Hannah kicked the sand. "I want it all. I told you that a long time ago."

"Listen, Hannah . . ."

But she wasn't listening. She was down on her hands and knees her fingers in the sand.

"Brian, look." She held a fistful of dirt out to me. "Gold!"

The others jumped to their feet and snatched up sand in their own hands. Swiftwater Bill hastily washed out his handful in his derby hat. "Yessir," he admitted, "There's a strong trace here. But this isn't where we'll find the streak." He looked around. "Up there. That's where this came from and that's where we'll find the rich dirt." He pointed to a stream about three hundred yards away. The stream emptied into the Yukon Flats from some hills to the west.

"Let's go." Hannah began running toward the stream.

We all followed. Me. Swiftwater Bill. John Tanner. Captain Murphy. Even the helmsman was roused from his sullen gloom at the prospect of gold.

We waded up the stream, stopping frequently to look for tracings of gold. Hannah and Swiftwater Bill were the experts. The rest of us listened to their discussions and judgments in fretful silence.

At last, after we'd waded a long mile upstream, stumbling over fallen timbers and slipping on submerged rocks, Hannah said, "This is where the rich dirt is. Right here."

"How can you tell?" The dirt I picked up there looked no better to me than the sand on the beach.

Hannah's eyes glittered. "Brian, I just have a hunch about this spot."

"Me, too," Captain Murphy said. "Maybe there'll be a *Titus J. Murphy II* yet."

"What have I got to lose?" Tanner asked. "Somebody tell me how to stake a claim in Alaska."

"It's pretty much the same as in Canada,"

Swiftwater Bill answered. "Five hundred feet along the stream, and from rimrock to rimrock."

Hannah took charge. "Brian, you pace off five hundred feet upstream. I'll stake my claim from here on downstream. That way the Young and Bonner Mining Company will have a thousand feet smack in the center of the new strike."

I didn't know whether to laugh or cry. The whole ordeal was starting up all over again and I had a notion she'd never be able to stop. "Whatever you say, Hannah." I faced upstream and began pacing.

THE END

This book is published under the
auspices of the
ULVERSCROFT FOUNDATION,
a registered charity, whose primary object
is to assist those who experience difficulty
in reading print of normal size.

In response to approaches from the medical world, the Foundation is also helping to purchase the latest, most sophisticated medical equipment desperately needed by major eye hospitals for the diagnosis and treatment of eye diseases.

If you would like to know more about the
ULVERSCROFT FOUNDATION,
and how you can help to further its work,
please write for details to:

THE ULVERSCROFT FOUNDATION
The Green, Bradgate Road
Anstey
Leicestershire
England

WESTERN TITLES
in the
Ulverscroft Large Print Series

Powder Smoke Feud
William MacLeod Raine
Shane
Jack Schaefer
A Handful of Men
Robert Wilder

FICTION TITLES
in the
Ulverscroft Large Print Series

The Onedin Line: The High Seas
Cyril Abraham

The Onedin Line: The Iron Ships
Cyril Abraham

The Onedin Line: The Shipmaster
Cyril Abraham

The Onedin Line: The Trade Winds
Cyril Abraham

The Enemy	*Desmond Bagley*
Flyaway	*Desmond Bagley*
The Master Idol	*Anthony Burton*
The Navigators	*Anthony Burton*
A Place to Stand	*Anthony Burton*
The Doomsday Carrier	*Victor Canning*
The Cinder Path	*Catherine Cookson*
The Girl	*Catherine Cookson*
The Invisible Cord	*Catherine Cookson*
Life and Mary Ann	*Catherine Cookson*
Maggie Rowan	*Catherine Cookson*
Marriage and Mary Ann	*Catherine Cookson*
Mary Ann's Angels	*Catherine Cookson*
All Over the Town	*R. F. Delderfield*
Jamaica Inn	*Daphne du Maurier*
My Cousin Rachel	*Daphne du Maurier*

By Command of the Viceroy
                              Duncan MacNeil
The Deceivers   *John Masters*
Nightrunners of Bengal   *John Masters*
Emily of New Moon   *L. M. Montgomery*
The '44 Vintage   *Anthony Price*
High Water   *Douglas Reeman*
Rendezvous-South Atlantic *Douglas Reeman*
Summer Lightning   *Judith Richards*
Louise   *Sarah Shears*
Louise's Daughters   *Sarah Shears*
Louise's Inheritance   *Sarah Shears*
Beyond the Black Stump   *Nevil Shute*
The Healer   *Frank G. Slaughter*
Sword and Scalpel   *Frank G. Slaughter*
Tomorrow's Miracle   *Frank G. Slaughter*
The Burden   *Mary Westmacott*
A Daughter's a Daughter *Mary Westmacott*
Giant's Bread   *Mary Westmacott*
The Rose and the Yew Tree
                       Mary Westmacott
Every Man a King   *Anne Worboys*
The Serpent and the Staff   *Frank Yerby*

We hope this Large Print edition gives you the pleasure and enjoyment we ourselves experienced in its publication.

There are now more than 1,400 titles available in this ULVERSCROFT Large Print Series. Ask to see a Selection at your nearest library.

The Publisher will be delighted to send you, free of charge, upon request a complete and up-to-date list of all titles available.

Ulverscroft Large Print Books Ltd.
The Green, Bradgate Road
Anstey
Leicestershire
England

1 ↔ RP   Discarded bc1 RP 11.28 (4, 3 / 22)

NNS/WFFS   NC

DISCARDED
BAKER CO. PUBLIC LIBRARY

SEP 11 2014